Family Ghosts

Sarah Quick

SHIPWAY

PUBLICATIONS

Shipway Publications
Copyright © Sarah Quick 2011
First published in 2011 by Shipway Publications
161 Hewlett Road, Cheltenham, Gloucestershire, GL52 6UD

Distributed by Gardners Books
1 Whittle Drive, Eastbourne, East Sussex, BN23 6QH
Tel: +44(0)1323 521555 | Fax: +44(0)1323 521666

British Library Cataloguing in Publication Data
A catalogue record for this book is available from the
British Library

ISBN 978-0-9566708-0-9

Typeset by Amolibros, Milverton, Somerset
This book production has been managed by Amolibros
Printed and bound by T J International Ltd, Padstow, Cornwall, UK

Family Ghosts

For Gwen and Rose

In memory of
Maud Mary Bryden née Shipway
(1897 – 1983)
and
Phyllis Emilie Quick née Williams
(1900 – 1982)

Prologue

Zennor lies on the north-western coast of Cornwall, not far from Penzance and St Ives. Storms rush in from the Atlantic and beat against the cliffs and granite hills. Abandoned homesteads, ancient tin mines and prehistoric barrows are ghost asylums. This was where she was born. A midnight birth. The rain lashing at the windowpanes and clamouring on the cobbles in the yard. A week later, her journeyman father drove his family away from this village to seek business in South Devon. His cabinet-making skills required a larger clientele than permanent settlement permitted. City life did not appeal to him. He took his family on a rootless existence from county to county. But now his second daughter is back at her beginning.

Great-Granny Zennor Anderson never believed she'd be the one killed in an accident; didn't think it could happen to her. But here she is, the other side of life, looking at her accidental death from afar. Here she is, waiting to return.

And she vows she will.

One

Hepsie Anderson bent down and scratched her big toe. It was annoying to do so, but she didn't want to face the stares of the other people in Siesta Café. Stroud locals were inclined to gossip, nudge one another, and generally know your business, whether you wanted them to or not. Her big toe felt hot and she could smell the sweat from the inner sole of her flip-flop. She always wore flip-flops, even in winter, if she could get away with it. Why her feet were like smoking coals on this breezy May morning, she didn't know. But then nothing was normal any more.

She glanced at her watch as she sat up again. 11.02 a.m. He hadn't turned up. Hepsie got out his business card that she had put in her wallet.

> ### *Mike Johnson*
> ### *Family History Researcher*
> ### *Reasonable rates charged*
> ### *Guaranteed results*
>
> #### *Special Interest: The Five Valleys, Gloucestershire*
>
> ### *Contact: 07089 666999*

Mr Johnson had sounded young and keen on the telephone, not at all as she had imagined. His low-key, mellifluous voice made her spine tingle. She felt drawn to him. Weren't family history researchers usually old, grey, retired individuals with time on their hands? Mike Johnson sounded about thirty years old, and not the sort of person to be the least interested in genealogy. Was something not right?

Hepsie nearly released a despairing sigh but quickly checked herself. She furtively glanced up to see whether any of her neighbouring café drinkers were watching her. They weren't. Siesta Café wasn't her usual café; however, it was so easy to bump into somebody you knew in Stroud. Hepsie was afraid someone, such as the likes of Joan Franklin, might spy her sitting alone at the back of the café and noisily greet her, putting Hepsie and her secret mission under the spotlight for ever more. At the tables around her married couples chatted, their heads almost touching above the steamy froth of their cappuccinos, whilst parents and their young children threw banter across the air like broken crockery, and teenagers joked about their next pub crawl or new boyfriend. Even Stroud had its café chain branch and the café's swish interior with its large modern windows, chrome lighting, mahogany furniture, burgundy sofas and uniform white crockery could be found in any town or city in Great Britain, or the world for that matter.

Mike Johnson had chosen a Saturday morning to meet up. The weekend before the late May Bank Holiday was busy. In the narrow, hilly streets outside Siesta Café, shoppers jostled on their way to the two local markets: the cobbled Shambles walkway leading to St Laurence's Church; and the larger Farmers' Market based in and around the old market hall. If

4

Hepsie hadn't been waiting for Mike Johnson on her blind father's behalf, she would have been meandering around the market stalls, smelling the freshly cooked bread, tasting the succulent olives, admiring the rainbow-coloured scarves hung up like festival bunting, and selecting fresh fish, cheese and flowers to take home with her to Amberley.

Perhaps Mike Johnson had got lost in all this? Hepsie had been short with him on the phone. She hadn't wanted to call him anyway. It was Eb's idea. Hepsie stirred her empty cappuccino cup, trying to convince those waiting for a vacant table that she wasn't finished. Perhaps Mike was circling the one-way system at this moment? She hadn't bothered to tell him which of Stroud's many car parks he should use. And she hadn't told him that Eb wouldn't be with her to meet him. How had she convinced Eb to stay behind? It hadn't been easy.

"It's for your best interests, Eb," she had said. "We don't know who this Mike Johnson is, what his real intentions are. A business card just dropped through the letter box is no guarantee of authenticity. He could be a con man.

"Why hasn't he given us his address details? Or more information about himself? I don't think he should come to our house."

Eb, her sixty-seven-year-old father, had stared ahead of him but didn't reply. Had he guessed her real intentions?

"If I arrange to meet up with him first of all, somewhere not too close to home, I can ascertain whether he's genuine or not. I don't want you clobbered over the head, because he sees you're blind and he can take advantage of you. There are too many muggings of elderly people nowadays, even in a village like Amberley."

5

"Who's been mugged here, recently?" Eb sounded surprised.

Hepsie twisted a strand of her hair around her finger. "It was in last week's local paper. A couple in their eighties had their front gate stolen. They could have been attacked in their home. We must be careful, Eb. You can get anybody knocking at your door pretending to be the gas man, the postman, even workers from the council. They've got false ID and...oops, before you know it, they've stolen your wallet and valuables behind your back." Did it matter she was lying? The couple were in their fifties and, although their front gate was unlocked, their front door was securely bolted against the night.

Eb smiled.

Did he know she was lying? Had he listened to the newspaper article on his talking computer? Hepsie knew how much he wanted to use Mike Johnson's services. If anyone had got the genealogy bug bigger and better than anyone else, then it would have to be Eb. And there was her problem. Eb was going to resist every attempt to dissuade him. Since she had made the mistake of reading out loud Mike Johnson's business card, Eb was determined that Hepsie and himself should follow this genealogical lead.

"A special interest in The Five Valleys, did you say?" Eb looked hopeful. "He might have some information on Amberley or, at least, point us in the right direction. We have exhausted every other possible source. Don't you think Mike Johnson might be the key to open the next door?" His voice was pleading for Hepsie to agree with him.

"It will cost money, Eb. He won't be cheap. Don't you think you should leave the family history research as it is? You've discovered a lot already. Aren't you happy with that?" But Hepsie knew he wasn't. Why did Eb have to get these obsessions, which he then took to the extreme? Perhaps he was insecure, since losing his sight and the early death of Sofia. He clung to the world through the safety net of his obsessions. But then that wasn't the whole truth, was it? Hepsie knew why she was really trying to scare away Eb's genealogical interests.

In Siesta Café the time was now 11.15 a.m. Hepsie put Mike Johnson's business card back in her handbag. She wondered whether she should wait any longer. In some respects she was pleased he hadn't turned up. So much easier to explain to Eb why the meeting hadn't worked. So much easier to scare away Eb's genealogical obsession. Hepsie started to pull on her jacket. She could see a couple hoping to sit down at her table. She picked up her handbag but before she could swing it over her shoulder, her mobile phone began to ring. By the tune she could tell it was her friend Sally.

"Hi, Sal."

"Has he gone then?"

"He hasn't turned up."

"You've been waiting all this time? You are noble, Hepsie."

"Don't be stupid! You know why I'm really doing this. I'm just about to leave."

"It's only been three-quarters of an hour. Don't you think you should wait another fifteen minutes?"

"Don't ask me to, Sal. Joan Franklin could spot me at any moment."

Sally chuckled.

"You should wait another 15 minutes. To make it look to Eb as if you've tried. You don't want him suspecting."

"I've got two people waiting to sit here. I can't just hang around."

"Glare at them, Hepsie. Stick out your tongue."

"Sometimes, Sally, I'm think you're more on Eb's side than mine."

"You're getting cynical for your age, old girl. Time to find yourself a man and settle down."

"Now that really is rubbing it in. You know I can't leave Eb on his own. There's no one else to help him."

"Sometimes, Hepsie, I think you're your own worse enemy."

"Would you leave Dan to look after your blind Dad?"

Sally paused.

"No, I would take Dan with me."

"Saint Dan!"

Hepsie felt jealous towards her friend. It was easy for Sally: boyfriend, career, even owning her own flat. If anything happened to Sally's parents, she could still look after them without entirely compromising her free-spirited, independent self.

"He is a saint." Sally sighed into the phone. "He's taking me out nightclubbing in Bristol tonight. He did suggest bringing you along, too, but I suppose that's out of the question?"

"Yes," Hepsie replied curtly.

"Never mind, old girl. If Mike Johnson doesn't turn up, you've got one over Eb. It might work and put him off the genealogical craze."

"I'll keep my fingers crossed."

"Got to go now. Keep me in touch. If those people have stopped waiting, you should stay another ten minutes in case the seductive Mr Mike Johnson turns up."

"Goodbye, Sally," Hepsie said firmly.

It was true. The couple had now found another table. She could wait here for at least another ten minutes. In some respects, she was curious to see Mike Johnson in person. The man behind the voice. Sally wasn't her friend for nothing. Ever since she had met Sally at Amberley Parochial School, all those many years ago when she was eight years old, Sally had always shown remarkable intuition about what Hepsie was really feeling. Perhaps Mike was delayed getting here? How silly of her not to have given him her mobile number. She had told Eb that it wouldn't be safe to do so. "If there's a problem, I can phone him," she had lied to Eb. Then why wasn't she calling him now? Hepsie knew full well why she wasn't.

To make herself look busy, she took out her hand mirror and lipstick from her handbag. Peering at her reflection under the unflattering artificial lighting of the café, Hepsie thought she noticed another wrinkle spreading claw-like from the corner of her eye. Thirty-two years old and developing into an old woman already! She could hear her classmates chanting "Witch! Witch! Witch!" as they ran around the playground at Amberley. "You're an old witch, Hephzibah!" Children are so unkind. Would they be calling her 'witch' now? Hepsie scrunched up her face to see how many other wrinkles appeared on her pale skin. Pre-school she had been known as 'Bah', because she couldn't pronounce Hephzibah. When she started school, she had chosen to call herself Hepsie, liking the soft hiss of the 's'. No one in their right mind would call her Hephzibah, such an old-fashioned name, but it took nine months, nearly a whole school year, before her village classmates allowed her to be one of them. Only red-haired, freckled-faced Sally drew close to her, knowing what it was like to be teased. "Carrot Face" and "Hephzibah-the-Witch" faded in time like the grey stone walls of the school.

9

Hepsie smoothed the luscious lipstick over her full lips. Nude Rose. Her favourite lip colour. It complemented the chestnut colouring of her hair. Her heart-shaped face peeked out of her long tresses like a pixie, her retroussé nose adding to the image. Only the mole on the bridge of her nose looked out of place. Hepsie hadn't bothered to disguise it, like she used to do as a teenager; but she knew from past experience that her mole could be considered one of her most attractive features. What would Mike Johnson have made of it?

In her free-spirited days, as Hepsie liked to call them, she travelled the world, boyfriend in tow, her life lying before her like a roaring waterfall cascading into a long, meandering, flowing river. Cares dissolved like spume on the water's surface or got whipped away along the current until they were out of her reach. She had travelled around Europe during her gap year between A levels and university and then, during her university vacations, she had explored South America, the African Congo, Sri Lanka and, after obtaining her English degree, the shores and mountains of exotic India. They had been her passport to further independence and freedoms. Eb and Sofia were good about such matters. Although she was their only child, they allowed her to find her way in the world and carve out a niche for herself. At the time of Sofia's cancer diagnosis, Hepsie was enjoying her job as an editorial executive at Acanthus Books, one of London's most innovative publishing houses. There were friends and colleagues to share her passions, and plenty of opportunities to explore and experience the myriad sights and sounds of London. A deposit had nearly been put down for shared ownership of a house with two university friends. Boyfriends needed her, desired her, but there was no pressure to marry and mate. Hepsie wanted to enjoy her freedom before the cares and commitments of motherhood entwined her life in the grasp of a child's hand.

She threw the lipstick and hand mirror carelessly into her handbag. Her father's hand was all she had to hold now. Dutiful daughter. Growing old alongside her father, taking the years gracefully as they slowly passed by, both of them collecting the dust like ancient relics. Whose mistake had that been? Hepsie had done worse than stub her own toe. And now this lie. Did Eb really believe her con-man theory? Why had he suddenly caved in at the last moment? She knew he wanted to meet Mike Johnson so much.

Picturing Eb at home, she saw a lonely, unseeing figure, waiting patiently for her to return. His fingers strumming the table to calm his nerves, or getting up to make himself another mug of coffee, slowly touching his way around the kitchen. He'd be longing to hear her exciting news about what Mike Johnson can do for him. Hepsie felt a twinge of guilt. Here she was, taking away an old man's pleasure, stealing his moment of limelight. And a kind man's pleasure, too. Eb had so little to live for, especially after all he had recently experienced, yet you couldn't find a kinder, more considerate person to bear that suffering. It was just that it involved her. And, now her con man.

She could see how easily Mike Johnson could be a con man. It was strange he hadn't turned up. If he was a fake, then why did he bother to set up the meeting with her? But then he hadn't. Not wanting Mike Johnson to visit her at home, deciding to meet up in Stroud in a café she never frequented, not telling him the easiest route into town and where to park: these were her ideas. Where was Mike Johnson? He must know Amberley because he'd dropped the business card through their letter box. Was he local? She hadn't seen or heard of him. He hadn't said where he lived. Hepsie begun to twist a strand of her hair tightly around her finger. In fact, he hadn't given much away when she'd spoken to him. He had asked for her number, but Hepsie had refused, saying she didn't like giving her mobile number to strangers. It was strange he wasn't in Siesta Café…unless he had another plan.

Hepsie pictured Eb again, sitting alone at home, not a soul stirring the peace except the chimes of the grandfather clock in the hall. Had Mike Johnson got lost and gone to Amberley? She imagined him arriving in his car and, not having their telephone number, knocking on the door of Peace Cottage. He would have to wait a while before Eb reached the door and opened it. She saw the surprise on Mike Johnson's face as he realised Eb was blind. This is going better than planned, he thinks. Kind, unassuming Eb invites Mr Johnson into his home. The door closes behind them. What happens next?

"Who's been mugged here, recently?" Eb sounded surprised.

"It was in last week's local paper. A couple in their eighties…"

Did it matter she was lying?

Hepsie grabbed her mobile phone and punched the connection to Eb's number. It rang for several seconds. *"You have reached the voicemail of Eb Anderson…"*

"Eb, it's Hepsie. Where are you? Mike Johnson hasn't turned up. Is he with you? I'll be back as soon as I can. Give me a call when you get this message. I love you, Dad."

Drat it!

Hepsie punched the connection to their landline number. The phone rang for several seconds. *"Sorry neither Eb or Hepsie are here to take your call, but please leave your..."*

"It's me, again, Eb. Where are you? Why aren't you answering your mobile? Mike Johnson hasn't turned up. I'm coming back as soon as I can. I hope he's not with you. I'll try Joan's phone to see whether you're with her. Hope to catch you. Bye."

Hepise punched the connection to Joan Franklin's mobile number. It, too, rang for several seconds. Was nobody at home? Joan's gushing voice succinctly enunciated her voicemail message. Hepsie took a deep breath.

"Hi, Joan. It's Hepsie. Just wondering whether Eb is with you. Not to worry if he isn't. Bye."

She didn't want to call Joan's landline number. Best not to get Joan too involved at this stage. Joan was always around when you didn't need her, and not there when you did. Was Eb lying dead on their kitchen floor? She waited a few seconds for her mobile to ring. Fearing the worse, and wishing now she hadn't convinced Eb to stay behind, Hepsie picked up her handbag and rushed out of the café.

Two

The kitchen of Peace Cottage smelt of fresh coffee and chicken soup. Hepsie watched her father carefully, as he raised his soup spoon to his mouth and sipped noisily on the soup. He repeated this action several times, totally unaware that Hepsie hadn't touched her soup. Crumbs of crusty French stick lay scattered across the table between them. Hepsie had switched on the overhead halogen lights because the kitchen faced the back garden and only got the sun in the evening. She sipped on her black coffee, letting its strong flavour absorb her embarrassment and shattered nerves.

Eb looked remarkably well for someone who could have been mugged an hour or so ago. His cheeks were ruddy from having been out in the garden, "enjoying the breeze", as he put it. He hadn't expected Hepsie to be back for some time and taking a stroll in the garden seemed preferable to staying inside. And why wasn't his mobile with him? Well, he'd forgotten to take it with him.

Since his enforced early retirement, Eb's body had become stockier, with a noticeable paunch to his stomach and a thickness to his jaw. Lines of suffering crosshatched his face like an etching. But he was still a handsome man. His limbs were long and added an aura of dignity to his person. A benign, amiable smile hovering across his features illuminated the depth and sadness of his sightless pale blue eyes. Thick, wavy white hair softened the crosshatched blows to his forehead and gave him a slightly Biblical appearance, as if he had stolen one of the crooks from his ancestor Ebenezer's workshop and stopped back in time to herd his sheep across the Cotswold hills.

This morning Hepsie had laid out a white shirt for Eb, together with his black cords and brown jumper. Sometimes, Eb liked to choose his clothes for himself, special audio tags on the clothes telling him what they were and their colour, but this often took longer, and she couldn't waste her time today.

Eb seemed unbothered by her recent anxiety. Perhaps he was hiding his true feelings? But Hepsie knew it was because he didn't believe her. She knew what he was going to say next.

Eb wiped his mouth with his napkin.

"Why don't we get in touch with Mike Johnson?"

He paused for Hepsie's reply.

Hepsie banged her cup onto her saucer. Words fell out of her mouth like angry bullets. "You could have been more concerned for your safety! I was worried sick about you!"

Eb tried to look contrite but the corners of his mouth were twitching.

"I rushed back home, and were where you? In the garden! And your first thought? For Mike Johnson!"

"I was disappointed he hadn't turned up. It was very kind of you to offer to deal with him in the first place, but I think this time I'll come along, too."

"Look, we still don't know who he is. Why didn't he keep the appointment?"

"That's what I'm wondering. I hope nothing bad has happened to him."

Hepsie got up to refill her mug with more strong black coffee, her chair scraping across the flagstones.

Eb tore his chunk of French stick in two. "I'm convinced he can help us. We were looking for a researcher interested in the Five Valleys area and his business card arrives through our letterbox like an omen. We can't ignore it."

"What do you mean 'we'? It's your idea. I never wanted to put up that advert at the local family history centre AND the County Record Office. It's been two weeks. No one's got in touch."

Hepsie pictured the advert pinned to the walls of her father's two most favourite establishments. He had typed it up on his talking computer and asked her to correct any mistakes before printing it out.

RESEARCHER WANTED!

Information required on The Five Valleys,

Gloucestershire.

Does any one remember Peace Cottage, Amberley?

If you can help with the above,

please get in touch with:

Eb and Hepsie Anderson,

Peace Cottage, Amberley, Stroud

However, she had omitted their telephone number. Eb didn't know about this.

"There's still time." Eb's mellow voice, weighted with patience, rang out across the kitchen. "I'm not going anywhere."

And neither am I, thought Hepsie. Ever since Joan Franklin had started Amberley Family History Group, there had been no peace in the village. Eb was coerced into researching his house details on the 1901 census. Luckily, he could do this on the computer; unluckily, he discovered he was living in the same house as his ancestors. To his amazement, Eb found an Ebenezer and Hephzibah Anderson, their widowed son George and his three children living at Peace Cottage, Amberley. Ebenezer, head of the household, was aged sixty-seven years old and worked on his 'own account' as a crook maker and umbrella mender. Hephzibah was aged sixty-one. George worked as a draper's assistant. His age was thirty-nine. Grandchildren Elsie, Clara and Georgie were all scholars and aged respectively thirteen, eleven and seven. The family's birthplaces were recorded as Amberley, Glos. Eb was interested to note that Peace Cottage, even back then, didn't have less than five rooms. Were these people his ancestors? If Hepsie had known then what she knew now, she would have had the foresight to whack the obsession on the head.

Encouraged by Joan, Hepsie found herself helping Eb research his paternal ancestry. They were indeed related to the 1901 Anderson family. Joan cooed persuasively in the background, telling her family history group members that the village was going to hold an exhibition in the Church Parish Rooms and it would be really lovely if Eb and Hepsie Anderson of Peace Cottage could prove their ancestors had also lived at Peace Cottage. In fact, the more information, the better. Hepsie felt herself dissolving into a world of musty records, half-baked facts, innumerable websites and microfilm madness. Not only had she joined the past century, where horses were the main form of transport and Peace Cottage had an outdoor privy, but she was also now a veteran member of the village. If I had a blue rinse, solid gardening boots, a face wrinkled by days spent in the harsh wind, spade in hand, and membership of most of the village societies, I could rightfully label myself OAP, she ruefully thought.

And there was no end to it. She could understand that the co-incidence of her family returning to live at the same house as their forebears was remarkable. Eb hadn't known, when he and Sofia bought the house in 1982, that his father Georgie had grown up there. Why should he? Grandfather Georgie hardly spoke about his past. They had his birth certificate, from after he died, but not once did either Eb or Sofia connect Georgie's past details to their home. There was no need to. The birth certificate had laid forgotten in a stored-away box with Grandfather Georgie's other possessions. It was nice to know Eb and herself were unwittingly continuing a family tradition by moving back to Amberley, but, reasoned Hepsie, why did Eb have to take it to new heights?

As if reading her thoughts, Eb plunged back into his argument. "It's more than just a co-incidence. Why Peace Cottage? Why didn't we move to one of the other houses in the village? It's the ghosts of our past knocking on our door. We've been brought back for a reason. I've got to go on with it. Maybe my ancestors have got something to tell me?"

Eb was starting to look mystical, as he usually did when espousing his favourite cause.

Hepsie filled her mug to the brim, trying not to spill the coffee because her hand was shaking so much with anger.

"Would you like me to get an Ouija board, Eb, so you can make contact with your ancestral spirits?"

Eb's face remained passive.

Hepsie sat down at the table. "I certainly don't feel the ghosts of our past are with us. Have you sensed any of our ancestors walking about the house? No! You're letting your imagination run wild. Why don't you find another hobby?"

"If you could find an Ouija board, Hepsie, that would be lovely. Perhaps that will help my ancestors deliver their message. We have got to get down to the root of the problem. If only Mike Johnson had turned up. I'm sure he could find a likely connection. In the meantime, we must play with the Ouija board." Eb bit into a chunk of French stick, the crust crumbs falling onto his brown jersey.

"You know I'm joking about the Ouija board, Eb. And don't go asking Joan Franklin for one. She's involved enough as it is." Hepsie stirred her soup, which was now thick and cold. She attempted to sip some from her soup spoon, but cold chicken soup was as unappetising as Eb's genealogical obsession.

"Did Joan say we must contact Mike Johnson again?"

Hepsie glared at Eb. Even though he couldn't see her, she hoped he felt her wrath. Joan had phoned just before lunch.

"Hepsie, darling, is everything all right?" Joan's voice gushed loudly and effusively from the handset.

"Fine."

"Is there a problem with Eb?"

"I've found him now." Hepsie faked a chuckle.

"That's good. I suppose you've told him all about your meeting with Mike Johnson. How did it go?"

Pause. Hepsie would have to tell Joan, because Eb would tell her anyway.

"He didn't turn up."

"Oh, no!" Joan affected sympathetic commiseration. "Why was that?"

Pause.

"We don't know."

"But you're going to try, again, aren't you? Eb must be so disappointed. I know his genealogy is a pet love for him. Thank goodness we started a family history group in Amberley. Your father would be so lost without it.

"Let me know how you get on. I'm still planning an exhibition for next spring, so any new information you get will contribute towards its success. You and Eb are going to be my star display!

"Must dash now, got some planting to do in the garden. Give me a call if Eb goes missing again. Bye, Hepsie."

From the hall the loud ticking of the grandfather clock could be heard. It was a quiet Saturday afternoon in Amberley, before villagers started moving about in their gardens or driving along the country lanes to the town shops. Through the kitchen window Hepsie could see the apple tree boughs trembling in the breeze. Covered in white blossom, they seemed like fluttering white rags of surrender. If she didn't tell Eb what Joan had said, then Joan would.

"Yes."

Eb smiled with satisfaction.

"I'm surprised she doesn't know of anyone who can help us. But she means well." Eb cleared his throat rather awkwardly. "I only gave in to your need to see

Mike Johnson alone because I thought you wouldn't go through with the meeting. I do understand that the genealogy is wearing thin for you. It's my obsession, not yours, and I'm sorry if you've been dragged through an old man's concerns. It can't be easy." Eb paused, in case she wanted to speak. "I do value your help, Hepsie. Not only with the genealogy, but with life in general. I do understand that if Sofia hadn't died, you wouldn't be wasting your important years on me."

Hepsie's eyes filled with tears.

Eb's right hand stroked his upper leg, up and down, up and down. He always did this when he felt emotional. Touching his body gave him the reassurance that his sightless eyes couldn't give him. Hepsie imagined his fingers feeling the soft ridges of his cords. And finding comfort in tracing these regular vertical lines, up and down.

Glaucoma should never have taken over Eb's life. There were supposed to be cures. But Eb's glaucoma had laid in wait, undetected, slowly damaging his eyes. If he had worn glasses and, therefore, gone for regular eyesight tests, the stealthy disease would have been treated in its early stages. Eb felt like a normal person, with no pain to warn him or blurry vision to trip him up. It was only when he thought he'd better get spectacles for driving, that he learnt the dreadful truth. And then something else went wrong. Did his eye pressure, which had damaged his optic nerve in the first place, respond badly to treatment? Or did Eb mess up his daily dose of eye drops? These were meant to lower the eye pressure, but were difficult to handle. Slowly, Eb's central field of vision deteriorated, leaving him unable to read or recognise people. He said he was experiencing tunnel vision, before his world became hazy, as though he was seeing through a net curtain. Light danced on the periphery of his sight and forms became shadows.

It was a big change for Sofia and herself. How do you adapt to your husband or father going blind? Then Sofia was diagnosed with pancreatic cancer.

Hepsie dabbed her eyes with a tissue. "You couldn't have coped, Eb. I'm your only daughter. There's no other family to help you. And I promised Sofia I would. It's been eighteen months since she died and..." Hepsie paused, her breath constricted in her throat.

Eighteen months since she decided to throw in her lot with Eb. Three years since she began her increasingly regular trips back home to help Eb and Sofia. Two years since learning that Sofia's cancer was fatal. Months of shedding her free-spirited, independent woman for a dutiful daughter's skin. She had made a mistake. But what could she do? Eb was alone in the world. Their neighbours, Eb's former colleagues, her school friends and teachers, even her friends in London: she had told them she couldn't possibly leave Eb in the hands of strangers. She couldn't leave Eb to cope for himself. She had raised their expectations and now she couldn't let them down.

Eb reached across the table, his hand stretched open, palm up, for Hepsie to take. She squeezed his hand tightly, feeling the warmth of Eb's thick fingers, before he released his grip.

"You should take more time away from the house and me. I don't mind if you want to spend evenings in The Black Horse, or drive to Bristol or Swindon. Why don't you look for a non-freelance job? I can cope well enough by myself, with Joan nearby."

Hepsie remained silent.

She hadn't been in The Black Horse for many

months, not since she, Sally and another old school friend met up for a 'reunion'. Village friends, school friends, university friends: their lives had changed. It was the school run, nappy changing, happy marriages, prosperous careers, resettling in the North, or in London, or abroad. Busy lives. Stressful lives. Fulfilled lives. *Their* lives. There was no time to see Hepsie for a few casual drinks or a trip to the theatre or to go shopping together. And there was no common ground. She had given up her MySpace website link because she felt nothing ever happened to her. At least, nothing that she would want to advertise to the world.

"Why don't you use the Internet to meet people?" Eb tried again. "I find it's very useful for making contact with people in a similar situation to myself. You don't even have to meet them. But, at least, you can get it off your chest." Eb chuckled, attempting to pass it off as a joke.

"I'll give it a go, Eb." Hepsie didn't like to tell him that the last thing she wanted to do was relive her daily life with those in a similar situation. She wanted to get away from this life.

"You can still have a future, Hepsie. Life isn't over: look at me!"

A future? What future was there for her? She would be here until Eb died. Her peers weren't thinking of their old age, but here she was, right in the middle of Eb's and her own. She even sounded like him. Never mind the blue-rinsed hair, the gardening club, the many wrinkled reflections: her voice followed the intonations of her parents' generation, whether she looked like an old person or not. Hepsie wondered whether Sally or Joan or anyone else had noticed the change in her conversation. She tried to imagine their faces, searching for any change in their manner that

23

might indicate that she was not the Hepsie they used to know.

Eb pushed back his chair and stood up, resting his hands on the table to steady himself. He felt for his mug, picked it up by the handle and found his way over to the cooker, where the coffee pot was keeping warm. Eb placed his mug on a non-slip mat on the sideboard before feeling for the lid knob of the coffee pot, which was placed on a back hotplate to stop him from accidentally knocking it off the cooker. Moving his left hand down the coffee pot, Eb located the riveted handle and grasped it tightly. Carefully, he moved towards the sideboard, feeling for the non-slip mat and his mug with his right hand. Eb tipped the coffee pot so that its spout rested on the rim of the mug. He poured. His plastic liquid level indicator bleeped. Hepsie knew Eb was mentally counting his steps back towards the cooker before correctly placing the coffee pot on the back hotplate. Simple tasks such as this had taken Eb months of training. He had to learn again as if he was a child. His rehabilitation officer eased him into a new world of gadgets and sounds. Eb had to learn where everything was, memorising items in relation to one another, remembering the feel of their surfaces and their individual smells. This was why nothing could be changed in the house. Not even from when he was first diagnosed. Peace Cottage stood in a time warp. And if Hepsie felt bored with it, well, she couldn't change it. Eb needed the security, as well as the practical mobility, of being able to live in a home he knew and that he could visualise in his memory.

Hepsie blew her nose. She knew what was coming next.

Eb placed his mug on the table before feeling for

his chair and sitting down. "Do you mind getting the Bible, Hepsie?"

"Why do you need it, again?"

"It makes me feel good. Maybe there's a clue there I've missed. I only want you to read the family inscriptions. Nothing holy!" Eb chuckled, trying to pass off the situation as another joke.

Hepsie got up and went to get the Bible from the living room. Eb had suddenly remembered the Bible and its inscriptions when they were doing the family history research. It had been put away with Grandfather Georgie's possessions. Eb had been surprised that Georgie had kept such a relic. He remembered opening the Bible and discovering the handwritten inscriptions on two blank pages at the front of it. When he had asked Hepsie to search for the Bible years later, he recalled the neat, rounded script written in a traditional hand.

The Bible's leather binding felt soft and worn in Hepsie's hands. It was a deep blue-black binding and contained the mustiness of many years. She sat down at the kitchen table and carefully opened the Bible at the two pages of inscriptions. The Bible's pages were unusually thin, like tissue paper, and the reader had to be gentle when turning them. Hepsie read the inscriptions out loud, reeling them off like a shopping list because she had read them so many times to Eb.

To Hephzibah Beard on her 16th Birth Day – 24th June 1855 – A gift from her dearest Papa and Mama

Hephzibah Beard and Ebenezer Anderson wedded 24th June 1859

George Anderson born 18th Day of November in the year of our Lord 1861

Zennor Mills and George Anderson wedded 14th October 1886

Elsie Anderson born 16th August 1887

Clara Anderson born 21st March 1890

George Ebenezer Anderson born 8th September 1893

Hepsie waited for Eb's response, but he was lost in a private world of ancestors and dates. It was always the same. As soon as she had found the remembered Bible, she was helping Eb to match the names in the inscriptions with those in the 1901 Census, before tracking down the birth, marriage and death certificates on-line. If they were in the mood, she and Eb could even visit the local graveyard to lay flowers on the tombstones of Hephzibah and Ebenezer Anderson and of Zennor Anderson. Eb had run his hands over the tombstones, moss crumbling away from the damp Cotswold stone. Hepsie had helped him to clean the graves so that their inscriptions were clear to read. They were surprised to learn that Zennor Anderson was only thirty-two years old when she died. The thought didn't send a shiver down Hepsie's spine. She was the same age, but people often died young in Victorian times and it wasn't surprising that her paternal great-grandmother should be one of them. Eb thought it was strange Zennor had been buried alone. But then they discovered Zennor's husband, George, and their two daughters, Elsie and Clara, had moved to Stroud to run the draper's shop after the death of its

26

proprietor. These were Grandfather Georgie's immediate relations, but he had never spoken about them. Eb, of course, had insisted on visiting the site of Davis and Co. Drapers in Stroud, now unrecognisable as a High Street chain store. And then hunting for the graves of George and his two daughters in the town's cemetery. Eb probably knew more about his ancestors than they did. There wasn't an area of their life he hadn't asked Hepsie to poke into.

And, now, I would like to get on with my own life, she thought. But where was she going? The local Salmon Mill Publishing Company needed her to finish proofreading the manuscripts on *Gloucestershire Customs and Traditions* by next Friday. No doubt, they would have some more work for her, but nothing as inspiring as her previous job as an executive editor in London. With her skills and experience, she should have been able to get a good job locally or, at least, in Bristol or Gloucester; however, the work commitment level expected of her would be high and she knew she couldn't juggle being there for Eb on a daily basis and pursuing her career. Freelance allowed her to work from home whilst keeping an eye on Eb. If there had been a local editorial job in an office for a few hours every day, then she would have taken it. Each week she scanned the local papers in hope.

Eb had closed his eyes. His brow was furrowed in concentration. Who needs an Ouija board, Hepsie thought; Eb's found his own way of communicating with the spirits. The grandfather clock in the hall chimed the half-hour as she got up to clear away their lunch from the table. It must be 1.30 p.m. From the living room, she heard the muted rings of their telephone. *Who's that?* Eb opened his eyes, his face alert.

"I'll get it." Eb began to stand up.

"Can you get there in time?"

Eb nodded.

Hepsie couldn't be bothered. She hoped it was someone Eb could have a chat with. Get him out of the kitchen whilst she cleared up.

She handed Eb his long cane and left him to find his way to the living room. The telephone kept ringing.

Eb must have reached the telephone before the caller could ring off, because he shouted from the living room:

"It's Mike Johnson!"

Hepsie dropped the drying-up cloth she was holding. Mike Johnson! But they were ex-directory. *It can't be Mike Johnson.*

She rushed into the living room. Eb was standing there, holding up the handset, his face grinning like a Cheshire Cat as he said:

"He discovered his mobile had recorded our number."

Three

Amberley 1894

Zennor Anderson was going back to the place of her
birth. Thirty-two years ago, Zennor Churchtown gave
her its name. For the first time since her parents left
that small Cornish community, taking her sister Rose
and brother Joe with them in an one-horse wagon to
a country estate in South Devon, she was to set foot
on Cornish soil. Her mother hadn't meant to give birth
to her there. Pa was taking the family to his next job.
She had been conceived during his commission at an
estate near Penzance. Before leaving, the family
detoured to Land's End, but Ma's growing labour pains
forced their stop at Zennor Churchtown. She was told
how the wind thrashed rain against the windowpanes
during her birth and the sea hollered turbulently.
There were times when she wished she hadn't been
born.

Zennor wrung George's shirt one more time
through the iron mangle. The wooden rolling pins,
made by her father-in-law Ebenezer, squeezed out the
excess water, wetting the grass beneath the mangle.
She and George's mother, Hephzibah, had decided

to do the washing outside. It was a breezy day late in May, with the sun warm in the sky and the clouds scurrying as quickly as they could across the spring blueness. Zennor watched George's shirt fall into the tub, which was piled high with damp, wrung washing. Her hands were red and raw from being immersed in water. The washtub had yet to be emptied and she had left a washing dolly, also made by Ebenezer, floating in the dirty water. Hephzibah was seated in a kitchen chair beneath the blossoming apple trees. The blossom would be like a billowing white sheet in a few days' time. Zennor wasn't sure where they were going to hang up the washing line. If she used the apple trees, the washing would be spoilt by the blossom.

As if reading her thoughts, Hephzibah said: "We can use the gate post and the roof of Ebenezer's workshop to string up the washing line. Ebenezer can bring us a stake to support the middle of it. He'll come out from his workshop when he sees us waiting." She nodded her head in confirmation of what she'd said, the frills on her lace cap nodding along with her. Hephzibah had kept her plain, middle-parted hairstyle fashionable from her youth. She wore a dark red and green paisley shawl wrapped tightly around her dress, "to keep the cold off her bones", so she said. Her sewing lay in her hands as she paused to look closely at Zennor.

Zennor flinched, trying to hide her reaction behind a smile. What was Hephzibah thinking of her now? "That will be good, Mama," she said. Best to keep on the good side of her parents-in-law.

She dried her sore hands on her apron. Washing day used to be a joint affair between Hephzibah and herself, but her mother-in-law suffered from arthritis and dealing with wet washing and heavy manual tasks made it worse. Not wanting to seem as if she was shirking her duties and making her daughter-in-law do all the work, Hephzibah had offered to sit out in the garden, keeping Zennor company. George's parents were often like this. Ever since her courting days with George, Peace Cottage was her home. Zennor had never had a 'proper' home. Her cabinet-maker father tired of places and sought work wherever it took him, his family following him like left luggage. No soon as the family had settled, then it was time to move on again: to find new friends, new habits, new schooling, new solaces. When Zennor arrived at the Andersons' home, she felt she had found the stationary world at the centre of her heart. The one she'd always been chasing. And now she was in danger of losing it.

If Ebenezer was going to put up the washing line, then there was no need to sort out the wrung washing until he appeared from his workshop. He was probably looking at them through the window, as he lathed a walking stick or mended the spoke of a neighbour's broken umbrella. Zennor sat down on the grass, stretching her legs out beneath her long skirt. She closed her eyes and silently breathed in the familiar smells of her home: apple blossom, grass, wet washing, Hephzibah's sweet violet perfume, Ebenezer's wood chippings, the straw from the hen house, and the flowering hawthorn in the hedgerows. Amberley had been her home for seven years. When she opened her eyes, she saw that Hephzibah had resumed her sewing. The regular rhythm of Hephzibah's stitching echoed the regular rhythm of Hephzibah's daily life.

"It's not long before George and you go away. Are you looking forward to your holiday?" Hephzibah didn't look up from her sewing as she spoke. The sun caught the silver threads of her pied-dappled hair that wasn't hidden by her lace cap and sent piercing daggers of light into Zennor's eyes.

Zennor lifted up her hand to her eyes to stop them from squinting. "Of course, Mama," she lied.

"You must be excited about going back to the place where you were born. George has worked so hard in Mr Davis's shop so that both of you can go to your sister's wedding in St Ives. He does want this holiday to be *special* for you, Zennor." Hephzibah still had her eyes focused on her sewing. Her carefully placed stitches mirrored her carefully considered words. "A change of air will be good for you. They say that the winds off the Cornish coast are very reviving, more so than our own very good air here on the Common."

Hephzibah still wasn't looking at her. Zennor put her hand down and stared into the blinding sun. Who's going to help me now? she despaired. But there was no one she could tell. It was mad to stare into the sun. Zennor closed her eyes and tried to stop the thoughts rushing to her mind: disjointed words, fragmented images, the sun being shut out of her world, the lid coming down on top of her. A chaffinch burst into song near her but she remained silent. She didn't trust herself to speak.

"It's no use. I can't sew any more today. My fingers are feeling stiff."

Zennor opened her eyes.

Hephzibah had laid down her sewing in her lap and was gazing around the garden, looking for a distraction to ease her irritation.

"Do you want to go indoors, Mama?"

"No."

"Do you need another shawl?"

Hephzibah shook her head.

Zennor tried to push her babbling thoughts to the

back of her mind. She must make conversation with Hephzibah, otherwise they'll think she was getting worse again.

"I'm looking forward to seeing my sister Roelinda." At least that was true. "It's been more than two years since we last met up." But would Roelinda notice a change in her? "In her last letter she said she was glad to be marrying and settling down." But did Roelinda know what married life was like? Zennor thought back to the last time George had taken her in bed. They didn't do 'that' any more. It was one of the reasons why George had promised to take her on holiday. He hadn't said so, but she knew it was there, on his mind. At one time their loving had come easily. Her body yielded to George's touch. After little Georgie was born they lost interest. No, that wasn't true. She knew why. And she knew why, and she knew why, and she knew why...why, why, why...

Hephzibah was interrupting her thoughts. "Is Roelinda going to leave service after her marriage?" And then more sharply when there was no reply: "Zennor! Did you hear me?"

Zennor faked a cough, using her hand to partly conceal her face. "I was imagining what it will be like in Cornwall."

Hephzibah nodded her head, pleased with her daughter-in-law's response. I suppose that means I'm on the road to recovery, Zennor thought ruefully.

"You mustn't worry about little Georgie. The girls and I will look after him carefully during your absence. He'll want his Mama to come back home hale and hearty." This time Hephzibah glanced knowingly at Zennor.

Zennor had no choice but to look directly at her mother-in-law's smoky-grey eyes and smile. They thought she was ill. In some ways, she was. They thought she was of unsound mind during Georgie's time in her womb. What did they mean by an 'unsound mind'? Zennor knew she couldn't touch her food. She swirled it around on her plate or gave herself smaller portions. She grit her teeth and forced herself to swallow. Nothing escaped Hephzibah's eyes. "You're not feeling yourself, Zennor," she would say. "That was a stinker of a cold you got at Christmas. Let me get you some more beef tea. It will help make you strong again." By the time of her lying-in with Georgie, her cheeks were pinched and no amount of beef tea or fresh Common air could bring the roses back to them. The family were worried she wouldn't bond with Georgie: George's first boy heir.

She shivered. Hephzibah would think she was "feeling the cold on her bones". Although the sun was warm, the air on these hills could still feel chill on a May morning.

Surprisingly, she did bond with Georgie. How could she not? Giving life seemed to awaken her from her walking nightmare. The baby curled up his fingers in hers as she clutched them for the first time. It wasn't his fault. Here was someone who needed her in a different way from how George and Hephzibah and others needed her. Little Georgie, like Elsie and Clara before him, gave her back the trusting innocence she had lost. She could see George and Hephzibah, and Ebenezer, too, watching her closely after her confinement: perhaps she was going to drop the baby or let him choke on his own sick? For her part, she took baby Georgie in his perambulator for walks along the Common, the wind tugging at Elsie and Clara's hair as they ran on ahead, whooping like the birds in the sky and clambering over the grassy undulations of the Bulwarks and hill fort. As autumn turned into winter, and Georgie grew his first tooth, the Severn could be clearly seen glinting on the horizon. It was then that the old nightmares returned. She searched for clues in Georgie's face and thought she found them there. Did they notice?

"Look! There's Mrs Mortimer walking along the lane." Hephzibah was peering beyond the garden wall, watching a beribboned straw bonnet bob its way up the steep lane.

Don't call out to her, Zennor prayed. Mrs Mortimer was one of those "God botherers": chapel folk who self-righteously nosed into your business and passed moral judgements. Zennor had felt the likes of Mrs Mortimer and other God botherers staring down at her, often through their pince-nez, ever since...

"I do believe she's not going to stop and greet us. Tsch." Hephzibah made disapproving noises with her mouth. She wasn't a chapel worshipper herself but she did like her fellow villagers to be polite to her.

Zennor felt even more uncomfortable. She knew Mrs Mortimer had been slighting Hephzibah because the God botherer had guessed. They had once crossed in the lane by the village shop and Mrs Mortimer had lowered her eyes rather than meet Zennor's directly. The woman clutched her basket closely to her dress, taking her daughter's hand firmly in hers, before turning away.

Hephzibah sighed and folded her hands in her lap. Zennor felt she'd better say something.

"Ebenezer won't be long now. It's nearing lunch time." She tried to force a joke through. "Knowing Papa, his hunger pangs will get the better of him."

Her mother-in-law didn't laugh.

"This washing needs hanging up. It won't get dry

35

in that soggy pile." Hephzibah pulled her paisley shawl more tightly around her bodice. She had a weary, resigned look on her fresh-faced features. "We can't sit here all day waiting for my good man to turn up."

"Shall I fetch Papa from his workshop?"

"We'll give him another ten minutes of his own peace." Hephzibah folded her arms across her chest and set herself to wait.

Zennor waited for her mother-in-law to make further conversation but Hephzibah's eyes slowly closed. It was easier that way. Perhaps Hephzibah was doing it on purpose? Zennor watched the clouds scurry over Peace Cottage. The Cotswold stone home was built into the hillside, which meant that the apple trees were on a par with the upper storey. In times of torrential rain the flagstone floors of the kitchen and scullery were often flooded, as the rain poured down the garden slope towards the back of the house. There was a grill in the kitchen floor that stopped the flooded water from reaching the front parlour. Moist, damp smells lingered for a long time afterwards. Gloucestershire was known to be wet and damp, but Zennor didn't mind, because it was her home. Her part of the world was called The Five Valleys: Stonehouse, Painswick, Slad, the Golden Valley at Chalford, and Nailsworth. Amberley and its Common lay between the Golden and Nailsworth valleys. Locals often called this part of the world Paradise. And so it was. But now paradise was slipping from her grip. What she had always wanted to obtain and hold on for ever more – a secure world with a stationary home, a husband, a family, and a community to bind them together like a tight bonnet ribbon – had become unravelled. What was she to do?

The sprouting apple blossom stirred in the breeze. Like her, it was blown one way, then another. Indecision drove her mad. Should she or shouldn't she tell George? But they didn't trust one another any more. George had been confused to find that his wife of seven years was of 'unsound mind'. "I want my old girl back," he would say. It was the sleepless nights that had disturbed him. Zennor tried to hide her tears in her pillow, her head and body turned away from George, and she was sure he never heard her. However, she couldn't stop the dreams from haunting her and making her cry out in her restless sleep. Did she chat a lot in these nightmares? George hadn't said anything to her. He snored deeply in his sleep. Had he heard? Why couldn't she ask him? Like she used to do, when they were first married and enjoyed paradise in the garden of Peace Cottage.

She suffered flashbacks. They didn't know about this, too. She'd be in the scullery when her mind would suddenly black out. In slow motion she saw it happening again. Felt the sensations. Cold sweat pouring down her back. The warm breath. She tried to block out these memories, to deaden the force of her imagination. She felt she was carrying a dead weight in her head. Somnambulistic, she carried out her daily tasks. "Where's my old girl?" George used to ask. Craftily, the memories knocked on the doors of other memories, memories she had kept hidden for many years. She thought she had thrown the key away. For the second time in her life, her flesh crawled with fear and loathing. Voices danced a clamouring polka inside her head. "You remember, Zennor. You remember." Zennor wanted to be sick. Her guilt returned. It churned up in her stomach like clods of earth being ploughed. But there was no new sowing or harvesting of the wheat for her.

"You're not yourself, Zennor," they would say.

George thought she should rest; read some of those books she loved reading. Zennor couldn't tell him that every time she looked at the pages her mind went blank. It never used to be like that. There were times in her life when she would have done anything to read a book. She read anything: newspapers, magazines, pamphlets, old and new novels. Her own Pa had insisted on hiding them from her because he didn't want her getting above her station. He had stopped her dream of becoming a school assistant. Her teachers knew she was an able and keen pupil who should be encouraged, but Pa was having none of it. "You're to go in service like your elder sister Rose. None of this book learning," he told her. Zennor didn't understand why a man as skilled as her father didn't want his children to better themselves. But then he was a 'doing' man. She had rarely seen him reading a newspaper, unlike her husband George.

Zennor didn't like taking a rest. It gave her time to dwell upon bad thoughts. She felt uncomfortable letting Hephzibah clean the kitchen grate and light the first fire in the mornings before everyone got up. That should be her task. She wanted to get up and do her household tasks like a dutiful daughter-in-law, wife and mother should. She didn't like, although they were too young, Elsie and Clara to see her like this. It was easier after Georgie was born, because she could hide her fears in smothering him with motherly love. But it was difficult. Fatigue draped over her like a heavy rug-covering on a parlour table. It followed her around the house in the form of Hephzibah, Ebenezer and George. "You don't want those migraines occurring again," they would reason with her (she had lied when they'd asked why she was in distress). She knew George wanted to ask her whether it was the baby. Hephzibah did once, placing her hand on Zennor's stomach and trying to persuade her to undo her tight corset and wear a loose dress in the house. Zennor was having none of it. Her indispositions with Elsie and Clara had been straightforward and, although the lying-ins were painful, there were no problems or infections. But it was something to do with the baby. They were right about that. 'Evil hands' were at work. Isn't that how the God botherers would describe it? She needed a good bout of hand washing. Zennor shivered. She had lost her faith in God. Social life in Amberley revolved around the Church or Chapel, but her universe was now under the influence of some higher cosmic order.

"Why, you're shivering, m'dear." Ebenezer's low, burred voice cut through Zennor's thoughts like a knife cutting ping! through a trapeze wire. "I saw two fine ladies by themselves in need of company and thought I would come and do the honour of talking to them. But my good wife is a-dozing and my daughter a-shivering. May I offer you my jacket, Zennor?"

"I am fine, Papa," Zennor quickly replied. She managed to smile at him. The grass felt damp beneath her skirt so she stood up, brushing off the stray grass strands before smoothing down her skirt and long apron. "Can I get you a chair?"

"He doesn't need a chair," Hephzibah cut in crossly. "We won't be sitting out for much longer. And I wasn't a-dozing. Just thinking."

"My dear wife." Ebenezer turned towards Hephzibah to make a mock bow, but she was having none of it. She waved him off with her hands.

"We want a clothes line putting up. Washing needs hanging up or else it won't dry."

Ebenezer's weather-beaten face creased into a smile, accentuating the dimples either side of his wide mouth.

He was still an upright man, with broad shoulders and a slender build. His long white whiskers, Dundrearies they were called, fluttered in the breeze. Zennor could smell the wood shavings on his crumpled corduroy suit. There was always a fine layer of sawdust wherever Papa went.

"But I be wanting a rest first. I've left my work to 'specially come and talk to you both." Ebenezer spoke his words as if he was lubricating them with the oil he used to mend unyielding umbrella spokes. "No, no...there's no need to get me a chair," he said turning towards Zennor. "The grass's good enough for me." He lowered himself to the ground, easing himself into a comfortable position. Hephzibah tut-tutted beneath her breath.

Zennor didn't know what to do. She felt awkward standing between her parents-in-law. Was Ebenezer up to something? He seemed to have an ulterior purpose for his need for conversation. She could have easily fetched him from his workshop.

"Well, m'dear, it won't be long now before you'll be a-going away. I trust you're looking forward to it." Ebenezer eyed her intently.

Zennor could only nod her head and force a smile. Then, finding her voice again, she said: "Mama and I were just talking about it. Weren't we, Mama?"

Hephzibah remained silent. She was looking at both Ebenezer and Zennor, with the expectation that Ebenezer was going to say something important.

"Well that's good, isn't it my dear wife?" Ebenezer glanced at Hephzibah before turning his attention back to Zennor. "You know, there's a wonderful quote in the Bible, which do fully put it no better. Let me see, what did the good Lord say..." Ebenezer tugged at his Dundrearies in mock thoughtfulness. "That's it!"

40

Raising his right arm in triumph, he broke into a dimpled smile. "Proverbs, chapter seventeen, verse twenty-two: *A merry spirit doeth good like a medicine: but a broken spirit drieth the bones.* What do you say to that?"

Zennor was lost for words. She felt as if she was a thread of cotton being continually tightly wound around a wooden reel. All tide up and impossible to unravel just when you needed a neat thread to pass through your needle. Hephzibah could see she was struggling. Zennor swallowed and came out with the first thing she could say: "Thank you, Papa." She didn't know whether she sounded sarcastic or not.

"Is that all!" Ebenezer exclaimed. "There's a wonderful moral hidden in that proverb. Can't you see it?"

Zennor shook her head. Her mind was spinning like a child's wooden top. She couldn't see how the Lord's proverbs had anything to do with her own predicament. Did Ebenezer mean that the Lord was going to save her, now? When it was too late?

Ebenezer also shook his head, but in disappointment. Zennor could see that his clear hazel eyes were not unkind. Making another effort, her father-in-law spoke again: "Look, the good Lord advises us to live life with a merry spirit because it will cheer us up. It's like the best medicine you can take. A broken spirit will only lead you to the grave. Nothing more than dry bones."

Hephzibah chuckled.

"What are you a-chuckling at, my dear wife?" Ebenezer glanced at Hephzibah, who for the first time that day was smiling.

"You'll never make a Chapel person," Hephzibah said, trying not to laugh at the same time. "They wouldn't have you interpreting the scriptures like that, as if God's best interests were only that we should be merry."

The situation had been defused. Her parents-in-law were chuckling together, careful not to let the noise drift over the garden wall to their neighbours' gardens and the Common. Pulling herself together, Zennor joined in.

"Well, it's certainly worked," Ebenezer said. "Look at us! You couldn't get a merrier crowd doing God's duty by taking the best medicine."

A part of Zennor wanted to laugh out even louder. To hit the very heavens. But she knew it would be more a scream of despair than of happiness. All around her the spring sunshine caressed the budding shoots and encouraged the virgin leaves to wrap the Cotswold countryside in a green blanket. On the Common buttercups smothered the grass, providing a golden carpet for the cattle and horses as they lazily grazed beneath the huge, open sky. White May blossom garlanded the bushes and hedgerows. Even here, in the back garden of Peace Cottage, yellow cowslips trembled delicately in the clean, fresh air. If only I could lift this burden, thought Zennor, I would be happy in this paradise.

Ebenezer and Hephzibah were still wiping the tears from their eyes. It was amazing how her parents-in-law still shared the same bond of humour after so many years of marriage. Zennor had once hoped she and George might grow into another Hephzibah and Ebenezer.

Her father-in-law stood up, not bothering to brush the grass off his suit. "I better go and get that stake for you," he said. "Can't keep the washing waiting." He winked at Zennor before strolling off to his workshop at the bottom of the garden. "Won't be long," he called over his shoulder to his wife.

Zennor fished for the washing dolly in the dirty washtub and threw it onto the grass. Soapy water splattered her long apron and dampened her rolled-up sleeves. She picked up the bucket she had discarded earlier and began to mechanically empty the washtub, taking bucketfuls to be sloshed over the garden wall adjoining the Common. She had to be careful that no one was passing by on that side or that Clara was playing there. Zennor hoped Elsie, who was at the Parochial School, would be back in time for lunch. Her girls never strayed far but the Common held many distractions. She would have liked to have grown up here. As it was, she wasn't a part of this community any more. Not even as a grown-up.

She paused in her work, glancing around her and over the garden wall towards the broad, sweeping Common. There was no one about apart from some grazing horses and a swallow swooping in the sky. Relieved, Zennor picked up the bucket and took her time walking back to the washtub. She knew the likes of Mrs Mortimer were gossiping about her. And not because she was of 'unsound mind'. They had guessed. She wondered whether Ebenezer and Hephzibah had, too. Their every conversation worried her. Had they noticed?

The village community was sacrosanct. Any one who threatened its tightly knit rules wouldn't be tolerated. Keeping up appearances gave you a ticket to village life. Once you betrayed that, the ticket was ripped up and you were outside, again. Everything she loved dearly, the status quo, the belonging, the completeness, would be lost. Zennor knew people in the village were gossiping about her as if they were wringing a chicken's neck. Not only the God botherers and her own family, but others.

Hephzibah had moved from her chair and was walking towards the house. I've forgotten the pegs, Zennor suddenly remembered. At least it gave her a few minutes' rest from her mother-in-law. The washtub was almost empty so she would have to wait until Hephzibah's return. Together they would drag the washtub to the garden wall and lift it up to tip the remaining water onto the Common. Ebenezer was taking his time with that clothes line and stake. She remembered washing days used to run a lot more smoothly before...

Maybe going on holiday was a good idea? To breathe an untainted air. If only things were going better between her and George. Maybe they were right? Going away from all this might make a difference. But could she tell George in Cornwall? Before it was too late and it was all there for him – and the whole of Amberley – to see.

Four

Hepsie was back at Siesta Café. She and Eb had been there since 10.30 a.m. because Eb wanted to get a table and settle down before Mike Johnson's expected arrival at 11 o'clock. They were sitting at the back of the café, "an old man and his daughter", as Eb had told Mike. Hepsie stirred the froth clinging to the sides of her empty cappuccino cup. She was still unsure whether Mike Johnson would turn up this time or not. Every so often she glanced towards the entrance door. She also glanced at the minutes ticking away on her wrist watch. Eb had finished his shortcake and coffee and was sitting calmly beside her. Hepsie knew he was certain that Mike Johnson was going to turn up. This morning he had decided to choose his clothes himself and had opted for a smart blazer, front-pleated trousers and an open-necked blue striped shirt. He had asked Hepsie to make sure that his thick wavy hair was tidy and his face smooth after shaving. She nearly asked him whether he also wanted a dash of cologne, but bit her lip in time. It was obvious to Eb that she didn't want to meet Mike Johnson.

No. That wasn't quite true. All week Hepsie had been dreading this Bank Holiday Saturday. The week had passed slowly by. Eb was in exuberant spirits, humming to himself, and telling Joan they were going to get Mike Johnson to open the next door, genealogically speaking, for them. Hepsie was sick of the genealogy. For her, today's meeting was a chance to undermine Mike Johnson's help. As soon as she could see a loophole in his offer to help, she would decline his services. Maybe he charged too much money? Hepsie was determined to find that loophole and sweep the Mike Johnson saga, along with Eb and Joan's blue-rinse genealogy, under the doormat. She would have to be sharp to make sure that Eb didn't undermine her plan. For all she knew, Mike Johnson might not turn up. She was hoping he wouldn't, because then she could dismiss him as a con man and say to Eb: "I told you so." "Mike Johnson's unreliable and we don't need his services any more."

Hepsie abruptly stopped stirring the froth in her empty cappuccino cup. She glanced at the entrance door, again. A man and a woman, who she presumed to be his wife or girlfriend, entered the café. Hepsie quickly turned away and looked at Eb instead. At least he couldn't see her. It was getting awkward looking at the door every time someone entered the café. Other customers were beginning to stare at her. Eb was fiddling with his talking wrist watch. No doubt he was waiting for it to announce 11 o'clock. Hepsie could hear her stomach rumbling. Luckily, the café was full and noisy, and she was certain her rumbling couldn't be heard. She hadn't eaten much for breakfast and couldn't face the thought of eating a chocolate-covered shortcake as Eb had done.

No. That wasn't true, too. Hepsie had been dreading this meeting all week. For some reason, Mike Johnson's low, mellifluous voice had been playing in her ears. And she didn't dislike it. Although she was planning

46

to undermine him at this meeting, she couldn't help wondering what sort of man Mike Johnson was. His voice put pictures in her mind. He was young; he was sexy; he was tall; he was good-looking; he was bored and wanted to play; he hated genealogy. Hepsie couldn't stop these mad thoughts. She tried to erase them by focusing on how she was going to undermine today's meeting. There was no need to worry because she was certain he'd be easy to scare away. One sight of blind Eb and his crazy carer of a daughter should be enough to scare away Mike Johnson in one go, she thought.

However, she had taken great care with her clothes this morning. Whilst Eb had deliberated over his choice of clothing, she had frantically rummaged in her wardrobe, searching for the right outfit. If she was going to scare away Mike Johnson, she reasoned, then she had better dress to make herself look confident and mature. So here she was, sitting in Siesta Café dressed in a short black skirt and fitted white shirt, with her favourite flip-flops exchanged for sheer black tights and three-inch-high court shoes. The heels made it a little difficult walking up the steep streets of Stroud with Eb holding onto her arm for support, but Hepsie was determined to look grown-up and in control. She didn't want Mike Johnson to think that she was nothing but Eb's little girl clinging to her father's apron strings.

Her low-necked shirt required her to select an eye-catching, chunky beaded necklace, and she matched this with similar coloured pierced earrings. Stroud was well known for its local craft designs and the meeting was a good opportunity for her to show off the local jewellery. She had washed her chestnut hair, making sure to condition it so that the light would pick up the red and gold tints in her predominantly brown

47

locks. There wasn't a wind today, but she lightly hairsprayed her long hair to stop her from running her fingers through it if she became agitated during the meeting. Even her make-up had been chosen carefully. Hepsie took out her lipstick case from her handbag and flipped open its lid. Peering at her lips in the mirror, she decided to refresh her lips with some more Nude Rose colour. She considered she didn't look too bad. Overall, Mike Johnson would be impressed with her appearance.

Eb coughed discreetly. She and Eb hadn't spoken much since sitting down at the table. Eb, probably from excitement, and herself, from nerves. There wasn't really any more to say. The events that led them to being here had already been dissected and argued many times over. Secretly, Hepsie was angry with herself for not remembering that mobiles recorded callers' phone numbers. Was she worried that Mike Johnson had been keen to contact them again? Why did she think he would be easy to scare away by only missing one meeting? As it was, his excuse was something about being involved in a road accident on his way to Stroud. He was driving uphill on the Painswick Road between Brockworth and Cranham, when an on-coming car overtook another car on a bend. Mike was forced to swerve to avoid a collision and his car ended up stuck in a ditch. He hadn't phoned them straight away because he had only their landline number and, knowing they would still be waiting for him in Stroud, decided to call them when he thought they might be back at home. Hepsie didn't know whether this was true or not. She tried to convince Eb that Mike's story could be another con man's ploy.

"But Mike would have phoned us," Eb said, "if you had given him a mobile number."

"I did that for our safety, Eb," she reminded him.

"Well, he's got mine this time."

Yes, Hepsie thought, and now Mike Johnson knows for certain that both of us will be in Stroud to meet him, he'll go to our empty house and rob it. This time Eb had given Mike details of car parks and the easiest route into town. He had asked Hepsie for advice whilst she was standing beside him during last Saturday's phone call. Eb had been quick to suggest to Mike that they should arrange another meeting. He also found out that Mike lived in Cheltenham.

"Eleven a.m." announced Eb's talking watch.

It wasn't a loud announcement, but customers sitting nearby turned to look at them. People didn't always notice immediately that Eb was blind. Now, they looked at him a little more closely. At her regular café, The Juicy Carrot, where she and Eb were known by both staff and regular customers, talking watches were understood and ignored. Eb hadn't told Mike Johnson that he was blind. Hepsie was secretly hoping that Mike Johnson might find Eb's blindness embarrassing and be scared away from helping them. Of course, it could go equally the other way.

"He's coming," Eb said, half to himself.

"Where...?" Hepsie said, looking towards the entrance door.

"He's late, I know. But he is coming."

Eb was obviously having one of his second-sight turns. He seemed to be intuitively tuned into Mike Johnson's vibes.

Hepsie continued to look at the entrance door, watching an elderly couple enter the café. They were followed by a family with young children and a pushchair. A younger couple left the café. Hepsie felt herself being stared at, again. She glanced at her watch.

11.05 a.m. She looked at Eb to stop herself from looking at the entrance door. Eb's face showed complete calmness. He smiled knowingly. Defying the staring customers, Hepsie glanced towards the entrance door. A man had entered the café and was looking for someone. He walked towards the back of the café. That can't be him, she thought.

The man glanced their way. Involuntarily, Hepsie raised her hand and waved. He smiled back. For what seemed like a long time, he approached their table.

Mike Johnson was a young man, of about her age, she guessed. He wasn't too tall. He wasn't large boned. He was lean and sinewy. And dressed in a fashionable grey pinstriped suit with an open-necked deep purple shirt. His fair hair was fashionably cut shorter at the sides and longer on top. She could imagine him ruffling his fingers through his top hair so that it stood up like the bristles on a brush. Was he handsome? All Hepsie could additionally take in at the moment was that he had a most charming smile: broad, friendly and humorous.

He stood before them. Hepsie felt herself smiling at him.

"Are you Eb and Hepsie Anderson?" he asked.

His low, mellifluous voice made Hepsie's heart jump. She offered her hand to him to shake. "Hepsie," she managed to say.

Mike's hand briefly clasped hers. Firm and warm.

She had better introduce Eb to him.

But Eb was already offering his hand across the table. "And I'm Eb. Very pleased to meet you."

Mike shook Eb's hand warmly. He looked closely at Eb but didn't show any surprise at greeting a blind man.

"Mike Johnson," he said. "Can I get you a coffee or anything else?"

Hepsie shook her head.

"I'll have another coffee, please," Eb said. "Thanks very much."

Mike went to the food counter to order. Hepsie tried not to follow him with her eyes. He seemed the most unlikely genealogist to her. Or else the face of genealogy was changing. She could still feel the warm clasp of his hand in hers. If she had seen correctly, then he was as much attracted to her on first sight as she was to him. There was an invisible rope drawing his boat towards her, as if he was destined to anchor at her harbour. She saw the instant attraction in what she could now recall as his pale green eyes. Green eyes that had seemed to swallow her up whole like a cat eyeing a saucer of creamy milk.

By the time Mike came back to the table with two coffees, Hepsie had managed to remind herself that the meeting was about undermining Eb's genealogical intentions and that Mike Johnson was her enemy. It was in her best interests to get the meeting over and done with as soon as possible.

First, though, they made polite conversation. Eb was not to be rushed. He asked whether Mike had found the car park alright. And said he was glad Mike hadn't had another accident on the way to Stroud. Mike apologised for not making the meeting last Saturday, explaining yet again how he didn't have a mobile number for them. Somehow, they got on to discussing the weather and how lucky they were with the good forecast for this Bank Holiday weekend.

Hepsie thought she'd better interrupt or else they would be here all day.

"We should really be getting on with the family history business," she said.

"Of course," said Mike.

"Good idea, Hepsie," said Eb. "What can you tell us about yourself, Mike? How did you get into this genealogical business?"

Hepsie leaned forward and rested her elbows on the table so that her hands were clasped under her chin. She must listen very closely to Mike in case there were any loopholes she could use as an excuse to decline his services.

Mike amicably explained that his interest in genealogy started with his own family history research. He enjoyed it so much he decided to set up his own business as a researcher. Such was the current craze in genealogy, he could see there was a need for his services, and he wanted to make the most of that opportunity.

"Are you busy at the moment?" Hepsie asked him. "Have you got a lot of research to do for other people?"

Mike ran his fingers through his hair before giving his answer. "To be honest, you're my first clients. The business is a new venture I've set up very recently."

"I couldn't find your website on the internet," Hepsie said.

"Neither could I," Eb added.

Mike looked worried, but it quickly passed.

"I want to keep the business local at first. Because of work commitments, I thought it would be easier to manage and for me to do the research properly," he explained. "I don't want to be snowed under with requests, especially if I can't fulfil them as professionally as I would like to do. Unthorough research would be very frustrating for both myself and for my clients."

"You work, as well?" Hepsie asked. This was most interesting.

"Yes," Mike replied.

"What do you do?" she probed further.

Mike seemed reluctant to reply but then said: "I work in marketing."

"Does that keep you busy?" Hepsie asked.

"I make sure it doesn't stop me from pursuing my genealogical interests, if that's what you mean?" Mike's pale green eyes challenged her for a moment.

But Hepsie was not to be deterred. "You're certain that your work commitments won't infringe upon your genealogical commitments?"

Mike smiled at her. "Oh, I don't think so," he firmly stated, as if drawing a line under their discussion.

"Hepsie works freelance – don't you, Hepsie?" Eb said.

She was about to reply when Eb continued: "You could do that, couldn't you Mike? Free you up to give you time for your genealogical searches?"

"Maybe," Mike replied non-committally. Then he looked at Hepsie and said: "What do *you* do?"

Eb butted in, again, before she could reply: "Hepsie works in publishing. For the local Salmon Mill Publishing Company. Have you heard of them?"

"Yes, I have," said Mike. "Are you editorial or marketing?" he asked Hepsie.

"Editorial," Hepsie quickly replied. "But I think we've better get on with the genealogical discussion." She glanced at her watch to make the point. Eb was making the situation between her and Mike far too personal.

"Sorry, I didn't know you were in a hurry," Mike remarked.

"We're not," said Eb. "I suspect my daughter is worried that we won't have enough time to discuss the family history research."

Mike smiled broadly at Hepsie.

Hepsie wished she could hide her embarrassment under her cappuccino saucer. She decided to try another loophole.

"So you have no website connections, yet?" she asked Mike.

His smile wavered briefly before he replied: "As I said, it's easier to keep the business local that way. If the business takes off and I find that I'm making money out of it, then I suppose there's always the option of cutting back on my marketing work." Then he added jokingly: "I feel like a change of scene, anyway. You never know, the business might go that way."

"But it seems unprofessional, to me, not to have a website for your genealogy business," Hepsie persevered. "Surely, you'll attract most of your clients that way?"

"I've got enough on my hands to keep me busy at present," Mike replied. "Distributing my business card at the County Record Office and the local family history centres will reach the right people."

Hepsie was about to ask Mike why he hadn't been inundated with requests so far, when Eb butted in with: "When I googled your name, there were thousands of hits for Mike Johnson. Even found a few who had pasted the results of their genealogical research on their website. We couldn't go through the whole lot, could we Hepsie?"

"No," said Hepsie, wondering what point Eb was trying to make. Was he trying to defend Mike's justification for not having a website?

"None of those were yours, then?" Eb asked Mike.

"No," said Mike.

Eb chuckled. "My daughter was worried you might be a con man. That's why she was frantically checking for your details on the NET."

At this point, Hepsie should have crawled into her empty cappuccino cup, but there was no escape. Eb had let the cat out of the bag. Why had he done that? Was she supposed to judge Mike Johnson's reaction to see whether he betrayed any guilt?

Mike laughed. He seemed to be taking the insinuation lightheartedly. Hepsie couldn't bear to look directly at his eyes to see whether they betrayed a flicker of guilt. She looked at the middle distance, hoping the moment would pass.

"Nowadays, you can't trust anyone," Mike joked.

"No," Eb chuckled.

How can I regain control of the situation? Hepsie thought. Speaking with concern, she said to Mike: "I have to protect Eb; it's for his own best interests. You do understand that?"

"Of course," Mike agreed. But there was a flicker of doubt in his eyes.

Hepsie wondered whether Mike's laughter was masking an underlying nervousness. She still couldn't understand why someone like Mike had been bitten by the genealogy bug. He seemed such an unlikely candidate. Unfortunately, she could also see that Eb was undeterred by Mike's lack of client experience or the fact that his genealogy business was no more than a hobby alongside his main work commitments. She would have to probe further. There must be a likely loophole hiding somewhere in Mike's conversation.

However, there was another problem. Mike's attraction for her was undermining her scaring-him-away intention. Every so often she caught him looking closely at her, with his broad, congenial smile and cat-like green eyes appraising her face and body. A part of her wanted to shout out: "Yes, I fancy you, too!", but this was not how her mind had planned it. She

55

noticed Mike briefly glancing at her mole and she couldn't help wondering whether he found it an attractive feature or an anomaly on her face. The thought worried her. Should she had covered it with concealer this morning?

The closeness of their seated proximity also worked the other way. Hepsie noticed that the pinstripes in Mike's dark grey suit were deep purple and that they complemented his deep purple shirt. She also noticed that he had a slight five o'clock shadow on his jaw. But he had splashed his face with cologne this morning, because the scent tickled her nose enticingly. Hepsie was glad that she had sprayed herself with her favourite Oriental scent before leaving the house. She knew the exotic perfume would be strong enough for Mike to smell. If he wanted to, of course.

She even mirrored his gestures. At one point, her hand fiddled with the handle of her empty cappuccino cup. Mike's hand reached out for his half-full cup of coffee, but instead of drinking from it, he also started fiddling with his cup handle. When Mike smiled, Hepsie found herself effortlessly smiling. When Mike shifted in his chair, Hepsie found herself shifting in hers to match his position. It was most irritating. Her mouth spoke with one will and her body with another. However much she tried to fight the instant attraction between Mike and herself, she or Mike did something to undermine it. She would have liked to have asked Mike whether he was coping with the same problem. But that, of course, was impossible.

"I was only making a joke, Hepsie," Eb said.

Their conversation with Mike was making Eb's benign face look lively. His pale blue eyes twinkled as much as the reflective graphite of his long cane when it caught the light from the overhead chrome lamps.

"You have to be careful what you say, Eb. We don't want to offend Mike." Hepsie knew this was a lie but she wanted to gain the upper hand.

Mike smiled pleasantly back at her.

She found another question to challenge him. "How much do you know about Gloucestershire and the Five Valleys?"

"There's so much information," Mike began. "It's probably best if you tell me what you and Eb need to find out or want to know. Perhaps Eb could expand upon what he told me on the telephone?"

"Of course," said Eb, only too willing to oblige.

Briefly, he told Mike about how their family history research had all started with the Amberley Family History Group and the 1901 Census, which led them to discovering that they were unwittingly living in the house of their ancestors. Mike listened with apparent interest as Eb outlined how much research they had already done and which sources they had exhausted.

"I couldn't have done all this without Hepsie's help," Eb finished his résumé. "She's not only my carer but my genealogical eyes and hands." He turned his head to the right, where he knew Hepsie was sitting, and smiled fondly.

"You are a very lucky man, indeed, Eb, to have such a helpful daughter." Mike looked at Hepsie as he spoke, his mellifluous voice caressing his words as though fingering silk.

Hepsie blushed. And then felt immediately silly for doing so. She seemed to spend most of this conversation being embarrassed by the men at her table. Unable to find the appropriate words as a riposte to Mike's comment, she glanced at the other tables of customers, envying their ordinary chat and mannerisms. No one was looking her way. Through the large modern windows she could see the day was developing into a sunny one. Customers now arriving for lunch or a late brunch were taking the option of sitting at tables set up outside Siesta Café, along the pedestrianised High Street. Hepsie would have liked to have sat at one of these tables, if she had been enjoying a lazy Saturday on her own, shopping, instead of talking genealogy with Eb and Mike.

"We have a photograph to show you," Eb announced to Mike. "Hepsie, can you get it out for him?"

Mike's had a lucky escape, Hepsie thought, as she unhooked the plastic carrier bag hanging on her chair. Eb had wanted to bring the family Bible with them, too, but she had persuaded him that it was unnecessary. The Bible was too old and its thin delicate pages might get torn; or it might get lost; or they might mistakenly leave it somewhere. Wasn't it too much to show Mike all at one go? Slowly, Hepsie had worn down Eb's persistence so that, now, she only had the embarrassment of the family photograph to show Mike.

She drew the large photograph from out of the plastic bag and laid it on the table between Mike and herself.

"These people are our ancestors," Eb explained to Mike. "I'm sure Hepsie will point out who's who in the photo. She discovered it in the box of my father Georgie's possessions. Unfortunately, I can't remember ever having seen the photograph, so Hepsie had to describe my ancestors to me." Eb chuckled, as if he was trying to make light of the point.

"It's a fine photograph," Mike said, perhaps diplomatically not wishing to be further drawn upon Eb's disability. "Late Victorian?"

"Hepsie tells me it's dated 1893. We think it's a

christening photograph of my late father, George Ebenezer Anderson. He was born on September 8th of that year and his baptism recorded in the Amberley parish church records in November. He's posing with his parents and grandparents, isn't he Hepsie?"

"Yes," Hepsie replied.

She was amazed at how closely Mike was studying the sepia-tinted photograph. To her, the faded photograph pasted to a piece of cardboard with curling edges was like any other old photograph. Her ancestors had posed in the local studio of J H Elliott, whose name was printed in florid lettering at the bottom of the photograph. Surrounded by potted palms and heavy drapes, the four grown-ups stared out of the photograph as if they had been trying not to blink for a long time. Their startled expressions made them look unhappy, although Hepsie thought this was more to do with the fact that they found posing in their best clothes an uncomfortably uncommon experience.

"The two men standing behind the seated women are Eb's great-grandfather, Ebenezer Anderson, and Eb's grandfather, George Anderson," she told Mike.

She followed Mike's gaze as he switched his attention solely to the two men. The elder of the men, presumably great-grandpa Ebenezer, had flowing white whiskers but no moustache, and was wearing a brown corduroy suit and bowler hat. He looked the most uncomfortable in his best clothes. The younger man, grandfather George, was sprucely dressed in a three-piece heavy-cotton suit, with a smart cravat, and a straw boater on his head. His fair hair was short and his moustache neatly clipped. He was the most comfortable in his smart clothes. Both men worn a watch chain hanging out of their, respectively, jacket pocket and waistcoat pocket.

"What did they do?" Mike asked, turning to look at her.

Before Hepsie could reply, Eb said: "My great-grandfather was a crook maker and umbrella mender; also, did a bit of wood turning on the side. Grandfather George was a draper's assistant at the time. You can see the site of his former draper's shop, Davis & Co., in the High Street. Have a look when you go out. It's now that clothes chain...forget its name, but you'll know it when you see it. Shame that all the old shop fronts have been knocked down to make way for new development. It would have been nice to have known what my grandfather's shop looked like."

"What about old photographs?" Mike suggested. "They're a good reference point."

"Oh, we've done that," Hepsie said. "Believe me, Eb has searched high and low for every possible source that might help him. You'll be at a lost to find something new to discover."

What she meant, of course, was that they wouldn't be needing his services.

"I'm sure there's something we haven't yet discovered," Eb quickly said. "I've great belief, Mike, that you'll point us in the right direction. You've got keys we haven't got to open doors."

Mike looked surprised at this admission. Hepsie thought she detected a slight uneasiness in his eyes. Maybe he was getting cold feet? Perhaps he could see that Eb was on a loony mission to take his genealogy to the ends of the earth? For the first time, she felt that scaring away Mike was within her grasp.

However, Mike's response was disappointing. Recollecting himself, he replied with great charm: "Thank you. It's very encouraging to have such faith placed in my abilities. I'll do my best to help you."

Trying hard to hide her annoyance, Hepsie turned their attention back to the photograph. "The elder of the women is Eb's great-grandmother, Hephzibah Anderson, and the younger woman, holding baby Georgie, is Eb's grandmother, Zennor Anderson."

Hepsie noted how Mike, again, studied the figures in detail. Great-grandmother Hephzibah was wearing a plain dark dress with tight sleeves and bodice. Her pied-dappled hair was drawn back off her face and covered by a small dark velvet hat with trimmings. Broad dark ribbons, tightly tied into a bow under her chin, kept the hat secure on her head. She was Hepsie's namesake, but Hepsie was not going to tell Mike that. Grandmother Zennor, seated beside Hephzibah, was wearing a paler dress. Her small hat was made of straw and trimmed with flowers. Without ribbon ties, it balanced precariously on her fuller, fair hair. She was gripping baby Georgie tightly on her lap, his long christening robe almost reaching the hem of her long skirt.

"Zennor's an unusual name," Mike said. "Do you know why she was called that?"

"She's our most interesting ancestor," Eb replied. "She was born at a small place called Zennor Churchtown in Cornwall and we presumed she was named after that. Coincidentally, she also died there. The report in the local paper said she was on holiday with her husband. An accident happened. She was only thirty-two years old. The same age as Hepsie."

Mike looked at Hepsie.

Hepsie blushed. She wished Eb wouldn't give Mike these personal details about herself. They were supposed to be scaring away Mike, not inviting him into the family. However, she also hoped Mike wouldn't think that thirty-two sounded old.

61

"My age, too," Mike said.

Hepsie stared at him in delighted surprise, before realising she mustn't do that.

"Zennor died the year after this photograph was taken," Eb continued. "Amazingly, her husband conveyed her body back to Amberley to be buried. George must have loved his wife very much to do that."

"That must be very satisfying for you to know," Mike said. "It's amazing what you can discover about your ancestors nowadays. You never know when you might find some skeletons rattling in your ancestral cupboard."

"Oh, we were very glad not to find any ancestors listed in the workhouse or at the local lunatic asylum. No one of 'unsound mind'," Eb joked.

"Have you got any skeletons rattling around in your family?" Hepsie asked Mike.

Mike laughed. He ruffled his hair with his fingers, making the longer top strands stand up like a brush, as she had imagined him doing.

"If I had, I wouldn't be telling you," he said non-committally.

Eb chuckled, taking Mike's reply for a joke.

"So, are you going to help us find any skeletons rattling in our family cupboard?" Hepsie challenged Mike.

"Depends what you're looking for next. You and Eb seemed to have done a lot already. Do you want to trace your ancestors further back?" Mike looked at Hepsie quizzically.

"We want more information about Peace Cottage, or even about Amberley, during the Victorian era," Eb replied for her. "Anything about the Andersons living there. That's why we put up the advert at the County

Record Office and the local family history centre. Even if you can't help us, perhaps you know of someone who can or who has contacts who might be able to point us in the right direction?"

"Yes, I saw your advert at the Record Office," Mike said. "That's when I decided to post my business card through your letter box. I would have phoned you, but there wasn't a telephone number on your advert."

Hepsie looked uncomfortable.

"Really?" Eb said, surprised. "I thought you'd put our telephone number on it, Hepsie?"

"I'm sure I did," Hepsie lied. And then, seeing Mike's doubtful expression, shrugged her shoulders and added: "I can't remember. I'm sure I would have done."

Mike shook his head, but he didn't say anything to contradict her.

Hepsie couldn't help smiling back at him for his silence.

However, Eb knew, for he said: "Well, never mind. Mike's here now. And helping us."

Hepsie bit her lower lip, as she attempted to quell the anger that was rising within her. For all his attractiveness and charm, she really must find a loophole to undermine Mike before his helpfulness took Eb's genealogy to new heights.

"Perhaps it would help you, Mike, if I explained to you in more detail what it is we're looking for," Eb continued.

"Please do," said Mike.

Hepsie knew what was coming next.

Eb leaned forwards as if he was creating a more intimate setting between them.

"It's what Hepsie calls my 'sixth sense moment'. But my intuition is that we have been brought back to Peace Cottage, our ancestral home, because our ancestors are trying to get in touch with us. Why else would this coincidence happen?"

"That's all it is, Eb," Hepsie butted in. "Just a coincidence."

Eb shook his head.

"I don't believe that," he said with conviction.

"It's a fascinating idea," Mike said.

"Yes, but it doesn't help with the family history research, does it?" Hepsie quickly added. "You're not going to start communicating with the spirits of our ancestors in order to find out further genealogical truths."

Mike laughed.

"That wasn't my intention," he said.

"Look, Eb, Mike will think we're completely wasting his time. We've done all the research we can. There's nothing new to find out or we would have discovered it by now." Hepsie hoped she sounded reasonable.

"But there's the Amberley Family History Group exhibition at the Parish Rooms next spring," Eb argued. "Joan wants us to find as much information as possible. She would love it if we were able to prove that our inhabitation of Peace Cottage was more than just a coincidence."

I bet she would, Hepsie thought.

Mike was nodding understandingly.

Hepsie decided she'd better change tactic. There were still means of persuading Mike that their genealogy request was not worth his while.

"How much do you charge for your services?" Hepsie asked Mike. "Unfortunately, we can't afford to pay very much."

Mike looked far from crestfallen.

"I understand," he said. "If money's a problem, I'll do it for free."

Eb's smile spread to the corners of his benign face.

Hepsie was momentarily stunned.

Before she could reply, Eb quickly said: "That's very decent of you, Mike. Are you sure you can do that?"

"It's really no bother," Mike replied. "I'm happy to do the research for free. You're my first clients, so I'm letting you have the benefit of the doubt."

He smiled charmingly at Hepsie.

Hepsie still couldn't find the words to speak. She knew if she opened her mouth the right words wouldn't come through. She wanted to say: "Eb! How could you?" but she knew that he had scored an ace point on her undermining-genealogy dart board. There was no way they could refuse Mike's offer of free research. Why hadn't she seen that coming?

She knew very well why she hadn't. Throughout the second half of their meeting the attraction between her and Mike had not gone away. Even now, Mike was looking at her in a rather admiring way. She wondered whether he had noticed she was trying to scare him away. And, if so, did he know why? However, another part of her was flattered that he had not given up the fight so easily. She couldn't help wondering whether the thought that he might want to see her again, lay behind his decision to continue with a blind man's crazy quest.

In the same way as she couldn't talk Eb out of the situation there and then, especially in front of Mike, so she couldn't ask Mike, there and then, what he was really feeling about her.

Instead, Hepsie found another loophole to undermine their genealogical quest.

"So, what are you going to do?" she asked Mike. "Do you have any idea of where you're going or what you're looking for?"

"I'll look into it," Mike replied. "And get back in touch with you when I find something."

"Come and visit us," Eb suddenly said.

Hepsie nearly choked with surprise. If her cappuccino cup had still contained liquid, she would have quickly downed a large sip. As it was, she had to cover her mouth with her hand and pretend to cough.

"Come and see Peace Cottage and we'll show you our research," Eb continued. "And then perhaps you can see where we need to go next."

Mike looked momentarily thoughtful, before nodding his head as if weighing up the problem. "That's a good idea," he replied.

Hepsie felt her spine tingle. The part of her that was following Mike leapt in her soul. She hoped her face didn't betray any of these emotions.

"Great!" Eb's face beamed with satisfaction. "When's a convenient time for you?"

"Weekends are best for me," said Mike. "Perhaps next weekend – Sunday?"

"That's fine with me," Eb replied. "Hepsie?"

Hepsie was glad Eb couldn't see her face. Having no ready excuse in her mind, she managed to mumble: "Maybe."

"If it's a problem…" Mike began.

"I shall be there," Eb butted in, "even if Hepsie isn't, so please don't feel your journey will be wasted."

Mike's pale green eyes briefly betrayed disappointment.

"Afternoon would be better for me," he said.

"Two o'clock?" Eb suggested.

"That's great," said Mike.

Hepsie checked her watch. It was nearly 12.00 p.m. If they weren't going to buy lunch, then they ought to really vacate their table. The café was still busy and in-coming customers glanced over at their table wondering whether Hepsie and her companions were about to leave.

Mike noticed her checking her watch and, as if reading her thoughts, he said: "Well, I'm sorry I can't stay longer, but I'd better be going."

"It's been a pleasure to meet you," Eb said, proffering his hand to be shaken. "We'll look forward to seeing you next Sunday at 2.00 p.m."

Mike warmly shook Eb's outstretched hand.

Hepsie noticed Mike took a moment to study Eb's sightless eyes. She also took the opportunity to notice whether Mike was wearing any rings on his fingers. He wasn't. What was she looking for? A signet ring; an eternity ring; perhaps even a wedding ring. Mike's fingers were long with prominent knuckle joints. His fingernails were cut short and square like a man's.

He stood up and turned to face Hepsie.

"Hope you can make next Sunday," he said.

Hepsie blushed.

"Good-bye," was all she managed to say.

But Mike's pale green eyes seemed to speak volumes. She didn't have a mirror to her face, but she was rather conscious that her blue eyes were saying the same.

Hepsie wished Mike would be gone before more damage was done.

Mike's broad, congenial smile rested on her face as he said his goodbyes to Eb and her before turning away from the table.

Hepsie willed herself not to watch him walk towards the entrance door. The door clattered shut. She quickly looked towards the door and just caught a flicker of Mike's grey and purple pinstripe suit as he disappeared from her sight.

Eb's talking watch announced: "Twelve p.m."

"We'd better be going, too, Eb," Hepsie said.

"Mike's a lovely bloke, isn't he?" said Eb.

Hepsie scowled.

"We'll talk about it later," she replied.

She didn't want to discuss Mike Johnson right at this moment. Why an attractive young man like him was involving himself in this crazy genealogical business, she didn't know. She had started out as pretending to be suspicious, but now she was genuinely suspicious. Eb, of course, would take any con man to his heart, if the con man was a genealogist.

Hepsie put the family photograph back into the plastic carrier bag. She couldn't help wondering whether their encounter with Mike Johnson today was a new beginning. But whether that was for good or bad, she didn't know.

Five

Zennor Churchtown 1894

Zennor stared at herself in the mirror. In the soft glow of the oil lamp, she could see that her complexion was pallid, her pale blue eyes strained and aching with tiredness. Behind her the brass bedstead gleamed where it caught the light. This was the bed where she and George were to sleep tonight. Their first and only night in Zennor Churchtown. In the very inn, the Tinners' Arms, where thirty-two years ago she was born. Zennor began to methodically brush her long hair again. Her straight hair was more honey than straw. At least the years hadn't changed that; and her heart-shaped face and retroussé nose. But she could see it in her demeanour, in the downward turn of her pale lips and the furrowing of her brow. She was once a young girl, with roses blooming in her cheeks and a smile hovering over her mouth. "Where's my old girl?" George would have said. Zennor rested her brush in her lap. "Where's my George?" she might well ask. Where was he on their only night at Zennor Churchtown? At St Ives, after Roelinda's wedding, he had promised her that their night in Zennor

69

Churchtown would be special. What had happened? She glanced at herself in the mirror. Her pale grey moiré silk dress shimmered in the light, highlighting the watermark patterns of the fabric. The silk had been a wedding gift from George, from Davis & Co. Drapers where he worked, and was intended for her bridal dress. Hephzibah had helped her adapt the dress for Roelinda's wedding. It now had fashionable leg-o'mutton sleeves and a plain skirt made full by petticoats instead of a cumbersome bustle. She had cut a dash at Roelinda's wedding and been admired, but during dinner this evening, at the inn, she had felt self-conscious. Now George's dream of a honeymoon was over. It was partly her fault. And what the innkeeper had said and the way the locals had treated her.

She and George arrived after midday and had entered the inn to book their room for the night. The locals abruptly stopped talking as soon as she and George walked into the bar. Whilst booking their room, George mentioned to the landlord that his wife was born at this very inn thirty-two years ago and named after the Churchtown. The landlord looked at him blankly, as if the information meant nothing to him. George tried again. "Perhaps someone here remembers her birth? She'd love to know which room she was born in – wouldn't you, Zennor?" he said. The room was quiet. "Where ye from?" the landlord asked. When George replied "Amberley, Gloucester", the landlord shook his head. From the back of the room a man spoke loudly. The only word Zennor could catch sounded like "emmet". These locals spoke a stranger language than her Gloucestershire neighbours. She wondered whether the landlord didn't understand George, too. Being misunderstood made her feel uncomfortable. As soon as the door closed behind them, she and George could hear the locals resuming their banter and guffawing.

They also liked staring at her. Zennor felt she had been stared at enough today by the locals. Ever since the carrier's cart from St Ives set them down by the Tinners' Arms, she felt she was being treated like a sideshow freak in a circus. What *was* wrong with her? The locals she met looked her up and down, not saying a word, almost rudely, judging her attire, her demeanour, her manners, her face, her voice. Zennor could see them now, following her reflection in the mirror, their penetrating gazes seeing right through her, as if they were reading her innermost emotions. Had they guessed, too? Did they know why it was hard for her to tell George? Zennor began brushing her hair, again, trying to soothe her fears away with each brushstroke.

After a quick late lunch, where neither of them spoke nor the remaining locals in the bar, she and George took a walk around the Churchtown before heading towards the sea. Previously, they had been excited about exploring Zennor Churchtown and seeing more of the sea. The thought had lifted Zennor's spirits. Both she and George were in better spirits after Roelinda's wedding. Her sister's happiness had brought back memories of her own wedding to George more than seven years ago. She realised she was longing to return to those early married days when George and her lived in Paradise. Making up with George seemed to be almost within her reach and the courage was growing in her to tell him. Walking along the cliff tops, with the wind tugging at the yellow gorse and bracken, and the emerald sea stretching out to the blue horizon beyond them, would have been an ideal moment to hold hands and kiss. Zennor imagined now how they would have stood by that Window Rock on Zennor Head, an exhilarating thrill rushing through them as they kissed in the exhilarating abandonment of the wind. As it was, neither of them spoke. They admired the view through the aperture in the Window Rock, and listened to the sea bash the white surf against the dark granite rocks in the coves below them. The cliff tops were treeless and open to the elements. Zennor had never seen a wilder, more restless terrain than this. She felt she had gone back in time. It was like a prehistoric country, or how she imagined one would be. She would have liked to have shared these thoughts with George. As it was, all she could taste was the salt spray on her lips.

Looking at her pallid complexion in the mirror, it was hard to believe that she had spent the afternoon in the warm June sun, with the fresh winds beating the sea air into her cheeks. Strangely enough, the most important sight that caught her eye that day was in St Senara's Church. The mermaid had looked back at her, gashed and struck by God-fearing parishioners. "She's blasphemous!" these angry parishioners had cried, eyeing the mermaid's naked body. Unashamedly, the mermaid showed her comely stomach, the blatant belly button set high above her fishtail, and her thick, flowing locks. In her hands she held the symbols of her worldly vanity: a mirror and a comb. Zennor paused, her hand holding up her brush in mid-air, the mirror reflecting her face. "Her sort shouldn't be seen in God's house. Wanton, she is!" Zennor shivered. She had been told about the fifteenth century mermaid, carved into a narrow oak pew end, by Roelinda's father-in-law. "Something you must see, if you're going to Zennor Churchtown," he'd said. And he told her the

72

tale of the mermaid, Morveren, and her lover, Matthew Trewella. When she returned home, she would have to tell Elsie and Clara it. A sad, magical tale of love and sacrifice.

"Wanton, she is!"

"Harlot!"

Zennor dropped the brush. It clattered onto the floorboards. She dropped her arm to her side.

The poor mermaid! At least, she found peace with her lover under the waves. They can't taunt her there, even if they can hack at her face and breasts in the church. Roelinda's father-in-law had told her that sometimes the mermaid's mirror was seen as an apple and her comb as a stringed instrument. Morveren had tempted Matthew Trewella to bite into her apple, as if she was Eve tempting Adam in the Garden of Eden. Then her stringed instrument – a harp, perhaps – had lured the sailor into the sea, so that he drowned and his beautiful singing could be heard no more in St Senara. The locals would have to wait for the winds to catch his voice under the waves and bring it to them. They have never forgiven the mermaid.

Was she another mermaid? Zennor wondered whether the locals were looking at her as if she was another mermaid. She imagined them chipping off bits of her face, disfiguring her in their minds. Hacking away at her guilt. No. Although it was not her who stared back at her in the mirror, her face still looked whole. She picked up her hairbrush and placed it carefully on the dressing table.

At dinner she had suffered a lack of appetite. She and George were eating alone in a different room to the locals, at George's suggestion. Seeing her pick over her dinner, George had said: "What's wrong with you, Zennor? Don't you like the food?"

73

Zennor paused before replying. "I'm missing Georgie. He'll won't like it if I'm not there to breastfeed him. I'm worried he won't take milk from anyone else."

George shook his head. "Georgie needs a mother who's well and eats her food. The change's supposed to be doing you good."

"But it don't seem right to leave Georgie at this time. He's only nine months old. He's never had milk from anyone else. I should be at home looking after him, like a responsible mother should do."

George banged his fork and knife onto his plate. "A responsible mother! You know very well why we've come on this holiday." His brown eyes glared at her, in a way they had never done so before. Zennor could see his lower lip trembling. The anger contrasted strangely with his neatly parted hair and clipped moustache. George's amiable face rarely showed anger. Zennor put down her fork and knife, giving up all pretence of trying to eat her food. She clasped her hands tightly together in her lap. She must try, again.

"But I'm missing Georgie. All you do nowadays is moan at me."

"Moan at you? Well, that's not surprising, is it?"

What did he mean by that? Zennor searched his angry eyes for any clues. Had he guessed? Her breath felt as if it was being squeezed out of her lungs.

"Why isn't it surprising?" she managed to ask him.

George looked directly at her, before lowering his eyes. "You know."

Zennor bit her lower lip. Why can't she find the courage to ask him any more? George resumed eating, his fork and knife scraping across his plate. He was eating quickly, as though he didn't want to continue their conversation. Zennor didn't know what to say.

74

She might say the wrong thing. But had he guessed? Was that why she'd been taken away from Georgie? A baby who needed her. This holiday had been arranged when she should've been at home, looking after her nine-month-old baby.

They spent the rest of the meal in silence. George was drinking a lot of ale. After the meal was finished, George said: "Do you want to come for a walk?" She had refused, excusing herself with a headache. This wasn't true, but she needed to be alone. She could see it was the last straw for George. He got up from the table and left the room.

It was now late. Dusk was turning to darkness. Zennor stood up and moved towards the open window. George was taking a long walk. Should she wait up for him? He might have got lost. But what sort of mood would he be in? Wearily, she drew the curtains and began undressing for bed.

Voices could be heard outside the window. Zennor strained to hear. First locals talking, and then George's voice. She couldn't understand what the locals were saying. But what was George saying? Something about a horse. Why does he need a horse? The rest of his words got carried away on the wind. She strained to hear more. The sea breaking against the cliffs at Zennor Head muffled the men's words. Zennor was alarmed that George and the locals could suddenly understand one another. What's going on? Then whistling pierced the wind. Not knowing why, Zennor swung round to face the door. There was no one there. But she felt uneasy. The whistling triggered a memory in her brain that she couldn't place. Whistling was a dangerous sign but she couldn't remember why.

Footsteps on the cobbles. They had finished talking. George was coming back to the room. Zennor hastily

75

finished undressing and got into bed. She didn't want to meet George face to face.

For a while she heard the sea moaning and the wind rattling the open window. She opened her eyes. The oil lamp was still burning. She pulled the bedcovers up so that her face was partially hidden. Fear nuzzled closer to her, sucking at her breast like a baby. No noise from George's side of the bed. "Be you a-sucklin' the babby?" she heard Ebenezer saying. She shouldn't be here; she should be at home, breastfeeding Georgie. What was George doing? Zennor bit her lower lip. Tears streamed down her cheeks. She couldn't stop them. Fear, deep as a well, and wide as a continent, filled her body. Sentences tapped out in her mind as though her head was receiving a telegram message: *They have sent her on holiday to Cornwall to get rid of her STOP It's part of a broader plan she hadn't seen until now STOP She had been blind STOP Locked up in her fears STOP Of what others were thinking of her STOP And now she had fallen into a trap STOP George was getting rid of her STOP…*

She was a wife no more. Or, at least, not a fitting wife. Why was George asking after a horse? Zennor wished she had listened more closely to what the locals were saying. She might have guessed some of their words or the gist of their meaning amongst their thick accents. Perhaps she hadn't heard George properly?

No – no, it was no good. Something wasn't right. The talk of horses sent fear whipping through her. "He's going to get rid of me," Zennor cried into her pillow. "He's guessed!"

She must have fallen asleep. The door was creaking open. Footsteps on the floorboards. The person stumbled and cursed. George. She listened to him moving clumsily about the room. Undressing. Splashing

76

his face with water at the washstand. Groaning. Zennor clenched her fists beneath the bedcovers. George crashed against the bed and cursed. The room was plunged into darkness. He climbed into his side of the bed, the bedsprings creaking beneath him. George groaned, again. Soon he was snoring deeply. She could smell the strong ale on his breath. He was drunk. There would be no intimacy between them tonight, as George would have liked. Wasn't that one of the reasons why he'd decided to take her on holiday?

Zennor let the tears trickle down her cheeks and fearfully wondered whether there wasn't another.

She awoke determined to tell George the truth. There was no other way. He had guessed, surely? She had nothing left but to make him change his mind. She would tell him during the morning whilst they were walking on the cliff tops again.

But George had made another plan. Two horses were waiting for them in the inn yard. She was to ride the mare.

Zennor realised that this was what George and the locals had been talking about last night. She wondered why George had decided upon this plan. He hadn't discussed it with her. She didn't even like riding horses that much: surely George knew that?

"But it's necessary," George argued. "Horseback will get us quicker to Zennor Quoit – look, you can see Zennor Hill from here." He pointed inland at an exposed, treeless hill. "You can't take a cart. And it's a long walk. Through uneven, hilly ground and gorse bushes. The horse dealers say only horse tracks lead to the tomb."

"The wind is up and stronger than yesterday," Zennor retorted. "We'll be blown around up there."

"I've hired the horses now. If I go back on the arrangement the locals won't be pleased. They'll begrudge us. And you won't like that, will you?" George looked at her knowingly.

"Why isn't one of them accompanying us? We don't know our way. We'll get lost up there."

"I thought you didn't want locals around you. Make you feel uncomfortable. An extra hand on a horse will cost me more, too."

Zennor couldn't argue with this. George had paid the money. It wouldn't be right to waste it. And, if she did decide to stay at the Churchtown, she would be left alone with the locals, eyeing her with suspicion.

Sitting on the mare, Zennor tried to calm her nerves. The mare swished her tail in irritation, flicking at the flies, and snorting discontentedly. Zennor tightly held onto the reins, her body perched side-saddle on the chestnut mare, wondering whether the mare was as docile as the horse dealers had said. She and George weren't really appropriately dressed for riding. Her corset had been laced too tightly and was digging into her ribs. Hat pins fastened her day hat to her hair but she was afraid the wind might loosen them. The locals' eyes sought her petticoats peeking out below her skirt. Zennor looked at George for reassurance but he was fiddling with his steed. He had swapped his straw boater for a cap. She thought the locals were laughing at her and George's day wear.

Leaving the inn yard, Zennor smelt fresh bread baking. The yeasty smell followed them out of the yard and along the road towards the base of Zennor Hill. For a moment, Zennor was reminded of the Dangerfield Bakery at Amberley, and she wished she wasn't here.

Throughout the ride to the top of Zennor Hill, she and George rode apart. This was inevitable. George's grey steed was much faster than her mare and he had more control over his horse. Zennor was constantly pulling on her reins to check the mare. The animal was carrying her head too high so that she evaded correct contact with the bit. As their rode further up the winding tracks of the isolated hill, Zennor found she had difficulty in turning her mare in the strong wind. There was no chance to talk to George. Prickly gorse straggling the narrow paths snagged the hem of her skirt and embedded thorns in her leather boots. She would have to pick these out later. George should have planned the ride more carefully; their clothes would be ruined.

Ahead of her, George reined in his steed. Massive granite boulders lay scattered in front of him. Some, like unrisen bread, were balanced on top of one another. It looked as if giants had casually picked up these slabs by hand. Zennor drew up alongside George. His cheeks were flushed by the wind. He removed his cap and put it, rolled up, in his jacket pocket.

"This isn't the Quoit," he said.

"Is it far?" she managed to say against the wind.

George glanced at her. "It shouldn't be."

She could tell him now. But their situation on top of Zennor Hill overawed her. The isolated wildness was more prehistoric than the coastline she'd seen yesterday. To her right, in the far distance Zennor Churchtown could be seen nestled amongst the ancient patchwork fields, which were sewn together with granite walls and hedges. Sunlight reflected the warm tones of St Senara's auburn granite tower. Beyond the cliffs the glimmering blue-green sea stretched away into the horizon. Zennor was sure she could taste salt spray blown inland by the wind. Endless sea and sky merged into one broad band streaked with cloud and surf. She and George were completely alone in this open, windswept universe.

Having gazed at the view and walked with her around the menagerie of granite boulders, both of them touching the mottled surfaces as if touching skin, George remounted his steed.

Zennor abruptly discontinued tracing her fingers along the contrasting smooth and abrasive texture of the boulder she was exploring and put her leather gloves back on. She hastily remounted her mare as George began leading the way along the path to the Quoit.

"Do you know where you're going?" she called after him.

"We're to follow the path eastwards," he called back over his shoulder.

She hoped the ride to the Quoit wouldn't be long. There must be a chance for them to talk. Maybe they could sit down at the Quoit and eat their pack lunch. That would be a good time to talk. After his evening of drinking, George had slept deeply, awaking to a better mood than the one he'd been in during dinner. But he was restless. It was almost as if he didn't want to talk to her. The landlord had provided them with fresh pasties and saffron cakes for their lunch. Surely George's appetite would get the better of him and they could eat soon?

They passed a derelict building, probably once the busy engine-house of a mine. It was a solitary sign of humanity amongst the empty moorland. Yellow gorse, bracken, ferns and purple heather, strewn with miniature granite boulders, were the only other sights until Zennor saw a tall chimney in the distance, perhaps the site of another abandoned tin mine. Further eastwards, she caught a glimmer of the sea on the south-east coast. George was slowing down in front of her. They must be approaching the Quoit.

Zennor gulped and pulled more tightly on her reins, forcing her mare to trot more slowly. She didn't know what she was going to say to George. The exact words evaded her mind. Perhaps it was best to blurt it out. Would he understand? Could she make him? Could she make him change his mind about getting rid of her? Surely, he would have to believe *her*. She must have the courage. Zennor wanted to look into George's eyes and see there that he did *believe* her, that he couldn't continue punishing her, by getting rid of her and by taking her away from Georgie when Georgie needed her most. George had noticed and guessed. Though, yes, he was right but, no, he was so wrong. And because of this wrongness she must find the courage to tell him. If only he would stop and listen for a while. Zennor wanted to see the trust in his brown eyes again. She wanted to end the mistrust that had grown between them like a poisoning cancerous tumour.

The Quoit stood in a grass clearing surrounded by granite hedges. George had dismounted his steed and was tethering the animal to the post of a granite stile. Zennor trotted up beside him.

"Are we stopping for lunch?" she said.

"No," George replied without looking at her. "It's too windy up here."

"But aren't you hungry?" she persisted.

George shook his head. "Not really." Then he looked up at her. "Wind given you an appetite?"

"Yes," she said firmly.

"So you be feeling better than yesterday?"

"Please sit down and eat here with me, George. It's such a marvellous place."

George didn't reply. He held her mare as she dismounted and then tethered the animal to the other stile post. Zennor waited to see what George would do next. He didn't reach for their pack lunch in his steed's saddle bag.

"George..." she tried again.

"I'm going to look at the Quoit," George said as he climbed over the stile.

Zennor felt the wind tugging at her hat pins as it tried to lift off her light straw hat. She decided to follow George over the stile. For what seemed a long time, but could only have been a few minutes, they walked around the outside of the Quoit. The ancient burial chamber was made of huge granite slabs. The capstone had fallen and was resting diagonally against the supporting boulders. Zennor discovered the grey mottled granite was rough to touch, crumbling away in her fingers. How different from the smooth, hard, black granite rocks at the base of the cliffs. Soft, springy lichens clung to the weather-beaten stone like leeches to skin. And all the time the wind buffeted her and George's bodies. It would be difficult to persuade George to eat lunch here. She would have to find another opportunity to tell him, before they reached civilisation again.

The Quoit was an eerie tomb. Why had builders chosen such a desolate place for the burial? It seemed unlikely that mourners would want to make the trip across the windswept moorland. To her, many centuries later, this mysterious, prehistoric tomb was an offering to the gods. Rain, wind, sun, snow, storms, all swept over the massive granite slabs whilst the chieftain's body slept inside. His soul sacrificed to the gods. Zennor shuddered. This sacrificial rite had taken place many centuries ago. But what would happen if the Cornish people, today, wanted to make the same sacrifice to the gods? Who would they choose?

Zennor wished she hadn't been called Zennor. The Cornish locals were a superstitious people. It was as if she had stolen one of their Cornish names by taking it out of Cornwall and, now that she had returned, they wanted something back from her. Her name needed returning to its roots. She was to be another sacrifice. Zennor was part of Cornwall.

Anxiously, Zennor looked for George. He was crouching on the other side of the Quoit, staring into the pit-black hole of what must be the tomb's entrance.

"George," she said.

George looked up at her. His neatly parted hair was uncharacteristically ruffled and his cheeks flushed.

"If you want lunch we best be off," he said.

"George—"

But George was getting up and walking towards the stile.

"George, there's something I need to tell you", she should have called out across the grass clearing. But she knew he wasn't going to listen to her. She wasn't the Zennor he used to know. Why heed a woman of 'unsound mind'? Zennor stared into the pit-black darkness of the tomb's entrance. Is that where he wants to put me? And the Cornish do, too? she thought. She couldn't be more cursed. Zennor gazed up at the broad sweep of the sky and the moorland. It seemed to her that not only George and the Cornish but the very gods and their universe were conspiring against her.

"Come on, Zennor!" George called out to her.

She turned towards him. He had already mounted his steed and was starting to trot back along the track.

83

If she didn't follow him, she'll be left alone in this eerie desolation. She had no choice but to mount her nervous mare and follow him.

Six

Hepsie was sitting on the boxed-stairs, listening to what was going on in the kitchen. Joan was making preparations for tea ahead of Mike Johnson's visit this afternoon and Hepsie could hear her neighbour banging cupboard doors and her heels echoing on the flagstone floor. No doubt Joan was using the best china, something Hepsie wouldn't have done, especially on this occasion. Hepsie listened for the chink of china on the tray. She also imagined Joan had brought her own homemade cake – probably her favourite coffee gateau with ganache and walnuts – which she would arrange on one of her own silver cake stands and serve in neat, generous slices with the silver cake forks that were never used at Peace Cottage. There would be fresh milk in a jug, sugar lumps in a bowl, and the kettle ready to boil. Hepsie didn't know what Mike Johnson would make of all this.

She was supposed to be upstairs, lying on her bed, pretending to be ill with a sore throat. But, when she heard Joan moving about in the kitchen and guessed that Eb was sitting in the living room, awaiting Mike Johnson's arrival, she had crept downstairs. Now she was sitting on one of the lower steps, her feet resting on the one below, with her knees almost drawn up to her chest as she leant forwards. Her hand was on the door latch and she was spying out of the chink between the stair door and the jamb. She could just make out the front door, but it was a strain to see more clearly. The first weekend in June and it was raining! The small window higher up the boxed-staircase wasn't letting in enough light. However, this might mean that she wasn't so easily seen and could be mistaken for one of the shadows lurking on the gloomy boxed-staircase. She had to be very still, in case the old stairs creaked. At least the treads were carpeted, although Hepsie could feel the metal nosing strip on the outer edge of the tread digging into her bottom through her jeans. The nosing had been put in for Eb's benefit as his eyesight deteriorated. That was why the carpeting, walls, stair door and handrails were in contrasting shades of colour: off-white blue for the walls, to reflect light into the stairwell; brighter blue for the inside of the stair door and handrails; and an in-between blue for the carpet, so that the metal nosing could be obvious to the eye. Eb, of course, now couldn't see this decoration, but the boxed-staircase was kept the same, just in case.

Dust tickled Hepsie's nose. She hoped she wouldn't sneeze. The boxed-staircase was stuffy and she was very aware that it hadn't been dusted for a long time. Loose cobwebs dangled high above her. She was very conscious of the sound of her breathing, which seemed to be louder than normal. She hoped no one could hear her intakes of breath. She tried to train them to coincide with the ticking of the grandfather clock in the hall. In fact, the hall was so quiet, she thought she could discern the cranking of the clock's pendulum as it swung from side to side.

All week she had been dithering about Mike's

forthcoming visit. However much she wanted to find another way to undermine Eb's genealogical quest, she couldn't find the will to do so or think of a 'reasonable' idea. She had tried telling Eb about her genuine suspicion that Mike wasn't the genealogy type. But Eb was having none of it.

"He's fine, Hepsie. We're lucky to find someone who's so keen," he said.

"Don't you think Mike Johnson's the sort of person who has better things to do in his spare time than genealogy?" she retorted.

Irritatingly, Hepsie couldn't conceive a good enough reason to compel Eb to cancel Mike's forthcoming visit. She hoped inspiration might arrive by the end of the week, but it hadn't.

Part of her problem was that she was undermined by her strong attraction to Mike. How had this happened? And, if so, was it really true? Hepsie considered giving herself a shock, wondering whether this might wake up her deranged mind and reveal to her that she'd been bored into making up something to lighten up her dull life as a dutiful daughter. On the other hand, if the attraction for Mike was real, then why wasn't she giving up the undermining-genealogy fight and solely looking forward to his visit on Sunday?

To be honest, she was apprehensive about Sunday. What if she discovered that Mike's feelings for her had vanished? What if the feelings were now only one-sided, and on her part? She didn't want to make a fool of herself. Anxiously, Hepsie wondered whether she hadn't already. As in times of stress, she begun to bite her nails. They would have to be filed and neaten before Mike's visit on Sunday. As the big day approached, Hepsie found herself recalling Mike's broad, congenial smile, his pale green eyes, the way he ruffled his fair hair into a brush with his ringless fingers, the scented notes of his cologne merging with the mellifluous notes of his low voice until she was delirious with the melody they played.

But she always came back to the idea that made her genuinely – GENUINELY – suspicious of his real intentions: he just wasn't her idea of a genealogist. This wasn't only due to his youth, but to his manner and attitude. Hepsie couldn't imagine Mike sitting down and devoting his spare time to this kind of hobby. And now he wanted to create a genealogy business? She shook her head doubtfully.

Of course, there was another option. She could phone him and ask him straight out: "Are you a con man?" But Hepsie felt it wouldn't be an easy task. She was afraid she wouldn't sound right. And what if she was wrong? Even if Mike was a con man, he would deny it, anyway. He had already done so at their meeting last Saturday. Or had he? Recalling what he'd said, Hepsie saw him in a different light: Mike trying to side-step the insinuation by turning it into a joke.

If she did call him, Hepsie reasoned, they would be talking about things other than con men. Didn't she want to know more about him? And didn't she want him to ask questions about herself? Anything but genealogy and con men.

This Sunday morning, Hepsie had awoken late after sleeping fitfully. She arose and decided she would lie to Eb and say that she had a sore throat. She told him she didn't feel well enough for Mike's visit. Eb was worried. Hepsie thought he was probably thinking she wouldn't be well enough to help with the preparations for the visit.

"I don't want to pass my germs onto Mike, especially when he's come all this way," she lied. She said this as a dig at the fuss Eb's genealogical obsession was giving everyone. Secretly, she was hoping Eb would cancel Mike's visit.

"I'll call Joan," Eb said. "I know it's short notice but she might be able to help us. We've depended upon her before."

Yes, Hepsie irritatedly thought, meddling Joan!

However, she said: "It's no good doing that because Joan is having guests for lunch today – her sister-in-law and husband, she told me."

But Eb decided he must call Joan. Out of kindness to Hepsie, because she might be feeling worse by the time Mike arrives, and because he didn't want to cancel Mike's visit when they'd got this far. He'd been looking forward to this Sunday all week. The genealogy files were prepared and ready for Mike's perusal.

Eb telephoned Joan. Joyfully, he told Hepsie that Joan had decided to help them. Her Sunday lunch had been cancelled because her sister-in-law's husband was ill and Joan's husband had decided to go golfing, or, any excuse, to the golf club because of the rain. Hepsie could imagine Joan's loud, effusive voice, warming to the subject along the telephone line: "I'll love to come and help and, of course, to meet Mike Johnson. I've heard so much about him. It really is so exciting!"

Hepsie grimaced. Joan's involvement made matters worse. And more embarrassing. Because Joan would be questioning her about Mike and watching them closely. She would be quick to pick up on the signs between Hepsie and Mike and notice how Hepsie reacted to Mike and vice versa. Hepsie didn't want to betray her attraction to Mike in front of Joan. If she did, Joan would give her no peace. And Mike wouldn't be hers.

So embarrassing. Joan would soon have the whole village gossiping about them: 'Hepsie and Mike'.

Hepsie decided to pretend that her false sore throat was worse. She was going to stay upstairs and lie down on her bed during Mike's visit. "I don't want to spread my germs around," she reminded Eb.

"It's a pity you can't be with us," Eb said. "I know how much you wanted to meet Mike again."

Eb's comment didn't arouse her usual feelings of exasperation. Instead, she felt alarmed. Had Eb guessed about her and Mike? Despite not being able to see, had he guessed by the tone of their voices and their choice of words that something more was going on other than genealogical discussions? Or was Eb making that comment to annoy her? Because he knows that she doesn't want any further involvement in the genealogical business and that she's been attempting to undermine him, again?

She decided not to answer back. After lunch Hepsie got Eb's genealogical files ready for Mike to see in the living room. Neatly, she piled them up on the low coffee table and then placed the Bible and the 1893 christening photograph, still in its plastic carrier bag, next to them. Fearing that Joan might arrive at any minute, Hepsie left plumping up the sofa cushions and hurried upstairs.

Hiding in her bedroom, Hepsie could hear Joan and Eb chatting below. She knew Joan was being very organised. She wouldn't have been surprised if Joan had found a duster and quickly wiped the ornaments in the living room. There wouldn't be enough time to hoover. At one point, Joan called up the boxed-stairs: "Do you want a hot drink, Hepsie? Or a slice of coffee gateau?" Hepsie had to do all in her power, the best she could pretending to have a sore throat, to convince

90

Joan not to come upstairs to see her. No, she didn't want a hot drink.

"Oh, you poor love," Joan shouted back, her slushy concern reverberating throughout the stairwell. "Eb says you were really keen to meet Mike again."

Hepsie knew Joan was waiting for some sort of confidential reply from her. What had Eb been saying to Joan? Thank God, I've made the excuse that I'm ill, she thought.

"I can't talk, Joan. My throat…"

Joan got the message.

Now Hepsie was sitting on the boxed-stairs. Joan had been in the house for half an hour and Hepsie could already feel that Joan's presence had permeated the grey stone walls of the building. The grandfather clock had struck the quarter-hour before Hepsie took up her position on the stairs. Anxiously, Hepsie bit her lower lip. She must have been waiting nearly ten minutes.

Suddenly, the grandfather clock's musical chimes echoed throughout the house. 2 p.m.

Mike could be here at any moment.

Joan's footsteps moved out of the kitchen and into the hall, her narrow heels tapping on the flagstones.

Hepsie held her breath. She prayed Joan wouldn't open the stair door.

Joan's footsteps vanished, presumably muffled by the living-room carpet. Hearing her speak to Eb confirmed this. Hepsie caught Joan saying: "Mike's late."

A golf-ball-size lump had arisen in Hepsie's throat. Her throat wasn't so much 'sore', but brimming with fear. Hepsie's feet felt sticky in her flip-flops and her palms were sweaty. She wished Mike would hurry up. The boxed-stairs were claustrophobic and she was conscious that her armpits were beginning to perspire and, also, her neck beneath her loose hair. Was Mike always late? Punctuality didn't seem to be his good point.

And then the thought stabbed her. Perhaps he's not coming after all? Mike Johnson was a con man. And he had been leading them on. Hepsie's palms were sweating more profusely now. She wondered how long Eb and Joan would wait before they realised that Mike wasn't turning up again. What would they do? She could still hear them chatting. Joan must have left the living-room door ajar. Hepsie tried to listen into their banal conversation and, at the same time, to concentrate on listening for Mike's arrival.

When the doorbell did ring, Hepsie jumped with shock. The stairs creaked beneath her and the door latch rattled in her shaking hand. She hoped the doorbell had drowned out these noises.

Her heart leapt in her. Hepsie moistened her dry lips with the tip of her tongue. She didn't want to lean further forwards in case she was noticed as more than a shadow in the chink between the stair door and jamb.

Joan's heels tapped across the flagstones. Hepsie caught a glimpse of Joan's pearly blonde bob and her olive and apricot striped top by the front door. She heard the front door opening. A draught of damp air entered the hall and Hepsie breathed in the smell of rain-soaked earth.

"Hello," Joan gushed, as if welcoming a film star. "Are you Mike Johnson?"

"Yes, I am," came Mike's surprised reply.

Hepsie could just about make out Joan clasping her hands together against her breasts in ardent admiration.

"I'm Joan Franklin, Eb and Hepsie's neighbour. So

pleased to meet you. Do come in." Joan stood back to let Mike into the hall. "I'm helping Eb out today because Hepsie's poorly."

"That's a shame," Mike said, speaking in the same low, mellifluous tones as he'd done at Siesta Café.

And then, as though realising his reaction didn't sound quite right, he corrected himself: "I mean, that Hepsie can't be here today."

Hepsie bit her lower lip to stop herself speaking out.

"That's quite all right," Joan effused. "We're sorry, too. She was so looking forward to meeting you again."

Hepsie grimaced.

She risked leaning a little further forwards, carefully keeping her hand steady on the door latch, so that she could glimpse a clearer view of Mike.

He looked the same, although this time he was casually dressed in black jeans, a white T-shirt and a light brown corduroy blouson jacket. His fair hair was damp from the rain and his cheeks glowed refreshingly.

Mike unzipped his jacket.

"Ghastly rain," Joan said conversationally. "You can tell it's summer! Are you very wet?"

"I'm fine, really," Mike replied. "It's more of a drizzle now."

Hepsie could tell by the way Mike spoke that he did not like Joan's fussing manner around him. She hoped Mike had wiped his wet shoes on the doormat, otherwise Joan might ask him to remove them.

"Eb's waiting for you in the living room," Joan said, slightly peeved.

Hepsie guessed Joan was peeved because Mike wasn't going to take off his damp jacket. She smiled at the thought.

"He's got his research all ready for you," Joan

continued. "Are you sure you won't let me hang up your jacket?"

"I'm fine, really," Mike replied, turning away from the front door and out of Hepsie's sight.

She clenched her left hand, the one that wasn't holding onto the door latch. Briefly, before turning away, Mike had looked in her direction. She wondered whether he'd guessed that she was sitting behind the door. Or, whether he was only looking around at the hall, maybe wondering where that door led to. For a moment, Hepsie thought how foolish she was to fake being ill. She could be talking to Mike now, looking into his pale green eyes and smiling back at his broad, friendly smile.

No. Not with Joan there. Joan, her considerate but interfering neighbour, watching them both and noting every tweak in Hepsie's face and, no doubt, Mike's.

As Hepsie followed Mike and Joan's footsteps across the flagstones, she caught a whiff of Mike's cologne: deep, sexy, earthy notes, the same as she'd smelt in Siesta Café. So she hadn't dreamt him up? Hepsie felt relief pouring over her like the rain on dry ground.

And then Joan shut the living-room door.

Hepsie cursed. Now she wouldn't be able to hear what was going on, or what was being said.

The grandfather clock chimed the quarter-hour.

Annoyed, Hepsie took out her mobile phone from the back pocket of her jeans. She switched it on and checked for text messages from her friend Sally.

She had told Sally about last Saturday's meeting with Mike. Sally had gobbled up her gossip about how unsuccessful Hepsie had been in deterring Mike's genealogical help. She laughed when Hepsie explained she was undermined by Eb's determination and Mike's willingness to help him.

"Is that all?" Sally had hinted, perhaps intuiting that something further had taken place that day and that Hepsie was withholding information from her.

"No," Hepsie had lied.

She didn't know why she didn't tell Sally about her and Mike's attraction for one another. Her 'carrot face' best friend, who she'd known for so many years and with whom she shared so many secrets, would have been so keen to hear all the gossip about that.

As it was, Sally persisted in her hints, until Hepsie decided to let slip that she thought Mike was an unlikely genealogist and she was genuinely suspicious of him. Sally laughed. Hepsie felt she had to defend her corner.

"Genealogy is hardly the hobby for a dedicated career man, with age and energy on his side," she argued. "Look Sal, who's heard of a marketing colleague wanting to give up his career to pursue a genealogical business that had started as a hobby? He seems totally unsuitable to be an obsessive genealogist. How does he have the time to do all these tasks? I think he's lying somewhere."

"You and your con man," Sally joked. "If he's as young and good-looking as you're making him sound, then why don't you get him interested in yourself? That might take his mind off the genealogy and get him back onto the path of the living. Maybe that's why he's been dedicating his spare time to genealogy – he hasn't got a girlfriend to brighten up his life."

"I don't care whether he's got a girlfriend or not," Hepsie crossly replied, stung by the thought that Mike could have a girlfriend or even another life she knew nothing about. She recalled Mike's ringless fingers.

"Well, I could look at it your way," Sally judged. "Mike is a con man. He might not work in marketing

95

and he's only saying that to make you and Eb trust him. You know, to make himself look good. And capable."

"That's true. We only have his word that his works in marketing." Hepsie hoped her voice hadn't dipped too much when she spoke. Secretly, she hoped Mike wasn't lying about his job. What if he really was an obsessive genealogist and the marketing job was no more than a façade? If so, he had certainly confused her.

"The point is," she continued, "he's making Eb's genealogical bug bigger. And we're wasting his time, because Eb's got all the information he needs and can find. How am I going to scare away Mike? Can you think of anything?"

"I've have to go away and get back to you when inspiration finds me," Sally replied. "Don't get too down. I'm sure he's not really a genealogist." She chuckled but Hepsie wasn't laughing along with her.

Now, Hepsie wondered whether Sally had guessed. That she, Hepsie, had fallen for this stranger. And, if he was to be believed, an ardent genealogist, too. No wonder Sally was laughing her head off. Hepsie's plan to undermine her father's genealogical obsession had gone awry. She didn't need to tell Sally the news. However, by not conceding her point, she had managed to prevent Sally from teasing her endlessly there and then.

But she was niggled by one of Sally's comments. The words floated in her brain as though waiting for her to find the hook to fish them out. "…*why don't you get him more interested in yourself. That might take his mind off the genealogy…*"

Hepsie read Sally's text message. It simply said: *how itz going.*

She texted back: *I faking sick.*

Then she switched off her phone in case its ringing tones betrayed her presence on the boxed-stairs.

She wondered what to do next. She could hear the voices in the living room rising and falling. Joan's loud voice was the most vocal. Eb's mellow tones and Mike's mellifluous notes mingled like a medley between Joan's shriller pitch. There was even laughter. Hepsie wanted to hear exactly what they were saying. She particularly wanted to hear Mike's voice. She told herself this was to find out whether he betrayed himself during his conversation with Eb and Joan. No, she wasn't anxious to listen to him because she wanted to find out more about him as a person. Anyway, she might discover the worse, that he was indeed nothing more than an obsessive genealogist.

Hepsie decided she couldn't sit on the stuffy boxed-stairs any longer. She felt like she'd been locked inside an airing cupboard. On the shelf, already! An old maid left to gather dust. Slowly, she opened the stair door, hoping its hinges wouldn't squeak. She stepped down onto the flagstone floor and moved towards the living-room door, making sure her flip-flops landed softly on the worn grey stones so that there was no flipping sound echoing around the hall. Hepsie put her ear to the closed living-room door. The loud ticking of the grandfather clock beside her drowned out some of the chat inside the living room. Hepsie cupped her hands over her ears so she could hear better.

She knew eavesdropping was stupid – even childish – but she wanted to listen into the conversation. Standing on the wrong side of the living-room door, she felt strangely excluded. What were they talking about? Hepsie knew she was being stupid because she knew they could possibly be only talking about genealogy.

And, indeed, they were. Their polite banter circled the banal glories of Eb's genealogical research. Hepsie was disappointed to hear Mike's amiable replies to Joan and Eb's questions and his willingness to ask his own questions. His attitude was no more than politeness, but this veneer irked Hepsie. She forced herself to listen in case Mike betrayed himself or the conversation took a more interesting turn. Why couldn't Joan and Eb ask Mike about his private life?

She didn't realise how intently she was listening to the conversation until she jumped when the grandfather clock struck the half-hour. Luckily, she prevented herself from gasping out loud just in time. However, this didn't make her move away from the living-room door. At one point she wondered whether she should get a glass from the kitchen and use that to put against the door in case it made the conversation clearer for her to hear. She was getting used to predicting the reactions of Joan, Eb and Mike to one another. Every time Joan made an overtly fussy or gushing comment to Mike, he retaliated by a polite put-down, which made Hepsie smile. He was handling the situation very well. She was still standing there, her ear against the door, when the grandfather clock chimed the quarter-hour.

Suddenly, Hepsie heard Joan saying she would get tea.

Hepsie quickly moved away from the living-room door and, as quietly as she could, rushed up the boxed-stairs. Her heart beat frantically when she thought she heard a stair creak beneath her footsteps. She had managed to pull-to the stair door after her but she didn't know whether it was still ajar or whether Joan might open it, perhaps to come upstairs to use the bathroom.

In the safety of her bedroom, Hepsie listened to the sounds of Joan moving about in the kitchen. Looking out of her bedroom window, she saw that Mike was right: the rain had turned to drizzle. The landmark solitary copse on top of May Hill was obscured by the wet mist. Her bedroom faced the front of Peace Cottage and on a clear day she could see the gently rolling hills on the other side of the Nailsworth Valley, as well as May Hill in the far distance. She looked down at the narrow lane outside the house. There wasn't a car parked there. Mike must have decided it was better to leave his car on the Common near the War Memorial, rather than drive it down the steep lane to Peace Cottage. Or was he worried that someone, maybe herself, might make a note of his car's registration number and trace his details?

Hepsie recalled snatches of the recently eavesdropped conversation. She didn't know what Mike was really thinking. He was supposed to be looking at Eb's genealogical research and deciding what to do next. She smiled as she imagined Eb boring the socks off Mike whilst Joan busied herself preparing tea for them in the kitchen. Unless, of course, genealogy was Mike's whole life and love and he was hanging onto Eb's every word. Hepsie grimaced.

Irritatedly, she drew the curtains further back, even though there was as much light as there possibly could be coming through the small windowpanes. She would have liked to have made herself a mug of tea. Her throat felt dry after being stuck on the boxed-stairs for half an hour. And straining at the living-room door, listening to a conversation from which she was excluded, was thirsty work. But Joan was in the kitchen and Hepsie wasn't going there.

Footsteps creaked on the stairs. Someone was

coming upstairs. Firm, agile footsteps. Not Eb's and not Joan's. Hepsie could still hear noise from the kitchen drifting up the boxed-stairs. The footsteps walked along the landing away from her slightly ajar bedroom door. She heard a door being shut and locked. The bathroom door.

What was wrong? Hepsie reasoned; wasn't their guest allowed to use the bathroom? But she realised she was holding her breath.

Hepsie waited. She heard the cistern flushing, the boiler revving as hot water was running, and then the bathroom door being unlocked.

She waited for the footsteps to go back downstairs. Instead, they walked along the landing towards her bedroom door. Half-way along, they stopped. Hepsie heard the floorboards creak. What was Mike doing? She guessed he must be standing near Eb's bedroom door. Surely he wasn't nosing about? Unless...

Hepsie brought her hands to her face in horror.

Taking a deep breath, she opened her bedroom door.

Mike looked momentarily surprised, then quickly composed himself. His mouth relaxed into his now familiar broad, congenial smile. And his pale green eyes revealed how pleased he was to see her.

Hepsie blushed. She thought she was doing so from anger, but her wildly beating heart told her otherwise. Unable to keen a stern face, she smiled back at him. She was conscious of feeling rather silly.

"Joan told me you were ill, so I hope I didn't disturb you just then," Mike said.

Hepsie nearly said: "No, I'm fine", but she managed to stop herself. Mike could probably tell, anyway, from looking at her, that she wasn't really sick at all. Eb, of course, couldn't see her and Joan hadn't seen her so far today.

"I was lying down," Hepsie lied. "I heard someone moving around and…"

She didn't finish the sentence. For some reason, she couldn't utter the words. She was going to accuse Mike of trespassing on private property with the intention of stealing. But she hadn't actually caught him red-handed, in the act of stealing, with, say, Eb's wallet in his hands. She didn't know for certain whether Mike had, indeed, entered Eb's bedroom and she couldn't go in there now and look for Eb's wallet or check whether any other items were missing; and she couldn't ask to search Mike's person.

The thought of touching Mike made her delirious. Her body tingled in delicious waves.

No, this approach wasn't going to work. But why was he nosing around upstairs?

As if reading her thoughts, Mike said: "Sorry for nosing around, but I was interested in your decoration." He indicated the colour-contrasting walls and skirting boards and doors. The skirting boards and doors were painted in a dark shade of green so that they stood out from the very pale green walls. Even the doorknobs were painted in pale green to make them noticeable against the darker door paint.

"I wondered whether the house was painted like this for Eb's benefit?" Mike continued, with the implied hint of "You know, because Eb's blind" being left unspoken.

"Yes, it was," Hepsie said simply.

"And the gadgets in the bathroom?"

Hepsie imagined Mike looking at the enlarged control knobs above the bath and in the shower cubicle. If he had pressed them, they would have told him whether the water was hot or cold. At least, he hadn't tried the talking scales. Having your weight spoken out loud wasn't always a very pleasant experience. It was best not to stand on them. And then there was the non-slip flooring and the non-slip matting on the shelf above the washbasin, where she laid out Eb's toothbrush for him every morning and night. And the colour-contrasting extended in a mad chain from bath tiles to toilet seat to toilet-roll holder to even the soap dish. Nothing had changed in five years. Mike must be wondering what sort of circus was going on here at Peace Cottage.

Without meaning to, she suddenly said: "Eb hasn't always been blind. The colour- contrasting was painted when we thought Eb's deteriorating sight might be saved. As it was, we decided to keep the décor – just in case."

Mike nodded sympathetically.

"I'm sorry," he said. "It can't have been easy for Eb or for yourself."

Hepsie was about to agree and tell him about Sofia's death, when she realised that their conversation was taking a more personal turn. Somehow, they had sunk to a more intimate level. This would have to stop. She was sharing her personal history with a stranger whom she had met only once. And one who she was supposed to be scaring away.

"No," was all she said.

There was an awkward silence between them that could have been for a few seconds but seemed to last longer.

Hepsie noticed Mike's pale green eyes hungrily absorbing her, taking her inside his being. She felt self-conscious. Although she had planned not to meet Mike today, she had washed her hair and applied make-up to her face. She had compromised this by wearing faded jeans and a plain white T-shirt. However, her flip-flops were her newest, favourite pair: pale blue inch-thick soles with silver and white beading on the thongs. Hepsie thought they perfectly complimented the silver nail varnish of her painted toenails. Finally, she had sprayed herself with her favourite Oriental scent, five minutes before going to sit on the boxed-stairs to await Mike's arrival.

Mike was looking good in his casual clothes. He had removed his corduroy jacket and Hepsie saw that his arms were tanned and well-toned. Not the unmuscular arms of a genealogy enthusiast who spends all his spare time tracing genealogical sources on his computer or searching for family records in the fusty archives of the Record Office. She wondered whether the man standing in front of her was more likely to go to the gym three times a week than to visit the Record Office. There was no trace of five o'clock shadow on Mike's firm jaw this time and, standing near to him, Hepsie could see that he was a few inches taller than herself.

At last, Mike said: "Well, I'd better leave you to recover in peace."

Hepsie smiled weakly and slightly nodded as if to say, yes, that's the answer she'd been waiting for.

She watched Mike turn his back on her and walk along the landing towards the staircase. Secretly, she was sorry to see him go.

At the head of the stairs, Mike suddenly turned round and smiled at her. "Hope you get better," he said.

"Thanks," Hepsie managed to reply.

Mike disappeared down the boxed-stairs.

Hepsie wandered back into her bedroom and pushed her door to. Downstairs, the noises had ceased from the kitchen and she guessed that Joan was now serving tea in the living room. She could hear their low chat rising up through her floorboards: a medley of voices with lyrics she couldn't interpret word for word. This time she couldn't be bothered to eavesdrop. Kicking off her flip-flops, she sunk down onto her bed. The duvet cocooned her in its soft padding. Her chestnut hair laid spread out on the innumerable cushions at the top of her bed. Hepsie closed her eyes. She wasn't ill, but she needed to compose her thoughts. For a while, she kept her eyes shut, until she realised that darkness brought no peace.

She opened them. Her bedroom was gloomy from the constant drizzle outside. She let her eyes gaze lazily around her room, randomly resting upon certain objects. There was a wooden carving of a giraffe from her travels in the African Congo standing on the mantelpiece above her small, unused fireplace. Conch shells from the Indian coast were arranged next to the giraffe and a dried starfish found on a beach of a South American country, she couldn't remember which one. Coral beads were draped over the frame of her dressing-table mirror, where a postcard of London, recently sent to her by an ex-colleague, reminded her of her independent days living in the city. Hanging on the back of her bedroom door was a long tie-dyed scarf in bright oranges and burnt browns. Hepsie guessed this also came from the African Congo. When she had first travelled to distant lands, she brought back lots of posters and postcards to adorn the plain walls of her bedroom. These in turn had replaced the pop posters of her teenage school years. Hepsie cringed at the memory of her taste in music.

Now, her bedroom walls were painted a pale blue and she liked to stare at the bare walls and lose herself in their tranquillity. On her bedside table there was a photograph in a silver frame. This was of her mother,

Sofia. Before the final signs of her debilitating cancer were etched into her face. Hepsie glanced up at the ceiling, also painted pale blue, and followed the line of the single exposed beam joist. Her gaze penetrated the ceiling right through to the attics above her. This was where they kept Sofia's possessions: her clothes; jewellery Hepsie didn't wear herself; school books Sofia had kept throughout her life; letters; official papers; walking boots Sofia would never use to tread on the Common again. Eb and Hepsie hadn't been able to throw out anything. Sofia's life was mummified in the attic like an ancient Egyptian's.

Hepsie brought her gaze back down to her bedroom window. Since childhood she had watched many sunrises from this view, seen changes of weather, experienced the seasonal moods of the Cotswold countryside, and waited for the solitary copse on top of the distant May Hill to reveal its secrets to her. Across the Nailsworth Valley, looking towards Woodchester on the opposite hillside, Hepsie could see a changing landscape, as housing developments, telegraph poles and, no doubt soon, wind turbines, nestled in between the pastures, hedgerows and woods. But there was still sky. Lots of it. And fresh, reviving air. And, despite sometimes hearing the low hum of traffic on the main roads, Amberley was a haven of quietness in a busy, busy world.

But did she want a quiet life? Hepsie's eyes rested on a perfume bottle made from coloured Murano glass, which she had watched being blown into shape during her visit to the Venetian island. It seemed to her that her whole life was contained in this room. Beside her on the bed lay her cuddly toys from childhood: teddies with torn ears, a pink elephant in checked dungarees, the fur worn away on his trunk, and her favourite rag doll – Molly Poppet – with her dangling legs and lopsided stitched smile. Hepsie ran her fingers through Molly Poppet's tangled woollen curls.

But it was the ornaments and souvenirs from her travels that brought her current situation home to her. The giraffe, the starfish, the perfume bottle: they were all reminders of a time when she was a free-spirited person, set on course for an independent life, away from the cosy homeliness of Peace Cottage. When she would never have dreamt of being a dutiful daughter to her blind father Eb, as she now was. How she would have laughed in disbelief, during her younger days, at the thought of spending her time trying to undermine Eb's genealogy obsession. That was all her life was now, wasn't it? All the hopes and promises and attempts at obtaining a life of her own, where had they vanished? She had had them there, all of them, in the clasp of her hand. Now her hands were empty. She was standing on her head, her life upside down.

Mike's face floated before her eyes. She ought to check her mobile for texts from Sally, but she couldn't be bothered. The grandfather clock could be heard ticking the minutes away downstairs. Hepsie couldn't remember whether she'd heard the clock strike the quarter-hours, so lost had she been in her reverie. Some things didn't change in her life: the regular chiming of the grandfather clock, marking the passing of time; the solitary copse on top of May Hill, a constant feature in a changing landscape. Symbols of security that a child might mark her life by. As Eb had said, if Sofia had been alive then Hepsie wouldn't be living with him at Peace Cottage.

Joan's voice, loud and clear, drifted up the staircase from the hall. Mike must have left the stair door open. Hepsie checked her bedside clock: 3.40 p.m.

Mike was leaving.

Quickly, Hepsie rose from her bed and ran barefoot to her window. She could hear Mike's voice in the hall and then the clicking of the front door as it shut. She watched Mike walk down the short garden path to the front gate. He was carrying a familiar plastic carrier bag. Hepsie recognised it as the one the 1893 christening photograph was kept in. Why was Mike taking that away with him? She was surprised that Eb had entrusted Mike with his precious family photograph. Why had Eb done that? But who knows what's going on in the mind of an obsessively crazy genealogist.

Mike stopped at the front gate and glanced over his right shoulder to look back at the house. No, he was directly looking up at her bedroom window. Before she could move away, Hepsie realised he had seen her watching him from the window. Mike smiled broadly and waved at her before opening the gate and strolling off along the narrow lane to the Common.

She hadn't waved back. Hepsie lingered a little longer by the window, watching the drizzle fall on the garden and hills.

Mike's possession of the photograph was, genealogically speaking, a bad sign. She hadn't managed to undermine the genealogy connection. However, Hepsie also felt pleased by the sight of the familiar plastic carrier bag in Mike's hands. Because this meant there was a chance she would be seeing Mike again.

Seven

Mike was washing up at his Granny Wilson's house. Whilst he scrubbed the saucepans, Kate, his aunt, dried up beside him. Both of them were silent. Mike was pleased about this because the respite gave him a moment to review today's afternoon meeting with the Andersons. On the one hand, the meeting had gone well. He hadn't betrayed himself or his real reasons for setting up the genealogy business. In fact, he was lucky. The genealogy charade – for that was all it was – had convinced the Andersons that he was an obsessive genealogist. Of course, he wasn't. He would hate to think that someone might see him as one. But at least he'd been convincing enough for Eb Anderson; although Eb was so keen, he was probably going to believe Mike whatever Mike did. Mike felt guilty about misleading a blind man but, for Kate's sake, he must swallow his convictions and not let his moral conscience get in the way of the charade.

He saw that Kate was intently drying up, her thoughts no doubt focussed on their snatched conversation before supper. He had handed her the Andersons' family photograph hidden in its plastic carrier bag and briefly told her the outcome of the meeting. She'd bit her lip. He knew in the few minutes between her taking the bag upstairs to her bedroom and then coming back downstairs for supper, that she'd fleetingly studied the photograph. During supper, they couldn't say anything about it to one another. Granny Wilson served supper and chatted amiably with them. Mike hoped she hadn't guessed that something was afoot between Kate and himself. He knew Kate was dying for the meal to end so that she could convince her elderly Mum to put her feet up in front of the telly whilst she and Mike cleared up. He thought Kate would want to talk about today's meeting in more detail. But she was silent. He didn't like to disturb her thoughts. Sometimes her intensity could make her fly off the handle and emotionally strike out at you, as if she was punching away at an invisible enemy. There was one more dish to scrub, so Mike took his time over it.

At first, he hadn't wanted to carry out Kate's plan. The idea seemed crazy to him. What if he was caught? But Kate didn't want to do it herself. She didn't – she couldn't – in case the Andersons discovered the real reasons behind her interest. And she felt she couldn't reveal those to anyone. She'd been through enough. Mike had found himself in a difficult position. Here was his little aunt Kate, who had been his friend and surrogate sister since he was born. Fifteen years separated them. He'd grown up with Kate always being there for him. Now it was his turn to be there for her. He had to be. He had promised himself he would. The family couldn't risk Kate overdosing on sleeping pills again. This thought had kept him going when his car accident on the Painswick Road nearly made him call off his first meeting with the Andersons. Mike felt guilty that he'd come so close to letting down Kate. If this bizarre charade made her feel better, helped her take her mind off what had happened, prevented her from trying to kill herself again: then that was good. Mike knew he must put her needs first, even before those of a blind man.

The plan was to get what he, or rather Kate, needed, return what didn't belong to them, such as the Andersons' treasured family photograph, after Kate had scanned a copy onto her computer, and, then, to depart from the Andersons' lives as unexpectedly as he had entered. However, Mike also knew this wouldn't be easy. Somehow he had complicated the situation. And he wasn't about to tell Kate why.

"So there weren't any complications this time?" Kate asked him, beginning her sentence as she completed drying her last saucepan.

Mike paused in his scrubbing and looked over his shoulder at Kate. Her face showed no sign of extreme emotion as she placed the saucepan on the kitchen table beside the other dried items. Despite not going out as much as she used to do, she still took care with her appearances. Mike noticed how her dark hair shone like smooth black granite under the halogen kitchen lights. She was only a short woman, roundly built, and, if it hadn't been for the hell she'd been through, which made her features taut and weary, young for her forty-seven years. Before the incident, Kate's face conveyed a lively expression, with blue eyes that were intelligent and interested in everything around them. With her chic, urchin-cut hairstyle, and strong make-up, Kate kept the encroaching years and her wrinkles at a trendy distance. That vitality was all gone now. The trendy, confident woman had been replaced by a little lost girl, more street urchin than street wise. Even her wrinkles and the shadows beneath her eyes couldn't scare away the vulnerability of the child Kate had become. Mike knew that she was referring to his car accident when she spoke of 'complications'.

He smiled at her before replying. "Only the Andersons' neighbour: a bossy Joan Franklin. But I survived her."

He hoped Kate would laugh. She smiled wanly.

"Why was she there?" Kate asked.

"Eb's daughter was ill. Mrs Franklin was helping him."

Mike hoped his face remained emotionless. He hadn't told Kate about his feelings for Eb Anderson's daughter.

"So this Joan Franklin wasn't a problem?"

Mike shook his head. The situation was getting far too complicated. To hide his face, Mike resumed scrubbing the now well-scoured dish. The problem was that he couldn't tell Kate the truth. Joan Franklin was interested in using his genealogical services. Very interested. In fact, she was persuading him to give a talk to her Amberley Family History Group at their monthly meeting. Mike couldn't see a reasonable way of refusing her. His excuses would have to come later, when he severed his contact with the Andersons. God knows what he was going to say. Having said he wasn't too busy, that his marketing job wasn't going to undermine his genealogy business, and that the Andersons were his first clients, Mike was reluctantly considering to tell them that, maybe, his mother had died, or, maybe less traumatic, that his mother had suddenly been taken into hospital for a life-threatening operation. He knew these were terrible lies to tell and he hoped they wouldn't revenge him by happening in real life. The family had been through enough as it was. However, he needed an excuse to get him out of this business. The plan was that he would tell the Andersons he was taking a break from his genealogical business for a while and then, behind their backs, he would change his mobile number so that they couldn't contact him again.

Therefore, telling Kate about the Joan Franklin problem wasn't worth it. He would only be giving her additional worry, which she didn't need. Mike thought it was a good idea to rinse the dish before Kate noticed how much it'd been scoured. Granny Wilson wouldn't be pleased if he'd wiped off the whole pattern. Mike placed the dish carefully on the drying rack and pulled out the sink plug. The foamy water gurgled as it swirled down the plughole, filling the silence between Kate and himself. He let the water go down before rinsing out the sink with fresh water and giving the washing-up brush a quick clean. Mike always washed up after his meals with Granny Wilson and Kate. Sometimes, his mother Margaret and his dad John joined them for dinner. They did this mostly for Kate's sake and to help Granny Wilson have some respite from looking after Kate. At eighty-one, Granny Wilson hadn't expected to be caring for her youngest daughter. Kate had been living her own independent life but now her tiny house in Cherry Tree Close was rented out and her working days spent with Granny Wilson at the latter's home in Leckhampton. Having to keep an eye on Kate daily was stressful for his Gran, but Mike could see that Gran was desperate to keep Kate going, whatever the cost. "Wouldn't you do the same for your own child?" she had said to her elder daughter Margaret. Mike's mum, Margaret, offered to accept some of the responsibility, but they both knew that the one place where Kate really wanted to be, after all that she'd been through, and where there was a possibility that she might heal, was her childhood home.

When Mike turned round to face the kitchen table, he saw that Kate was sitting down, her hands cupping her chin in a thoughtful repose. He pulled out a chair and sat down beside her. She didn't look at him.

"So there weren't any other problems?" she asked.

Mike wondered why she kept asking him this. Had she guessed? He didn't think he had betrayed any of his emotions. In fact, he had done his best to avoid mentioning Hepsie Anderson in their conversations. Did Kate's intuition tell her that something else was wrong? Mike hoped she wouldn't guess.

"I don't think so," he lied. "The Andersons are very nice people. I don't think they'll give us any more trouble if we don't continue with this situation. I'm just sorry they couldn't provide us with any information on the Zennor Anderson secret."

"They made no reference to it?" Kate asked.

Mike shook his head. "None, as far as I could see. I looked through Eb's genealogical notes but...nothing. Not even a reference to your great-grandfather."

"Their research isn't as comprehensive as ours?"

"No. The old man offered me his genealogical files to take home but I refused. I made some notes in my notebook, if you want to look at those, but there's nothing new, apart from the photograph."

Kate looked amazed. "So the Andersons don't even know that Zennor's younger sister, Ivy Mills, married our ancestor, Neville Dangerfield, the year after Zennor's death?"

"They had no record of Ivy Mills being married. Either they don't know about Neville Dangerfield. Or, maybe, they're hiding their knowledge."

Mike looked at Kate and she looked at him.

"Can we be sure that they're hiding that knowledge?" Kate asked.

"No."

"But the blind man seems to think there's something going on?"

Mike sighed. He ruffled his hair with his hand before replying. "Eb Anderson believes he has been brought back to the former home of his ancestors because they're trying to get in touch with him."

"If only they could!"

"Of course, it could just be a co-incidence." Mike knew he was mirroring Hepsie's thoughts.

"If only his ancestors could talk," Kate repeated, wistfully this time.

And then, almost jokingly, she added: "You can't convince the Andersons to employ a medium?"

Mike laughed.

A smile broke out on Kate's face. For a moment she almost looked like her old self. Mike hoped this was a sign that the genealogical obsession was beginning to bring her out of herself.

To please her, he joked: "Shall I ask them next time I see them?"

"Well, something's got to happen," Kate said. "I wonder…" But she didn't finish the sentence. Her face resumed a perplexed frown.

Mike waited for her to speak. In the quietness he could hear the humming vibration of the fridge. It was still light outside. When he'd been washing up he had glanced out of the window and seen Granny Wilson's washing line glistening with bead droplets of rain. He would have liked to have picked up this necklace of watery beads and fastened it around Hepsie's slim neck.

Kate was still lost in her perplexed thoughts. Mike decided he'd better give her another five minutes before he started getting coffee ready. Granny Wilson didn't mind them chatting in the kitchen whilst she watched television but she would be wanting her coffee soon. The kitchen clock showed that it was nearly eight o'clock.

Hepsie's face brightened up his thoughts. He noticed the way light caught the golden and copper glints in her chestnut hair; and how her round blue eyes communicated her feelings so intelligently and sensitively. He had even noticed the mole on the bridge of her retroussé nose: a feature that he found attractive, even sexy. Her exotic scent still tickled his nostrils. Even her defiance of him, when she was confusingly trying to undermine his genealogical assistance, made him feel good. It was odd how she kept trying to scare him away. To him, the attraction between them was strong and obvious. It had certainly made the meeting at Siesta Café less arduous and more interesting for him. But why was she outwardly denying her feelings towards him? Mike had to try hard to restrain himself from revealing any anxious signs of emotion in case Kate woke up from her deep thoughts and noticed him.

Why was Hepsie ignoring this strong attraction between them? Mike could only think of one reason. Hepsie had a boyfriend. Mike felt cross. Why didn't Hepsie say so? But, of course, she wasn't going to do that. He had been mad to even consider there could be something developing between them. A strong attraction was a strong attraction: nothing more. Mike knew he should leave this genealogy charade behind him and get on with his life. The situation he'd talked himself into was complicated enough.

However, today's Sunday visit had loomed large in his mind. The difficulty of his task was made more bearable by the thought of seeing Hepsie again. Of checking to see whether the strong attraction between them was still there a week later. And the competitive urge in him, created by the thought that she might have a boyfriend, made him want to fight even more for her attention. Therefore, he had gone off to the Peace Cottage meeting in good spirits. He was nervous, but hopeful. That was why today's meeting, on the other hand, hadn't gone so well.

It was a blow when he heard that Hepsie wouldn't be playing a part in the afternoon meeting. Mike realised he would have to go through the whole charade, not only hiding his deceit, but also his disappointment. He had lied about needing to use the bathroom. The truth was that he was keen to explore Hepsie's home, to see whether he could find out more about her and her lifestyle. What sort of person was she? Unrealistically, he hoped he might bump into her upstairs, although she was supposed to be sick with a sore throat. After using the bathroom, his curiosity had dared him along the landing and made him nose into a bedroom. This was where she had caught him. Mike felt guilty, because he knew he looked suspicious. But she had been very nice about it. They had almost moved on to talking about her private life when she'd suddenly clammed up. Mike wondered now whether it was because she was ill, although she looked in good health to him. Of course, he should have used their brief chat to ask her about her boyfriend. Or used his exploration of the upstairs to look for evidence of any signs of one in Hepsie's life. But he had left the house not knowing. Even talkative Joan Franklin hadn't divulged this secret.

After their brief chat on the landing, the rest of the afternoon's meeting had rushed by. He found he could bluff his way more easily through the genealogical discussions with Eb and Joan. And, then, she'd been waiting for him at the bedroom window. Mike sensed he was being watched as he walked down the garden path. He couldn't restrain himself from turning around and waving at her. She hadn't waved back. Strangely enough, her eyes seemed to be focussed on the plastic bag he was carrying.

Eb Anderson hadn't asked Mike to take the photograph away with him. Mike knew that the old man wouldn't be too pleased that his treasured family photograph was now in Mike's hands. Mike knew it was wrong of him to surreptitiously take the heirloom away with him. But it had been easy for him to do so. Eb was blind and Joan was fussing over the used tea crockery. He had put on his jacket and was about to leave the living room. All it took was for him to clasp the plastic carrier bag, with the Andersons' photograph he'd put back in it, by the handle and carry it outside the house. Simply done. Ignored in the confusions of saying goodbye to Eb and Joan and promises to get in touch soon.

Well, of course, he would be getting in touch soon. To apologise about inadvertently taking the Andersons' photograph. Of course, he would have to return the item. That very next weekend. He would call the Andersons' landline tomorrow evening and explain. He imagined Hepsie answering the telephone. Mike knew he could call Eb's mobile but there would be less likelihood of Hepsie taking the call. Kate would have six or seven days to study the original photograph before she was left with only a scanned copy. When Mike had told her about the 1893 photograph, describing the figures in detail to her as best as he could, she had urged him to get her a copy. Mike tried to explain that this wouldn't be easy for him because he had no valid reason for taking the photograph. That was why, in the end, he had resorted to – no, you couldn't really call it stealing – to borrowing the item. Now, of course, Kate had what she wanted and he had an excuse for meeting Hepsie again.

No, the situation wasn't as simple as that. He was supposed to be returning the Andersons' photograph, very apologetically, and somewhat foolish at his mistake, before quickly driving away and probably – no, hopefully – never to return to Peace Cottage and the Andersons' lives. That's how he should play it.

But Mike knew, whilst he sat at the kitchen table, that he wasn't going to be able to stick to this plan.

The old, sepia-tinted photograph was inexplicably linked to his vision of Hepsie and himself. This heirloom was like his passport into another world. When he handed it back to the Andersons next weekend, he hoped it would lead to further encounters with Hepsie Anderson. The trouble was, how could he convince Kate to change her mind about ending all contact with the Andersons?

Mike couldn't imagine Kate wanting to continue with their genealogical charade. She had more genealogical information on the Andersons' family than they did. Unless…Mike held the thought in his mind for a second. Unless he continued with the genealogical charade by himself. He knew this would be very dangerous. And that he might blow his cover. But Kate wouldn't have to know about it. If he was caught, however, he might have to reveal her part in the charade and her reasons for instigating it. She wouldn't like that. And Mike was unsure whether she would be able to cope.

Kate's chair scraped across the lino as she pushed it back to stand up. Mike glanced at the kitchen clock and realised they'd been sitting in silence for about ten minutes. Granny Wilson would be gasping for her after-dinner coffee. He could hear the television in her living room. She must have turned up the volume.

He watched as Kate set up the coffee pot on the hotplate and measure spoonfuls of rich roasted coffee into the filter. Realising she'd forgotten to line the filter with a filter bag, Mike leapt up from his seat and rushed to get one from out of the cupboard.

Kate saw what he was doing and smiled apologetically. He emptied the measured coffee from the filter into the paper filter bag. Granny Wilson still liked to use this old-fashioned method of making fresh coffee. Kate had brought her cafetière from Cherry Tree Close but Granny Wilson complained that the residue left at the bottom of the cafetière created a dirty mess in her sink and clogged up the plughole. Mike switched on the kettle.

"I don't know what I would do without you, Mike," said Kate. She was putting three mugs onto a tray ready to take into the living room.

Mike squeezed Kate's shoulder. "I'm always here for you," he said.

He unscrewed the top of Granny Wilson's biscuit barrel and chose three chocolate digestives and three iced mocha biscuits to put on a side plate. Kate put the plate on the tray.

She smiled generously at him. "I really do appreciate the risk you took in getting the Andersons' photograph for me," she said.

"That's all right," said Mike. He wondered whether the change in Kate's mood might make it easier for him to persuade her to keep in touch with the Andersons. "You never know," he added, "the photograph might lead to other connections. Why don't you study it for a bit and see whether you can think of any new excuse we could use to try and get the Zennor Anderson secret out of the Andersons?"

Kate looked interested. "Yes, I can't wait to look at the photograph in more detail. 'Though I don't know how I will feel about it...you know, looking at *her*."

"But we don't know whether Granny Wilson's story is true," said Mike, trying to sound as sympathetic as he could. "Our ancestor could have made it up."

"Well, that's why we're researching the matter," Kate retorted, as if Mike was thick.

He didn't mind. When she was focussed on her genealogical quest, Kate's obsessiveness often made her speak like this. In fact, he was pleased to see her behave with some of the spirit of her pre-incident days. At times like this, you couldn't imagine her ever trying to commit suicide. Mike was glad Granny Wilson had inadvertently blurted out the family secret to Kate one day. At first, they thought the confession had made Kate more disturbed but, then, she became obsessive about finding out the truth. She wanted to find out everything about Zennor Anderson. Seeing the Andersons' advert at the County Record Office, on one of the rare occasions when she did go out, propelled Kate to devise the genealogy charade.

Mike was surprised how Granny Wilson hadn't guessed how far the genealogy obsession had gone. She knew he was helping Kate research the Dangerfield and Anderson family lines and she was interested in sharing the research results with them. However, if Granny Wilson knew how far he'd allowed Kate to take matters, he knew she would label them both mad. He imagined her berating them: Kate she could understand, but not him. Mike turned round to face the cooker so that Kate couldn't see him gulp. He poured boiled water from the kettle into the filter. The rich aroma of coffee stung his face as the hot water seeped into the ground coffee. Granny Wilson didn't know about his fear. His fear that, if he didn't help Kate with this crazy charade, she might overdose again. He was afraid of her relapsing. Only recently, Granny Wilson had remarked that since Kate's mind had been focussed on the genealogy, Kate had been suffering from less nightmares and flashbacks. Her youngest daughter was even showing signs of being unafraid of the dark.

Kate had placed a saucepan of milk to heat up on the cooker and was sitting at the table when Mike turned round to face her again.

"I wish Gran had a photograph of Neville Dangerfield," she said. "You'd thought she would, being his granddaughter. I would've loved to have seen what he looked like."

"No hope on the Web?" Mike asked.

Kate shook her head.

"Maybe the Andersons are hiding one," she said.

"Who knows?" Mike proffered. He was thinking that he would have to wait for Kate to come round to deciding whether to keep in contact with the Andersons or not. He didn't know whether she would. He hoped he sounded as if he was encouraging her without being pushy. As though the thought was to come from her, not him.

"I'd better go and sit in the living room with Gran," Kate suddenly said. "She'll be wondering where we've got to."

Mike agreed.

"Tell her, coffee will be about five minutes," he called after Kate as she left the kitchen.

Mike stared at the liquid coffee as it filtered through

into the coffee pot. He was reminded of an hourglass. Flowing coffee was measuring his life like grains of shifting sand. Mike wondered how much longer he had left. If he turned the coffee pot and filter upside down, as if his life was being turned on its head, would that make any difference? Would he be a happier person? Granny Wilson wouldn't be pleased because all the liquid and coffee granules would dirty her clean cooker. Perhaps that was what he was afraid of? He was afraid of displeasing people. Of letting them down.

All his life – thirty-two years of it – he had striven to do his best. He had chosen a straightforward route and stuck to it, obtaining what he had set out to do. From studying Marketing and Business Studies at university to his present job as a Marketing Executive at Thomas Clarksons, Mike knew he'd been lucky in his career. However, it wasn't enough. In the six years he'd been at Thomas Clarksons, a local educational publishing firm that had grown in size and international reputation, Mike's future hopes had disintegrated. He could almost rub the crumbs of his remaining hopes off his clothes.

You would think that as a Marketing Executive he would have enough money to buy his own home. But as house prices whistled up, faster than an unattached balloon caught in the wind, his hopes of creating his own nest faded. At the moment, he was emotionally empty. Seven months ago, he'd been ready to move into a freehold flat with his girlfriend, Selina. Her parents were contributing towards the cost of a deposit for a new flat in the Lansdown area. The problem was that Selina didn't want to buy the flat in their joint names. Mike had offered to contribute a small amount towards the deposit. Selina wanted the flat to be hers outright. She said because they were unmarried she thought it would be safer that way. Mike had argued that if they were staying together, then the flat should be in their joint names. Selina moved out of their rented flat. He lost both her and the chance of owning a place he could call home.

Mike's old school friend, Eddie, took Selina's place as flatmate at a terraced Regency house near Suffolk Parade. The friends recalled their teenage days as aspiring bass guitarists in a local Indie band. Mike very rarely picked up his guitar to play it nowadays. Music, like love and laughter, had lost its fascination for him. Mike longed to rediscover that youthful vibe from his youth. When he was freewheeling around the world and discovering what it was like to live. He thought maybe part of his current problem was that he'd been washed back onto the shores of his hometown. Having left home to attend university and then to take up a graduate traineeship in Birmingham, Mike had made the mistake of resettling in Cheltenham. It seemed to him as though he'd got somewhere only to find that he had gone nowhere. Mike smiled cynically, as he imagined himself as a mad Zebedee spinning round and round on a Magic Roundabout. Surely Zebedee had the magic or wits to get off this constantly revolving Roundabout? Wasn't Zebedee supposed to have springs? But Mike's Zebedee never made the leap to freedom. Zebedee kept on spinning – round and round – with his curled black moustache twirling in time to the vicious music of the Roundabout.

The coffee pot was filling up. He would have to take the tray through to the living room in a minute or two. Mike closed his eyes to block out the world. But his thoughts didn't go away. Tomorrow would be the same for him as all the other weekdays of his present life. A day of going to the office, earning money to pay the rent and bills, a joke with his colleagues, a new marketing project to present, a trip to the supermarket, drinks with Eddie in Montpellier in the late evening. Mike wondered whether this daily rhythm would change if he moved away from Cheltenham. Perhaps he was getting old and set in his ways? Why didn't he look for a job that paid him more money, so that he could afford that dream home and have something to show for his hard work other than his job title? He was lucky that he wasn't the type of man to be attracted to drugs or alcohol abuse or to escape through sex. A quick fix didn't grab him as it grabbed some of his friends and colleagues. And he was glad of this. He knew from close experience where that sort of behaviour bitterly led.

No. What Mike needed was the courage to give up his job. To trade his structured marketing career for a freewheeling sabbatical. That small deposit he was going to give towards his ex-girlfriend's flat could easily become a passport to a year's freedom. Mike had often thought he'd lost out on seeing the world. Well, now was his chance. So why was he holding back? He was worried. Worried that he would lose his footing on the career ladder; worried about letting go of his finances, however inadequate they were in today's housing market; worried that having put so much of his youthful energy into achieving his career goals, the younger years of his life would be wasted if he were to give up his job. He wasn't even sure whether it was a good idea to let his bosses know how he felt. In case they marked him down or passed him over for promotion.

Mike could smell the milk heating up in the saucepan. He ought to check the milk to see whether it was beginning to boil, but he couldn't be bothered to open his eyes.

Was Kate holding him back? Kate's predicament made him feel just how sick he was of the world: of its ugliness, its evil, the degradation of British society, the atmosphere of diminishing hopes and of limited horizons. Crime was up; taxes were higher; debts greater; money tighter; morals and human values eroded. Law and bureaucracy played against the good and honest members of society. Even the Human Rights Act no longer served the genuine victim. The victim was always the criminal: either she was prosecuted by the criminal who had wronged her in the first place, and who now saw himself as the victim of the incident; or she was condemned to lose her case over some minor technicality that the criminal had thought right to appeal. That was why Kate was having doubts about going to court. On top of all her hurt and shame, she didn't want the additional humiliation of being portrayed, however crazy it seemed, as the one who was the criminal. Life was unfair, thought Mike bitterly. Why else would he be involved in a crazy genealogy scam on behalf of his aunt? How could he refuse to help her, having seen what she'd gone through and what else she still had to suffer?

He recalled Joan Franklin's chat about Hepsie. She had told him that Eb's wife had died of cancer less than two years ago and that Hepsie had given up her job and life in London to return to Peace Cottage to look after Eb. Mike decided that Hepsie must be a very caring person to do something like that. It wasn't often that younger people put their lives before their parents. He was full of admiration for her. Hepsie's fine face brightened up his thoughts again. She had a distinctive way of smiling at him. He couldn't quite put his finger on it. Did she remind him of someone?

It didn't matter. Mike had decided he mustn't lose this chance of emotional happiness. He was looking forward to ringing Hepsie tomorrow evening and hearing her clear voice, even if she was defiant in her attitude towards him. He prayed Eb wouldn't answer the call. Tomorrow's Monday would be different from all his other weekdays. Phoning Hepsie would change the daily rhythm of his Monday. And maybe of his whole life...

"Mike, what are you doing?"

Kate's puzzled voice awoke Mike from his reverie.

A burning smell was permeating Granny Wilson's fresh, clean kitchen.

Mike grabbed the milk saucepan off the hotplate. The milk had almost boiled over. The bottom of Granny Wilson's favourite milk saucepan was burnt. Mike cursed. He emptied the burnt milk down the sink plughole, squeezed a large jet of washing-up liquid into the saucepan and filled it up with hot water to soak.

"Gran did wonder what was going on," said Kate, ironically.

"I'll get her a new one," Mike said.

He swapped the filter on the coffee pot for a lid and began filling up the three mugs.

"Penny for your thoughts?" Kate looked at Mike more directly than she'd done all evening.

Has she guessed? Mike thought. He tried to think back to their earlier conversation. He didn't think he had revealed his feelings about Hepsie.

"I was only thinking about the genealogical research," he lied. "Whether there was anything else we could do to keep the Andersons interested. In case they revealed the Zennor Anderson secret."

126

Kate nodded.

"I've been thinking, too," she said.

Mike raised an eyebrow. He didn't know what she was going to say. He put the still-warm coffee pot back on the hotplate.

"I don't want to give up the Anderson link; especially now you've got a foot in their door," she said. "But we do need an excuse to carry on with their genealogy. I was wondering..."

Kate looked pleadingly at him.

"It's a big deal to ask you, Mike," she continued, "but do you mind?"

"Mind what?" he asked.

"If you give the Andersons my research on Zennor Mills's family." Kate took a deep breath, as though she had released a long-held thought.

"Zennor Mills's family?" Mike asked, in some disbelief.

Kate nodded again.

"You said the Andersons don't know about the Ivy Mills and Neville Dangerfield link," she said. "Well, don't you think, if you give them this genealogical link, it might jog their memory or mean something to them?"

Mike ruffled his hair several times.

"Well...yes," he eventually replied.

"So you'll tell them that?" she asked. "Either tomorrow or when you see them next weekend?"

Mike couldn't help smiling. Unbelievably, Kate was saying she wanted to continue with the Anderson connection.

He squeezed her shoulder tenderly. "Of course I'll do it for you," he said.

Kate's smile showed how grateful she was. For a brief moment, her blue eyes flickered with a lively intelligence Mike hadn't seen in a long time.

"Shall I tell Gran about her saucepan, or shall you?" she said.

Mike grimaced.

"I will," he replied.

Kate managed a little laugh.

Her first laugh for a long time, Mike thought.

He took out a bottle of milk from the fridge and topped up their mugs with cold milk. At last, the tray was ready to take into the living room.

As he followed Kate out of the kitchen, Mike couldn't help thinking that, although their genealogical scam was crazy, both he and Kate had a lot to gain from continuing with the Andersons' connection.

Eight

Zennor was in the hands of time, falling slowly through the years. Although she beat her heart, no one heard her. She could have roamed the moorland surrounding the strange Quoit on Zennor Hill; or she could have bashed her soul against the granite cliffs at Zennor Head, as the Atlantic Ocean did. She could have vented her anger in thunderstorms that rained hard against the auburn stone of St Senara's church tower; and curled up in the arms of the wooden mermaid on the pew end, weeping her woe into the harlot's tresses. But she did none of these things. Zennor had expected to hear the mermaid Morveren and her lover Matthew Trewella singing beneath the waves. But they were silent. She had nothing to do but to sing to her lonely self.

Bending down, Zennor picked up a pebble from the wet sand and stroked its smooth surface. She held it in her hand as though it were a precious stone and not just a plain pebble. Thrilled, she gazed at it wide-eyed like a child. This pebble was like her former life. She curled her fingers around it and grasped tightly. How she'd wished she'd done so with her own life. That stationary world at the centre of her heart – the one she'd always been chasing – and which she had treasured like an expensive diamond, was really no more than an imperfectly shaped plain pebble like this one. Those who didn't know its worth, who wouldn't even give it a glance, would have hurled the pebble into the sea and left it to sink, forgotten, beneath the waves. But Zennor knew its worth. And that's why her heart ached.

Now she's unleashed from her world, cut adrift and rootless as her nomadic childhood. Like a clumsy piece of driftwood, she found herself sullenly floating in stagnant waters, willing the strong sea to rush in, swirl her around and return her to life. But that moment never came. Zennor was treading time like treading water.

She had expected to meet those she'd lost in her life, such as Charlie. He was her younger brother by eighteen months and her confidant. Poor Charlie! How she had missed him after he was buried. Ten years old and in the grave. Zennor closed her eyes, shutting out her guilt. She had often wondered whether his death from pneumonia was her fault. It was she who had taken him out to play that day, a fine, hot summer's day, when she and Charlie were going to seek coolness in the shade of the riverbank. They didn't notice the gathering storm clouds. The blocking out of the sun. They had laid down on the riverbank and fallen asleep in the protective long grass. Thunder woke them up. Before they reached home, their skins were drenched by flooding rain. She was strong and able to shake off a good soaking. Charlie, her Charlie, shivered like a jelly until the wetness penetrated his soul. He had a wonderful smile, as though he was always imagining sunshine and butterflies and scented hollyhocks before him, and she remembered how the ghost of this smile still seemed to hover over his face after life had left his sick body. But where was he now?

It was after Charlie's death that she'd began to read. Words became her imaginative friends, replacing Charlie as her confidant. When she read of Little Nell's death in *The Old Curiosity Shop* she cried. Beneath the floorboard of the bedroom, Zennor had hidden a stone, a chestnut leaf, and a shrivelled conker on a string. The last time she'd looked at these memories of Charlie's life, the chestnut leaf had wilted. She should have pressed the delicate leaf between the pages of a book before consigning it to beneath the floorboards. This time, Zennor carefully prised open the loose floorboard and put her hand into the narrow gap. Her fingers grasped for the hidden items. There was nothing there. Frantically, she ran her fingers as far into the gap beneath the floorboard as she could. Her skin was scraped sore by the rough wood. When she pulled out her hand, it was dirty and covered in thick, grey dust and there was a splinter dug deep into her little finger. Zennor bit her lip as tears flowed down her cheeks. How had Joe guessed? Why had he known where to look? Her body shook as she tried to hold to her heart what remained of Charlie and her memory of him.

Of course, the family had moved away after that. Charlie lay buried in some forgotten graveyard, where no one visited him and where, Zennor now guessed, no one bothered to pick fresh flowers to put on his grave. She sighed. Why did people like Charlie die and people like her elder brother Joe...? Zennor's gaze drifted out towards the sea but she neither saw the rolling waves nor heard the seagulls screaming in the sky. What Joe had done to her was bad. So very bad. Zennor shook her head, closing her eyes to seek inner peace. Brothers but so unalike. She wondered, as she had done many times before, that if she hadn't taken

131

Charlie out that day of the thunderstorm, if he had lived to spend her childhood years with her until she left home, she wondered whether the...Zennor let the guilt and the shame wash over her, until she was drowned in sorrow. Such a bad thing to happen. If only she had known how to stop...

Zennor opened her eyes. The wind was changing. She could feel it moving against her body, wrapping her long skirts around her legs so that she was unable to walk without stumbling over. She had tried to pass on her love of reading to her children. Elsie was only six years old but she could already pick out a few sentences in the books Zennor read to her before bedtime. Four-year-old Clara was still prattling in her baby language. She loved to sit on Zennor's lap and be read to. Soon she would be like Elsie, stringing words along like beads on a thread. Zennor had high hopes for her daughters. She wouldn't get in the way of their chances in life. Pa's discouragement of her ambition to be a school assistant had made her determined not to underestimate her daughters' worth. They'd be no...Zennor shivered in the wind. She wrapped her arms around her chest and allowed the wind to rock her from side to side. What were her children doing now? She wanted the wind to whip the words from her lips and carry them across the world: nothing had broken her spirit more than the seeds of her womb.

Baby Georgie. His first milk teeth were coming through. His face was plump and his fists strong. She could have lived for him. But had George guessed? Zennor shivered more violently as the wind turned icy. Of course George had. She wouldn't be here otherwise. Zennor gritted her teeth. George had taken her away when she should have been at home. Now the worse had happened: she'd lost her children. They needed her and she wasn't there for them. What sort of mother was that? Zennor felt her broken spirit crushing the vertebrae of her spine, as she watched the seeds of her womb – Elsie, Clara and Georgie – turning to fallow dust. This was what she had tried to avoid. The reason she was hanging on to life like a fly caught in a spider's web. But she had still lost them.

The north-westerly wind was kicking up a drenching spray. Salty seawater stung Zennor's face. She would have to move away. But where to go?

Zennor knew where to go. She'd been there a few times in the last...Well, she didn't know how many days or hours or years it'd been, but she'd been there. To spy.

Today – was it a Tuesday? – she found herself staring out of the mirror. Into someone else's reflection. The woman was a brunette likeness to her own fair reflection. The same retroussé nose, heart-shaped face, demeanour: as though the other woman could have been a part of her. Zennor felt she ought to know this woman. But who was she?

The woman was brushing her teeth with a bright red toothbrush. Zennor watched in amazement as the woman rinsed her toothbrush with running water from a tap. A properly fitted bathroom! The people who lived in this house must be very rich. Zennor had never been in a house with running tap water. Her former employers, Richard and Dorothea Langley-Smith, had a WC in their house at Lansdown Road, where Zennor had worked as a housemaid before marrying George. It was Zennor's duty to clean this WC daily, but never to use it herself. Servants were told to use the outdoor privy at the back of the house or a chamber pot. Zennor remembered the arduous trips up and down stairs, straining her back with heavy pails of hot water, as she laboured to fill up the hipbaths in her employers' bedrooms. Then she would have to take, with the kitchen maid Ellen's help, bucketfuls of dirty bath water all the way back downstairs, to be emptied out in the street drains or to 'refresh' the back garden. But these people – this household – had a bath! A proper bath with taps. Zennor sighed. Such luxury!

Her mirror image was washing her face. Zennor watched as the woman splashed her skin with water and then patted her face dry with a towel. She was surprised that she could smell the fragrant soap the woman had used to clean her skin. Zennor closed her eyes and breathed in the familiar scent, last smelt by her long ago, of camomile. When she reopened her eyes she realised that her mirror image was talking.

"What are you saying?" she said, her breath rushing to the glass.

The woman kept on talking.

Zennor shook her head in dismay.

"I can't hear you!" she said more loudly.

The woman kept on talking.

Zennor was silent. And then she understood the woman was talking to herself. Was this a sign of madness?

Zennor cocked her ear to the glass and closed her eyes to concentrate on the woman's words.

"...I don't care want Eb thinks. This is the only chance I can use to speak to Mike without Eb being there...I don't know why he 'accidentally' took the photograph...Eb should be glad he's bringing it back..."

There was silence.

Zennor opened her eyes and turned to face the glass. The brunette woman had paused in her self-absorbed chat and was admiring her reflection in the mirror. Zennor noticed that there was a mole on the bridge of the woman's nose. She wondered whether the woman could see her.

"Can you hear me?" she shouted.

Her words reverberated off the glass and back onto her face.

Zennor sighed.

The woman began talking again. She shook her head, as though in no doubt about something.

"...of course he's annoyed about it...but I knew he wouldn't be able to get out of it...Joan's got him fair and squarely nailed..." The woman chuckled. "...who cares that I told him that Sunday morning was the only time Mike could visit us..."

Zennor was surprised to see the woman's round blue eyes dilate with strong emotion. And then the woman blushed.

Who was this Mike? This Eb? Zennor could tell that the woman was 'in love' with Mike. She felt a hollowness in her stomach. A long-forgotten urge gnawing away at her innards. For a moment she was almost somewhere else. From the locked rooms of her memory, a key was turning in a door, allowing her to peep into a room she'd never wanted to visit again.

Zennor banged on the glass, her knuckles rapping against the hard surface.

The woman didn't flinch. Instead, she carried on talking.

"...I know I shouldn't lie to him...but what can you do?...I need to be alone with Mike..."

Zennor banged more urgently on the glass.

"Listen to me!" she yelled.

With dismay, she noticed her breath reaching the glass without misting it.

The woman began brushing her long hair.

Maybe she's deaf, Zennor reasoned. Maybe it's not me. Maybe she's...

The thought struck her like a slap across her cheek. The woman was pretending deafness! She was doing so on purpose. Why?

Zennor stared into the woman's eyes, seeking for answers or a sign of recognition. That she, Zennor, was her reflection. But although the woman's mid-blue irises were as clear and luminous as the sea on a bright summer's day, they yielded less secrets regarding Zennor's existence than the opaque depths of the Atlantic Ocean.

The woman moved away from the mirror.

Looking at the glass, Zennor realised it was empty of reflections. Her pale blue eyes weren't watching her in a mirror image. Zennor ran her fingertip over the glass. It seemed solid enough.

"Hepsie!" A male voice called out from somewhere. "Hepsie!" He sounded like an older man.

"Coming, Eb!" The woman's voice echoed through the bathroom.

Zennor heard the woman mutter: "A dutiful daughter's work is never done! What does Eb want now, I wonder?"

A door was unlocked and Zennor heard footsteps walking along creaking floorboards.

Zennor wondered whether the old man – the one the woman called Eb – might be The Blind Man. She had come across him during her spying. Strangely enough, she could see him without the mirror's help. Unlike her experience with the woman, Zennor felt that The Blind Man could sense her presence. Maybe she should...

Looking around her, Zennor began to think the

place looked rather familiar. There was something about the layout of the ceiling beams and the shape of the mullion windows. She couldn't remember the walls ever having been painted in these contrasting tones of bright colour, but if the walls were whitewashed they would look very familiar. Zennor shook her head in denial. She must be imagining things.

Slowly, she rested her hand on the doorknob and turned it. The door pulled towards her. She opened it wider and peeked out into the corridor.

If she could get The Blind Man to speak, maybe he could help her? Unlike the woman, who must be his daughter, he seemed to be aware of her. The problem would be in getting him to listen. Surely he wouldn't ignore her or pretend deafness as the woman had done? Zennor hoped his blindness might make him kind towards her. Not that she looked a fright. She smoothed down the skirt of her dress, caressing the silkiness of its fabric with her fingertips. No. At Roelinda's wedding they'd said she'd looked very fine in her former wedding dress. Hephzibah had even helped her to make leg-o'mutton sleeves. So fashionable! Really, it was a shame The Blind Man couldn't have seen her.

Zennor stepped out into the corridor. She paused. Where had she last seen The Blind Man? Doors led off into rooms around her. She ought to begin her search for him soon. Today, if she was serious.

She raised her hand to knock on a door but then thought better of it. Somewhere in her head, she could hear the ticking of a clock. Tick-tocking time with mechanical precision. Zennor put her hands over her ears. The clock boomed loudly in her head as it struck the half-hour.

This was no good. She must get a move on. Zennor

removed her hands from her ears and slightly pulled up her skirt so that she could run along the corridor more quickly.

The open window told Zennor that the time of year must be summer. She could smell freshly cut grass and scented roses and honeysuckle. Birdsong sweetened her hearing. The grey stone walls of the house cocooned the room in a cool slumber, safe from the sun's heat. A fire screen hid the unlit grate. Zennor admired the collage of painted flowers and fruit on the screen. Peaches, pears and plums were beautifully rendered so as to be good enough to eat. Raindrops glistened on the painted leaves and an inquisitive fly squatted life-like on the fair skin of one peach.

Thursday. How did she know today was Thursday? Ever since the clock had been ticking in her head, the counting of hours and days had come more easily to her. A clock, of course, can spend all its time counting time, but she couldn't. She was surprised when her mind decided today was Thursday. Why had she taken so long to find The Blind Man?

For there he was. Sitting in an easy chair by the fireplace. His eyes closed. His chest rising with each breath.

Zennor stood there watching him. His white hair was the same whiteness as Ebenezer's but without the flowing Dundrearies. She was able to see the wrinkles on his kind face: a cross-hatched etching of care, laughter, sadness and patience. As for his apparel, she was interested to note that he was without waistcoat, his checked shirt was open-necked, and his shirt sleeves rolled up. Was he taking a break from his labour? She didn't know what sort of trade a blind man might do. He must be hot, for he had removed his neck'chief. On his lower half he was wearing crumpled cords, again like Ebenezer, but without the sawdust. Looking at his feet, she was curious to see that he was not wearing a labourer's hobnailed boots. What was he wearing? The toes of his green socks were peeping out from a buckled strap. There was another strap around his ankle. Sandals? Zennor had never seen a man wearing sandals before.

She coughed. The Blind Man didn't stir. She watched his chest heave as he took another breath.

She coughed again. The Blind Man grunted.

Zennor leant forwards to peer more closely at him. He could be sleeping. She tapped him on the shoulder. His eyelids fluttered for a moment before his head lolled forwards.

She cleared her voice.

"Sir," she said, "I am Mrs George Anderson. I would like to request the pleasure of your help."

Taking a deep breath, she waited for him to reply.

The Blind Man snorted.

Zennor gasped. She rested her hand on the armrest of the easy chair.

"Can you hear me?" she asked.

The Blind Man's eyelids fluttered again.

Zennor cleared her throat.

"Please listen to me," she pleaded.

She watched his chest rise and fall to the rhythm of her own apprehension.

It was no good. Zennor grasped his upper arm and briefly shook him.

The Blind Man's eyes momentarily opened before he closed them again and his head lolled sideways, so that he was almost touching her as she leant across the armrest.

Zennor bit her lower lip. She could feel tears pricking her eyes. Knowing it was wicked of her to do so, she gave him a sharp pinch on his bare lower arm.

He didn't flinch. Or so much as snort.

And then his mouth opened.

He was mumbling. Zennor leant closer so that she could catch his words between the breaths of his heaving chest.

"...got to find out...there must be a reason...it's in there somewhere..."

Zennor held her breath. Was he helping her?

She listened more carefully.

"...Hephzibah...Ebenezer...Zennor...they're all there...got to be a reason...oh...why can't I find it?"

Zennor's mouth dropped open in amazement. She clutched at her skirt, bunching up the fabric into a tight ball inside her clenched fist.

"Please, Sir," she begged, "I'm here. It's me. Zennor...I mean, Mrs George Anderson."

She didn't dare to shake the old man's arm again. He was waking up. He would be able to help her. He seemed to know her. And her parents-in-law. Was he an acquaintance of the Andersons? Maybe Hephzibah had been kind to him. That was so like Hephzibah, for her to make a blind neighbour a coltsfoot jelly or bring him a mug of hot beef tea. Did he live far from Peace Cottage?

Zennor clutched her skirt even more tightly. She breathed in deeply. Soon, soon, this nightmare would all be...

But what was this? The Blind Man's head was lolling forwards, so that his upper body was almost bent over his lower half.

She listened to his steady breathing.

If he wasn't careful, he'd fall out of the chair.

And then his body lurched back and fell against the easy chair's cushions, his head resting on the chair's back and his arms limp like a rag doll's.

Zennor banged her fist on the armrest. A few minutes ago she wouldn't have dared to do this, but it was obvious to her that The Blind Man had not fully woken up. Lost in his slothful slumbers, he was blissfully unaware of her.

She looked around her. She must wake him up. This was her only chance. Her eyes skimmed the contents of the room. Easy chairs. A sofa. Walls lined with books. Sofa tables. And many ornaments. Zennor glanced more closely at what lay on the sofa table nearest to her. A silver frame holding a photograph. She gasped in amazement. A coloured photograph! The hand tinting was superb, rendering the details of the figures and the background they stood in as though the photographer had memorised each tiny dot of colour. Next to this lay a large conch shell, and beside this...Yes, this was it.

Zennor gazed at the smooth roundness of the glass paperweight. She marvelled at the intricate strands of coloured glass twisted into an eye-catching pattern inside the paperweight's transparent surface. Cautiously, she touched the ornament, running her fingers over its form. It was completely solid. Not a single hairbreadth crack. Zennor sighed. She didn't really want to break it.

Looking around her, she saw there was nothing else she could use. And then she smiled. She realised she was standing on carpet. Yes! Carpet! Thick, luxurious carpet, that she'd only seen in rich people's houses. How could The Blind Man afford such a thing as a carpet? But perhaps this wasn't his house. Zennor paused, doubtful as to whether she should continue.

But it shouldn't matter, she reasoned; no damage would be done. Or so she hoped. She knew it was very naughty of her. If her Pa had been here, if he had found out, he would have...Zennor shuddered. Slowly, that key was turning in her mind, the door to the room was opening a little wider. Pa used to thrash her brothers with his thick leather belt if he'd thought they'd done wrong...indeed, he would've done so to her, if Ma hadn't stopped him...but why should she have been the one to be blamed...they knew it was him...there was one time – no, many times – when Pa should have thrashed...Zennor closed her eyes, hoping the darkness would shut out the gruesome thoughts swelling up in her mind like a throbbing wasp sting...oh, the pain! She put the back of her hand to her forehead, but there was no sweat dripping on her skin or heated fever raging through her head. Zennor dropped her arm to her side. She stood limply for a few moments, waiting for the puppeteer to pull on her strings tightly again.

There was nothing else she could do. Lifting up the paperweight, Zennor felt how heavy it was. She hurled it onto the carpet. The room echoed with the hard thud sound of its impact. She waited, her chest heaving with anticipation.

The Blind Man snorted. And started out of his sleep. He blinked for a second or two, as though wondering where he was. Blindly, he sensed the atmosphere, moving his head from side to side, perhaps listening.

"Is anyone there?" he said. His voice was low and mellow.

Zennor caught her breath. Now was her time to speak. But her words got stuck in her mouth. She opened her lips wider to get the words out but The Blind Man was talking again.

"Who's there?" he barked.

She pulled herself together and stood ramrod, as she used to do whenever her former employers ordered her to their study or drawing room. Her hands should be behind her back and she was also very conscious of not being dressed in her black taffeta afternoon dress and frilled apron and cap, as a housemaid should be.

Her voice quavered as she said: "Sir?"

She waited for The Blind Man to reply.

He blinked again. Sniffed. In silence he waited.

From outside the room, Zennor could hear the ticking of a clock.

"Sir?" she repeated.

The Blind Man looked her way. But, of course, he couldn't see her.

Zennor coughed, to let him know she was standing there.

The Blind Man gazed right through her.

Zennor couldn't bear the tension any longer. She knew it was rude of her but she shouted so that her words reached the very rafters of the attics: "CAN YOU HEAR ME?"

The Blind Man continued gazing through her. He made no sign that he had heard her.

Zennor sighed. She gripped at her skirt in frustration. Was he pretending deafness like his daughter? Despair swung from side to side in her stomach like a clock's pendulum. Did the woman and The Blind Man think they were too good to talk to the likes of her? Zennor wondered whether the village had been gossiping about her – perhaps, that Mrs Mortimer – or, any other of those God botherers – any one who thought Mrs George Anderson was a shame to the neighbourhood. Zennor could have wept.

Her eyes searched around the room. Of course, if it got out that she'd been throwing other people's property around – that she'd entered their house without a formal introduction and was trespassing on their property and behaving like a naughty child…Zennor stopped abruptly. But was this someone else's house? The room looked very familiar to her. There was no centrally placed table with a heavy rug covering, as there was in the front parlour of Peace Cottage; and she couldn't remember the far wall being lined with books, or the bare walls being painted in shades of warm apricot but…She looked more closely at the chimney breast of the fireplace. Yes, there was a broad length of timber set in the limestone chimney breast. Although, in Peace Cottage the limestone had been hidden beneath a layer of whitewash. Zennor wondered why, if the owners of this house could afford a properly fitted bathroom and a carpet, they had left the limestone exposed on their fireplace. Maybe they hadn't got round to whitewashing it yet?

The ticking of the clock was growing louder. The regular rhythm made the atmosphere in the room reminiscent of Peace Cottage. Zennor shivered, although she should have been glad to hear such familiar sounds. Her eyes glanced around the room one more time. She gasped. A blue-black Bible lay on a low table in front of the sofa. Ignoring The Blind Man, who was still gazing through her, she walked over to the low table and opened the Bible. There they were: Hephzibah's handwritten inscriptions. Why had Hephzibah given her precious Bible to The Blind Man? This Bible only left Peace Cottage when Hephzibah took it to church. Zennor couldn't imagine why The Blind Man should be in possession of it. He couldn't read. The woman, his daughter...Zennor ran her fingers over the delicate tissue-thin pages of Hephzibah's Bible. Strangely, there was a very musty smell emitting from the tome, as though the precious Bible had been left mouldering, forgotten, in the attics. Zennor rubbed her fingers against her skirt to get rid of the lingering smell of mustiness on them.

Moving away from the low table, she turned towards an open door. The ticking clock was almost a part of her now. She paused on the threshold of the door. She thought she could hear the cranking of the clock's pendulum as it swung from side to side. Then three chimes reverberated through her head and filled the room. Zennor's heart leapt. She caught her breath. The musical chimes sounded as though they'd emanated from the belly of an old oak grandfather clock.

Zennor stepped into the hall. There it was: the old grandfather clock that used to stand in the hall of Peace Cottage. The same worn wood, polished to a lustrous glow by Hephzibah. The yellowed clock face with the painted sun, moon and stars. And there, set in the lower clock case, the glass lenticle, where, if she'd bent down, she would have seen the clock's pendulum swinging hypnotically from side to side. But the rest of the hall looked familiar, too.

She glanced at her feet. She was stepping onto well-scrubbed flagstones. They led to a front door and to the door of a boxed-staircase. How did she know that door led to a staircase?

Zennor clenched her fists. Her suspicions were confirmed. The keeper of time – the grandfather clock – had proved her doubts were right. This was Peace Cottage. But, although this was her home, it was not her home. The familiar rooms were unchanged but changed. Zennor shook her head in disbelief. Why were The Blind Man and his daughter living here? Where was her family? Why have The Blind Man and his...?

They were thieves! The Andersons had been robbed of their most precious possessions. Perhaps even turned out of their own home. Zennor thought of all the wedding presents she and George had received: the silver-plated cutlery set from her Ma and Pa, the three-tiered Staffordshire cake stand from her sister Rose, the damask tablecloth from Richard and Dorothea Langley-Smith...where had all these gone?

She felt betrayed. She knew that if she went upstairs to the bedrooms and to Elsie and Clara's room in the attic, she would make the same discovery. What had happened to her family? What did The Blind Man and his daughter know? They had betrayed her, because they must know and they were refusing to speak to her. They must know that George killed her. That her death wasn't an accident. Well, that's what she believed. She couldn't trust him and he couldn't trust her. But where was he now? Had he taken the children away with him? Far away from Peace Cottage where he knew she would try to find them. And were The Blind Man and his daughter part of this conspiracy? They must be. George had even left some of the furniture for them.

Zennor longed for the truth to be told. Was that why she had returned? After all these years. She didn't know how long The Blind Man and his daughter had been living in this house. But it was only yesterday when she remembered Elsie and Clara and...the tears welled up in Zennor's eyes, ready to rain an ocean on the world. Georgie. Georgie with his tight fists and his smile so like...

She could have crumpled up on the flagstones.

Her mind whirled around like the mechanism of a clock. Each cog, however tiny, worked against another cog, until the thoughts in her mind were working like clockwork.

I must get The Blind Man and his daughter to notice me, she thought.

But how could this be done? They were already blind and deaf towards her. She might need to disrupt their lives in some way. Zennor knew this was naughty of her. But if she couldn't attract their attention, then how could they answer her questions? To tell her the truth. About what had happened. And about her children. She would have to be clever. Her options were limited. She must begin today.

Lifting the latch, she opened the door of the boxed-staircase and begun walking up the creaking stairs.

Nine

"And Sunday morning's the only time Mike can visit us?" Eb asked.

"That's the second time you've asked me in an hour," Hepsie replied, crossly.

"He can't come another day?"

"No!"

Eb could imagine the frown on Hepsie's face.

"Surely you don't want him to hold onto your photograph for longer?" she added.

She had a point there.

"No, but—"

"Then what's the problem?"

"I—"

"You're going to ask me the same question, again, aren't you?"

"I don't understand how someone could 'accidentally' take a photograph like that."

Now he could imagine Hepsie shaking her head in irritation. If she was wearing her hair loose, her long chestnut locks would be glinting in the sunlight and air.

"Look, Eb, I don't know why Mike took the photograph 'accidentally', but at least he's bringing it back. You should be pleased with that."

Eb sighed. They'd been arguing like this ever since Hepsie had told him the news. Unfortunately, he had been in the bathroom when Mike called them on Monday evening. For some reason, Mike had used their landline number. Fool! Eb was sure he'd told Mike that it was best to use his mobile number. He thought maybe Mike understood that Hepsie wasn't too keen about him helping out with the genealogy.

Now Eb wasn't too certain about Mike. Why had he 'accidentally' taken the photograph? Eb shook his head in disbelief. There was no following comment from Hepsie, so he presumed she hadn't noticed him or was ignoring him. Perhaps she was gazing out across the valley to the hills beyond? It had been a hot day and he could still feel the heat caressing his body. On good days, Hepsie would have described the view to him, but not today. He would have to guess how the view looked, remembering the green fields and woods and the hazy May Hill from his memories of being able to see.

"At least you can believe me now," Hepsie said.

"Believe you?" He affected surprise.

"Yes. You'd thought I'd hidden the photograph."

"No, I didn't. I—"

"And then, when you called Joan, who confirmed what I'd said – that Mike was carrying the photograph's plastic carrier bag when he left – you still didn't believe me. Even when Joan suggested you call Mike, you still didn't believe he'd taken it. 'Wait a day or two,' you said, 'in case the photograph unexpectedly turns up somewhere. We don't want to accuse Mike of something he hasn't done.'"

"But Mike said he didn't want to take anything. I certainly wouldn't give him the photograph to take – there's no reason to." Eb found himself gesturing with his hands, which was so unlike him. "Mike is such an intelligent man: I can't believe he'd do something like that by mistake."

Eb could hear flies buzzing near him. And then the angry flick of the cow's tail as the animal swiped the irritating flies off its flanks. He hoped Hepsie hadn't brought them too close to the cattle. The cow couldn't be far off. He could hear munching and the long grass swishing as the cow shifted its hooves. A low snort confirmed his fears. Surely the cow's pungent breath was only a head away?

"Aren't we too near the cattle?" he anxiously asked Hepsie.

"No, Eb. They're standing over by the bushes."

"Are you sure?"

"It's too hot for them. They're in the shade."

I shall have to believe her, Eb thought. Although it seemed to him that the cattle were a lot nearer. This was the trouble with being blind: you had to trust others so much. He tried to remember where the bushes were situated in relation to the seat they were sitting on, but it was many years since he'd last seen this part of the Common and he couldn't remember exactly what Hepsie had told him. The seat was situated on the Common above Peace Cottage and was set several yards from the War Memorial, on the hill slope overlooking the Nailsworth Valley. This was Sofia's commemorative seat. In early spring, neighbours, villagers, Sofia's former friends and colleagues, had gathered with Hepsie and him on this hillside for the ceremonial erection of this seat, dedicated to Sofia's memory. Hepsie had read the commemorative plaque to him: *In memory of Sofia Anderson who loved walking on Amberley Common.* He'd been told it looked like any other outdoor wooden seat, with a back and armrests and enough room to seat three adults. Now, he rubbed his fingers along the seat's slats, feeling the smooth wood where it hadn't yet been roughened by the elements.

"You don't have to do the reading," Hepsie said.

Eb gave a laboured sigh.

"You know I can't let Joan down. She's depending upon me."

"What? She can't get any other disabled person to do the reading?"

"Oh, what do I care!" Eb exclaimed. "It's too late now. If I had spoken to Joan earlier in the week, perhaps we could have made other arrangements."

Hepsie was silent. Eb knew she was probably aware that he was having a dig at her. The trouble was that she was quicker than he was answering the telephone this week. Consequently, it was Hepsie who had spoken to Joan and told her about Mike's visit clashing with Eb's church reading on Sunday morning. Before he could decide for himself, the two women had arranged for Joan to take him to the parish church and for Hepsie to collect him after the service, when Mike had left. Cornered like this, Eb felt he couldn't find a reasonable way to cancel his church reading. Faking sickness wasn't a possibility because Hepsie would surely argue with him that, if he was too unwell to give the reading, then he was too unwell to be meeting Mike. Anyway, Eb didn't like to admit to illness. He didn't want the congregation to add towards their pity for him.

"Have you read through the passage?" Hepsie asked.

"No."

"Well, aren't you leaving it a bit late?"

"Religion's not my kind of thing. I don't even know what part of the Bible it's from. The parable of the good Samaritan or something like that. The last time

I read that was years ago at school." Eb chuckled, hoping Hepsie would pick up on his age joke.

She didn't laugh.

"Hasn't Joan given you a Braille copy to learn?"

Eb nodded.

"I could go through it with you, whilst you read aloud. It'll be good to have a practice before Sunday."

When he didn't reply, she continued: "Next time you'd better refuse Joan. You know she's always meddling in other people's business."

Eb was almost certain he could detect a hint of a smile behind Hepsie's words. Yes, she was right. Since Sofia's illness, Joan had been slowly infiltrating his daily life. And without realising it, he had become more dependent upon her. There was no doubt it was useful to have such a helpful neighbour when you were blind and your wife was dying. But he would never have agreed to do something like the church reading before Sofia's death. What had he got himself into? True, Joan was on the Church Committee and very chummy with the vicar. In fact, Joan was on most committees in the village: the Mother's Union, Amberley Parochial School, the WI, the Gardening Club and, of course, Amberley Family History Group. She might well have devised this church service with its theme of recognising disability in the community. He was an obvious target. Here's our local man with 'impaired sight': let us show the strength of our community by including this disabled man in our village life. Disabled! The last thing Eb wanted to term himself was 'disabled'.

"My problems are with this world, not the next one," he said.

"I'm not saying you should take up religion. It's just that, now this reading is going ahead, you really ought to—"

152

"I know, I know..." Eb found himself gesturing again. As though waving his hands might make the whole situation evaporate into the evening air.

He wasn't sure whether Hepsie had deliberately misread him or not. 'My problems are with this world, not the next one.' But he wasn't talking about just religion. There were times when he wanted to shout to the world: "I haven't changed! I'm still the Eb you used to know." He found it hard to explain to people – to strangers, to his neighbours, to his friends – that he didn't like being treated as though he had become someone else. This was what blindness did to you. "I'm still here," he wanted to say, but the world now saw him as 'Eb the blind man', 'Eb the disabled', 'Eb the dependant'. There were times when he began to doubt himself. Who was he? There seemed to be two Ebs, facing each other as though they were strangers.

The world had changed when he'd thought he had known it inside out. Eb admitted he was afraid of totally losing his grip on life. And after, it seemed, he had come through so much. Learning to cope with the realisation of his increasing blindness and the problems of adapting to a sightless daily life were challenges enough. And he thought he had conquered these mountains. But having got over, or if not that, then learning to accept his plight, he was now discovering that his problems weren't solved. His blindness – or his 'impaired vision' or 'disability', as others liked to politically correctly call it – had struck at his self-identity far deeper than he could have ever imagined.

Take for example, his weekly visits to The Black Horse. What had happened to them? Eb used to enjoy his sociable draught of beer at the village pub. The friends he'd made there, mostly from Amberley and the surrounding hamlets and nearby Minchinhampton, would have enlivened his retirement for many years. But as soon as his eyesight started to deteriorate, and he couldn't throw a dart so straight, and he couldn't keep up with the team during Quiz Night, and he couldn't smile at his friends as they pulled a pint at the bar, then his trips to The Black Horse whittled away until he was left at home holding a glass of beer by himself. "Let us know, Eb, and we'll come and collect you," various friends had said to him, but Eb found it increasingly difficult to 'let them know'. He felt their hassle at having to treat him like he was...disabled. "Can I get you a pint, Eb?" they said, when he did come to the pub; but he used to sit in the corner, unsure of them, unable to see their faces and to join in fully with their conversation. Even if Hepsie accompanied him, it wasn't the same. Eb licked his lips, tasting the hops from the sly glass of beer he'd sipped before coming out for a stroll with Hepsie this evening.

It'd been such a hot day, that Eb had waited until evening to take a walk. He'd had to wear trousers and socks, because he couldn't see the thistles and Hepsie couldn't always notice the confounded prickly weeds before he took his next step. Even now he could feel a thorn itching his flesh through his sock. If he'd been able to see, he would have removed it.

Hepsie yawned beside him. He felt her shifting her position on the seat. She hadn't asked him whether he wanted to move on. He could smell her perfume. That exotic, Oriental one she'd been wearing lately, since their first meeting with Mike Johnson. Eb couldn't help smiling to himself. The intonation of Hepsie and Mike's voices, their choice of words, their comments to one another, revealed to him their mutual attraction. They probably thought he couldn't guess because he couldn't see them. No doubt, Hepsie's recent speedy answering of the telephone had something to do with this mutual attraction. He wasn't going to ask her. That would be stepping on her independence. And he knew he'd done that enough.

Through losing his own independence, his only daughter had seemed to have lost hers, too. Blindness harnessed them together like prison chains binding them to a shared cell. Neither of them wanted this loss of independence. He and Hepsie had always shared a close father and daughter relationship. But, now, his blindness and the lack of independence it brought them was driving them apart. Well, who would blame Hepsie? He was piling problems onto his daughter's back when she should have been living her own life. She had no young family of her own, her career was 'on hold' and he had probably ruined her life. He didn't want to do this. There were times when he wondered whether a daily carer wouldn't be better for him. But, after Sofia's death, Hepsie had insisted she must live with him permanently. His daughter was stubborn like that. And he was weak like that. He couldn't deny that having Hepsie back at home would make him happy – far happier, than if he'd chosen to live alone with a daily carer visiting him for an hour or two each day. Maybe he was afraid of being alone.

Occasionally, he wondered whether, if he hadn't been blind, he might have remarried. He knew that no one could replace Sofia in his affections, but maybe he might have liked a companion to see him through his lonely, retired years. But who's going to love a blind man? Who's going, when they are elderly themselves, to care for someone like him? Not an easy task. Meanwhile, Hepsie would be waiting by his side, in danger of developing glaucoma herself. Eb hadn't know that he was in danger of inheriting this disease;

155

the doctors thought its origins were likely to have come from his mother's family, whom he hadn't been in contact with for years. This was why it was important that Hepsie took regular eyesight tests and saw the world and lived her life before the disease might take over. Of course, in several years a permanent cure for glaucoma might have been discovered. If only he hadn't messed up his eye drops...perhaps he might have saved everyone all this trouble.

Eb felt something tickling the hairs on his arm as it crawled up his skin. Angrily, he swiped hard, hoping to hit the creature off his arm.

"What are you doing, Eb?" Hepsie asked.

"I think it's a fly," he said.

"You don't need to injure yourself," she said, ironically. "You could have asked me."

"I'm always asking you."

"Let me have a look."

Eb could feel Hepsie's breath as she leant in front of him. Her fingers gently brushed against his arm.

"Just a small fly," she said.

A strand of her long hair touched his shoulder as she moved away from him.

"Do you want to move on?" he asked.

"No. Do you?"

Eb thought he detected a reluctant note in Hepsie's voice, as though she was wishing he would say no, too. This was most unlike Hepsie. Normally, she would be sick of hanging around places because he didn't want to move. Her elderly, blind father, slowing down the world. Eb was intrigued. What was she up to now?

"Let's sit for another five minutes," he suggested.

"Ok."

"Before the heat and the flies get to me." He chuckled, hoping to make light of the situation.

"Five minutes it is then." Hepsie sounded as though she was biding her time.

In the village, a lawnmower started up, breaking the peace. Eb could smell the sweat on his body. Hepsie had persuaded him to wear a cotton hat on his head, despite his initial objections that they weren't going out in the midday sun. Now, he could feel his hair was sticky where the crown of his hat pressed against his forehead.

"Have you told Joan about Thursday?" Hepsie suddenly asked.

Oh. That's why they were still sitting here for another five minutes.

"No."

"That's probably a good idea." She laughed.

He didn't join in.

"You don't believe me, do you?" he said.

"What? About the ghost?"

"I told you. Someone threw Sofia's paperweight onto the floor."

"And that's why you were crawling on the carpet when I came back home?" By the tone of her voice, Eb could tell that Hepsie was never going to believe him.

"Why else would I be crawling on the floor? It's not something I normally do."

"And neither do you normally talk to ghosts nor surprise poltergeists throwing objects around the room," said Hepsie. "You must have been having some really weird dream to knock Sofia's precious paperweight off the side table. Are you sure you didn't stumble when you got up from the chair?"

Eb sighed with exasperation.

"Now you're saying I can't be left on my own," he said.

"It's not that I don't care, Eb. I DO. But I'm worried now, that if I'm out of the house and you have a fall, you might be injured or...even worse."

"What? The poltergeist might hit me over the head?"

"No, I don't mean that!"

"You should be more worried about a poltergeist roaming our home."

"If you think I'm going to believe your story about the return of our ancestor, 'Zennor Anderson', and poltergeist activities in the house, the answer is NO."

"But it was her," Eb insisted.

"How do you know? You can't see."

Eb was silent. Hepsie was presuming that he'd seen the vision of his ancestor, Zennor Anderson. Had he? He remembered a woman talking to him in his sleep and that he had woken up, startled out of his dreams. And then? He'd been so surprised, he couldn't speak. He had merely...watched? Eb shook his head. He must have dreamt her. What other explanation could there be? But then...the paperweight. How did that get onto the floor? For all Hepsie's insinuations, he was definitely certain that he hadn't fallen out or stumbled when he got out of his armchair and that he hadn't knocked Sofia's paperweight off the side table.

"She told me," he replied. "'I'm Mrs George Anderson,' she said."

"I bet she did!"

The lawnmower whined to a spluttering stop in the village. Voices drifted over from the road running across the Common.

"Perhaps you're doing too much genealogy," Hepsie continued. "It's giving you hallucinations."

"That's exciting."

"Exciting?"

"Yes! Not only have we be brought back to live in

the house of our ancestors, but they're trying to communicate with us."

"Your genealogical powers must be improving," she said, sarcastically.

"Quite. Maybe all our genealogical research has unleashed the poltergeist."

"Well, that's lovely! Who wants a dangerous poltergeist inhabiting their house? I don't!"

"Why don't you take up another hobby?" she continued. "One that doesn't involve communicating with the dead spirits of your relatives."

"I'm not going to give up the genealogy. Not now."

Eb began stroking his thigh, up and down, as he always did when he was upset.

"Why?"

"I enjoy fitting the jigsaw of my family research together. Individual pieces randomly slotting together. The picture is still incomplete but more whole than when we'd first started."

"And what happens if you can never complete this jigsaw?"

"Why does it have to be completed?"

Hepsie remained silent.

"Just think how much we're finding out about ourselves," Eb continued. "My father Georgie never spoke about his family. This is new ground for me. We're learning about who we are, Hepsie, and our place in history."

"We're learning about the past, but I can't see how that affects us now. We can't change the past. It's said and done."

Eb wished he could see Hepsie's face. What was wrong with her? He wanted to gauge her expression, to see why she was so against his genealogical journey of self-discovery. Maybe it was because she was young.

Eb had to admit that in his younger days he had been unbothered about finding out about his family roots. What he would give now to hear his father Georgie speak about his youth at the turn of the last century and the family members who lived then. Had Grandmother Zennor Anderson really appeared to him in a…dream? Was it her communicating to him? Perhaps Hepsie was right. The genealogy was becoming more than an obsession for him. But he was not going to give it up. Not now.

"I do remember meeting my aunts," he said.

"I thought you said you didn't have any contact with Georgie's relatives."

"The memory came back to me quite recently, after we'd been researching Elsie and Clara's lives. I'm sure Georgie took me to a small market town where I met two spinsters. They could have been my aunts."

"But you're not sure?"

"No."

He would have liked to have been sure.

"What are you going to say to Mike when you see him on Sunday?" he asked, conscious that he having another dig at her.

"I'll just thank him for returning the photograph. Hopefully, he won't have too much to say."

"No? You're not going to offer him coffee or a slice of Joan's gateau? He was rather partial to her cake last time."

"There's no point in him staying longer than he has to, Eb. He's a working man. He's probably got more important things to do."

"That's a shame. I thought you got on rather well with him at the café."

Hepsie shifted uncomfortably on the seat beside him, and coughed.

Eb stopped stroking his thigh.

He was thinking it would be good for Hepsie to be alone with Mike. If, as he suspected, they were attracted to one another, then there was a chance Mike might still be at Peace Cottage for longer than Hepsie envisaged. And he did want to speak to Mike. To ascertain that Mike was still this trusted person he'd met last Sunday. Had the boy foolishly taken his photograph by mistake? Or were his daughter's con-man doubts taking hold of his mind? If Mike was the con man Hepsie had originally thought him to be, then she couldn't be left there on her own, in case...But why hadn't Mike struck sooner? A con man took the first opportunity that came his way. Unless, of course, Mike was waiting to be alone with...No, it didn't make sense.

Eb wondered whether he could do it. He knew Joan might be displeased. But what was a little lie? In his mind he counted how long it might take him. The chances were that he would be cutting it tight but, at least, he'd given it a go. That would rest his mind.

Impulsively, he began to hum to himself. He was looking forward to Sunday.

"Do you want to return home?" Hepsie asked.

Eb paused in his humming to reply that he did.

He groped for his long cane, which he had propped up against the armrest of the seat. Clasping it's ball handle, he used the cane to ease himself up. He waited, until he could feel Hepsie standing next to him, before he allowed his fingers to find the crook of her elbow.

"I'm going to start walking," she said.

She moved forwards with him keeping at least half a pace behind her. Eb prodded the ground with his long cane in his spare hand. He broke off from his humming to tell her to avoid any thistles she could

161

see. His foot still itched from that one on the outward walk.

The evening air was cooling down. Eb was glad. When he got home he could remove this confounded sweaty sunhat. His talking watch announced the time as eight o'clock. He imagined the grandfather clock chiming in the hall. And he wondered whether she would be...Really, he and the ghost had a lot in common. Not just because they were related. They were both of this world but not of this world. A part of it but not a part of it. Like islands, they floated in the oceans of life, occasionally touching the human world but always returning to their own isolated darkness.

Ten

The grandfather clock struck the quarter-hour. Mike was late. Hepsie frowned, irritated that fifteen minutes of her time had already been lost. She peered out of the living-room window, looking to see whether Mike was walking along the lane. He was due to arrive at 11.00 a.m. Why were men so unreliable? If Mike didn't hurry up, there wouldn't be enough time to speak to him before she had to collect Eb from the church service.

Friday's heat had continued over into Sunday and Hepsie could feel the warmth coming through the open window. Bees buzzed noisily amongst the brightly coloured stocks in the flower bed below her and a pair of Painted Ladies fluttered delicately by the rose bushes growing over the front garden wall. She had made certain that Eb was ready to leave when Joan picked him up at 10.30 a.m. For some reason, Eb had cheered up about the reading. Perhaps he had been suffering from nerves. But she felt sure he could give a competent performance to Amberley's congregation – whether he liked religion or not. Despite the short time he'd given himself to familiarise the Bible passage, he was handling it very well by the time she listened to him reciting the words out loud. His fingers had traced over the Braille characters with an ease she found admirable. It was amazing how her father had learnt to read like this and how he had conquered each difficult step in adapting to his blindness. She didn't know what motivated him. Would she have given up, if she'd been him? Would she have succumbed to a dark and lonely world? If Eb was determined not to be isolated by his impaired vision, not to be cut adrift from the living, seeing world, then she admired him even more. Good for him! Good for him for trying!

This morning she had watched Eb select his best clothes. Despite the heat, he was wearing his navy-blue blazer, smart trousers and a short-sleeved white shirt, with polished black loafers. He'd asked her to make sure his loafers were shiny enough when she was polishing them for him. Finally, he'd chosen a tartan handkerchief for his top blazer pocket. She didn't ask him why he was suddenly so conscientious about his appearance. Perhaps he had decided to enjoy his uncustomary trip to church.

Hepsie was relieved Eb had said no more about Mike's visit and its unfortunate timing. She was getting tired of lying to him. To make up for the inconvenience of 'accidentally' taking their precious photograph, Mike had asked her when was the most convenient time for him to visit on Sunday. She, of course, had told him 11.00 a.m., when she knew Eb was committed to Joan's church service for the disabled. She had also lied to Joan, telling her that, despite Mike's visit, Eb would still be willing to take part in the reading. "That's so thoughtful of Eb," Joan had gushed. "The parish could do with more committed people like him."

This morning Joan had bossed Eb into her car. But Eb hadn't seemed to mind. He kept on humming, that silly tune he'd been humming since Friday evening.

"Oh, I know that tune," Joan said, making sure Eb's seat belt was fastened. "Let me see – is it a hymn?"

Eb nodded his head.

"*He who would valiant be?*" Joan suggested.

Eb broke off from his humming. "I don't think so. It's one I remember singing at school – but that was such a long time ago, I can't remember the title or words of it." He chuckled.

Joan laughed. She always did when Eb made one of his embarrassing age jokes.

"You'll have to try it on the vicar. Or, maybe, the organist," she said. "Oh yes, Mr Mortimer is bound to know it." She shut the passenger door with a jaunty swing.

There was a niggling doubt in Hepsie's mind that warned her Eb might be up to something. But she couldn't think what. She was pleased she'd got him out of the house and off to church, as planned. She was afraid Eb might have cancelled or wormed his way out of today's commitment. Or pretend to be ill and then, suddenly, be better upon Mike's arrival. In fact, she was surprised he hadn't asked her to ask Mike how his research on the Andersons was going. And to check whether their precious christening photograph had been returned in good condition and not used in any way. "You will probe Mike further, won't you?" she imagined Eb pleading, "And find out exactly why he took the photograph 'accidentally'." She had to admit to herself that it was odd why Mike had 'accidentally' taken a large Victorian photograph with him. Unless, of course…Hepsie couldn't help smiling to herself. She lifted the window catch and opened the window wide, so that she could lean out over the mullion sill. Wood pigeons cooed to one another in the beech copse next to the house but, although she strained to hear, she couldn't pick up the noise of a car or footsteps on the lane down to the front of Peace Cottage. The idea had occurred to her that the 'accidental' taking of the photograph by Mike was an excuse on his part to return to Peace Cottage. Why else had he stupidly taken it? Hepsie felt a slow blush suffusing her cheeks. I'm hot, she thought. But she knew full well why she was blushing.

She leant back and put the window back on the catch. Idly, she walked around the living room, her legs kicking against her long, crinkly skirt. If Mike didn't hurry up, her plans would be wasted. Should she text him? Hepsie walked over to the low coffee table where her mobile lay. Her fingers hovered over the slim case before she withdrew them. No, that would be stupid. If he was on his way here, Mike would be driving and unable to answer his mobile. Anyway, she thought, she couldn't contact him like that: it might make her look...keen? Or silly. Or, even worse, desperate. But wasn't she desperate? Hepsie fingered her throat as though she was nursing an irritating tickle in it. This was stupid. She was behaving like a lovesick teenager on her first date instead of a mature, experienced woman in her fourth decade. Hepsie abruptly stopped caressing her throat. Her hands naturally fell into a tight clasp at the front of her body. Perhaps Mike couldn't make it. Had something more important got in the way? And, instead, he was going to visit this afternoon? When Eb was here. The three of them would talk boring genealogical talk. And she would be none the nearer to getting to know Mike. Hepsie raised her eyes heavenwards. Men!

She was planning to offer him a coffee, hoping it might make him linger and chat to her. But it was getting too late for that now. Each regular stroke of the grandfather clock cut into her throbbing heart as though carving the minutes on it. She was due to pick up Eb at 12.15 p.m., which meant leaving the house by at least 12.05 p.m. to give her time to walk to Holy Trinity church. Eb had hoped to be picked up at twelve, but Joan had asked Hepsie to arrange to meet him a little later after the service had ended, so that there was a chance for the congregation to talk to him and for the vicar to thank him properly. Hepsie had said to Eb she would try and get there as soon as she could. This was partly to deter Eb from deciding to make his own way home. Which, slow as he was, she could see him doing.

Hepsie released her hands from their tight clasp.

"Chill out!" she spoke out loud, as though the streetwise words were an incantation.

Don't look at your watch, she hissed in her mind.

Feeling that movement was the best way of calming herself, she walked into the hall. She tried to cheer herself up by thinking that she was lucky to be missing the church service, which, no doubt, Joan would have persuaded her to attend. "Of course, Hepsie, there's a place for you," Joan would have gushed. "Plenty of seats! You can't miss out on your father's reading. And the parish needs your support as much as Eb does."

There was a mirror on the wall next to the front door. Hepsie found herself gravitating towards it. Just one little look, she promised herself. She glanced at her face in the mirror, studying the mole on her nose and seeing whether her mascara had smudged around her eyes. The heat had made her normally pallid complexion glow lustrously. She was pleased with her appearance. If only Mike would hurry up. Despite her anxiety, her expression looked relatively calm...almost hopeful. And then she remembered something else

Mike had said and her brow furrowed into unattractive wrinkles.

Mike mentioned that he had done some research already on the Andersons and that he was bringing it today. However, she remembered now, it wasn't about the Andersons, as such, but her great-granny Zennor Anderson's family, who were called Mills. Why had Mike decided to do research on this family line? He was supposed to be finding out about Peace Cottage and the Andersons. Maybe he was trying to whet Eb's appetite and prove he could do genealogical research. Of course, she hadn't told Eb because it would only make matters worse. He might have been doubly keen to not attend the church service. Anyway, she was going to leave the Mills research for Eb to sort out later. She certainly wasn't going to discuss genealogy with Mike. No way!

In fact, that was why she had set up this meeting to see Mike alone. Urged on by Sally's hint "...*why don't you get him interested in yourself? That might take his mind off the genealogy...*", Hepsie was hoping to encourage Mike to talk about himself. The plan was three-pronged: (1) to undermine Eb's genealogical obsession; (2) to prove or disprove her suspicions about Mike's genuineness as an obsessive genealogist; and (3), more importantly, she wanted to find out more about him because she was attracted to him and she believed – no, she knew – he was strongly attracted to her. So she was not only trying to scare away the genealogy but she was also aiming to get something out of it for herself.

Of course, she hadn't told Sally the whole truth. Her freckled-faced best friend presumed Hepsie was doing this for a tease. During their last telephone conversation, Sal encouraged Hepsie to: "...give it a

go. You never know, Mr Handsome might fall for you!"
Hepsie had bitten her tongue. She still didn't want
Sal to know her innermost feelings about Mike
Johnson. Especially, when she wasn't sure herself.

Hepsie turned to glance anxiously at the grandfather
clock. 11.24! The faded painted sun and moon seemed
to mock her from their unsmiling position on the clock
face. She wished she could turn back time to 11 o'clock.
Here she was, hoping to keep Mike talking for some
time, but her plan, until now perfect, was being
undermined by Mike's unpunctuality.

The doorbell rang piercingly through the house.

Hepsie gasped and then jolted into action.

Why hadn't she heard him walking up the garden
path?

Quickly, she unlatched the front door.

Mike smiled broadly back at her. And then, as
though suddenly aware of the purpose of his visit,
changed his expression to an apologetic grin.

Hepsie felt her blood rushing to her head. Or
should it be her heart? With great control she managed
to keep her hand steady as she held the door open.

"Hello," she managed to say.

Mike's pale green eyes twinkled hungrily at her.

Hepsie gulped.

"Hi," he said. "Sorry I'm late, but there was a slow
tractor which left a tailback on the Painswick Road. I
hope you and Eb weren't beginning to think I wasn't
going to turn up."

"Eb's not here," she suddenly blurted out.

Mike looked surprised.

Hepsie felt the colour rising in her cheeks, which
she was sure were now glowing lustrously, not only with
the heat, but also with the sweat she felt forming on
her face.

"He's got another appointment," she quickly continued. "He's sorry he can't make it."

Mike looked as though he'd been given a highly intoxicating cocktail.

Wishing to get the genealogy business out of the way, she glanced to see whether Eb's precious plastic carrier bag was in Mike's hand. Mike's eyes followed hers. He grimaced apologetically.

"So foolish of me," he said. "I don't know why I picked it up. It must have been in the confusion of saying goodbyes – you know, how everything happens at once."

She didn't believe him.

Unsure whether her face betrayed her disbelief, she said: "Eb's just really glad to have the photograph back. Really, it's no problem."

Mike looked relieved. But he didn't hand over the plastic carrier bag.

She waited, the ticking of the grandfather clock filling the awkward silence between them. She presumed the christening photograph *was* in the plastic carrier bag. The shape filling out the bag was characteristically flat and square. So why wasn't Mike handing the bag over to her?

However, one problem was cleared up. Mike was wearing trainers. That was why she hadn't heard his soft tread up the garden path. Taking a second to glance beyond him, she also noticed that he hadn't shut the gate properly, so there had been no hope of her hearing it clicking through the open windows.

The grandfather clock chimed the half-hour between them.

Hepsie looked at Mike and he looked at her.

Time was rushing on. She reached out towards the plastic carrier bag.

"Oh, how stupid of me," Mike said, as though suddenly waking up. "This is yours." He proffered the bag to Hepsie.

She took it, feeling the warmth of Mike's fingers around the handle. She ought to check inside the bag, just in case, if only to stop Eb asking her silly questions later on. Peering inside the bag, Hepsie saw her family's photograph and...

"My research on the Mills family's also in there," Mike explained.

Hepsie quickly closed the plastic carrier bag. "Eb will be delighted. I'll leave it for his return." She smiled at Mike, wishing she could think of a better reason to ask him into the house. Her mind raced around searching for an alternative. No, it was no use.

She took a deep breath and said: "Why have you done research on great-granny Zennor Anderson's family?"

Mike smiled broadly.

"There's another interesting link with Amberley," he said.

"Really?" Hepsie knew she didn't sound in the least interested.

Mike, however, seemed to take hope from her question. "I could discuss the research with you, if you like," he said. "It might help when Eb asks you about it."

And, then, when her lack of excitement must have shown in her face, he continued: "Or, if you prefer, I could telephone Eb and discuss—"

"Oh no, I couldn't waste your time," Hepsie quickly injected. "Come into the living room."

She stepped back, allowing Mike to enter the hall.

She was conscious of the minutes ticking away on the grandfather clock. There *was* no time to offer Mike

171

a coffee, but she reckoned she could risk half an hour with him. Here was her chance to find out a little about the real Mike Johnson. Of course, she wasn't going to sit and discuss genealogy with him during this half-hour. Five minutes, maybe, but that would be enough.

Her heart fluttered as she closed the front door behind them. Mike was wearing white jeans and a black T-shirt. Hepsie noticed the form of his biceps beneath his T-shirt sleeves.

He followed her into the living room. Hepsie placed the plastic carrier bag on the coffee table before she sat down on the sofa. She hoped Mike would sit down next to her. He did. Together their scents – hers, exotic Oriental, and his, sexy earthy notes – mingled above the two-seater and entwined together in the cool shade of the room.

Hepsie was conscious of Mike's eyes upon her. She had chosen to wear a white sleeveless T-shirt that showed off her recently tanned arms and shapely chest. A studded, brown leather belt was slung low over the top of her long, crinkly skirt. She had brought this skirt back from India and its swathes of patterned crimson, pink and orange kept her untanned legs hidden from Mike's view. Finally, a favourite but worn pair of leather flip-flops with white sequins, which she had picked up in an African market, completed her look. No, that wasn't quite true. Mike's eyes lingered a little longer over her ankle bracelet, with its glittering dropped-beading and miniature coins. She tried to look relax, spreading her arms across the top of the sofa's back and the armrest.

Mike smiled back at her. He had also spread his arms across the back of the sofa and along his armrest. Hepsie wondered whether their hands might touch on top of the sofa's back. Her fingers trembled. Slyly, she glanced out of the corner of her eye at Mike's hand resting on the top back of the sofa. No, his fingers weren't trembling. Hiding her disappointment, Hepsie calmed herself by noting that his long, knuckled fingers were still ringless.

He's waiting for me to say something, she thought. But she couldn't bring herself to start talking about the genealogy. She was supposed to be doing the opposite.

As though reading her mind, Mike eased himself from his comfortable position and placed the plastic carrier bag on the sofa between them. He pulled out his research notes.

"Do you want to look at these?" he said, offering the notes to her.

Hepsie indicated with her hands that she didn't want to accept them. "Oh no, I'll leave them for Eb to look at."

"I'm sure they will all make sense," she added, as she saw a hint of disappointment behind Mike's lively green eyes.

"Zennor Anderson had a younger sister called Ivy – did you know that?"

Hepsie looked at Mike blankly. He was still holding his research notes.

"No," she said. "Eb and I haven't bothered researching Zennor's Mills family. Eb's interest is focussed on the Andersons."

Mike put down the research notes. He clasped his hands together eagerly, an attractive smile spreading across his face.

"Ivy Mills married the local baker, Neville Dangerfield. Have you heard of him? His family ran a bakery in Amberley."

Hepsie shook her head.

"I can see the genealogy has kept you very busy," she said. "Does it give you time to do anything else?"

"Not much," Mike joked.

"There must be plenty of distractions in a town like Cheltenham."

Mike paused, as though unsure of what to say next.

"Yes. But the genealogy takes up most of my time."

Hepsie knew she looked crestfallen. "Oh," she said.

And, then, getting a hold of herself, added jokingly: "You must miss your social life!" She chuckled, hoping Mike would, too.

Mike chuckled, but nervously.

For a moment, Hepsie thought he was going to take up her bait and talk about himself.

"Genealogy is amazing," he began.

No, that's not what I want to hear, she thought.

"It shows what a small world we live in," he continued. "Here, we have two sisters, both outsiders, marrying men from the same village community. The Dangerfields, the Andersons and the Mills families all became connected to one another. And, presumably, through co-incidence..." Mike looked at her expectantly.

Hepsie was puzzled. Was he hoping for her to start an in-depth discussion about genealogy with him?

Well, she wasn't going to take his bait, too.

"Where do you work?" she asked.

Mike scratched his head before ruffling his fingers through his hair, which stood up like a brush when he'd finished.

"I think I told you the first time we...er...met."

"Oh, yes. I remember now," she said. "You're a marketing executive. Do you work for that large educational publishers...what is it called...Thomas...?"

"Thomas Clarksons," Mike stated.

"A good company to work for," she said. "Have you been there long?"

"Six years." Mike gave her a direct stare.

Hepsie felt herself blushing. If she'd been more modest, she would have lowered her eyes. She challenged him back.

"Do you live alone?"

If Mike was taken aback by her direct question, he didn't show it.

"No," he simply said, before glancing at his research notes.

Hepsie's heart plummeted to the pit of her stomach. She swallowed, hoping he wouldn't catch sight of her swallowing the poison he'd just given her.

"Do you have any photographs of Ivy Mills?" he asked, smiling broadly at her as he did so.

She should have been irked, but Mike's smile melted her yet again. Struggling to contain the conflicting impulses fighting within her, Hepsie managed to shake her head.

"Or of the Dangerfields?"

One of conflicting impulses inside Hepsie broke free.

"No," she snapped back.

Mike swallowed, as though unsure whether to continue.

You'd better not! she thought; I'm not sitting here for half an hour talking genealogy with you. No way!

But Mike wasn't listening to her inner voice.

"Ivy Mills married Neville Dangerfield the year after Zennor died. It makes you wonder whether, before she died, Zennor was instrumental in setting up the relationship between her sister and the local baker. What do you think?"

A trapped fly buzzed angrily against one of the closed windowpanes.

Hepsie couldn't answer his question. She wanted to know who he lived with. Her question danced around in her mind to a taunting rhythm. This other person...was *she* an obsessive genealogist, too? Did *she* and Mike spend their evenings together, sharing cosy chats about whose ancestor had married whom?

Looking at Mike you wouldn't have thought so. Hepsie allowed her eyes to follow the line of his body, tracing the shape of his sinewy muscles and tanned skin, but always coming back to his face, with that broad, congenial smile and the humour radiating from his intelligent eyes. He hadn't seemed to have changed since the last time she saw him. But how was she to know? She barely knew him.

As for her suspicions about his genuineness, he was proving her wrong. If Sally were here, she would be laughing her head off at them both. Hepsie couldn't see how things were to progress between herself and Mike, despite their mutual attraction. In fact, the more she took him off his genealogical point, the more he wanted to talk about it. He was becoming more like...

Hepsie inwardly groaned.

Mike was still waiting for her to answer his question.

She looked into the middle distance of the living room, pretending to stare at nothing.

Yet, despite Mike's obsession for genealogy, there was still a nagging doubt at the back of her mind. She couldn't think what it could be. If he was a con man, surely he would have struck by now? But, if that wasn't his intention, then what was it? She realised she was becoming more intrigued. Which was fatal. Mike didn't live alone. And Mike was a genuine genealogist. Hepsie inwardly groaned, again. Not only Eb, but now Mike. She was sandwiched between two fanatics.

Giving up, Hepsie decided to answer his question. "I don't know. I wasn't there."

Mike laughed.

Hepsie felt pleased for making him laugh. Perhaps she'd been taking the wrong approach. Mike needed to see his genealogical research in a different way. If she could coax him to see the funny side of his obsession, maybe he would open up about himself.

"That was a stupid question for me to ask you," he said. "I sometimes think this genealogy is going to drive me mad." He ruffled his fingers through his hair, as though – and here, Hepsie's heart leapt up back to its rightful place in her breast – as though he was almost embarrassed about his genealogical obsession.

"It's already driven me mad," she said.

Mike laughed.

She joined in.

It was strange how they were sharing this little joke over the madness of genealogical research.

Mike gave her a broad smile, which she couldn't help returning.

"I suppose you have better things to do with your time," he said. "Work, boyfriends, social life."

His pale green eyes gazed intensely at her.

But Hepsie couldn't meet his gaze. She lowered her eyes, pretending to fiddle with the fastening of her belt. Her social life? She felt so embarrassed. Boyfriends? Did Mike Johnson believe she was living a fast-paced social life, with blind Eb and his genealogy clinging to one arm, and her dutiful daughter to another? Oh my God! she thought. She didn't want to tell him the truth. That Hepsie Anderson was no better than an old-fashioned spinster left to dry out on the cupboard shelf.

She raised her eyes to look at Mike. "There's not a lot to do in Amberley."

"You like going to Bristol, or Swindon?"

"Occasionally."

Mike looked as though he would have liked her to have said more. He seemed to be weighing up something in his mind. He gulped.

"So, your boyfriend, what does he do?"

Hepsie nearly fell off the sofa.

"My...what?"

"Your boyfriend."

Mike's body appeared to be leaning more towards her. She could almost catch the fast intakes of his breathing.

Hepsie felt herself blushing. He was nailing her fair and squarely. She would have to come out with it. If she pretended she had a boyfriend, their conversation could revert to genealogy speak. And she wasn't having that. Not now she had got him speaking about...well, they weren't speaking about him. Mike had reversed their roles.

"I don't have a boyfriend," she said. "There's not much chance of a...a good social life living with Eb. You know, it can make it difficult."

Mike's pale green eyes glowed more intensely.

Hepsie fingered the bangles on her wrist. She was surprised at how much better she felt for telling Mike the truth. Was it that the coolness of the living room had lifted the outdoor heat from her body or was this new lightness she felt around her shoulders something to do with a subtle shift in her and Mike's relationship?

And then the thought stabbed her. But Mike had a girlfriend.

"I know, family obligations often get in the way," he said. There was an underlying trace of irony in his words. "I have the same problem, too."

Hepsie gave him a puzzled stare. What did he mean? Was his girlfriend pregnant?

"Kate—"

Mike suddenly broke off, gesturing apologetically with his hands. "Sorry, I shouldn't be loading you with this personal stuff."

"Kate?" Hepsie couldn't stop herself from reiterating the girlfriend's name.

"It really doesn't matter," Mike said, getting more embarrassed.

Hepsie realised she must have looked cross – maybe Mike could see the imaginary dagger she was clasping in her hand – because he added: "She's my aunt."

"Oh." Hepsie didn't know whether she believed him or not. If Kate wasn't his girlfriend, then why his confusion?

Mike looked as though he could have kicked himself. He was still holding his broad smile but his eyes were slightly uneasy.

A string pulled on Hepsie's heart, making her pulsating organ twinge with hopeful resonance. Mike was having second doubts about his insensitivity. He was admitting he had been unkind to her.

Hepsie twirled a strand of her chestnut hair around her finger. But she still couldn't let him off the hook. She couldn't let him leave the house without finding out that his girlfriend – *this* Kate – was living with him.

"You share a house with her?" she asked.

"Him," corrected Mike.

"Him?"

"Yes, my friend—"

The ringing doorbell sliced through Mike's words.

Startled, they looked at one another guiltily, as though they'd been disturbed in some intimate act.

Mike raised his eyebrow.

She did the same.

Finally, after what seemed like five minutes but was probably only a second or two, she said: "I'd better go and answer it."

Mike nodded.

Reluctantly, she got off the sofa and walked into the hall. Looking at the grandfather clock as she passed by, she nearly choked. The clock hands were positioned at thirteen minutes past twelve. How had time passed so quickly? She was due to meet Eb in two minutes. He would be annoyed waiting for her at Holy Trinity church. She would have to see off this person at the door, explain she was in a hurry, before seeing off – and here her heart plummeted back down to her stomach – Mike. How had time passed so quickly? She calculated she might be able to get to Eb by 12.30 p.m., unless, of course, someone had...

Hepsie's heart did a double belly-flop in her stomach. Grabbing the door latch, she wrenched open the front door.

Eb was standing on the doormat. Leaning on his long cane, he looked very pleased with himself.

She glanced over his shoulders, but there was no one else with him or any sound of a car being driven away. Luckily, Eb couldn't see her face. She could feel the heat – or was it her anger? – rushing to her head. Her hand fiercely gripped the front door as she stood blocking Eb's entrance into the house.

"Is that you, Hepsie?" asked Eb.

"Who else would it be?" she said, unable to keep her crossness out of her voice.

There was an awkward pause between them.

"Mr and Mrs Dangerfield gave me a lift back," Eb eventually explained.

"But I thought you were to wait until I picked you up?"

"Well, it's 12.15 p.m. now. You're late, anyway." And, then, he added hopefully: "Is that because Mike's still here?"

Hepsie didn't want this to happen. But she had no choice. Eb would have to come into the house.

"Yes," was all she said.

Standing beside Eb on the doormat, she lifted his hand and placed it in the crook of her elbow.

"I'm walking inside, now," she said.

Carefully, she led him into the hall. The tapping of his long cane's pencil tip on the flagstones echoed throughout the house.

"I'm pausing now, to close the front door," she said.

She swung the brightly painted blue door so that it shut with a bang, making the old house shudder.

"Is Mike in the living room?" asked Eb.

"Where else would he be?" Hepsie replied, sarcastically. Did he expect Mike to be up in her bedroom – half-undressed?

She led him into the living room. Mike got up from the sofa to greet Eb. The expression on his face was amused. She wondered whether he'd been listening to her and Eb's scenario on the doormat. The two men exchanged pleasantries, with Mike apologising for his foolish mistake of 'accidentally' taking Eb's photograph home with him. Eb seemed to take this well, his pale blue eyes glinting keenly as he assured Mike he understood.

Hepsie kept her hold on Eb's arm. She did not steer him to his armchair. Once seated, he might start talking genealogy speak with Mike. And she didn't want that.

"Has Hepsie told you I've got some research for you?" Mike asked.

"No, she hasn't," said Eb, before she could speak for him. "That's quick of you."

"It's only about great-granny Zennor Anderson's family – you know, the Mills connection," she interjected before Mike could reply.

"Mills?" Eb sounded surprised.

"Yes," Mike began to explain, "there's an interesting connection—"

"I can tell Eb all about it, if you need to get home." Hepsie looked at Mike pointedly.

Mike raised his eyebrows.

Hepsie gripped Eb's arm more firmly. "Eb's had a long morning. He's probably in need of rest after his church reading."

Eb shook his head in denial. "I'm fine, really—" he began.

"You should have a rest, Eb."

Hepsie continued to look pointedly at Mike. She could tell he was dying to pick up his research notes and read them to Eb. Oh, why did she have to be stuck between these two fanatics?

"It's my fault," she added. "I should have picked you up sooner, as I was meant to. Luckily, you were given a lift."

Yes, she'd been lucky Eb hadn't tried to walk home by himself. Even with his long cane and counting the steps he'd remembered taking on their previous walks from Holy Trinity church to Peace Cottage, he might have ended up in someone else's garden.

Mike appeared to waver for a few seconds before saying: "Well, I suppose I'd better be going. But if you want to discuss any of the Mills research, then please give me a call." He smiled broadly at Hepsie, his pale green eyes full of hope that she would be the one calling him.

"You don't have anything on the Andersons and Peace Cottage yet?" asked Eb, trying to stall Mike's departure.

"No, but I will be looking into it. The Mills research is just something to be going on in the meantime. Perhaps when Hepsie," – here, Mike looked at her meaningfully – "reads it out to you, you might be able to—"

"Yes, I will," Hepsie said, anxious to stop Mike from talking more fully about his research.

Relief showed in Mike's face. Hepsie felt conscious that she couldn't hide the relief in her own face. Relief that the genealogy speak was coming to an end.

She released her hand from Eb's arm and moved towards the hall, hoping that Mike would follow her.

"Will we be hearing from you soon?" Eb asked.

"I hope so," Mike said. He sounded as though he meant it.

As Hepsie opened the front door, she hoped Mike meant it, too. Although Mike came hand-in-hand with the genealogy, today had shown there was another side to him, and, therefore, hope for herself.

Mike stood beside her. He smiled warmly at her as he said: "His name's Eddie."

"Eddie?"

"Yes."

"Who's Eddie?"

Mike laughed.

"My flatmate."

Hepsie blushed. She continued holding the door open for Mike, hoping he would leave before she became too embarrassed, but at the same time willing him to stay.

"Well, goodbye, then," Mike said.

"Goodbye," Hepsie said simply.

She thought there was a touch of regret in Mike's pale green eyes as he turned his back on her to walk down the front path.

When he came to shut the gate, Mike turned round to face her.

Hepsie was suddenly conscious she was still holding onto the open front door.

But when Mike waved at her, her heart leapt like a kite released in the wind. She waved back.

Mike looked pleased. He glanced at her lingeringly one more time, before he headed off along the lane.

Hepsie closed her eyes, allowing the hot sun to roam over her face. If only she could get to the bottom of *this* Kate problem.

Eleven

Zennor picked up the pen and gazed at the empty lines on the page. She paused, the pen's nib poised above the page, before she decided to put the pen back down. She wanted to steal another look out of the bedroom window. At the view she remembered seeing from her and George's bedroom. The heat of this warm day bathed the distant hills in a blue haze, like the aura bathing the Florentine hills in Italy. Or that was what Ebenezer used to tell visitors, although he'd never set foot further than Gloucester to his north and Cirencester to his east. Someone must have told him.

The lonely copse on May Hill was now fully grown. It stood out against the sky like a coronet on a queen's head. Zennor tried to recall that poem by Baynes, the one called *Hampton Common*, but her mind was too full of other memories. The pine copse had been planted in celebration of Queen Victoria's Golden Jubilee. George, Hephzibah, and Ebenezer had attended the opening ceremony, but she'd been big with child. 1887 was the year Elsie was born. For seven years, Zennor had watched the fledgling copse growing into a landmark, its growth noting the changes in the grain of her own life. There were times when she used to whisper her secrets to it, conscious that the hill's mystical powers might be listening to her, and, she hoped, evoke the luck that had recently evaded her.

But it wasn't quite the same view. The bare hillsides had become a patchwork of sprawling villages, woods and fields. And amongst the birdsong, Zennor could hear the hum of harsher sounds, which reminded her of the machinery in the mills along the Nailsworth Valley. She wondered whether the walking-stick manufacturers, who had set up in the former woollen cloth mills, were still operating. There were also umbrella manufacturers settled in the area. She remembered that Ebenezer's self-employed trade had been struggling against these new inhabitants of the Five Valleys. That had been a whetstone in George's argument not to follow in his father's trade. Wood turners, crook makers and umbrella repairers had been an Anderson tradition for generations. By fingering the fineness of satin, silk and muslin, George was defying his father's authority and love of wood. Now, it seemed, there were plenty of trees on the hillsides to keep not only Ebenezer's tradition going but the mills in the valleys.

However, one feeling hadn't changed. Zennor breathed in the fresh, scented air and felt herself in a world where the sun always shone on Paradise. Through the open window, out in the garden, she imagined Elsie and Clara playing beneath the warm sun, their childish shouts and cries hitting the broad sky. Hephzibah was putting out the washing in the back garden and Ebenezer was lathing a rolling pin in his workshop. Zennor smiled as she remembered Hephzibah constantly sweeping up the trail of sawdust and wood shavings that Ebenezer left behind as he moved about the house. Wood and Ebenezer were inseparable. She heard the cries of baby Georgie, and then…The front gate swinging on its hinges, as George returned from work, the train having set him down at Woodchester Station, one-stop on from Dudbridge and his journey on the *Dudbridge Donkey* from Stroud. She watched his straw boater bobbing along the garden path and saw his shadow approach Peace Cottage's front door. Zennor's stomach knotted. She heard baby Georgie's wails.

Hush, she wanted to say. It's all right.

But as she rocked Georgie's cradle, she knew it wasn't.

Zennor shuddered at the memories this bedroom brought back to her. She wanted to lock the door that was beginning to be opened more widely by her memories. But the harder she tried to turn the key in the lock, the more resistance she felt against her hands.

She took some comfort in the fact that the bedroom now belonged to someone else. Zennor guessed it was the girl's room. The whitewashed walls were now painted a delicate pale blue and the room was very comfortably furnished. There was even carpet covering the floorboards. The Blind Man and his daughter were certainly rich. But why? And why were they living in a small, old house like Peace Cottage? There were bigger and better houses in the village, more suited to a wealthy family. Zennor's suspicions increased.

That was why she was sitting here at this desk by the window. The desk was small and lightweight, with slender legs and a long drawer at the front. Zennor hadn't dared to open the drawer, leaving the key with its white tassel untouched. However, lying on the worn painted surface of the desk, fresh and pristine against the turquoise stippling, were the open pages of a journal. Zennor had carefully lifted the ends of both sides of the journal to examine the binding. The covers were decorated with strips of richly patterned fabric that were interweaved with silver and gold threads. The bold colours spoke of exotic, far distant lands. Zennor could even smell the whiff of incense hanging over them. She had paused, unsure of what to do next. She had hoped to find the name of the journal's owner embossed on the front cover. Her fingers had toyed with opening the journal at the beginning, but good manners held her back. What if the journal's owner suddenly arrived in the room and caught her in the act of reading their innermost secrets? Zennor knew that she wouldn't like anyone else reading her journal, if she'd had one.

So she had consoled herself by running her fingers over the fresh, virgin pages left open for her. It had taken her some time to devise this plan. She'd moved restlessly through the house, seeing how her former home had changed but was still unchanged. She half-expected to find George's *The Stroud Herald* folded up by his easy chair. Or Hephzibah's sewing box left unopened upon the parlour table. Time must have passed since the Thursday she'd devised her plan to gain The Blind Man and his daughter's attention. Whilst she moved about the house, she could hear the ticking of the grandfather clock and the seconds, minutes and hours must have sunk into her mind, for she picked up the pen and wrote on the first line of the first page:

Sunday a.m.

Zennor paused, amazed at what she had done. She had found this open journal and pen as though waiting for her to write in. That's when the idea had presented itself to her. But did she have the nerve to continue? Zennor examined the pen more closely. It had a rounded ball tip from which ink seemed to flow freely. The casing was of a pretty floral design and...Zennor sniffed the pen's nib. Yes! It did smell of fragrant flowers. She knew that if she didn't continue, she would never be able to find out the truth. Why were The Blind Man and his daughter living in her home? Where were Elsie and Clara and Georgie? Where had George taken them? She was certain The Blind Man and his daughter knew something about the truth, that they were part of George's conspiracy against her. How long had they been living here? Was Peace Cottage their barter for helping George?

She also knew that if she didn't continue, she would never be able to tell the truth of what happened to her. Of why she...

Zennor wrote:

Dear Madam,

It is with great trepidation that I write this short letter to you. For many years I have been bereft of my home and of my children. It is my belief that you are knowledgeable in such matters. I beg of you to reply to me by way of return.

Yours respectfully,
Mrs. G. Anderson
(Formerly of Peace Cottage, Amberley)

Zennor admired her handwriting. She felt the same pride she'd always felt after having written a piece well. The characters of her copperplate hand were neat and well-formed. She was also pleased, and slightly surprised, that the pen had left no ink splodges to mar the clean page and for her to blot. Glancing over the other paraphernalia on the desk top, she searched for an inkwell and for blotting paper. There were none. She'd been lucky that the floral scented pen had served her well.

Making sure the pen was neatly placed where she'd found it between the open pages of the journal, Zennor read through her letter one more time, breathing in the scented ink of her words. Reluctantly, she got up from her chair and walked out of the room.

She couldn't wait. The seconds, minutes and hours drummed a steady beat in her mind until she was back in the bedroom. Outside, the day was overcast, the warm heat having fled from the pursuing clouds. Zennor could tell by the smell of the earth that it was going to rain soon. She sat down at the girl's desk. The journal was still open at the same pages. She sighed. The regular lines of the pages were untouched apart from her own letter to the girl. Had it been read? Zennor didn't know. There was nothing to show that it had: no fingerprint, or crease on the page, or stray wisp of hair caught in the binding.

Zennor glanced around the room. Had anyone been here since she was here last? The bed was made up the same as it was before, with a plump eiderdown and countless cushions arranged at the bedhead. Zennor was surprised to see how many toys the girl owned: bears, an elephant and a rag doll. Elsie and Clara would be lucky to have one apiece between them. If she had been...Zennor swallowed. If she had been meeting Elsie and Clara she could have taken one – maybe one of the old bears with torn ears and worn paws – which she was certain wouldn't be missed by the girl. But what was she thinking of now? The Blind Man and his daughter certainly knew how to manipulate her into a criminal. Firstly, she was encouraged to damage someone else's personal property and to throw objects around their home; secondly, she was now being encouraged to steal from them. Never in all her eight years as a domestic servant had she considered cheating on her employers. She shouldn't be about to start now. But The Blind Man and his daughter weren't her employers. She shouldn't be deferring to them like this. She was as much their equal as...

As George was. Or had he encouraged them to spite her as others, in the village, did – that Mrs Mortimer, for example – or, Mr Beard, who owned the village sweet shop? None of these people had treated her with the same due respect after she had...Zennor flinched. When she was first married, she'd loved approaching the shop counter and being addressed as "*Mrs Anderson*". But she felt that by the time she'd been...yes, afterwards, they wanted to call her something else. She saw Mr Clutterbuck in his striped blue and white apron standing in his butcher's shop, his coarse moustache sharp above the thin lines of his lips as he mouthed that other name. Or names. Why stop at just the one? It had taken all her courage to take herself around the shops of Amberley: the butchers, the grocers, the Post Office, the shoemakers, the tea merchant and, God forbid, the bakers. Zennor pushed the thought away from her, as though scaring off a swarm of wasps. But it wasn't easy to hold a swarm of wasps at arm's length.

Resignedly, she picked up the pen and wrote:

Monday p.m.

Dear Madam,

It is with great trepidation that I write further to you. I beg of you, did you read my letter of Sunday a.m.? Time is passing and I am no nearer to the truth. If you would so kindly oblige to hold a correspondence with me in these pages, I can set you right about what really happened. And you – YOU can tell me what happened to Elsie, Clara and Georgie Anderson. I know they were taken away from here. Peace Cottage was their former home. So, I beg of you, please write by way of return. I am depending upon your confidence in this matter and have faith that your understanding of a mother's love for her children will eventually decide you.

Yours respectfully,
Mrs. G. Anderson
(Mother of Elsie, Clara and Georgie Anderson)

Zennor put down the pen. She had filled one page of the journal. This time she wasn't so proud of her neat handscript or her ability to compose sentences or her avoidance of splattering the page with ink splodges. She was subsumed by what her words meant to her. Half of her smelt the strong-scented ink the pen had left on the page; the second half of her was alert to sounds outside the bedroom door. She hoped to hear a footstep on the stairs, a door being banged shut or the grate being raked in the kitchen. The house was far too quiet. What would happen if The Blind Man and his daughter had gone away? Who would be here to hear her? Zennor bit her lower lip. She shook her head. She couldn't accept that they had gone away. Maybe the girl was taking her time before replying to her. Zennor could understand, that if the girl was guilty, replying to Zennor's letter would not be an easy task for her. Maybe she was weighing up her conscience, either consulting with The Blind Man or not, before committing herself on page. Zennor hoped, with all the stitches straining to contain her broken heart, that her second letter would sway the girl's mind.

Getting up from the chair, she gazed disconsolately at the solitary copse on May Hill, before leaving the room.

She hadn't said a prayer to May Hill. But she did hope it might evoke some luck for her. Coming into the bedroom for the third time, she noticed the bed had been slept in. Someone had also thrown a dressing gown over the desk chair, which was now placed in front of the dressing table. Zennor's heart somersaulted in her breast. She ran to the desk. The journal was still lying open on the desk top. At the same pages. Her own writing stood out clearly on one page. The other page was...

Zennor sunk to the floor on her knees. She rested her arms on the desk top and buried her face in them. The fine moiré silk of her sleeves felt cool and smooth against her hot cheeks. She wetted the fabric with her tears.

They were ignoring her. The Blind Man and his daughter despised her. She was sure the girl could read and write. Anyone who lived in such a wealthy house must be educated. Even if they were not a lover of education. Unlike her. This thought stung Zennor's pride. She knew, that if she'd been allowed to be a school assistant, the things that happened to her wouldn't have happened. She wouldn't have gone into service in Stroud, she would never have met George at Davis & Co. Drapers in the High Street, whilst out shopping with her mistress, she would never have come to Amberley, and she would never have met...Zennor closed her eyes so tightly shut she thought she was in danger of never being able to open them again. If she could find the wheel of her life, she would spin it around in the opposite direction. Pull a different cart. With a different load. And travel along another road.

Zennor sighed. These things were so easy to say as words but she knew she couldn't turn back the wheel of life. What about her children? These seeds of her womb would never have been born. As it was, she had lost them. No, she couldn't turn back the wheel of life but she could try to find them. To discover the truth about what happened to them. And to make up for the time she had lost with them. Her poor baby Georgie! She feared he wouldn't remember her. How many years had passed since she'd last seen him? Was he still yearning for the milk from her breast?

In some respects, she was hoping he hadn't grown. It was not only because she didn't want to miss his baby years. George might think he was right. Well, he was, but he wasn't. But how could she explain to him? Or, to anyone?

The sound of rain splattered against the windowpanes. Zennor forced herself to open her eyes. She lifted her head and stared at the raindrops running down the small panes. Raindrops bigger than the tears she'd just wept.

Pulling herself up from the floor, Zennor turned to face the bedroom. Reflected in the dressing-table mirror was a bookcase. A tall bookcase, with shelves full of books. Zennor looked at the wall opposite the mirror. She had never owned so many books as she now saw filling up the long shelves. As soon as she'd collected a few – Charles Dickens, Mrs Gaskell, the penny dreadfuls – Pa would confiscate them. "I ain't having my daughter losing her head in books," he berated. "You're to know your place in life. And reading books won't help you get there." Zennor remembered flinching, aware that Pa could strike her with his heavy leather belt, the one that was holding up his trousers. He was a skilled craftsman, a cut above a common labourer, but his cabinet-maker's trade still left wood chippings on his trousers and sawdust on his hands. Why wasn't he proud of his second daughter's ability to read? Yes, he wanted his children to read and write, but once school was over – for some of them, at twelve, for others, like herself, at fourteen – they had to earn a living. And Zennor knew the many schools she'd attended wouldn't have paid her for school room assistance, not until she was of a maturer age. For a year she had stayed at home, helping Ma bring up the younger children after her elder sister Rose had left to go into service. "And a lot of fine help you are, too," Pa had complained, his whiskers twitching as his mouth sarcastically voiced his concerns about her. "Joe says he caught you at it again!"

Zennor blushed. "Joe says he caught you at it again." She knew what Joe meant. And she knew he was not only ruining her love of reading. Zennor shivered, although the shut windows made the room warm. When did it first start? A key turned in another lock. Her fear increased as the door creaked open a crack. The door should have been locked. There were three of them sleeping in the one big bed. Ivy lay between

Roelinda and herself. Ivy was seven years old; Roelinda twelve. Both were sleeping soundly, lost in their dreams. Only Zennor heard the soft tread of footsteps across the floorboards. And then...here, she gasped, unable to contain the constricted breath in her throat. Bedclothes lifted. A nightdress being pulled up. Hands stroking her skin. Familiar hands. Rough from sawing wood all day. And the guilt.

Even today, Zennor could feel the guilt dripping from her head like sweat. First the pleasure. Sensations awakening within her as his rough hands discovered her body. Her surprise. And then the pleasure turning to sickening fear, as she realised what he was doing to her. And what he continued to do to her. And how it...

Zennor broke free from his embrace and slammed the door shut. She pushed her palm flat against the door until she felt it straining at the hinges. One more thought escaped from her. He had made doors like this.

Just before her sixteenth birthday she'd been glad to leave home to go into service. This door – this door she hadn't wanted to open again – had tipped her into obeying her Pa's wishes.

And the door should never have been opened again. If only she hadn't...Zennor remembered the lack of appetite that had attacked her when she was big with Georgie; the sleepless nights and the lying to those nearest and dearest to her. That's when the door was unlocked. Trying to escape from one room, she had fled into another. It seemed to her she was trapped by the four walls. She didn't want to live in either room.

Books. Their spines rose out of the bookcase towards her and she was reminded of why she was here. Of course. The girl *was* educated. She must be able to read. And the owner of so many books would also surely be able to write.

Unhesitatingly, Zennor reached for the dressing gown on the chair in front of the dressing table and threw it onto the unmade bed. She dragged the chair across the floor, not caring whether the chair legs scuffed the precious carpet. Setting the chair before the desk, she sat down and picked up the pen lying by the side of the journal. On the clean second page, she wrote:

Tuesday p.m.

Dear Madam,

I beseech you to write to me. Your silence is deafening. Perhaps I do not explain myself enough. For eight years I was the happy inhabitant of this home, Peace Cottage, where I lived with my husband George Anderson, his parents, and our three children. Papa was the local crook maker and umbrella repairer; his wife Hephzibah took in sewing and sold her rose-hip syrup for a penny. George worked as a draper's assistant in Stroud. He had a good position and we would have moved to Stroud to live over the draper's shop when Mr Davis died. George would have become the proprietor. Our lives would have—

Zennor broke off writing. *Our lives would have changed,* but she could not bring herself to write this. She knew how much George wanted to move to Stroud. How he viewed their simple village life in Amberley with bored disdain. He hadn't told Ebenezer and Hephzibah this. He knew they would be hurt. But he also knew that Hephzibah, at least, would understand his reasons why. At the beginning of their marriage, Zennor quickly realised that George's relationship with his mother was close. When she was confined with her children, she learnt why. Poor Hephzibah had suffered many miscarriages and George was the only pip from her apple core to sprout new life. There was no orchard of fruit-bearing trees, only George. And he was more precious for that. That was why Hephzibah sided with George when he denounced his father Ebenezer's local trades and pleaded for a draper's apprenticeship in Stroud. If she was honest with herself, Zennor was loathed to leave Peace Cottage. She had come to love it and Amberley more than anywhere else she'd been in her life.

She resumed writing.

—become better off.

Yes, that was it. *Our lives would have become better off.* And George would have worn his smart straw boaters and silk cravats. And she would have had all the choice of fine fabrics – plaid, sprigged muslin, bombazine, rich velvet – to clothe herself and her children. Kid gloves, manufactured lace, chenille tassels, gaily patterned ribbons. A wealth of material to replace what she had lost. And no chance of meeting him...

Zennor steeled herself to continue writing.

Perhaps this is where George and my children are living now. Misfortune took me away from them and I am trying to trace their whereabouts. As the new inhabitants of this—

Zennor swallowed hard, before continuing:

—home, I do believe you know of such matters, or might have a forwarding address. If you could enter into a correspondence with me, I would be much obliged.

Believe me to be true and sincere,

Yours respectfully,
    Mrs. G. Anderson
    (also known as Zennor, formerly Mills)

Zennor dropped the pen onto the open pages and leant back, exhausted, against the chair. She closed her eyes momentarily, listening to the rain droning a rhythmical pattern into her heart. Without expectations, she vacated the chair.

Her fourth visit. The evening sun had moved round to the back of the house and the girl's bedroom was covered in shadows. However, it was still light enough to see by the window. Zennor set herself down by the faded turquoise desk. She could hear noises in the room below her. Voices, like people talking through a muffled megaphone. And other noises she couldn't distinguish, but which reminded her of the rumbustious machinery in the mills.

Ignoring the noises, Zennor dared to glance more closely at the journal. She gasped.

The journal was open at a new page.

And someone had written on it.

Zennor's heart raced like a whipped horse in a steeplechase. For a few seconds she stared at the handwriting on the page. It had been written in a shaky hand, as though the author was nervous or suffering from a malady. Yet, it was definitely an educated hand. Indeed, the author was confident enough to deviate from the copybook style she must have learnt at school. Or, with her governess. Zennor guessed, with a guilty jealousy, that the girl was far better educated than herself. She might even have been away at a ladies' establishment to broaden her education.

With her hopes lodged in her mouth like a horse's bit, Zennor began reading the handscript. The correspondence was undated: she didn't know whether the girl had written in the journal yesterday evening or sometime during today. Wednesday. The mechanism of the ticking grandfather clock told her that. Zennor felt she had stored countless minutes and hours in her mind since returning to Peace Cottage. She was keeping more perfect time than George's pocket watch, an inscribed gift from his dearest Papa and Mama. In time, he would pass the pocket watch onto Georgie, as a family keepsake. Little did he know that—

Zennor hurriedly resumed reading the note left for her. She presumed it was for her, because the note was not addressed to her. Zennor tried to brush off this slight, as though it was an oversight on the girl's part. Although you would have thought that someone who had been well educated would have minded to conduct themselves with propriety in such matters. Was there another reason behind this? Reading on, Zennor could only feel her hackles rise in wounded indignation:

Who are you? What do you want? How come you're
writing in my notebook?
—I

Zennor frowned at the girl's messy crossed-out
pronoun, before continuing.

I cannot believe my eyes. How do you do this? Or
shouldn't I ask?
My God! I think the world is going crazy.
It's Eb. He's got to me. His loony genealogy has—

Why am I writing this? I'm not writing to anybody.
I'm writing to myself—
But then how did these LETTERS get here?
Am I going crazy?
Did I write these LETTERS? I'M
SLEEPWALKING?
JESUS!

Zennor was taken aback by the girl's emphatic
blaspheming of Christ's name. She would never have
dared to write anything of such nature. Her situation
in the village was bad enough as it was, without her
being condemned as an atheist and a blasphemer.
Although there were those in the village community
who probably thought she was, in her own way, as
bad as one. Sinning took many forms but, to the
moralist brigade, the condemned shared the same
heavily loaded basket of guilt. Murderers, adulteresses,
thieves, atheists, forgers: they were the spoiled goods
of a wasted shopping trip, pennies ill spent. Zennor
blushed as she re-read the girl's words. Another
uncomfortable feeling jostled behind her discomfort,
like an advancing horse fast on her tail. If she didn't

gallop faster, this uncomfortable feeling would overtake her.

The note was unsigned. Was this another slight? Zennor presumed, because the journal was in this bedroom, that the author was The Blind Man's daughter. But she had no proof. The only way to find out would be to reply to the note. Zennor felt her pride smarting under the whip of the girl's ill-considered words. For all her fine education, the girl's lack of propriety in such matters made corresponding with her more difficult. Zennor's fingers hovered above the floral scented pen. The advancing horse in her mind, whose hooves she could hear tearing up the turf behind her, and whose breath she could feel closing upon her flanks, decided her. She picked up the pen and wrote:

Wednesday, Dusk

Dear Madam,

It is with great joy that I hear from you. Although your words are somewhat unexpected in their form, it heartens me greatly that you have entered into a correspondence with me. I have been waiting many years to hear news of my beloved children and I am confident that you are the one who will bring me such good tidings.

Believe me to be good and true in my intentions,

Yours respectfully,
    Zennor Anderson

(P.S. Perhaps you could be so good as to inform me of your name. I would like the pleasure of addressing my letters direct to you.)

The evening shadows were lengthening in the room and the light was fading from the window. As Zennor put down the pen, she became aware that the noises in the room below her were becoming more distant. Feeling that she was no nearer to winning her race, and conscious that the advancing horse was almost a head's pace upon her, Zennor drew the curtains and shut out the dusk.

Walking into the girl's bedroom the following day, with the midday sun shining across the blue-speckled carpet, Zennor noticed that something had changed in the room. The bed was unmade and clothes were strewn across the floor. This dishevelment extended to the faded turquoise desk by the window. Zennor's heart missed a beat. Where was the journal? The desk top was covered in loose papers, some of which were held down by a weighty dictionary, and, on another pile, by a used wine glass and a bottle of wine. Zennor approached the desk. The wine bottle was uncorked and she could smell the intoxicating fumes of the alcohol. The heady notes hit the back of her head and made her senses swim for a second. Ugh! The wine must be a very strong claret. The sort that George, and occasionally Ebenezer, liked to drink. She and Hephzibah preferred the sweet elderberry or dandelion infusions that Hephzibah brewed and which were kept, unwisely or not, in Ebenezer's workshop. Sometimes, the homebrews didn't make it back into the house. And Ebenezer would be quietly burping throughout the evening as he digested a bottle of elderberry wine with – thanks to Mrs Beeton's recommendation – half a pint of brandy added to every gallon.

There was a smudged pink lip stain on the rim of the wine glass. Another sign of the girl's wealth. Zennor used to pinch her lips to make them look redder or to rub a rouge powder onto them, but she could never have afforded such a pretty pink as the girl was using. Not that the local God botherers would have approved. Zennor was relieved that the girl wasn't one of them.

But where was the journal? She searched amongst the paraphernalia on the desk top, carefully moving the heavy dictionary and the wine bottle and glass to look beneath the pile of loose papers. The girl seemed to be in possession of some printed manuscript, but Zennor was too busy to read what was on the pages. She peered at the other items sitting on the desk top: an exotically patterned receptacle containing pens and pencils and other writing tools; a prickly plant that she guessed to be a cactus, such as those she'd seen in pictures in *Wonders of the World* or *Girls' Own Encyclopaedia*; a carved giraffe with black markings; and another jungle animal, which looked like a hippopotamus to her, but was painted bright pink. Zennor wondered whether the girl had kept these animals from a Noah's ark. How Georgie would have loved to have played with such toys. That is, once he was out of his baby frocks.

Her hand moved towards the key of the desk drawer. She fingered the long, soft fringes of the white tassel attached to the key. Slowly, she turned the key in the lock and then pulled out the drawer. Nothing. Zennor ran her fingers along the inside of the drawer but could only feel the smoothness of the wood.

She turned to face the room. Where was it? She glimpsed the desk chair reflected in the dressing-table mirror. Various apparel had been discarded over the back of the chair. Shirt sleeves and trouser legs overflowed onto the seat. Peeping out from beneath this was the corner of a page.

Zennor rushed over to the chair and flung the clothes onto the floor. There was the journal. Opened at a new page.

Breathlessly, she picked up the journal and saw that the girl had written on it again. Zennor closed her eyes momentarily and then steeled herself to read the girl's words:

> *PLEASE LEAVE ME ALONE!*
> *Mrs Zennor Anderson or whoever you are.*
> *It got so bad I drunk a whole bottle of wine last night – and – thanks to you – or whoever you are – I'm much worse for it.*
> *I was hoping to stay up all night – well, the wine was supposed to help me – but I fell asleep.*
> *Now I'm so hung over, I don't know whether I did or I didn't—*
> *But I can't have done?*
> *Yesterday's letter proves it – I didn't write that <u>Dusk</u> letter – that wasn't written when I was sleeping – I can't be sleepwalking and writing letters—*
> *I'm going mad—*
> *It's Mike—*
> *It's Eb—*
> *It's both of them—*
> *Him and Eb*
> *There's got to be a rational explanation for this—*
> *FOR CHRIST'S SAKE! – WE CAN'T HAVE A POLTERGEIST IN PEACE COTTAGE!*

Zennor clasped the journal against her chest. She curled the ends of the pages within the tight fists of her hands. Anger welled up in her like the mechanical punch of a Jack-in-the-box, ready to spring out of the confines of its wooden box and shake on its withering coils in the face of the unlucky recipient. She flung the journal from her. She would write in it no more!

The journal, its silver and gold threaded cover glinting in the sunlight, fell with a thud to the floor. It lay shut upon the luxurious carpet.

If she was going to be treated like this, then she would have to find other means to gain the attention of The Blind Man and his, oh, so arrogant, daughter. Poltergeist? Is that what they thought she was? Zennor shuddered. I'm no poltergeist, she told herself, clasping her arms around her body and swaying from side to side. The rocking motion lulled her into calmness. Like she used to lull Georgie to sleep in her arms. She imagined his soft cheek against hers and his tightly shut eyes. "I'll do this for you, Georgie," she whispered; "It's not what I want to do – it's what I have to do."

She planted an imaginary kiss on Georgie's brow and thought she felt him wiggle in her arms.

The wind rattled the open window behind her. Zennor unclasped her arms and, as she walked out of the girl's room, shivered as she saw Neville Dangerfield's shadow falling across the bedroom walls.

Twelve

"Why don't we ask Joan whether her Family History Group has any photographs of the Dangerfield family?"

"Don't be stupid, Eb. We don't want to get involved in that side of Mike's research. He's only using it to keep us interested until he finds new information on the Andersons." Hepsie hoped that would be end of the conversation. Eb had been pestering her about Mike's research on the Mills and Dangerfield connection ever since last Sunday.

Eb's long cane tapped on the wet tarmac as they walked along the narrow lane towards the former Methodist Chapel. A morning of torrential rain meant Eb's weekly trip to Amberley Post Office to collect his pension had been delayed until after lunch. She was walking half a pace ahead of him, the sleeve of his Barbour chaffing against the shiny smoothness of her anorak as he gripped the crook of her arm. On her feet were an old pair of pink flip-flops and, to take her mind off how irritating Eb was being, she deliberately splashed into the streams of water overflowing from the gullies running down the sides of the steep lane. She felt the cold water soothing her toes and awakening her senses.

"But he did seem very interested in this connection," Eb persevered.

"I told you, it means nothing."

"He asked you for photographs. He wouldn't have done so if there wasn't a good reason why."

Hepsie sighed. "You sound more suspicious than I was at first. Don't you trust Mike now?"

Eb was silent.

Hepsie wished she had never told him what Mike had said in addition to the notes she'd read out to him. How had Eb wheedled this information out of her? She blushed. She knew full well. One lie to cover another. Just imagine Eb's face, if he'd heard Mike and her sharing a joke about how mad the genealogical research was driving them. That was the Mike she was longing to get to know. Not the one who shared Eb's genealogical fanaticism. However, there was another problem growing between the floorboards and ceilings of Peace Cottage. A problem that had made the world seem mad for five days but that she couldn't possibly share with Eb.

"Mr Jones seemed certain that the Post Office petition would go through," she said, changing the conversation.

"Yes," was all Eb replied.

"Well, aren't you pleased about that? We don't want to lose Amberley Post Office. I would have to drive you to Minchinhampton to pick up your pension. And we might lose the village shop, too. Isn't that why we signed Joan's petition?"

"Yes."

Eb was being unusually reticent. What was wrong with him? Joan had organised the whole of Amberley into signing her petition against the closure of their Post Office by the Government. If Will and Pat Jones lost their Post Office subsidy, Amberley's only shop would be in danger of closing down. Although the small market town of Minchinhampton was only across the Common, Hepsie would need to drive Eb there. Talk about decreasing your carbon footprint! At the emergency meeting held at the Parish Rooms, Joan had argued that the Post Office was part of their heritage: there had been a Post Office in Amberley since the 1860s and it was now the only remaining retail outlet in the village, since the closure of the former Dangerfield bakery fifteen years ago.

Hepsie grasped her hand more tightly around the shopping bag she was carrying. She had bought fresh bread, a packet of chocolate digestives, a cauliflower and, for herself, *The Stroud Herald.* She didn't know what she would do, if the village lost its only retail source. Did she see herself driving Eb regularly to Minchinhampton? Or did she see herself using the increased distance as an excuse to take an even longer walk to the shops, arguing that the walk across the Commons between village and town would tire out Eb? She often used Amberley's Post Office and Stores as an excuse to get away from him and Peace Cottage. Her present trips to the local shop seemed a long way away from her trips there with Sally when they were children. She and Sally used to ask the then current owner – a Mr 'Alliday – for liquorice shoelaces, marshmallows and pear drops. And messy sherbet dips that used to cover their mouths and clothes in a fine layer of yellow dust.

The Old Chapel was getting closer. Hepsie could read the wording on the commemorative plaque set above the arched main door, which told her the Wesleyan chapel was built in 1790 and renovated in 1887. With its tall gothic windows and the glimpse of the graveyard at the back, you wouldn't have thought the chapel had been renovated into a residential home after its closure in 1990. The gate to the old graveyard was kept locked, but the New Room next door was still used for social functions, some of which Hepsie had recently attended in her reluctant capacity as a member of Joan's Family History Group.

"I'm turning the corner to the right in about five paces," she warned Eb.

When he didn't reply, she added: "Be careful you don't slip. There's a lot of water overflowing down Chapel Hill."

Eb grunted his acquiescence.

As she turned the corner, Hepsie noticed the mist rising off the wet hills across the valley looking towards Woodchester. The heavy rains had made the Cotswold stone houses greyer and damper than usual. She hoped their kitchen and utility room wouldn't be flooded upon their return to Peace Cottage. Springs did have a habit of suddenly usurping through the flagstones during times of torrential rain. It didn't help that their house was built into the hillside. She believed at one time Peace Cottage used to have a flood grill in the kitchen to prevent the rest of the downstairs from flooding, but this had been removed during renovation in the 1970s.

Hepsie glanced back to see how Eb was coping. His usually benign face was strangely blank. She couldn't tell what he was thinking. A part of her did wonder whether he had guessed. Although, she had been careful to hide her growing anxiety from him during these last mad five days. Her head still ached from that bottle of Jacob's Creek she had foolishly drunk on Wednesday night. She didn't think Eb knew about that. But just in imagine, if she had told him about the entries in her notebook: it would be like setting fire to rum poured over a crêpe Suzette. Eb's genealogical flame would be re-ignited until it was burning like the Guy Fawkes beacon that used to be lit on the Common, before Health and Safety banned all public bonfires.

Of course, what was irritating, was that he'd been right all along. He had encountered a poltergeist in the living room. Oh, how he would love to read those notebook entries. Hepsie could imagine him declaiming: "I told you so! We've been brought back to the home of our ancestors because they have something to tell us." He would believe that the poltergeist was his grandmother, Zennor Anderson. Hepsie had no such feelings. The author of those letters could be anyone. Neither she nor Eb knew about Zennor Anderson's private life, apart from the few facts they'd discovered about her and the Anderson family, and she could no more believe this 'Zennor Anderson's' desire to find her lost children than she could imagine herself taking up genealogy as an obsessive hobby.

However, there was another greater problem lying behind her uneasiness. How did you cope with a poltergeist? When Hepsie had drawn her curtains on Sunday night, she believed she might have been hallucinating. Had Eb and Mike's genealogical fanaticism gone too far in her own mind? That she, Hepsie Anderson, was now thinking, breathing and hallucinating about her ancestors in the same insane way as Eb and Mike. Or, if not that, maybe her attraction for Mike had sent her crazy? She was lovesick and hallucinating ancestors in order to be closer to him. Or, and this seemed the most likely reason to her, she'd been living too long with Eb and, consequently, had been too long out of life and the real world. A

211

poltergeist? Hepsie shivered within her anorak. On the Monday morning she had hoped to find the page in her notebook blank. It wasn't.

By the Wednesday night, after she'd discovered the poltergeist had written in her notebook only minutes beforehand, and had even drawn her bedroom curtains, Hepsie was beginning to feel her world dissolving around her. A part of her wanted to deny what was happening. Maybe Eb was writing in her notebook. Although, he was blind, and couldn't possibly have done such a task. Maybe she was writing the letters when she was sleepwalking. But she had never sleepwalked and the letters always appeared before she went to bed. Was she hallucinating? Hepsie saw how she was like a dog chasing its own tail. Her scepticism followed her fear and incredulity in a foolish circle. She'd hoped the letters were temporary. She even, half-heartedly and half-madly, wrote to the poltergeist, her fingers trembling as she did so. Then the poltergeist flung her clothes around and moved the furniture. Every step Hepsie took to calm herself was undermined by her growing lack of control over the situation and her mounting uncertainty of what the poltergeist might do next.

They were passing the Old Bakery. Hepsie glanced over her shoulder at Eb. She didn't like him being as silent as this.

"We're walking along Bakery Hill now," she told him. "It won't be long before we get back home."

"This uphill climb always does me good," Eb said.

Hepsie felt relieved. So he wasn't ignoring her. As she led Eb along the steep lane, she couldn't help glancing at the twin bay façade of the former bakery. She remembered buying bread from there when she was a child. Thick, crusty bread ripe from the oven.

The crust was hot to touch and the smell of yeast lingered on her fingers long afterwards. Nowadays, Eb made fresh bread in their kitchen at Peace Cottage. He had learnt not to trust his nose but to use a kitchen timer to cook his bread. Hepsie pictured Eb in the kitchen, feeling the bottom of his loaf to see whether it was firm and crusty, before giving it a tap to test for hollowness. Talking kitchen scales helped him to measure the flour and tactile markers, known as 'bumps-on', enabled him to use the oven controls.

"Shame the Dangerfields aren't still living there," Eb suddenly said.

"They weren't running the bakery when it closed," Hepsie remarked.

"I know that. But it would have been useful for us. We could have asked them."

"About what?"

"Neville and Ivy Dangerfield."

"You never give up."

"They're still some Dangerfields living in the neighbourhood," Eb continued, as though ignoring her. "They might be descended from the bakers. We could ask them."

Hepsie glanced back at Eb. His face was lively. And there was a keen glint in his pale blue eyes.

"What is the point?" she said. "You're going off on a tangent."

She wished Mike had never brought the Mills family research with him on Sunday. A part of her, since reading the poltergeist's notebook entries, was more determined than ever to persuade Mike away from his genealogical obsession. She wondered how long it would be before he got in touch with them again.

"I'll ask Joan," Eb said. "She might know them."

"You're making the genealogical research more

complicated, Eb. Why don't you give it a break?" Hepsie walked a little more quickly, forcing Eb to quicken his pace. She knew she shouldn't do that, but she was determined to bring Eb's genealogical musings to an end.

Eb tapped the point of his long cane more emphatically on the wet lane, splashing dirty rainwater on her bare legs as he did so. She slowed down so that they were both walking evenly uphill. Eb was catching his breath.

"The lane's levelling out here," she told him. "We're passing the Common."

The War Memorial stood out against the overcast sky, buttercups shivering in the drenched grass around it. Hepsie led Eb along the winding lane, telling him when the lane sloped downwards and when they had reached the front gate of Peace Cottage. Slowly, she led him along the damp path until they reached the bright blue front door set within its white frame. This door was another bit of colour-contrasting painting from Eb's pre-blind days, when his deteriorating eyesight could still distinguish colours.

Hepsie put down her shopping bag and searched for her keys in her anorak pocket. She unlocked the front door. It swung open, raindrops glistening on its bright blue paint. Hepsie led Eb into the hall. They were greeted by the ticking of the grandfather clock. Eb released his arm from the crook of her elbow and stood as she closed the front door and...

The picture had moved. No, not just one picture. All of them. Various prints of old-fashioned coaching scenes and rural views of Gloucestershire, which Eb and Sofia had collected since moving to Amberley, and a framed painting of Peace Cottage that Hepsie had made at the Parochial School, and a textile collage of flowers on the Common made by Sofia at one of Joan's evening classes and...They were all lopsided or turned upside down. Her own painting of Peace Cottage looked as though it was about to fall off its hook. Hepsie contemplated moving from her frozen spot to set her painting right, in case it did fall off the wall and alert Eb to what was going on. Eb was still standing in the middle of the hall, waiting for her to lead him into the kitchen. Hepsie swallowed. She glanced around the rest of the hall, scanning the flagstones and the door of the boxed-staircase, which was still closed as she had left it before they went out to the Post Office.

"Is everything all right?" Eb asked.

Hepsie moved towards the living-room door.

"Yeah," she said, straining to keep her voice level.

She quickly peered around the living-room door. It was the same scene. But worse. Pictures, prints and photographs were lopsided or thrown on the floor. Books had been flung from their bookshelves. One side table was tilted upend against Eb's armchair. The brass fender from the fireplace had ended up in the newspaper and magazine rack. Hepsie trembled. What was she going to do? How was she going to clear this up without Eb knowing?

She turned round to face Eb. He looked puzzled. She was relieved he couldn't see the damage to their home.

"What is it?" he asked.

Eb's instinct must be telling him that something was wrong. Hepsie wondered whether he could feel a change in the atmosphere. She shivered. Apart from the ticking of the grandfather clock, the house was very quiet.

"Nothing, Eb. We're going into the kitchen."

She placed Eb's hand in the crook of her elbow and led him along the passageway to the kitchen. The flagstones smelt moist beneath their footsteps. She hoped the rain hadn't seeped through the back doors. Otherwise, she would have a lot of clearing up on her hands today.

On the threshold of the kitchen, Hepsie couldn't help gasping.

"Is something wrong?" Eb asked.

Hepsie stared at the kitchen. Saucepans had been flung from their place on the saucepan stand. A chair was upturned. Another was facing the wrong way, back-to-front at the table. Cupboard doors had been left open. And brightly coloured drying-up cloths scattered all over the kitchen like confetti.

Eb's grip tightened on her arm, as though he sensed the adrenaline racing through her heart.

"Is something wrong?" he repeated.

Hepsie couldn't speak. Whilst one part of her mind wobbled like jelly, another part was thinking whether she could pass off this disturbance as the work of burglars. What had been taken? The front door hadn't been forced open and, as far as she could see, neither had the living-room and kitchen windows nor the back doors. In fact, from what she could see beyond the open door on the opposite side of the kitchen, the utility room hadn't been disturbed.

Maybe the burglars had broken into upstairs. But Hepsie was unable to see how they could have got up there, unless they'd borrowed a ladder or scaled up the walls Spiderman style.

Eb was shifting impatiently beside her. She would have to tell him something. He was probably getting annoyed because he knew something had happened but he couldn't see it for himself.

"We've been burgled," she blurted out.

"Burgled?" Eb sounded surprised.

"Yes. I'll have to look upstairs. They don't seem to have forced their way in downstairs." She was trying to keep her voice level, but she could feel the hysteria rising in her. This household disturbance was several million times worse than the mysterious letters in her notebook.

Abandoning Eb, who was still standing on the threshold of the kitchen, Hepsie raced upstairs, her damp flip-flops pounding on the flagstones and then on the creaking stairs. She ran along the landing, opening closed doors and looking into the bedrooms, the bathroom and the airing cupboard. They were just as they had been left. Even her bedroom, which she had tidied up after the poltergeist's visit yesterday lunchtime, when she had found her clothes flung off her chair and her notebook thrown onto the floor, remained untouched.

Hesitatingly, Hepsie unlatched the staircase door to the attics and begun to ascend the narrow, spiral stairs. She didn't come up here often. The air smelt stale and musty, as though she'd walked into an enclosed tomb. Eb wasn't allowed to come up these narrow, winding stairs since he lost his eyesight. Hepsie noticed cobwebs dangling from the walls and mildew sprouting over the yellowed ceiling.

The attics ran the length of the house. There wasn't enough light coming through the shut skylights, so she nervously switched on the ceiling light. In the glare of the uncovered light bulb, their boxes of stored possessions, suitcases waiting to go on holiday, Eb's unused golf clubs, her school hockey stick, tennis rackets that Sofia would never now use to hit balls, and other discarded paraphernalia, were as stationary

217

and as tidy as Hepsie had last seen them. She breathed in deeply. As children, she and Sally had played hide and seek up here, their girlish giggles penetrating the stuffy atmosphere and their constant chat enlivening the forgotten piles of possessions. More recently, she had packed away Sofia's personal possessions and unearthed the family Bible and 1893 christening photograph from Grandfather Georgie's box.

Hepsie switched off the light, which flickered for a few seconds before shutting the attics in gloom. Gingerly, she walked down the narrow, spiral stairs, holding onto a rope handrail. The thick rope felt rough and dusty in her hand. When she clicked the staircase door latch closed, it was as though she was sealing up the attics and her memories for another discovery. Like an archaeologist, she would unseal the tomb and discover new objects long since forgotten by the living.

Where now? Hepsie paused at the head of the boxed-staircase. If she went back to Eb and told him, yes, Peace Cottage had been burgled, then he might ask her to call the police. She knew she couldn't take the problem that far. Not that the police would come to Peace Cottage, anyway, or, at least, immediately. They never did. Burglary was considered to be a lesser crime and only took place to meet their performance targets. Something to do with a lack of human resources and Government statistics. If she did report Peace Cottage's burglary, it would only become another form-filling exercise, which Stroud Police might or might not bother to investigate. When she was a child, there was a village bobby available to contact. Now, Amberley residents were more vulnerable to crime. Hepsie couldn't help smiling as she suddenly thought of Mike and her lie about him being a potential con man. What would the police have done if she'd discovered he had been conning her and Eb? Despite Mike's superb performance as a fanatical genealogist last Sunday, there was still a part of her that wasn't sure that he was a hundred per cent genuine, but she couldn't think why.

Feeling that she was getting nowhere, Hepsie walked back into her bedroom. Resignedly, she unlocked her desk drawer. On the left-hand side lay the Salmon Mill Publishing Company manuscript she'd been proofreading, which she had put away out of sight in case the poltergeist scattered the pages around her bedroom. Next to this was her notebook. Hastily, Hepsie picked it up and, scarcely breathing, thumbed through the pages. There were no more entries. She breathed out in relief. The last entry – her own incoherent scrawl – stared back at her in all its embarrassing damnation of the poltergeist. For a moment, she was relieved that Eb was unable to see. But he wouldn't need to know what she'd written. Her hands trembled as she took the notebook out of the room with her.

Back in the kitchen, she found Eb sitting down at the table. He had removed his Barbour and draped it over the back of his chair.

"Is that you Hepsie?" he asked, as her footsteps echoed on the flagstones.

There was an expectant expression on his face, as though he guessed what was coming next. Hepsie scowled, annoyed that what she considered to be their bad luck, would be good news to Eb.

"They're not burglars," she blurted out. She removed her anorak and flung it onto the chair that was facing back to front.

"What's happened?" Eb asked.

"The downstairs has been ransacked," Hepsie said, forcing her words out between her clenched teeth. She sat down opposite Eb and opened her notebook at the first letter. The neat copybook hand gazed solidly back at her.

"But if they weren't burglars—" began Eb.

"It's the poltergeist."

Eb's pale blue eyes lit up. A broad smile flushed through his face.

"Well, don't look so happy about it," she continued. "Poltergeists are dangerous. If you could see what she has done—"

"She?"

"Yes."

"How do you know it's a she?"

Now there was no backing down.

Reluctantly, she said: "She's been writing in my notebook. Ever since last Sunday morning."

"Granny Zennor Anderson?" Eb sounded surprised.

As well he might be, Hepsie thought.

"Yes," she managed to reply.

"Then I was right. It was her who threw the paperweight on the floor." Eb looked joyful.

"We can't have this, Eb."

"What?"

"We can't pretend that this poltergeist *is* our ancestor, Zennor Anderson. Just because she – I mean, it – says that's who she is, doesn't—"

"What did she write in your notebook?"

Hepsie sighed.

"Letters. Four of them."

"Why didn't you tell me about this?"

"You know very well why I didn't."

Eb leaned across the kitchen table, his face lively with eagerness.

"What did she say? Has Granny Zennor Anderson got a message for us?"

220

Hepsie felt she was dealing with a school boy. But there was no turning back. Once whetted, Eb's obsession would have to be appeased.

Resignedly, she said: "I'll read them for you."

Eb clenched his thick hands into tight fists on top of the table. He moistened his lips.

In a quiet monotone, she begun to read Zennor Anderson's letters to him.

Not once did she glance up to look at Eb's face. She could guess his reaction to each new piece of information. How his eyes would light up at each personal comment the poltergeist made about the Andersons and Peace Cottage. Not once did he interrupt her but she could feel his enthusiasm hungrily eating up every word she read out.

She did not read out her reply written in mad haste to the poltergeist on Wednesday morning. Lying, she told Eb she had penned a few lines in her notebook just to see whether she got a direct response from the poltergeist or not.

"And did you?" Eb asked.

"She – I mean, it – did reply," Hepsie admitted, reluctantly.

"What did she say?" Eb persisted.

Hepsie didn't want to read out the poltergeist's final letter because she knew what was coming next. She cleared her throat, trying to delay the moment, but she could feel Eb's anticipation almost picking up the words he couldn't see.

She read the letter to him. The letter that told him that Zennor Anderson was pleased to hear from someone and that she would like to know their name.

Eb gasped. "And did you?" he said, the words tumbling out of his mouth like pennies in a slot machine.

"No."

Eb looked crestfallen.

Before he could ask, she explained: "I thought it would be stupid to write another reply to the poltergeist – which is what 'she' is. I didn't think it was wise to give this 'thing' my name. Come on, Eb, she – I mean, it – has attacked us again. And badly this time."

"But that's what she wants," Eb said.

"To attack us?" Hepsie looked at Eb as though he was mad.

"No! She wants us to reply to her."

"But I have." And, unknown to you, a second time, too, she thought.

"No!" Eb was getting exasperated. "We need to reply to her fourth and final letter. Tell her who we are. And that we want to meet her."

Hepsie banged her notebook onto the table. "Meet her! Are you mad?"

"She wants to get in touch with us. She wants us to tell her about her children. She hasn't seen them for many years."

"She's not likely to. They've been dead for several decades."

"This is a one in a million chance, Hepsie. Why do you think we've been brought back to the house of our ancestors?"

"Because you and Sofia liked the house and the location."

"No! Because they've got something to tell us. This is more than just a coincidence."

Hepsie shook her head in disagreement. She moistened her lips, hoping her saliva would cool her parched tongue. Staring passed Eb, she could see the apple trees through the kitchen window. They were bent and twisted, almost as diagonal as the steep slope of the back lawn upon which they stood. White blossom had metamorphosed into leaves and budding fruit.

Brushing away the thought that these apple trees were probably growing here in great-granny Zennor Anderson's time, she said: "We should exorcise her."

"Exorcise her!"

"She's dangerous, Eb. We can't have a poltergeist disrupting our lives. And damaging our home. If you could see the mess she's made—"

"I'm not exorcising my ancestor. No way!"

"She's not your ancestor. There's no proof that she is. I've now got to clear up the whole of the downstairs. And then there's the worry she could strike again. We're not safe, Eb."

Emphatically, Eb repeatedly tapped his finger on the table, as he said: "That's why we must write to her again. Here, I will dictate a letter to you. And you must write it down in your notebook."

Hepsie shook her head. "I'm not doing this."

"Please, Hepsie," Eb pleaded.

She bit her lip. Closed her eyes, so that she didn't have to look at Eb's excited sightless face. She saw the patience and care etched into his worn skin. And his pale blue eyes alive with enthusiasm but unseeing of her. What he would give to see those notebook entries himself. If he ran his fingers over the pages he would feel where great-granny Zennor Anderson had pressed her pen down firmly on the lines. He knew she hadn't made up the letters. He believed her, and, she had to admit, that gave her some comfort.

Opening her eyes, she retorted: "All right, then. But only ONE letter."

Eb reached out across the table, his fingers searching to grasp her hand. Hepsie briefly squeezed his fingers before retracting her hand. She didn't want him to feel she was willingly condoning his mad plan.

She found a pen on the sideboard and sat back down. Placing her notebook before her, she turned to a clean page, mindful to avoid her final incoherent entry.

"I'm ready," she said.

Eb sat thinking for a few moments and then, in a slow, measured voice, he begun. Hepsie picked up the pen and wrote:

Friday p.m.

Dear Zennor Anderson

It is with great pleasure that we, the present inhabitants of Peace Cottage, introduce ourselves to you. I am your grandson, Eb Anderson, and the young lady whose notebook we are writing in, is your great-granddaughter, Hepsie Anderson. She has read your letters to me and I would very much like to enter into a correspondence with you. Or, even better, to meet you in person.

At this point, Hepsie paused and gave Eb a dirty look, before forcing herself to resume writing.

Whichever you decide is best, please feel that you have our best interests at heart. We would love to hear more about yourself and, in return, we can tell you about your children—

Eb trailed off, unable to finish his dictation. Hepsie glanced up from her writing. Eb's eyes were moist with tears. She waited for him to resume speaking. After about a minute or two, Eb sniffed and cleared his throat.

"Sorry, but the thought of telling her that her children have..." He broke off, again.

"She's only a poltergeist, Eb. It's not going to bother her that much."

Eb shook his head.

"Do you want to finish the letter?" she asked. A part of her deluded herself that he might say no.

"Yes. I need to sign off."

Hepsie sighed. Resignedly, she listened to Eb's final dictation and wrote:

> *I look forward to having the pleasure of getting to know you better,*
>
> *Yours sincerely*
> *Eb Anderson*
> *(only son of Georgie Ebenezer Anderson)*

"Can you read the letter back to me, please," Eb said.

Hepsie did so, without emotion.

"Well, what do you want me to do with it?" she asked.

"As you did before."

"You want me to leave my notebook on my desk?"

"Yes. That's where she knows where to find it."

"Thanks!" Hepsie angrily closed her notebook. "Let's invite the dangerous poltergeist back into my room. I can tidy up the mess she's sure to make after I've finished clearing up downstairs."

Eb leaned across the table so that he could speak more urgently to her. "Please, Hepsie. It's important that we treat the poltergeist in this way. If she reads my letter, she might think twice about disrupting the house."

"I bloody hope so!"

Eb leaned back in his chair, his expression unmoved.

"And what happens if the poltergeist doesn't reply to your letter?" she asked.

Eb thought for a moment before replying: "We could hold a séance."

"A séance!" Hepsie studied Eb's face closely to see whether he was joking.

"Yes," he said earnestly.

"And who's going to hold this séance?" she retorted.

"I'll have to ask someone."

Hepsie shook her head. She decided not to bother carrying on this conversation with her deranged father. Her chair scraped across the flagstones as she stood up to leave the table.

"Are you getting tea?" Eb asked.

"No!"

She knew she should have removed Eb's wet shoes and brought him his slippers. And their coats should have been hanging up on the coat hooks in the utility room to dry off. But she couldn't be bothered. Exasperation and desperation dug through like a skewer, as though she was a lump of meat on a kebab.

"I'll get tea myself," Eb said. "Do you want a cuppa?"

"No," she repeated.

Hepsie knew she should tell Eb she was going upstairs, but she snatched her notebook from the table and walked out of the kitchen. The flapping of her flip-flops on the limestone slabs would tell him that she was leaving.

Back in her bedroom, she paused at her desk. Reluctantly, she placed her notebook on the desktop and opened it at Eb's letter. She hoped the poltergeist didn't reply. But if that happened, then there might be another disturbance in the house. Eb and she were not safe. If the worse came to the worse, she would have to contact an exorcist herself. No way was she going to allow Eb to hold a séance. Where did he get that mad idea from? Another worry, was that he might tell people in the village – especially Joan. Hepsie could imagine Joan arriving at their front door with either a medium in tow – one of her spiritualist chums from Stroud – or a reporter from *The Stroud Herald*. "This will really put Amberley on the map," Joan would gush. "The village could do with the publicity. It might help to raise funds for the church and village amenities. Do let us get involved, Hepsie."

In despair, Hepsie sat down on her bed. What was she to do? She could call Sally. Her childhood best friend always made her laugh. But she hadn't told Sally yet about the mysterious letters and the poltergeist activity. Somehow, the thought of explaining it all to Sally and of having to go through every small detail of the tortuous time she'd been going through these last five days, didn't appeal to her. Sally might even not believe her. Her red-haired friend would spend her time laughing at Hepsie and teasing her that Eb's genealogical obsession was taking a stronger hold over her than before. Well, it was. But not in the way Sally could ever imagine.

Hepsie picked up her mobile phone from her bedside table. Futilely, she flicked through her contacts list. Mike's number caught her eye. What was his number doing on her phone? She knew full well. Last Sunday – well, maybe before that – she had surreptitiously taken his business card from Eb's genealogical file and recorded his mobile number on her contacts list.

Impulsively, she selected the text message option. In a few seconds she had inputted her message. Hepsie read it back to herself:

HI MIKE

GENEALOGY PRBLM @ PEACE COT. DONT KNOW WHAT 2 DO. CAN U HELP?

HEPSIE :~(

Her finger hovered over the send command before she, eventually, pressed it. Too late, now. The message whizzed off to Mike's phone. She'd had no excuse to previously contact him. But now, as the grandfather clock struck four o'clock, excitement shivered through her body as she realised that the poltergeist could be bringing them closer together.

Thirteen

Hepsie found Eb lying on the kitchen flagstones. She had been reclining on her bed, thinking of Mike, when she heard a clatter from below. Guiltily, she had suddenly thought of Eb.

"You shouldn't have moved from the table until I'd come back downstairs," she said, bending down to give Eb a hand up.

Eb groaned. He looked dazed.

"I wanted to get a mug of tea," he mumbled, "but I think I must have stepped on one of the saucepans grandmother Zennor'd disturbed."

He groaned as Hepsie led him to the kitchen table and helped him sit down.

"Are you hurt?" she asked.

Eb shook his head. "No, just winded."

"Well, that's a relief. I thought the poltergeist had come back to bump you off."

Eb smiled grimly at her joke.

Still feeling guilty, she added: "We could both do with a cuppa. I'll make us tea before clearing up this" – Hepsie looked around the kitchen – "bloody mess."

There was no response from Eb towards her last retort. Privately, Hepsie hoped he was having second doubts about the poltergeist's attack. She wanted to say to him: "I told you so. You shouldn't be encouraging dangerous poltergeists." But she knew he wouldn't listen to her. He was winded but not defeated.

She took an hour to clear up the kitchen, hall and living room. Eb tried to help her in his own slow way. When pictures, furniture, cushions, and saucepans were all straight and orderly again, Hepsie began to prepare supper. It was only when she was slicing through a cucumber that she remembered her text to Mike. Fearing that Eb might guess something else was bothering her, she continued to prepare supper, mixing their salad and laying out their cutlery and plates on the kitchen table before putting a ready-made red-pepper-and-bacon flan in the oven.

"I'm just going upstairs for a moment," she called out to Eb as she passed the living room. He was having an aperitif whisky – to calm his nerves, so he said, after a rather exciting afternoon – and Hepsie knew he would be unlikely to disturb her until supper time.

Her bedroom was as she had left it. Hepsie found her mobile phone amongst the folds of her duvet. She grabbed it and saw that Mike had tried to call her just after she'd gone to attend to Eb. There was also a text message from him. Quickly, Hepsie clicked on the icon. Mike's message was brief:

HI HEPSIE

CAN U CALL ME B4 8 2NITE

MIKE

Hepsie sighed. She had missed him. She glanced at her bedside clock. Calling Mike after supper would give her more time to talk to him. She was still unsure whether telling Mike about the poltergeist was a good idea. He might not believe her. Her situation was not an easy one to explain to a...well, a stranger. She was no nearer to knowing Mike as well as she would have liked to have done. Wondering what Mike was doing after eight o'clock this evening, she reluctantly placed her mobile phone on her bedside table. She hoped her phone would still be there after supper. But you could never be certain with a poltergeist roaming your home.

Anxiously, she glanced towards her desk. Her notebook was still lying open at Eb's letter. She walked over to her desk and, more dutifully than fearfully, checked for the poltergeist's reply. There was none. Hepsie sighed in relief. She could see her exorcist plan winning.

At supper, Eb had an expectant look on his face. Hepsie knew he guessed something was going on. She was finding it hard to hide her nervous excitement at having to call Mike after supper. Her voice seemed to quaver slightly every time she spoke to Eb. He probably thinks great-granny Zennor has written a reply in my notebook, she thought, and he's waiting for me to own up. But, of course, she wasn't going to do that. Eb knew she was against any further civilised communication with the poltergeist. He would believe she was holding back in the hope of convincing him to hire an exorcist to extinguish his ancestor. Surprisingly, Eb didn't ask her once during supper whether there was a reply to his letter.

When she was sure Eb was settled in the living room with a mug of coffee, Hepsie returned to her bedroom. Her hands shook as she dialled Mike's number. He was quick to answer. She warmed to his low, mellifluous voice as she had done that first time she'd called him. They exchanged brief pleasantries.

"So what's the problem?" Mike asked.

Hepsie hesitated before taking the plunge: "Peace Cottage's been attacked by a poltergeist."

"A what?" Mike sounded disbelieving.

"I'm thinking of calling in an exorcist," she hurriedly continued. "The situation's really bad. She's vandalised the downstairs rooms. Eb and I are living in fear of her next attack."

"She?"

Hepsie bit her lip. Damn it! Now she would have to tell Mike.

"The poltergeist wrote letters to me. Signed them as though she – I mean, it – were Zennor Anderson."

"Your great-grandmother?"

"Well, she's not. It's a poltergeist."

"That's amazing!" Mike seemed genuinely impressed. "But you haven't spoken to her yet? Or met her?"

"I wouldn't want to!"

"She might be able to tell Eb and you about her past," Mike continued. "Did she write about it in her letters?"

Hepsie didn't understand. From being disbelieving, Mike was now as firmly on the poltergeist's side as Eb was. Didn't these genealogical fanatics have any qualms about dangerous poltergeists invading their homes?

She remained silent.

Mike appeared to swallow hard before he said: "Of course, I understand that you're worried about your own safety. Who wouldn't be?" He paused as though he was hoping she would end her silence.

Hepsie took her chance. "That's why I want to hire an exorcist. It's no good encouraging great-granny – I mean, the poltergeist – to communicate with us. We've got to get this harmful presence out of Peace Cottage."

And then she added for extra affect: "I'm really scared, Mike. This isn't any normal genealogical problem."

"Quite," Mike agreed.

Hoping she was nearer to getting him on her side, Hepsie continued: "I need to persuade Eb to hire an exorcist – for his own safety. He doesn't understand."

"I can see his point," Mike said.

Hepsie nearly dropped her mobile phone in exasperation.

"Before you hire an exorcist," Mike hurriedly continued, "shouldn't you wait in case Eb and you do find out more about great-granny Zennor? Why don't you reply to one of her letters? That way, you'll really know whether she's real or not."

"We have already," Hepsie replied crossly.

"And?"

Mike's voice sounded as though he was balancing on a trapeze wire.

Hepsie sighed.

"Ok," she finally relented. "Yes, she did."

"Wow!"

Hepsie grimaced. She would have to find another argument to get Mike on her side.

"We're waiting for her to reply to Eb's letter," she proffered, "but she hasn't done so yet. Eb wants to arrange to meet her, which, of course, she isn't going to do."

"She might," Mike said. And then, perhaps sensing he was making her more cross, he joked: "Although, I don't want her killing off you and Eb. Any more attacks and she'll definitely have to be exorcised."

"Eb's already fallen over a saucepan," Hepsie said, taking advantage of Mike's change of tone.

"Poor Eb!"

And then they both laughed. Somehow, they both

had an amusing image of poor, blind Eb tripping up on one of the saucepans that had been carelessly flung by the poltergeist. They both knew it wasn't kind to laugh but, really...Hepsie wiped a tear from her watering eyes.

"Look," Mike said, "I've got to go out soon, but let me know whether there're any further developments. Let me know that you're safe – I don't want to think the poltergeist has bumped you both off."

Hepsie felt a warm glow flush through her. So he did care about her.

"Going anywhere nice?" she asked. She wished she was sharing the rest of her evening with him.

"Oh, nowhere special – drinking with Eddie, maybe a nightclub later on tonight. The same routine." Mike laughed, as though he was shrugging off his social life as something to be considered ordinary and boring.

"Anyway, don't feel you can't text or call me," he added.

"I'll keep in touch," Hepsie promised.

They said their brief goodbyes and then Mike's phone clicked off.

It was all right for Mike, Hepsie thought. He was going out, having a good sociable time this evening, whilst she was trapped at Peace Cottage with a crazy obsessive genealogist and a dangerous poltergeist. If there was one way in which her conversation with Mike made her feel better, it was in her new feeling of security. A problem shared was a problem halved. He seemed to believe her, or wanted to believe her. And he was concerned for her safety. Hepsie felt half her battle had been won. Maybe next time, she could convince him completely to take her side. For the moment, she felt less scared of the poltergeist and more in control.

She didn't glance at her notebook until she was going to bed. There was still no reply. Ideally, Hepsie wanted to lock away her notebook in her desk drawer. But a part of her was worried that this might excite the poltergeist to make a further attack. And she didn't want to risk being disturbed in her sleep. If the poltergeist came and wrote in her notebook during the night...Hepsie shut the thought out of her mind. She prayed the poltergeist might have gone away – for good.

Snuggled up in bed, Hepsie checked her mobile phone. There was a text message from Mike. She read:

HI HEPSIE

NOT HEARD FROM U. R U STILL ALIVE?

MIKE

After his name, he had added the 'fingers crossed' symbol: *X=*. Hepsie smiled to herself. Encouraged, she texted back:

HI MIKE

STILL ALIVE!

HEPSIE :-)

She would have liked to have added more, but felt there was nothing else she could say within the boundaries of their present conversation. Instead, her unspoken thoughts chased each other in her mind: *How are you Mike? Are you enjoying yourself at that nightclub? Why haven't you asked me to come with you? Is that Kate with you? Who is she? When will I see you again?*

Why don't we hire an exorcist tomorrow and say goodbye to the genealogy forever?

Hepsie waited a few minutes after sending her text, in case Mike replied immediately. When he didn't, she switched off her bedside light and laid her head on her pillow, her heart pumping joyfully and warmly within her breast.

During the night she slept fitfully. At one point, between sleeping and dreaming, she thought she saw the shadow of a large man on her bedroom wall. This struck her as strange: if the shadow was the poltergeist, then shouldn't it be a woman's shape? Hepsie shivered, but she didn't know from what. She turned over in her bed and drifted into another disturbed sleep.

Next morning, she awoke early. Blearily, she reached out for her mobile phone on her bedside table. There was one text message. But it was not from Mike. Disappointed, Hepsie read Sally's text:

NOT HEARD FROM U L8LY. R U OK?

From the time the text was recorded as being sent, Hepsie guessed that Sally must have spent the early hours of today at her boyfriend's favourite nightclub in Bristol. She scowled. Lucky Sally! Putting her mobile phone back on her bedside table, she was relieved that there was no point in replying to Sally's text there and then because her red-haired friend would still be asleep.

She got out of bed and decided to make herself a mug of tea. On her way along the landing, she paused to knock gently on Eb's door. Eb called out that he was awake and, yes, he would like a mug of tea if she was making one. Hepsie wondered whether he had slept as badly as she had.

Upon entering the kitchen, she nearly fell over a saucepan lying by the doorway. Quickly, she looked around her. The ceiling lights had been switched on and all the halogen bulbs were flickering. Hepsie thought she had switched off the kitchen lights before going to bed. She didn't think Eb had been down to the kitchen during the night and forgotten to switch them off. Only one person – or 'thing' – could have done this. More saucepans had been flung onto the flagstones. And Eb's gaily coloured liquid level indicators thrown across the kitchen table like tiddlywink counters. Cupboard doors were open and cutlery spilled out of a drawer tipped upside down on the sideboard.

Above her, Hepsie could hear Eb's long cane prodding the bathroom floor. What was she going to do? Admittedly, her first thought upon waking had been about Mike and not about checking her notebook to see whether the poltergeist had written a reply. She would have to check her notebook. However, she was pleased: because now there was further proof that the dangerous poltergeist was causing more harm at Peace Cottage. She decided she would use the camera on her mobile phone to record this latest attack. Proof would be needed to show the exorcist that the poltergeist was real.

She rushed upstairs, calling out to Eb that tea would soon be on its way but she had to do something first. In her bedroom, she glanced at her notebook. She was right. The blank lines after Eb's letter were proof that the poltergeist preferred a more violent means of attack. Hepsie grabbed her mobile phone and rushed back downstairs. Before she returned to the kitchen, she peered around the open door of the living room. Yes! Total chaos! Hepsie took several photographs with her mobile phone camera. This time she noted that books removed from the bookshelves along the far wall had been placed carefully on the carpet rather than flung. She wondered why the poltergeist had done this. There was almost a reverential feel to the way the books had been positioned neatly on the cream carpet.

Back in the kitchen, Hepsie efficiently took her photographs. Surely, no one would think she and Eb had created this mess themselves? That the poltergeist's attacks were a charade invented by herself and/or Eb because they were attention-seekers? She decided to make tea first before getting dressed and clearing up the poltergeist's mess. There was no point in Eb coming downstairs for breakfast until the kitchen had been cleared up. Falling over another saucepan wouldn't be good for him. She would also need to get the flickering ceiling lights working properly. Thank God there was no disturbance upstairs for her to clear up! All this constant tidying up made her more determined to exorcise the poltergeist.

Eb's face was expectant when she took him his tea. His white eyebrows were raised quizzically. She spoke before he could ask her. And then she told him the bad news. Well, the poltergeist's latest attack was bad news to him, if not for her.

"I wonder what's wrong," Eb said, more to himself than to her.

"What's wrong? I can tell you what's wrong. A dangerous poltergeist is roaming our home, that's what's wrong!"

Eb's demeanour was stubborn. "I didn't hear anything during the night," he said.

He doesn't believe me, Hepsie thought; he thinks I've created the mess myself in order to consolidate my exorcist argument. And then, pausing to think for a moment, she couldn't remember having heard any loud noises, too. Did the poltergeist's attack happen during the night or early this morning? She didn't know.

Back in her bedroom, Hepsie checked her mobile phone. There was no message from Mike. He was probably still asleep after his night out. She sent him a text:

HI MIKE

SHE ATTACKS AGAIN.
NOT HURT.

HEPSIE :~(

She hoped it wouldn't be long before she heard from him. Re-reading Sally's text, Hepsie knew she should send her best friend a reply. But she couldn't be bothered. Somehow, events had developed so much since last Sunday, she felt Sally had been left too far behind for a brief explanation in a text message. No doubt, Sally would catch up with her later. And, hopefully, when Hepsie had her exorcist argument on more solid ground.

During breakfast, Eb was very quiet. Hepsie wondered whether he was chewing over his reluctance to hire an exorcist. Maybe he would change his mind about their situation. He was certainly upset the poltergeist hadn't replied to his letter. She left him to think in solitude and went to tidy up the disturbance in the living room.

"I'm going to Stroud," she told him later. She wanted him to come with her. Eb wouldn't be safe staying at

Peace Cottage by himself. But Eb refused. Hepsie guessed he wanted to stay at home in case he encountered the poltergeist.

"It's for your own safety," she insisted. "I don't want to come back home and find you've been killed."

But Eb wouldn't change his mind. Hepsie had no choice but to leave him behind. She had to go to Stroud because they were low on food and essentials that she could only buy from town. Of course, now that Eb wasn't accompanying her, she could go to Waitrose. Eb hated her shopping at these out-of-town supermarkets. He thought – and quite rightly so – that they took away trade from the independent shops in the centre of Stroud. But Hepsie loved shopping at Waitrose: the experience reminded her of her London life when she shopped at the Finchley Road branch. No doubt, Eb guessed she was going to the supermarket, so he must be doubly keen to stay at home instead of discouraging her.

After she'd taken her shopping back to her car, Hepsie checked her mobile phone for text messages. She didn't think Eb would send her one. He was either waiting for the poltergeist to suddenly appear and say 'hello' to him or he was dead. In the car she could smell the warm, fresh French stick she'd bought for their lunch and the ripe organic strawberries grown in Herefordshire. Eb would be disappointed if he wasn't alive to eat this delicious food. Disliking supermarket shopping never prevented Eb from enjoying the food she bought there.

Hepsie's heart leapt. There was a text message from Mike. She quickly read it:

HI HEPSIE

LOOKING 4WARD 2 C-ING U 2MORO.
SÉANCE: A GR8 IDEA.

MIKE :-)

She re-read Mike's message several more times. There was only one reason why Eb had stayed at home. She flung her mobile phone into her handbag and started up her car. There was no point in speaking to Eb there and then. And there was no point in calling Mike until she'd spoken to Eb face to face. As she turned out of the car park, she knew she shouldn't have told Eb about the photographs of the kitchen and living-room mess that she'd taken for the exorcist.

Upon her return to Peace Cottage, Hepsie dumped her shopping bags in the kitchen and stomped into the living room. Eb didn't glance up. He was sitting at his computer, listening to *The Daily Telegraph* on-line. He couldn't hear her because he was using earphones to listen to his computer's Narrator facility. Hepsie tapped him firmly on the shoulder. Startled, Eb pulled out his earphones and turned round.

"Is that you?" he asked. But he looked disappointed.

Hepsie guessed he was hoping the poltergeist had tapped him on the shoulder.

"Yes, it is," she replied angrily. "And what do you mean by inviting Mike to a séance?"

"Hey?" Eb seemed surprised, as though he'd been up to nothing.

"You know very well!"

She breathed over him, unable to restrain the heavy gusts of breath she felt tunnelling up within her.

When Eb didn't reply, she added: "Mike sent me a text. You must tell me what's going on."

Eb's sightless pale blue eyes gleamed intelligently. He smiled wanly before daring to break into a broader smile. "I called Mike. After I had called Joan."

"Joan!" Hepsie felt the living-room floor dissolve beneath her flip-flops. "What's she got to do with this?"

"I asked her to hold a séance for us tomorrow."

"A séance? But Joan knows nothing about hosting a séance."

"Yes, she does. She told me she's experienced several séances at her spiritualist friend's house in Stroud."

"That doesn't mean she's qualified to tackle a dangerous poltergeist." Hepsie swallowed hard before she could continue. "And you haven't given a second thought about how dangerous it is to tell Joan about our poltergeist problem. She'll never keep it quiet."

A pleased look passed across Eb's benign face. "Don't worry, I made her swear not to tell anyone – even her husband."

"She's the last person I would have trusted with a secret," Hepsie retorted. She imagined not only the whole village wagging their tongues about the Andersons' ancestral visitor, but Joan arriving at Peace Cottage's front door with a reporter from *The Stroud Herald* or, even worse, a television crew from South-West News.

"You told Mike," Eb said pointedly.

Hepsie blushed. When she didn't immediately reply, Eb continued: "Mike seemed surprised to hear from me; he was expecting a call from you. When I told him about my plan for Sunday, he admitted he already knew about the poltergeist because you had told him." Eb's eyes twinkled mischievously.

Brushing off Eb's insinuation, she replied, half-lying:

"I had to tell someone – it might as well be Mike because he's the only other genealogical fanatic I know who might be willing to believe our situation."

Eb chuckled. "That's what I thought," he said, obviously pleased there was at least one point they seemed to agree upon. "I couldn't leave Mike out of tomorrow's séance. He would love to read my grandmother Zennor's letters and to meet her."

Hepsie closed her eyes in exasperation for a minute and wished she could force herself out through the rafters of Peace Cottage. She clenched her fists and released them before she could trust herself to speak.

"But why tomorrow? Don't you want to wait in case the poltergeist replies to your letter? She might."

Hepsie knew she was stalling for time. She was annoyed because Eb had beaten her to it: he had made arrangements for a séance before she'd had time to search for an exorcist on the Internet. No doubt, telling him about this morning's attack and her photographic recording of the poltergeist's mess had encouraged him to act quickly. Why couldn't she always see through her father's silences? She could never trust them now.

"Tomorrow's the earliest I can bring everyone together," Eb replied. He didn't refer to his letter.

She could see that he was determined to hang onto his hopes, however much he might be grasping at straws blowing around a windy farmyard. He was wounded that his courteous letter had failed to work on the poltergeist.

Seeing that she was getting nowhere, she asked: "What time is the séance tomorrow?"

"3 p.m. Mike's arriving at 2 p.m. and—"

"Joan, no doubt, any time before that," Hepsie finished for him.

"I can't back down now," Eb protested. "It's all arranged. Look, if the séance doesn't work—"

Hepsie raised her eyes to heaven and, fed up, left the living room, leaving Eb still talking to her.

Monotonously, she put away the shopping and prepared lunch. She only once spoke to Eb, to call him into the kitchen when lunch was ready. They spent the meal in taunt silence.

Afterwards, Eb announced he was going out into the garden. Hepsie watched him as he got up and made his way outside. The weather had improved since yesterday morning's torrential rain. Through the kitchen window, she could see the sun peeking out from behind the clouds. The twenty-four hours' respite from the rain would have given the grass time to shed some of its sodden wetness. She hoped so, because Eb hadn't bothered to put on his outdoor shoes.

Wondering what she was going to do this afternoon, she was about to pick up her and Eb's dirty plates when her mobile phone rang. Hepsie jumped. Her phone's musical ringing tone brought her back into the real world. She glanced at the incoming call's number. It was Mike.

Quickly, she flipped open her phone and greeted him.

"I've been waiting to hear from you all morning," Mike said. "Where have you been? I was beginning to think the poltergeist had bumped you off before the séance could be held."

"Eb phoned you," Hepsie simply stated.

"I was expecting to hear from you," Mike said. "It was a bit of a shock to hear Eb's voice."

Despite her annoyance with Mike, Hepsie couldn't help feeling pleased with this admission.

"We need to call off the séance," she said. "Eb's got

244

this crazy idea that he's going to call up the ghost of his ancestor. You'll have to help me tomorrow by convincing him to give up this crazy idea. Will you refuse to take part in the séance?"

There was a pause at the other end of the phone before Mike replied: "To be honest, I only agreed to be taking part in Eb's séance because I thought it best to humour him. He does seem to be very excited at the idea of calling up his grandmother Zennor. Which is not surprising, of course, because a visiting ancestor *is* a very rare occurrence. However, I don't think the séance will work."

Hepsie felt relieved. She didn't want the séance to take place tomorrow but she also didn't want to miss the opportunity of seeing Mike again. His visit was the only good aspect of Eb's crazy plan.

"So you'll take my side?" she urged him. She waited for his reply, her breath suspended.

There was another pause at the other end of the phone before Mike, in his low, mellifluous voice, replied: "I'll try to. It might be difficult because Eb's so keen and you've got that other—"

"Joan," Hepsie finished for him. "Joan Franklin, our neighbour. You met her on your first visit to Peace Cottage. She's no idea how to hold a séance. I think our task will be easy. Neither Eb nor Joan will be able to create a séance."

"But you'll have to come and support me," she quickly added, anxious that Mike might decide it was not worth his time coming tomorrow.

"Oh, I wouldn't miss tomorrow for the world!" Mike exclaimed.

Hepsie laughed, nervously. She hoped that some of Mike's enthusiasm was not only due to his genealogical excitement but was also for her.

Tomorrow's séance didn't seem such a stressful afternoon with Mike there to calm her.

Audaciously, she said: "I'm pleased you're going to be there." She could almost feel Mike's warm breath at his end of the phone.

"Yeah, I'm looking forward to seeing you, again," Mike said. Hepsie felt her heart swing up high, and then low, as he added: "And Eb."

"Well, I'd better let you get on with your Saturday," she said more tersely, "before our poltergeist takes over your whole weekend."

Mike chuckled good-humouredly, as though he hadn't noticed her change of tone. Did he think their poltergeist problem was a laughing matter?

But then he said: "I'll keep texting you until we meet tomorrow – just in case the poltergeist tries to bump you off. Oh, and Eb."

Hepsie smiled. Mike seemed to have a peculiar way of balancing his genealogical concerns with his concern for her safety. Was this her getting to know Mike? She felt that Mike without his genealogical concerns would be an easier person to understand.

They said their goodbyes with more good humour than when they'd first spoken. Hepsie wished she had asked him how his night out had gone. *Which nightclub did he go to? Was* she *with him?* But there was no hint of his girlfriend accompanying him. Or, of her being involved in Peace Cottage's poltergeist problem. Hepsie didn't believe that *this* Kate was his aunt. His unopenness about his girlfriend worried her.

However, for now she had more pressing concerns on her mind. Looking out of the kitchen window, she saw that Eb was still sitting on the bench in the garden. Hepsie left their dirty plates on the kitchen table and went upstairs to her bedroom. The letters in her notebook were a problem. Both Joan and Mike would want to look at these letters. And that was a problem because they would see what Eb couldn't see: her own incoherent replies to the poltergeist.

Tearing out the pages she'd written on wasn't a good idea because they were written on the back of the poltergeist's letters. Her only possibility was to scan the poltergeist's letters onto her laptop and save them onto CD. This way she could lie and say that she'd done this for Eb's benefit, so that he could listen to the letters using the Narrator facility on his own computer. "How thoughtful of you, Hepsie!" she could imagine Joan saying. And then she could say that as the CD was in the living room, Mike and Joan might as well look at the letters on Eb's computer, too. At least, she hoped this would work. If one of them did ask to see the actual letters in her notebook, she could lie and say that she thought it best her notebook shouldn't be handled in case the poltergeist's letters got damaged in any way – she might need to show them to an exorcist as evidence. That's, if the séance didn't work. Which, of course, she knew it wouldn't.

Upon entering her bedroom, Hepsie was relieved to find it undisturbed. No clothes flung on the floor or books thrown off her bookshelves or chairs left upended. Perhaps the poltergeist was having a holiday. She sat down at her desk and picked up her open notebook to move it so that she could use her laptop. She nearly dropped the notebook. On the page opposite Eb's letter there was a reply from the poltergeist.

Her heart beating, Hepsie clutched her open notebook in her hands. She saw the now familiar handwriting, with its neat and well-formed characters. Gulping deeply, she read:

Saturday, Noon

Dear Mr. E. Anderson,

It is with great pleasure that I request to meet you and your daughter in person.
  Would three o'clock tomorrow Sunday afternoon be convenient for you?
  I await your reply.

Yours sincerely,
    Mrs. G. Anderson

Slowly, Hepsie let her notebook slip out of her hands. It landed with a thud onto her desktop. For a moment she gazed out of her bedroom window at May Hill, hoping the solitary copse on its crown would give her mystical powers. Yesterday's grey clouds were falling away, leaving the hill bathed in golden sunlight. Hepsie closed her eyes, imagining the warm sun bathing her own face.

When she opened her eyes again, she tore out the page with the poltergeist's last letter on it, screwed it up and threw it into her wastepaper bin.

Fourteen

The curtains were drawn and the lights switched off. Mike moved the second armchair so that both armchairs and the sofa were almost touching one another. Joan had asked for the low coffee table to be left in the middle of this seating arrangement. He knew very little about séances but he guessed this was in case the poltergeist decided to communicate by knocking her replies on the smooth glass table top. The living room was now ready for the séance, due to take place in fifteen minutes' time. From the hall, the grandfather clock chimed the quarter-hour. Mike looked around him. Although the living room was gloomy, he could still see the furniture, the fireplace and the books on the bookshelves along the far end wall. Sunlight from outside trickled through the gaps in the thick curtains at the front of the room. Hepsie was in the kitchen, helping Eb and Joan prepare tea for after their séance. Taking the opportunity of being alone, Mike sat down on the sofa.

He could hear the chatter of his guests' voices in the kitchen. Joan's gushing shriller notes topping Eb's low hum and Hepsie's clear melody. There was a note of anxiety in Hepsie's voice. Mike could tell she was trying to hide it from them, but he'd noticed how nervous she was every time the grandfather clock chimed. Was she afraid the poltergeist would appear? But, like him, she didn't think their séance would work. So why was she nervous? Mike had flattered himself that their recent contact with one another since yesterday afternoon had made Hepsie feel safer. She had replied to his regular texts with what seemed like gusto. Didn't she say she needed his support here today? Mike wondered what was bothering her, unless...

When Hepsie'd texted him on Friday afternoon, he'd been more than pleased to receive her text. Ever since seeing her last Sunday, he'd been trying to think of a reasonable excuse to get in touch with her. He was anticipating some mundane genealogical problem or, even, some information about the Zennor Anderson and Neville Dangerfield connection. He certainly wasn't anticipating a genealogical problem of this proportion. A poltergeist? Mike thought Hepsie's voice sounded sincere when he spoke to her Friday evening. There was desperation behind her words. And she was frightened for her and Eb's safety. Of course, he didn't know her. She might be given to making up fantastical lies. Or, the situation could be a trap. Mike was beginning to wonder whether the Andersons had set up a charade. Could it be possible that they did know something about the Zennor Anderson and Neville Dangerfield link and they were using this poltergeist and séance charade in the hope that it might confuse him and scare him away? Hepsie certainly seemed very nervous about something this afternoon. The only way for him to find out, was to go along with this séance.

At least, the Andersons hadn't asked him to hold the séance. That would be out of the normal range of even a genuine genealogist. As far as he knew, genealogists dealt in facts, not the paranormal. However, Mike couldn't help admitting to himself that he was intrigued about partaking in a séance and whether it might work. God! some of Eb's enthusiasm must be rubbing off on him. It was so easy to get caught up in other people's search for their ancestors. He knew, if Hepsie found out about his growing interest in their séance, she wouldn't be very pleased. Their chance of intimacy was already undermined by his charade as an obsessive genealogist. Mike wished she didn't see him as one because it couldn't be further than the truth. How much simpler their situation would be if he didn't have to play the fanatical genealogist. The only encouraging information he obtained last Sunday was that Hepsie didn't have a boyfriend. But, surely it was not only his genealogical charade that was undermining their mutual attraction for one another? There must be another reason why she was scaring him away. And, Mike had to admit, he found this intriguing. Why was it important that he shouldn't find out what the Andersons were trying to hide from him?

The grandfather clock ticked loudly from the hall. Joan's voice could still be heard in the kitchen. She, Eb and Hepsie would be joining him in the living room very soon. Mike exhaled deeply. He was worried about blowing his cover. As he nearly did last Sunday. Kate's name had fallen from his lips before he realised what he was doing. He hated lying to Hepsie and wished he could tell her the truth. Mike wondered now whether Hepsie wasn't trying to find out more about him not because she was attracted to him but because she suspected something was wrong. He tried to think back to their conversation last Sunday: had he said something to give his game away? Was his attitude wrong? But all he could think of was her intelligent, sensitive blue eyes looking at him and the light bouncing off the red and gold glints in her long chestnut hair. No, she was trying to find out whether he guessed they knew more about the Zennor Anderson and Neville Dangerfield link than they were admitting. He wished he could tell her the whole truth, but he couldn't. For Kate's sake.

Mike reminded himself he wasn't only here to see Hepsie. Kate had been very excited when he'd told her about the Andersons' latest developments. Mystery letters from a poltergeist who said she was Zennor Anderson, attacks on Peace Cottage, and, now, a séance. Didn't she say the Andersons needed to hire a medium? Well, here was the chance to get their ancestor to talk. How she wished she could take part in the séance, too. There was so much she wanted to ask Zennor Anderson. If it was true. But, of course, she couldn't come with him. There was the danger she might speak out and betray herself and his charade. She would be so embarrassed. Humiliated. She didn't want to reveal to strangers what had happened to her. It was so disgusting. The Andersons' perception of her would change. They would see her as a different person. She would be branded in their eyes for ever more. She would never be rid of the taint that had swept over her like a big, ugly splodge of red paint. No amount of scrubbing with soap and water or white spirit or turpentine could remove that taint.

Anxiously, Mike ran his fingers through his hair as he thought of Kate's tired, urchin face as she said these words. He could only agree with her. The danger was that Kate might relapse again. He was only too aware of how her memories of that fateful night could make her seem unbalanced. She took anti-depressants – Cipramil – to stop her crying and breaking down. She was not the Kate he used to know. The Kate he knew would have laughed at him for taking part in a séance to contact a dangerous poltergeist. "You're pulling my leg," she would have joked with him. As it was, he was relieved she wasn't here at Peace Cottage today. Mike was afraid, that if the poltergeist did appear, if she was Zennor Anderson and she did tell them the truth about what happened, the implication of finding out might be too much for Kate. She was so determined to absolve her great-grandfather of any blame. Neville Dangerfield couldn't have behaved as he said he did. His words were those of an old, sick man incoherently rambling on his deathbed. Mike wished Kate didn't have this fixation with her great-grandfather's final confession. The story could have been made up by Granny Wilson's mother. But what could he do? After her incident, it wasn't surprising she reacted in this way. She'd been there herself. For her own peace of mind – and there certainly wasn't much of that left since the incident – she had to find out and absolve not only her ancestor's conscience but her own.

Hepsie's flip-flops resounded on the flagstones in the hall. Alert, Mike looked up, but her flip-flops vanished up the boxed-stairs. Glancing at his watch, he saw that their séance was due to start in less than ten minutes. He still hadn't told Kate about his feelings for Hepsie. Kate would warn him how stupid and dangerous he was to get himself more embroiled with the Andersons. He was supposed to safely find out what he could before disappearing from the Andersons' lives forever. However, he knew this was impossible. He was hoping to find a chance of emotional happiness with Hepsie. And, in view of his present life, he didn't want to miss that chance. He knew the thought would haunt him for months, if he didn't. So, here he was, making the best of a difficult situation, awaiting not only genealogical developments but personal ones.

Heels resounded sharply on the hall flagstones. Joan's. Mike grimaced. He wanted to get up and pace the living-room floor but managed to will himself to sit still.

"We won't be long," Joan trilled, as she poked her head around the living-room door. She flashed a beaming smile at him. "Bet you're excited! I'll just have to see to something before I'll begin the séance."

Mike nodded his head, trying his best to smile amicably at her. To his relief, her head disappeared and he heard her heels tapping back towards the kitchen.

Ever since his arrival at Peace Cottage this afternoon – and he had made sure he was early this time – he had been worried that Joan might ask him to set a date for the genealogical talk she wanted him to give to Amberley Family History Group. During his drive to Amberley, he'd been preparing excuses in his mind. Various delaying tactics were devised and then rejected before Mike decided that it might be best to allow Joan to set a date and then he could pretend to be sick or, he knew it was bad of him, to say his mother had suffered a stroke. Anyway, he planned to wheedle his way out of this difficult situation. No way was Mike Johnson going to stand up before a crowd in a village hall and talk genealogy for an hour.

Throughout the fifty minutes he'd been at Peace Cottage, he was nervous every time Joan opened her mouth to speak. Which was often. After their welcoming pleasantries, and before he volunteered to arrange the furniture for their séance, Joan had got him involved in asking about the poltergeist's letters. She wanted to read them. Mike did, too, but only for

Kate's sake. Hepsie showed them the scanned copies on Eb's computer. The letters were convincingly written in an old-fashioned style and sounded genuine enough. Mike privately studied Joan's manner to see whether she betrayed any knowledge of a plan against him. But he couldn't detect anything suspicious behind her gushing enthusiasm for the poltergeist's letters. What was odd, was Hepsie's demeanour. Despite encouraging him and Joan to read the scanned copies on Eb's computer, Mike couldn't help noticing the nervous flicker in her eyes as she did so. Perhaps the letters weren't real. And, when Joan asked whether she could see Hepsie's original letter to the poltergeist, the colour rose in Hepsie's face. He could almost see her mole twitching on the bridge of her nose.

"Oh, no," she hurriedly explained. "I'm afraid the originals might get damaged if my notebook is handled too much. There's not much to see, anyway. Only two polite lines – nothing more." She shrugged her shoulders to further emphasise that her letter to the poltergeist really was nothing.

Joan looked crestfallen. She turned to Mike for support.

"But we would love to see the originals at some point, wouldn't we?" she said.

Mike smiled lamely. He was about to say that he didn't want to cause too much bother, when Hepsie interjected: "I'm keeping them safe for the exorcist, Joan. In case the letters are needed as evidence." Mike thought he detected a hint of maliciousness in her voice.

"Hepsie's afraid the séance's a bad idea," he said, hoping to get on Hepsie's side by offering his support to her. "Aren't you worried that calling up a disruptive poltergeist might be dangerous for us? That we could be killed?" He dared to look directly at Joan's eager brown eyes, magnified today by a pair of large mauve glasses.

She clasped her hands together in front of her chest. Staring directly back at him, she said: "Eb does so want me to hold this séance for him. We can't let him down, can we? It's for his benefit."

Mike gave Hepsie a sidelong glance. He knew she was thinking the same as him. Joan wasn't doing this séance for Eb's benefit. It was for her own. A slight smile hovered over Hepsie's lips but she said nothing. Perhaps she was trying not to laugh. Joan Franklin, spiritualist of Amberley, takes centre stage. Another bow to her meddling fiddle.

Joan caught the look that passed between himself and Hepsie. Strangely enough, she seemed to be encouraged by this. Her brown eyes sparkled intelligently behind her large glasses, as though she was pleased to see the innuendo between himself and Hepsie.

Without waiting for a reply, she continued: "I think the poltergeist will behave more properly after our séance. It will show that we do want to meet her. I can see Eb's point of view. We don't want an exorcist to extinguish your ancestor until we're certain that no contact with her can be made at all." And, then, seeing the cynicism in Hepsie's face, she added: "At least, give the séance a try, Hepsie. Don't you want the chance of meeting your great-granny Zennor Anderson? You might find the experience very illuminating."

If the poltergeist is true, Mike thought. Kate had asked him to obtain copies of the poltergeist's letters. Now was probably the best time to do so. Before Hepsie and Joan came to blows over holding the séance.

Turning to Hepsie, he said: "I would like to have

printed copies of the poltergeist's letters. Is that possible?"

She looked at him as though he was mad. God! she probably thinks I'm being the fanatical genealogist, again, he inwardly groaned. How he wished he could tell her the truth. He no more wanted printed copies of the poltergeist's letters than he did salt in his tea.

But before Hepsie could reply, Joan interjected: "That's a brilliant idea, Mike! I could have some for Amberley Family History Group's archives. Can you print them off from Eb's computer, Hepsie?"

"No!" Eb exclaimed.

They all turned to look at him. He'd been sitting quietly in his armchair throughout their conversation.

Joan looked surprised. "Why not, Eb?" she asked.

"No," Eb mumbled, rather self-consciously, "Or, at least, not yet. I did ask you Joan not to tell anyone about our poltergeist problem. Have you?"

She raised her eyebrows in mock innocence. "Of course not!" she exclaimed. "You swore me to secrecy, Eb, and I've kept to it."

Hepsie's expression was disbelieving. Mike felt she would have liked to tell him how Joan Franklin was the last person to keep a secret. Wasn't their neighbour on most of the social committees in the village? He was warming to Hepsie's point, when she looked directly at him and asked: "And what about you? Have you told Kate?"

The living room swivelled uncomfortably around him for a second before Mike could regain the breath blasted out of him.

"Kate?" he managed to say. "No, I haven't told Kate, or anyone." He hoped his lie sounded convincing. Despite wearing a T-shirt, he felt hot around the collar. He held Hepsie's defiant gaze for a moment before

257

he glanced at Joan. She smiled warmly back at him. He waited for either her or Eb to ask him who Kate was. But Eb simply said: "I'm sorry, Mike, I think it's best you don't take away any copies of great-granny Zennor's letters just yet. Hepsie and I would like to keep our poltergeist problem secret for a little while longer." And, then, brightening up, he added: "If our séance's successful, maybe you can take copies home with you."

Mike acquiesced but he noticed Hepsie glaring at Eb. He wondered why Eb wouldn't let him have any copies of the letters. Normally, Eb was keen for Mike – who he saw as a fellow fanatical genealogist – to have as much information about the Andersons and Peace Cottage as was available. Mike felt Eb was holding something back from him. Perhaps the Andersons were betraying him. And the poltergeist and the séance were no more than a charade. Because the Andersons wanted to hide information from him. But why? Wasn't it far-fetched of them to make up a charade like this? However, Mike had to admit, that if Eb and Hepsie found out about his own charade – as a fanatical genealogist – and the reasons why he was doing this, they would be just as disbelieving.

The grandfather clock was still loudly ticking the passing minutes in the hall. Glancing at his watch, Mike saw that it was five to three. Hepsie, Eb and Joan would be joining him in the living room at any moment. He could hear the floorboards creaking upstairs in what must be Hepsie's bedroom and he exhaled deeply as he heard the creaking move towards the landing and boxed-staircase. The thought of seeing Hepsie today had kept him sane. He wished he could spend more time alone with her, so that he could get to know her better. At least, this weekend had opened up the possibility of being more easily in touch with her. Mike felt he could now freely text and call her. In some respects he hoped their séance didn't work this afternoon. Hepsie would need his regular contact in case the dangerous poltergeist was still roaming Peace Cottage and she – oh, and Eb – were attacked. Perhaps she might even ask for his help in getting an exorcist. Although, Kate wouldn't be pleased about this. He would have to argue with Kate that helping Hepsie to hire an exorcist would be in their best interests. Anything to stay in touch with the Andersons in case he did discover they were hiding information about the Zennor Anderson and Neville Dangerfield connection. An inner warmth spread through Mike's body as he envisaged his future contact with Hepsie. He began to feel more sure of himself.

Joan's heels tapped neatly along the flagstones in the hall, followed by the tapping of Eb's long cane. Mike grimaced. He'd hoped Hepsie would get here before them, so that he could have a minute or two alone with her. Putting himself on his guard again, he turned to smile at Joan and Eb as they entered the living room.

Joan's face was full of excitement. Her brown eyes gleamed as much as her pearly blonde bob. She was wearing comfortable grey slacks and a light mauve T-shirt that matched her mauve glasses. Eb's face was suffused with expectation. He was wearing beige cotton trousers, with neatly pressed front creases, and a brown and green checked short-sleeved shirt. Joan led him to his armchair, which Mike had positioned on the fireplace side nearest to the door. She sat down in the armchair next to Eb and opposite to himself. At that moment, Hepsie came into the living room and shut the door behind her. She breathed deeply before walking over towards their group, her eyes focussed on the bookshelves on the far wall beyond Joan and himself. Sitting down on the sofa beside him, she glanced towards the living-room door as though making sure it was firmly shut. Mike could sense she was still anxious about something. Since being upstairs she had applied a fresh coat of lipstick and sprayed herself with more of that exotic scent that seemed to envelop him in sensuousness every time he met her. Slowly, and with precision, the grandfather clock struck three o'clock, each chime resounding loudly throughout the house.

Hepsie had jumped at the first chime and Mike noticed how she kept her lips firmly closed as though she was biting her lower lip. After the third chime, she glanced at the living-room door, again. Mike was sure he could hear her heart thumping wildly beneath her cerise T-shirt. He glanced at Eb and Joan to see whether they were betraying any similar emotions. But Eb's benign face was still expectant and Joan had her eyes shut, as she prepared herself inwardly for the spiritualist task ahead of her. Suddenly, she opened her eyes and exclaimed: "Let the séance begin!"

She raised her arms high in the air and then, glancing at Mike, reached out to take hold of his right hand. He felt her long nails digging into his palm as she tightly gripped him. She turned to her right and took hold of Eb's hand. Eb firmly squeezed her fingers in reply. Hepsie reached out for Eb's left hand. She looked at Mike as she took his hand in hers. Mike couldn't help a smile spreading across his face as he touched the warmth of her soft flesh. He was sure he caught a flicker of a smile hovering over her lips. Her grasp was light and his larger hand protectedly enveloped hers. At least, her painted nails didn't dig into his flesh like Joan's did. He squeezed Hepsie's hand in the hope that it might make her feel less nervous. But she didn't respond. Instead, she glanced towards Eb and Joan. When Mike did the same, he noticed Joan was smiling at them both in a knowing way. He was relieved when she shut her eyes and told them to do the same.

"Is anyone there?" she intoned slowly and deliberately to the living room.

Mike could hear their shallow breaths and a fly buzzing behind the thick drawn curtains. Steadily, the grandfather clock was ticking in the hall. Although the living room was shaded from the afternoon sunlight, he was still conscious of light prickling at his shut eyes and trying to prise them open. It was too pleasant a June afternoon to be shut inside a gloomy, stuffy room. The only good aspect was being able to hold Hepsie's hand.

He managed to keep his eyes shut as Joan repeated: "Is anyone there?" Her grip was tighter than ever around his hand. He could hear her breathing more deeply, as though she was willing the poltergeist to appear. Mind over matter. Or, was it spirit over matter? He would have liked to have opened his eyes and seen the expressions on their faces as they concentrated on calling up their poltergeist. However, he must keep up his pretence. It wouldn't be good to give away his charade just now.

There was a slight movement on the sofa from Hepsie's side. He was conscious of Hepsie looking at him. Quickly, he opened his eyes and glanced at her. But she was faster than him and had closed her eyes again. He admired her profile for a moment before taking a brief glance at Eb and Joan. Although sightless, Eb had his eyes closed and there was a look of serene concentration on his face. Joan was still breathing deeply, her nostrils flared and her large mauve glasses balancing precariously on the bridge of her nose. Mike could see she really fancied herself in the role of spiritualist leader. Eb had told him, during their telephone conversation yesterday, that Joan had attended séances at her spiritualist friend's home in Stroud and was confident that she could replicate a working séance at Peace Cottage.

Suddenly, Joan put more pressure on his and Eb's hands, and cried out: "Is anyone there?"

Mike quickly closed his eyes.

"We are awaiting your presence!" she added in gong-like tones.

He could feel her hand shaking with the intensity of her emotion. Maybe she was going to conjure up their poltergeist solely by the power of the warm current emanating from her hands. He wondered whether Eb was receiving an electric shock, too. Hepsie's hand felt warm and comfortable in his, but he didn't know whether the tingles he felt in his flesh were due to Joan's electrical current or to something belonging only to him.

The ticking grandfather clock filled up the silent minutes after the living room echoed with Joan's words. A car could be heard driving along the narrow lane outside Peace Cottage. And then a whirring lawnmower started up in a neighbouring garden and shattered the lazy afternoon peace. Mike waited for someone to get up and shut the windows but no one moved. He was relieved because the living room would have been unbearably stifling. Daring to open his eyes, he caught Hepsie glancing at the living-room door. Her manner was less nervous now. As though she was relieved something had passed. Perhaps she was scared at the beginning of the séance because she didn't want their poltergeist to be called up in case they were attacked. Unless, something else was bothering her. Was she nervous about betraying him? And that he might discover the poltergeist and séance to be only a charade?

Mike quickly closed his eyes as she glanced back towards their group. He felt her eyes linger over him for a second. Had she guessed he'd been looking at her? Mike squeezed her hand in the hope of indicating to her that he was aware she was worried about their safety, if the poltergeist did appear. He hoped she would find this contact reassuring but she didn't respond. When he arrived at Peace Cottage this afternoon he'd been relieved to find that she and Eb hadn't been bumped off by the poltergeist. It would have been too sad if they had been killed by their ancestor, particularly as Eb was so looking forward to meeting his grandmother, whilst Hepsie was planning to exorcise the poltergeist before she and Eb could be killed.

Pins and needles were developing in Mike's legs. He wanted to stretch them out but they were wedged in between the sofa and the low coffee table. If only Joan hadn't insisted on the table being placed in the middle of their tight circle. Even the poltergeist would have difficulty in knocking her replies on such a low table. The whirring lawnmower abruptly cut off. Mike could hear Joan's breathing relax as the living room returned to the sound of the grandfather clock ticking in the hall. He was half-expecting Joan to invoke the poltergeist again, when there was a knock.

Hepsie's hand tightened her hold on his. For a moment, Mike thought maybe he had misheard the knock, which didn't seem to be coming from the low coffee table near them. A second knock, firmer and louder, confirmed his suspicions. Opening his eyes, Mike glanced towards the living-room door. He saw that Hepsie already had her eyes open. He squeezed her hand. She looked at him, both surprise and fear flickering through her round blue eyes. Mike glanced at Eb and Joan. They both had their eyes shut. Joan was frowning with intense concentration. There was a third knock at the door. A look of triumph passed across Joan's face.

"Please show yourself!" she exclaimed.

Mike glanced back at Hepsie. She was not daring to look at the living-room door. He could hear her heart thumping in time to the ticking of the grandfather clock. He held on tightly to her hand, taking the opportunity to feel the vibes of her throbbing heart pulsating through the warm, soft flesh of her palm.

"Please show yourself!" Joan repeated. Her voice was loud and shrill and Mike thought she was about to collapse with spiritualist concentration. Or, excitement. With his limited knowledge of séances, he wasn't sure whether she wanted the poltergeist to appear in the living room or for the poltergeist to communicate with them by further knocking.

He glanced towards the living-room door and was in time to see the doorknob slowly turning. The living-room carpet was thick and the door dragged across the cream carpet as it was opened. Hepsie quickly glanced towards the door.

"If you are there, please knock three times!" Joan exclaimed.

"I think, Joan, you'd better open your eyes," Mike said.

"Shush!" she hissed. "You'll disturb her!"

"Joan, you'd better open your eyes," Hepsie reiterated.

Joan sighed with exasperation. Unwilling to relinquish her role as spiritualist leader, she reluctantly opened her eyes.

Mike noticed Eb had opened his eyes. In fact, Eb looked as though he had...well, as though he had seen a ghost. Wonder and shock made him seem lost for words. Was Eb experiencing a blind man's sixth sense? Poor Eb, Mike thought, he can't see what we can see.

Peering around the living-room door, her hand on the doorknob as though she might quickly close the door and flee, was a woman. A woman dressed in old-fashioned clothing. Her skirt was floor length and her corset tight. Sleeves ballooned out at her upper arm before narrowing down to her lace cuffs. Lace inserts decorated the bodice of her fine grey dress, which even in the gloom of the living room gleamed like silk. Mike's breath was nearly taken away. When he looked at her face, he thought she reminded him of someone. But her hair piled up on her head was honey-toned and her eyes the palest blue he'd ever seen. Paler than Eb's sightless blue eyes. She couldn't have been much older than Hepsie and himself. Her free hand clutched at her skirt, crumpling up the fine silk fabric and exposing a grey laced boot poking out from beneath her petticoats. She was the woman in the 1893 christening photograph.

She wasn't smiling. Her expression was as anxious as her ready-to-flee stance. Mike thought he detected anger in her pale blue eyes. He hoped she wasn't about to attack them.

"My!" Joan exclaimed. "We've done it!" She released her grip from both Eb and Mike's hands and grasped her hands together with a clap against her chest. "Do we have the pleasure of meeting Mrs George Anderson?" she asked with condescending politeness.

The woman at the living-room door stared in fear at them. Mike could see she wanted to flee but something was holding her back. To his dismay, Hepsie released her hand from his. The circle was broken when she released her hand from Eb's. Mike hoped his disappointment didn't show in his face. He could feel the warmth of her touch lingering in his hand. Hepsie was staring intently at the woman. If she was nervous that the poltergeist might attack them, she didn't show it. Eb was still musing over some inner wonderment.

"It's all right," Joan continued, "we called you up for a very good reason."

"You didn't reply to my letter of yesterday," the woman blurted out.

"Your letter?" Joan asked. She raised one eyebrow quizzically. "Do you know anything about this, Eb?"

"No," Eb simply replied.

There was an awkward silence.

"I'm not a liar," the woman said. "You can look in the girl's journal. I wrote to a Mr Eb Anderson yesterday noon. Why haven't you replied to my letter?" There was a rising note of hysteria in her voice.

Hepsie closed her eyes. Mike wondered whether she was scared the poltergeist was going to attack. He was about to touch her hand to reassure her, when Eb spoke.

"Do you know anything about this, Hepsie?" he asked.

Hepsie gulped. She reopened her eyes.

"Yes," she said.

Joan gasped.

266

"Mrs George Anderson wanted to meet Eb and me at 3 o'clock today," Hepsie continued, "but I didn't think it would be safe. That's why I didn't tell you. I thought we would be better holding the séance and finding safety in numbers. She's a dangerous poltergeist who can't be trusted. How do I know that she wasn't planning this meeting to attack us? She could still kill us now."

The woman let out a moan. Mike saw tears well up in her pale blue eyes. Her look was desperate.

"How dare you!" she decried. "I'm not a poltergeist! I'm a mother who's lost her children. I did what I did, because I had no other choice. You," – she glanced accusingly at Eb and Hepsie – "you wouldn't have anything to do with me. Although you live in my former home and you take my family's name, yet you do disdain to tell me the truth. The truth about my children's whereabouts and my husband's part in my—" She broke off, her words seeming to stick in her throat. "What are you trying to hide from me?" she asked. "Why are you tricking me?"

This is most interesting, Mike thought. The poltergeist suspected Eb and Hepsie of hiding something from her. But why would they be tricking the poltergeist? What did they know about the Zennor Anderson and Neville Dangerfield connection that Zennor herself didn't know?

"We are not tricking you," Eb replied. He spoke with extreme kindness. "I'm sorry Hepsie – my daughter – didn't reply to your letter of yesterday but—"

"How were we to know, Eb?" Hepsie butted in. "She's behaved like a dangerous poltergeist in the last few days. You were worried for our safety, weren't you Mike?" She glanced at him. Her fine blue eyes were compelling him to agree. Mike remembered the touch of her hand in his and wished they were sitting alone instead of in this mad séance group.

"I was very worried," he replied, hoping to earn Hepsie's approval.

She was about to smile back at him, when Joan interjected: "You're a kind girl, Hepsie, and a dutiful daughter to Eb. Of course, you were worried for his safety, and for ours. But don't you think" – and, here, Joan rolled her magnified brown eyes behind her large glasses – "don't you think, perhaps, you're going over the top?"

Hepsie scowled instead of smiling. She made no reply.

Joan's smile broadened so that she showed teeth almost as pearly as her bob. She leaned forwards and, pointedly looking at Zennor Anderson, said: "This chance for us of meeting an ancestor is not one to be missed. I know how much Eb has wanted to meet – or, at least, speak – with his dear grandmother. We, too, are very grateful for this opportunity to meet her."

If Joan was hoping to appease Zennor and get her to smile back at them, it didn't work.

"I'm not a grandmother!" Zennor exclaimed. "I'm a mother of three young children. And I'm very sorry I haven't been here to look after them as a mother should. If you can tell me where my children are now living, I promise I will not desert them again." Her pale blue eyes looked at them pleadingly.

Joan glanced at Hepsie. "There," she said, "I told you so. There was no need for an exorcist. You've got to give these situations a try. Just wait until I tell Amberley Family History Group about our successful séance."

"No!" Hepsie and Eb said simultaneously.

Joan affected surprise.

Before she could speak, Eb said: "Look, Joan, I did ask you to keep this problem a secret. I think it's better that way, just for the moment. We don't want to scare away Zennor by putting the spotlight on her."

Disappointment showed on Joan's face. Mike tried not to smile. He knew Joan was congratulating herself on finding a new niche as a spiritualist. She wanted to tell the whole world that she had powers to call up the dead. But he wasn't so sure that she was the one instrumental in doing so on this occasion. Neither Eb nor Hepsie had complimented her on her spiritualist skills and, looking at them both now, he wondered what it was they were trying to hide. And why they wished to protect their newly arrived ancestor from becoming public knowledge. He thought it was suspicious that a passionate genealogist like Eb didn't want to share his discovery with other genealogists.

At least, Kate would be pleased. He would have to spend the remainder of his afternoon at Peace Cottage trying to find out more. The woman standing by the living-room door was real enough but he didn't know whether she'd been set up by Eb and Hepsie to mislead him and Joan, or whether she was genuine.

The grandfather clock struck the half-hour. Joan took this opportunity to regain her composure and said: "I think we should have tea. I've brought some of my homemade coffee gateau, Mike, that you loved so much last time."

He smiled back at her as pleasantly as he could. To be honest, he couldn't remember Joan's cake. Hepsie was the only delightful memory he'd taken back with him after his visit.

Glancing at Zennor, Joan asked: "Will you join us for tea, Mrs Anderson? We would so love your company."

Zennor stood motionless by the living-room door. Although she had released her hand from her skirt, her other hand was still clutching the doorknob as though she might flee. She shook her head.

The ticking grandfather clock filled up the stifling silence of the room. Mike could tell that Zennor was longing to turn her back on their séance group and run out into the hall beyond their reach. Fearing that he might lose his only chance of speaking to her, he blurted out: "Did you know Neville Dangerfield?"

Zennor's pale blue eyes widened. She looked back at him...well, she looked back at him as though she'd seen a ghost.

Fifteen

Eb could see her. This was their second meeting and, no, he wasn't dreaming. He'd been right that Thursday, nearly a fortnight ago.

Zennor sat opposite him at the kitchen table. He could see her pale grey dress and her face and honey-coloured hair. But the light around her was blurred and shadowy. Although he could feel the hard wooden surface of the kitchen table beneath his hands, he couldn't see it.

She wasn't looking very pleased at the moment. Having wandered into the kitchen early this afternoon and found him sitting there, she had since been seeking an explanation from him. Why were they tricking her? Why were they living at Peace Cottage? What had happened to her children?

The last question was proving difficult for Eb to answer.

"Surely you must understand a mother's love for her children. If you do, then you must answer me truthfully." Zennor's pale blue eyes pleaded with him. Her lower lip trembled, as she continued: "A mother needs – and should – find her lost children. Why can't you help me?"

Eb felt awful. He knew the truth would only add

to her despair. But he couldn't lie to her. She hadn't believed him when he'd said he was her grandson and Hepsie was her great-granddaughter. He would have to try again, as best as he could.

Taking a deep breath, he replied: "They left Peace Cottage with George, when he took over as owner at Davis & Co. Drapers in Stroud."

Zennor leaned forwards, her lace cuffs gently brushing the table top. "How long ago was that?"

"That was some time ago," he admitted. "Your daughters were grown up and...er...baby Georgie – my father – had left home."

"Left home?" Zennor's mouth gaped open in surprise.

"That was after the Great War of 1914 to 1918. He left Amberley for good. Before that, he'd been living with his grandparents here at Peace Cottage and working as a labourer." Eb shifted uncomfortably in his seat.

"I don't understand," she simply said.

He nodded sympathetically. "I know, it's a lot to take in."

Zennor banged her fist on the table top. "You're tricking me! You and your daughter! Why do you call yourselves my grandson and great-granddaughter and take our family name? Why do you know all about my children's lives when I know nothing more than what I knew – and what I lost—" She broke off, as she gasped to push her remaining words out of her mouth: "—before death torn me away from them and Peace Cottage?"

She had said it. The word none of them, either yesterday during and after the séance or himself here in this kitchen this afternoon, had dared to say to her. If his grandmother knew she was dead, then her – and his – problem lay elsewhere. Eb was suddenly very conscious of the passing of time. How could he tell Zennor they were not talking about days, weeks or even months, but years? And many years, generations ago, in different centuries?

"Many years have passed, Zennor, since you were last at Peace Cottage," he told her gently. "Your children grew up and lived through many changes in a new century. That century has also gone and, with it, your children. I am Georgie's only son and I live in the present century. By chance I came back to live at Peace Cottage, not knowing it was my ancestors' former home. It was here, Zennor, that I discovered through records about what had happened to you and your family. And, believe me, I do care about you and—"

"You know what happened?" Zennor's voice rose hysterically. "How can you know what happened? Has George told you? What has he told you? He's guessed?"

"I know nothing except the facts I found in the records," Eb replied. "Look, I'm sorry to have to tell you this sad news. I know it's not easy for you. When you're ready, I can show you copies of the records, so you can see proof that your dear children and husband are" – Eb swallowed hard before he could find the strength of voice to continue – "indeed dead."

He hoped the tears moistening his eyes might convince his grandmother Zennor that he was telling her the truth. Surprisingly, she looked relieved.

"George is dead?" she asked.

"I'm afraid so."

"He murdered me," she blurted out.

Now it was Eb's turn to feel disconcerted. He wondered whether he had heard her properly. He was about to ask her when she added: "You don't believe me, do you?"

Her pale blue eyes stared back at him honestly. Eb noticed the way her silk dress gleamed as it caught the light from the halogen lamps above them. He hadn't seen fabric for a very long time, except in his memory and through the sensations of touch. Did she know that he could see her? He stared into her eyes, but she didn't flinch or show any sign that his eyes were nothing more than a sightless mirror to her.

"Why do you think he murdered you?" he asked, hesitantly. Her death certificate certainly hadn't stated she'd been murdered. Killed in an accident, yes. Taken back to the Tinners' Arms at Zennor Churchtown where she died and, according to the local newspaper, a coroner's inquest was held, before her body was taken back to Amberley by her grieving husband.

Zennor glanced down at her hands and twisted her fingers. Eb waited for her to speak but he could see she was reluctant to tell him. His father Georgie had never mentioned a murder in the family. He wondered what Georgie would have made of his mother's admission and, if it was true, what it would have been like growing up with a psychopathic father. No, Zennor's admission couldn't be true. George would have murdered again, surely, if he'd been psychopathic.

Without looking up, Zennor quietly asked: "Did George murder my children?"

His conversation with his newly found grandmother was getting increasingly more complex. They seemed to be on two different mind waves. Both of them were as incredulous of the other. Eb thought he'd better answer as honestly as possible, given the limited facts he knew.

"No, he couldn't have done. My father and his sisters were still alive when George died."

Zennor sighed in relief. She stopped twisting her

fingers and looked up again. Unaware that he could see her, she studied his face. Eb wondered whether she was looking for some form of family resemblance. Did he remind her of anyone? Or, was she still trying to gauge whether she could trust him or not? Ever since her return to Peace Cottage, he'd been hoping to have a long chat with his grandmother about her life, the lives of his other ancestors and what it was like living in nineteenth century Amberley. However, trying to break down the stranger's barrier between them was making this a difficult task for him. How could he ask his grandmother about her past when she was so obviously upset by it? He would have to clear up quite a few problems – such as, Zennor's inability to accept her children's death, and why she believed George murdered her – before he and Zennor could comfortably sit down and talk about her past.

"I'm not proud of what I did," she blurted out.

Eb raised his eyebrows.

Seeing that he didn't understand her, she continued: "For behaving like a poltergeist. I'm not proud of having caused a disruption in Peace Cottage. It's not how I normally behave. You do understand, don't you?"

Eb smiled back at her. "Oh, definitely. I've been in a few compromising situations myself lately, where I've been accused of not behaving normally." He thought of Hepsie finding him crawling on the living-room carpet, as he searched for the paperweight that Zennor had thrown to gain his attention. Hepsie hadn't believed him. She thought he was a doddering old fool who'd fallen out of his armchair and knocked the paperweight off the side table. He would have to be careful that she didn't find him crawling on the floor again.

"I had no other way of gaining your attention. You

275

and your daughter were ignoring me," Zennor said. "But I had good reason to act so. For my children's sake. I know I shouldn't have behaved like a poltergeist, but you all had no right to call me one."

Eb nodded sympathetically. "I'm very sorry for that, and I would like to apologise on everyone's behalf. Please don't feel you aren't welcomed at Peace Cottage."

He hoped she would stay. Indeed, he was lucky she was sitting here with him today. Yesterday, during the séance, he'd been afraid she was going to flee and never be seen again. Particularly after the mention of Neville Dangerfield. A change had come over Zennor's face when Mike had asked her about the baker. Eb didn't know whether it was the mention of the baker's name or Mike himself who had produced that look on her face.

There was something strange about Mike's persistent probing of a connection between Neville Dangerfield and Zennor. Mike was a likeable bloke, but he did do some strange things. Such as, 'accidentally' taking away the 1893 christening photograph with him, when it was obvious that this wasn't an accident. Mike was far too bright a chap to do a stupid thing like that. Maybe he was following a genealogist's instinct that there was something interesting lying behind the Dangerfield connection. He wanted to confirm whether his instincts were correct or not. Then why didn't Mike, Eb reasoned, approach Joan and her Amberley Family History Group to help him? Maybe Mike was intending to do so, when their poltergeist problem interrupted their lives. Mike decided to take the chance of directly asking one of the participants – namely Zennor – instead of relying on secondary sources. Well, any professional and dedicated genealogist would have done that. Maybe, Eb reasoned, he was being too hard on the chap. He didn't know Mike well, anyway. Best to let him get on with the job. Although, Eb suddenly thought, would he be needing Mike's services now? Mike would presume that Grandmother Zennor would be telling Eb all he needed to know about his ancestral background.

Eb smiled to himself. There was one reason why Mike might decide to keep in touch. And, even if he didn't do any more genealogical work for them, he would want to know about their relationship with Zennor and what she had to tell them.

What she had to tell them. That was the problem. How could Eb get his grandmother to talk about herself and her past without further upsetting her? In her fragile emotional state, she might decide to flee from Peace Cottage forever. And he would lose his only chance of finding out about his ancestors and what went wrong. He must keep her here. Make her feel welcomed. Until she was able to tell him. He could understand why she was accepting her children's deaths with difficulty. He still missed Sofia. Why hadn't Sofia come back to Peace Cottage, like Zennor had? But it was probably too soon. Sofia would come back and find him one day. And then they would speak again.

Eb wondered whether sharing his grief with Zennor might help her with her own, but he was afraid that he might start crying, and two upset people would be worse than one. He noticed she kept glancing nervously to her right. What was over there? He couldn't hear any noise apart from the low vibrating hum of the fridge, birdsong coming through the open kitchen window, and the grandfather clock ticking in the hall. He didn't think anyone was standing over there. But Zennor kept glancing nervously in that direction. There was the door to the utility room but Eb was certain he'd closed that before lunch. She couldn't be looking at the washing machine and wondering what it was.

"Is someone else with us?" he asked her.

Zennor looked startled. "Why do you ask?"

Of course, he'd forgotten she didn't know he could see her.

"I thought I heard a footstep," he lied.

Fear flushed through Zennor's face, widening her pale blue eyes.

"I can't see anyone," she said.

He had said the wrong thing.

"Sometimes my hearing isn't too good," he lied. "It was probably a sound from outside."

But Zennor was still agitated. She glanced, again, towards the utility-room door, as though she was expecting someone to open it.

"I'm sure there's no one else at home, apart from ourselves," Eb continued. "My daughter Hepsie has gone out."

Zennor glanced back at him. Her lower lip was trembling. Eb could see she couldn't speak. Afraid that she might flee, he quickly said: "You are welcomed here, Zennor. This is as much your home as it is mine and Hepsie's. You are my...er..." He was going to say grandmother, but looking at her now, he saw how ridiculous that was. She was many years younger than him, more like Hepsie than his grandmother. "You are my relative and Hepsie and I would love you to stay with us," he concluded. "Do say that you will."

But Zennor shook her head. With tears welling up in her eyes, she got up from her chair and left the kitchen.

Damn it! Eb thought. She had done that yesterday. They were busy getting tea in the kitchen and taking the tea paraphernalia into the living room, when someone noticed Zennor had vanished. "Oh, what a shame!" Joan had decried. "I was so hoping that a nice cup of tea would make her feel comfortable and get her to talk with us."

Get her to talk with us. Eb hoped this wasn't the last he'd seen of Zennor. He remained sitting in the kitchen, his world completely shadowy again.

The following afternoon Eb was weeding in the front garden. Hepsie had taken him to a part of the flowerbed by the front wall and he was now kneeling on his garden cushion and digging up the weeds he could feel with his bare hands. He fingered the stems and leaves of the plants to guess whether they were weeds or garden flowers. Around him he could hear the buzzing of the bees as they sought nectar from the scented rose bushes growing along the front wall. He should have worn his hat because the midsummer sun was beating down upon his head. Why hadn't Hepsie thought of that? She'd gone out to the village shop, so he decided he would wait until her return instead of rummaging around in the house for it himself.

"Eb! Coo-eee!" Joan's voice shouted across from her garden.

He laid down the weed he had just pulled up and raised his head.

"Eb! Can you hear me?" she shouted.

He'd better acknowledge her.

Slowly, he raised his arm and waved in the direction where he knew she would be standing. There was the lane and Joan's own garden wall between them but this never stopped Joan from holding a conversation with him whilst he was situated in his own garden.

"How are you getting on?" she asked.

Eb knew what she meant but he decided to pretend otherwise. "The weeding's not too bad," he shouted across to her. "I'll soon have them cleared up." He smiled pleasantly, hoping Joan wouldn't pry any further.

Unfortunately, he heard her garden gate clicking open. Her footsteps patted across the lane towards where he was kneeling. Within a minute he sensed her standing on the other side of his garden wall.

"Sorry," she whispered, "I forgot to keep IT secret. So, how *are* you getting on? Is she talking to you?"

Eb heard Joan lean across the top of the garden wall. Her breath smelt of strong peppermint. He knew she liked to suck extra-strong mints whilst she was gardening.

"She hasn't said much," he lied. He certainly wasn't going to tell Joan that his grandmother believed her husband had killed her.

"But, at least, you've seen her again," Joan whispered. "You must get her to talk about herself and what Amberley was like in the Victorian era."

Eb smiled as pleasantly as he could.

"Well, she's a bit shy at the moment," he said. "I may have to wait sometime until she's more trusting of me."

"Oh, I quite understand," Joan whispered confidingly to him. "She is keen on fleeing."

There was a pause between them. Eb could smell the freshly mown grass in a neighbouring garden. He knew what was coming next.

Still whispering, Joan said: "Amberley Family History Group would so love to have any details of your conversations with your grandmother. You know, when

SHE is no longer a secret. You could even give a talk to the Family History Group. They would love that! There's going to be a lot of interest in your grandmother, which is sure to put the Family History Group and Amberley on the genealogical map. We can't miss it!

"You know what? I could get in touch with Radio Gloucestershire and arrange for them to do an interview with you – and Grandmother Zennor, if she promises not to flee. And there's South-West News and *The Stroud Herald*. You and your grandmother could do an awful lot for Amberley. We could raise funds for church repairs and all the other village amenities in—"

"Joan!" Eb said somewhat more crossly than he would normally speak to her. "Joan, please don't tell anyone yet about Zennor. You must keep her return secret until—" He broke off, trying to find the right words without giving away Zennor's – and his – problem. "—until I've spoken further with her. There's no need to hurry into other matters. We will only end up scaring her away. And we don't want that."

"It's Hepsie, isn't it?" Joan said, dropping her conspiratorial whispering. "She's still trying to convince you to hire an exorcist."

Eb wavered for a moment. He shouldn't really do this. But he was still unsure that he could trust Joan to keep quiet and not gossip to her many friends and associates in the village. She had too many prominent roles in Amberley's public and social committees and she was already straining against his gagging order.

"Yes," he lied. "It's funny how the young never see our point of view. Although, I'm sure Hepsie will come round to accepting her great-grandmother eventually. Maybe she's in shock. But for the meantime, you mustn't make Zennor public. In case Hepsie does carry out her exorcist threat. We don't want that, do we?"

"No," Joan agreed. "Should I have a chat with Hepsie? Try and make her see our point of view?"

"Oh, no!" Eb quickly replied. "She might be more compelled to hire an exorcist, if you advise her not to. We must tread carefully."

"Oh, dear," Joan sighed. "Well, do let me know if she changes her mind. And," – she lowered her voice to a conspiratorial whisper again – "if Grandmother Zennor has anything interesting to say to you."

Eb could imagine Joan's eyebrows arching with innuendo. The smell of peppermint moved away from him as he guessed she stood up from leaning across his garden wall. He was relieved when they said their goodbyes. Joan's disappointment might have momentarily sapped her gushing enthusiasm, but it was only a stopper to a champagne bottle whose cork was going to burst out and shower everyone with bubbling excitement. If only he could work out Zennor's problems before Joan made her first move. He supposed he'd been lucky Joan had given him a day's grace.

Feeling uncomfortable kneeling upright, he shifted himself on his garden cushion and bent back down to continue his weeding. He didn't believe that Hepsie would hire an exorcist now. Before and during their séance he'd been worried she might still do that and that was why he'd disagreed with Joan about making Zennor's return public. But there had been no more talk of exorcists from Hepsie. Indeed, they hadn't even discussed Zennor's recent return. Was this because neither of them wanted to give into the other? He had won but Hepsie had also changed her mind about hiring an exorcist. Eb guessed this was because she saw that her great-grandmother was human. And, like him, she was also intrigued by Zennor's reaction to Mike's question. Neither she nor himself liked to ask the other. They were afraid of rocking this boat that they had been tumultuously sailing in ever since he set out on his genealogical crusade.

Eb stabbed at the earth with his trowel, digging the dry soil away from the root of the weed he held in his other hand. Once he was certain the weed was less embedded, he yanked it out and flung it into a wicker basket by him. If only solving his family problems could be as easy for him as removing these unwanted weeds.

By Thursday, Eb was wishing he could hold another séance. Grandmother Zennor seemed to have fled Peace Cottage permanently. Sitting in the living room, he sipped at his morning coffee and felt the warm sunlight falling on his body through the open windows. Hepsie was upstairs and he could hear her creaking around on the floorboards. Or, at least, he thought it was her. He listened more acutely, his mug paused halfway to his mouth. The creaking became louder. Eb was certain it was not coming from upstairs. He was about to raise his mug to his lips when a light touch on his shoulder made him jolt and spill his coffee.

"Oh, I'm so sorry," Zennor cried out.

The hot liquid soaked through his shirt and stung his skin. But Eb didn't mind. He was so relieved to see Zennor.

She stood beside his armchair, in the same pale grey dress she'd worn before. Eb watched entranced, as the sunlight danced over her fair hair and gleaming silk dress. He experienced a moment of elation as he saw

283

a human face for the third time in less than a week. His grandmother reminded him of Hepsie. Not in her colouring, with her fair hair and pale blue eyes, but in her demeanour. Something about the shape of her face and the set of her mouth. Eb guessed Zennor could be as defiant as Hepsie. Her expression now, however, was full of contrition.

She wrung her hands and crumpled up the sides of her skirt.

"I didn't mean to do that, sir," she said. "Please don't ask me to go. Shall I get a cloth to dry you?"

"No, I'm fine, really. And please call me Eb." He would liked to have added "I'm your grandson" but he didn't want to upset her further.

He was still holding his wet mug in his right hand. As he reached out to place it on the side table next to him, Zennor grasped her hand around his and helped him lower his mug onto the drinks mat. Her hand was solid and didn't evaporate as she touched his skin. Quickly, she released her grasp before Eb could release his own fingers and touch her.

"Please sit down," he said, gesturing towards where he knew the sofa to be.

Zennor paused, turning to look at the sofa and then back at him. To his relief, she smoothed out her skirt and sat down opposite him.

He would liked to have asked her where she'd been these last two days. But he didn't think this would be wise, in case she fled again. Zennor looked as though she wanted to tell him something but was unsure of how she should. Both of them sat there, the ticking grandfather clock filling up the unspoken gaps between them. Eb watched Zennor as she glanced around the living room. She was unaware that he could see her. He wasn't going to tell her. She might not believe him.

He hadn't even told Hepsie. His daughter *certainly* wouldn't believe him. He was as isolated in his newly discovered secret as he was in his blindness. The grandfather clock struck the quarter-hour. Zennor glanced towards the open living-room door. An idea seemed to occur to her.

"I'm so glad, sir, that the grandfather clock still stands in the hall."

"Eb. Please call me Eb." He smiled encouragingly at her, hoping to gain her trust. "I didn't know the grandfather clock was originally part of Peace Cottage. I inherited it from my...er...Georgie, who inherited it from his sister Elsie. When we moved here it seemed natural that it should stand in the hall."

"The clock belonged to my parents-in-law and had been passed down throughout the years, from generation to generation. My husband George must have stood it in his hall at Stroud and – and—" Zennor stumbled with her words, as though the exact meaning of what she'd said, and what she was about to say, hit her with enormous implication. "And now," – she took a deep breath – "the clock is back at its rightful home, Peace Cottage, and belongs to you, Eb."

A warm glow suffused Eb's heart. She had called him by his name. The realisation had been enormous for her but he could tell she was beginning to slowly accept what had happened to her children. Maybe there would be a place in her life for him. Not as 'sir', but as Eb, her grandson.

"I shall listen to the grandfather clock's ticking with renewed delight, now that I know I am listening to the ticking of my ancestors," Eb said.

For the first time since he'd met her, Zennor smiled. "That clock was ticking away well before my father-in-law Ebenezer inherited it. My Elsie and Clara used to sit in front of the clock case and watch the pendulum swinging inside the glass lenticle. Their grandpapa would come along and watch with them, saying that they could never be considered Andersons until their eyes had been hypnotised by the clock's pendulum. His apparently had been. Hephzibah and I used to get cross and tell him off, saying he was making the children cross-eyed and that they would never be able to read properly. My dear father-in-law would shrug his shoulders and say 'What do you want with reading, anyway?'."

Eb nearly leapt out of his armchair. Here she was, his paternal grandmother, telling him about her past and that of his other ancestors. He must keep her speaking like this. If he made her relaxed enough, she might even tell him about George and why she believed he'd murdered her.

He chuckled in response to Zennor's depiction of his great-grandfather. "That's a delightful anecdote of past times at Peace Cottage. Is there anything else that has stayed the same?" He couldn't keep the tone of keen hopefulness out of his voice.

Zennor, however, looked pleased by his reaction. "The apple trees I saw from the kitchen window, when we were talking the other day. They're more bent and twisted than I'd remembered, but it was like looking at old friends again."

Eb nodded encouragingly.

Zennor smoothed down her skirt. She was sitting ramrod on the sofa, her retroussé nose twitching slightly with nerves. "Every early October Hephzibah and myself used to pick the apples and lay them in their russet rows upon sheets of newspaper in the attics. The frost wouldn't get at them there. But we had to be careful of the girls. They slept in the attics and wouldn't leave those dessert apples alone. Ashmead's

Kernels was the name. They grew all over Gloucestershire.

"Taking a bite of them was like taking a bite of Paradise."

"Yes, they still taste good," Eb told her. He recalled the apple's rich scent as he'd bitten into its slightly rough but pleasingly green-brown skin. The flesh was sharper and juicier than those shiny modern varieties Hepsie bought out-of-season from the supermarkets. He was glad he hadn't chopped down the apple trees. And, now, they were another link to his past and that of his grandmother's.

"When they are ripe on the trees again, you must come and help Hepsie and me eat them," he added.

If he'd expected Zennor to look delighted, he was disappointed. She seemed to be lost in her thoughts, his words hanging over her like unripe apples that she didn't want to pick. Instead, she said: "There were times when we were happy. Living at Peace Cottage was like how I imagined Paradise to be. We had everything we wanted. Family, home, a loving marriage and a place in the village community. But then our lives changed. Perhaps we took too many bites of Adam and Eve's apple. And in tasting the flesh of Paradise, we incurred the wrath of the God botherers." Zennor cast him an anxious look, as though gauging his reaction. Eb didn't blink. He didn't want her to stop talking. Was she about to tell him?

Zennor was silent for a minute. The *God botherers* hovered over them like vicious crows. She opened her mouth, as though she wanted to speak, but no sound came out. They sat in silence for another minute.

He must help her. Speaking gently, he said: "I'm pleased that you were once happy at Peace Cottage, but what went wrong?"

287

The smell of baking bread crept into the living room. He had made a batch of loaves this morning and they were rising in the oven, ready for him to turn out and test for hollowness before lunch. He was looking forward to feeling the hot bread in his hands and tearing off thick crusty chunks. Butter smothered over his slab would ooze oily and golden through the bread's flesh and melt in his mouth.

Zennor ignored his question. Instead, she suspiciously sniffed the enveloping aroma of baking bread. Her expression became more disconcerted. Eb thought he'd better explain.

"I bake bread," he told her.

She stared at him wide-eyed. Anxiously, she clutched at her skirt, bunching up the gleaming silk in her tight grasp. Still she didn't speak.

Believing that more chat from himself would make her feel more comfortable, Eb said: "We used to buy our bread from the local bakery – you know, the one on Bakery Hill – before it closed down." Seeing her look of surprise, he continued: "I believe it used to be the Dangerfield Bakery in your day. Your sister Ivy married the—" Eb broke off, as he suddenly remembered he wasn't supposed to be mentioning Neville Dangerfield.

"Who did Ivy marry?" Zennor asked.

She was looking at him in a very peculiar way. Eb didn't want to tell her. He knew she wouldn't like his response. The grandfather clock struck the half-hour. Taking a deep breath, he replied: "One of the Dangerfield bakers."

Zennor raised her eyebrows. He knew she'd guessed. They both sat there, the other knowing what the other one was thinking, but neither daring to say the name. Zennor's lower lip trembled. Tears sprung up in her pale blue eyes. She tried to stay seated on the sofa. But the word formed itself out of her mouth.

"No!" she shouted. And then she was gone.

Eb felt like crying. What was the problem with Neville Dangerfield? Why didn't his grandmother want her sister Ivy to be married to him? What should have been a genealogical dream was becoming a nightmare. He didn't like these unanswered questions.

Upstairs, Hepsie creaked on the floorboards. Although he could feel the warm June sun touching his body, he was back in darkness. Now that Zennor had gone, he couldn't see the sunlight gleaming on her silk dress – like he had once seen sunlight gleaming around him everywhere.

Hepsie. Maybe that what it was. Zennor's problems were too personal a matter to tell someone like him. His grandmother needed a woman's understanding. As a Victorian woman, she wouldn't want to confide in her grandson, particularly – as he guessed – these personal problems concerned herself and George. She needed to pour her troubles into another woman's ear. Maybe Hepsie could be this other woman and, doing what he couldn't do, coax Zennor to open up about herself. And, maybe, only then would he be able to find out why she believed his Grandfather George had murdered her.

The smell of baking bread was getting stronger. His kitchen timer would be bleeping soon. Eb felt his appetite diminishing. He must be careful baking bread again. He had never known the delicious aroma of baking bread to have such a devastating affect on anyone as it had on Zennor.

Sixteen

Hepsie stared up at the blue sky. She was lazing on Eb's favourite deckchair beneath the apple trees. A slight breeze shifted the leafy branches so that the fragments of blue sky changed shape. Eb's deckchair was an old-fashioned one, with a strong wooden frame and broad stripes, which he had found amongst Grandpa Georgie's possessions after Grandpa's death. Eb couldn't sit in it now because he had trouble getting up from the low-slung seat. Hepsie had propped up her head with a cushion from the living room and was very comfortable in her lazy position. Her arms hung over the sides of her deckchair, the long grass tickling her fingertips. She should be mowing the lawn, but after lunch she'd left Eb listening to his Audio Description TV – the one where the narrator irritatingly comments on every action, gesture and expression for the viewer – and dropped herself into this deckchair. On the grass beside her, also within easy reach of her fingers, was her mobile phone. Ever since Sunday's séance, Mike had been in touch with her.

Hepsie was surprised by this. After their successful séance, she'd thought she would be seeing less of Mike. There was no need for his genealogical services now that her and Eb's ancestor, Great-Granny Zennor, had returned to Peace Cottage and could tell them all about the past. Although, Hepsie was sure Mike would have been likely to have contacted Eb about what Great-Granny Zennor had to say. So she was really pleased when he'd texted her last Sunday evening and then, when she had called him back, they had joked about Joan's performance as a would-be spiritualist. Somehow, neither of them managed to mention genealogy. Hepsie thought this might be a one-off, but their subsequent conversations and text messages proved otherwise. Her heart beat loudly as she thought there must be more to Mike's behaviour towards her than merely obsessive genealogical interest.

His touch had been reassuring during Sunday's séance. If slightly embarrassing. At one point, she thought Joan was going to say something about how much she and Mike liked one another. Another reason to avoid Joan. She was relieved Sunday's séance was over. Mike had noticed she'd been nervous. He had squeezed her hand to make her feel calmer. Although, this didn't exactly help her to relax. In fact, the sensation of Mike's touch contributed to the adrenaline pulsating through her. At any moment, she thought their poltergeist was going to walk through the living-room door. She was sure Mike suspected something was wrong. And then he kept catching her looking at the living-room door. In the gloomy light of the living room she had also stolen a few glances in Mike's direction, nearly being caught out once when he'd opened his own eyes. At least he had taken her side against Joan and, particularly, during that uncomfortable moment when her ancestor had revealed that she'd written a letter requesting to meet them that day. Hepsie felt her cheeks flush hotly as she remembered what she'd said to justify her reasons for not telling them about Great-Granny Zennor's last letter. *Safety in numbers.* Did they really believe that? Of course, she couldn't lie and say she hadn't looked at her notebook because (1) Eb knew she had scanned the poltergeist's letters onto CD for him on Saturday and (2) Joan and Mike might ask to look at her notebook, which would be even worse. They didn't know she had thrown Zennor's final letter away. And no way must her own incoherent replies be seen. Seriously, for the first time Hepsie considered throwing away her notebook. It wouldn't be needed now, anyway. Great-Granny Zennor had returned and they wouldn't be exorcising her.

The smell of barbecuing sausages drifted across from a neighbouring garden. Hepsie closed her eyes and breathed in the delicious aroma of charcoaled meat. She could hear voices and imagined a family group or a party of children congregating around the barbecue fire, heated baps, fried onions and tomato ketchup at the ready. Beyond the uppermost branches of the apple trees a helicopter whirred into the distant blue, maybe on its way to fly across the River Severn. Hepsie pushed her head further back into her cushion and let the patches of warm sun coming through the gaps in the leafy branches dapple her body like dancing laser lights. She was just about to slip into an apple-scented dream when a familiar musical tinkle made her start up. Quickly, she reached out and fumbled for her mobile phone in the grass. She hoped it wasn't a text from Sally.

Relieved to see Mike's number, she read:

R U OK 2 MEET WEDS 8 PM?

MIKE :-)

Without thinking further, Hepsie replied:

OK. WHERE?

HEPSIE :-)

She laid back on her deckchair, clutching her mobile phone in her hand. She hoped Mike would reply quickly. She liked to think he was sitting at home in Cheltenham, as bored as she was. Maybe he was lying in the sun, too, thinking of better ways to spend his time and the things they could be doing together. She closed her eyes, waiting for the love call of her mobile phone to arouse her.

He had told her about *Kate*. Apparently, she had misunderstood him by thinking that *this* Kate was his girlfriend. Mike had explained that Kate was his aunt and an important person in his life – more like a big sister than an aunt to him. Kate had experienced problems recently and he was trying to help her out. He didn't say exactly what these problems were. Hepsie guessed that he wanted to tell her more but he was holding back. That was ok. It was none of her business, anyway, and she could always find out more later, after she and Mike had got to know one another better.

Someone was watching her. Hepsie heard the grass rustle beside her. A faint whiff of lavender and marjoram hovered in the air. She opened her eyes.

There she was. Standing beneath the apple trees, her dress as old as the bent and gnarled bark but her face as young as Hepsie's. Great-Granny Zennor was looking at her hesitantly. The filtering sun through the apple branches played over her honey-coloured hair and splashed patterns of light over her face and dress. She wasn't clutching at her long skirt this time but held her hands together composedly below her bodice. Hepsie blinked. It was like looking into a mirror image, except someone had dyed her hair and given her contact lenses to change her eye colouring. She even shared the same retroussé nose, delicately tip-tilted and with discreet nostrils so that no-one could consider her turned-up nose to be unattractive.

Eb had told her to be respectful towards her great-grandmother, but the woman standing before her was more like her sister. Hepsie had replied to Eb that she wasn't surprised he had given their ancestor Zennor a fright when he'd called her Grandmother. Particularly, when he looked more grandparent than thirty-two-year-old Zennor did. What he really meant was that she was not to call Great-Granny Zennor names, such as poltergeist. Well, of course, she wasn't going to do that. She could see that her great-grandmother was a very human person. That was why she hadn't hired an exorcist. She had believed their poltergeist might harm them, but she had also kept Great-Granny Zennor's final letter a secret from Eb because she didn't want him cancelling the séance and, therefore, Mike's visit. Eb had won. Their poltergeist was their relative and had been trying to get in touch with them.

However, it wasn't until Thursday lunchtime that she and Eb had broken their stubborn silence and discussed the return of their ancestor. Hepsie could see that her father was upset. When he asked her to do a favour for him, she agreed. There was also the problem of Joan. For reasons similar and dissimilar to Eb, she was dreading the arrival of Joan at their front door or telephoning them. Every time she walked along the lane outside Peace Cottage, she was sure she could feel Joan's curtains twitching as Joan watched from her upstairs windows. She hurried along, mindful that if Joan wasn't indoors, she might be in her garden. Hepsie was relieved Eb had taken her side on this matter. She guessed he had done so during the séance because he was afraid she might hire an exorcist if Joan made Great-Granny Zennor's return public. However, since his talks with his grandmother, he had become even less keen to let his meddling neighbour have her way. And, Hepsie had to admit, it was not only the fear of their ancestor becoming public that made her eager to help Eb. She was intrigued.

The problem was waiting for Great-Granny Zennor to appear. There was no way of knowing when she might suddenly decide to talk to you. Hepsie had hoped it wouldn't be at a most inconvenient moment for her, such as when she was taking a bath. How could she have a serious conversation with her great-grandmother like that? But, now, here was her great-grandmother, come to find her outside. Perhaps Great-Granny Zennor thought, too, that she needed to confide in another woman and tell her great-granddaughter what she couldn't tell her grandson Eb.

Hepsie smiled encouragingly. Seeing her great-grandmother still hesitating, she sat up and indicated towards the garden chair beside her that she'd placed there for Eb.

"Do feel free to sit with me," she said.

Great-Granny Zennor smiled back politely. She glanced at the comfortable garden chair, with its padded back and seat, before slightly lifting up her long skirt and perching, ramrod, on the edge of the chair. With the breeze gently stirring the wisps of hair framing her face, she folded her hands in her lap.

Hepsie wondered what she could say to make her great-grandmother talk openly about her past. She was aware of having to proceed carefully in case she upset her great-grandmother and scared her away. Eb would never forgive her for that. A hedge cutter revved into action in the distance. Its harsh hum continued to disturb the rural tranquillity of Peace Cottage's garden.

"Are there mills nearby?" Great-Granny Zennor asked.

"Mills?" Hepsie was puzzled as to why her great-grandmother had asked her this.

"Yes. There were never working mills by Peace Cottage when I lived here, but I'm sure that I can hear machinery."

"Oh, that's a hedge cutter," Hepsie explained. There were going to be lots of things that her great-grandmother wouldn't know about. She probably hadn't even seen a telephone.

"That young man, who was with you in the front parlour on Sunday, is he a hedge cutter?"

Hepsie tried not to show that she was momentarily surprised by Great-Granny Zennor's reference to Mike. My God! Had her great-grandmother noticed, too? Was nothing secret in Amberley? A slow blush tingled through her cheeks, as she replied: "Mike? Oh, no, he's not a hedge cutter. That's the name of the machine."

Great-Granny Zennor stared back at her uncomprehendingly. "Does he work in the fields, then?"

"No."

Hepsie wondered why her great-grandmother was curious to know what Mike did. Then she remembered how Great-Granny Zennor had reacted to Mike's question during Sunday's séance. Of course, her great-grandmother was still upset about Mike's reference to Neville Dangerfield. Mike, in his genealogical fanaticism, had stepped on Great-Granny Zennor's wounded pride just like she had done by calling her great-grandmother a poltergeist. But his genealogical instincts had been proved right. If only she could get Great-Granny Zennor to open up about herself and tell them what had gone wrong.

"Look, I'm sorry about Mike's behaviour on Sunday, but he really didn't mean to upset you. Honest." Hepsie gave her great-grandmother what she hoped was a reassuring look.

"Is this...*this* Mike local?" Great-Granny Zennor asked falteringly.

"No. He's from Cheltenham." Hepsie had tried to say this as dismissively as possible, but her great-grandmother's constant attention on Mike made her more self-conscious. She should steer the conversation away from him.

Taking the plunge, she asked: "Was Neville Dangerfield one of those God botherers?"

Great-Granny Zennor looked surprised.

Hepsie waited anxiously, hoping her great-grandmother wouldn't become upset and flee. Eb had told her about Great-Granny Zennor's dislike of these *God botherers* in the village. He'd thought his grandmother hated the mention of Neville Dangerfield because the local baker was a God botherer. And that was why his grandmother was so upset by her younger sister Ivy's marriage to the baker. Hepsie knew they could ask Joan and her Amberley Family History Group for further information, but that wouldn't be wise. Joan would want to know why they were interested and if it was something to do with Great-Granny Zennor's chats to them about her past. Hepsie had no choice but to ask her great-grandmother directly.

"Not him."

Great-Granny Zennor's words came as a surprise. This must have shown in Hepsie's face, for her great-grandmother added: "The Dangerfields weren't Chapel people. Neville Dangerfield was a childhood friend of my husband George. They were good friends until…" She bit her lower lip, as though she shouldn't be saying any more.

The hedge cutter came to an abrupt stop in the distance. Hepsie could hear the chatting of her neighbour's guests. The smell of barbecuing sausages whetted her appetite. Could she ask her great-grandmother any more? The gentle breeze continued to stir the wisps of fine hair around Great-Granny Zennor's face. Hepsie felt she was looking at her sister. Didn't sisters like to share secrets? Eb was right. A woman's understanding might encourage her sisterly great-grandmother to talk. She was about speak when Great-Granny Zennor hesitantly asked: "Did Ivy and Neville have any children?"

Great-Granny Zennor's pale blue eyes were lowered, concentrating on her fidgeting fingers. Hepsie tried to think whether Mike's family tree of the Mills family contained any references to children born to Ivy and Neville Dangerfield, but she couldn't remember. Why hadn't she paid more notice to these matters? Lying, she replied: "I believe so." And then, feeling this wasn't adequate enough, added: "Mike's given us your family tree. If you like, I can double-check on there."

Great-Granny Zennor glanced up. Her eyes were wet. "How could he?" she asked, her voice full of hurt.

Hepsie was at a lost as to what to say. Was her great-grandmother referring to Mike or to Neville Dangerfield? If she said either name, would her great-grandmother flee? Great-Granny Zennor had turned away from her and was now looking towards the back of Peace Cottage. Her attention seemed to be focussed on the utility-room extension. Particularly, the back door. As though she was expecting someone to open it and come out into the garden. Was she afraid Eb was about to join them? But why should that scare her? Eb was not an unkind person. He'd been doing everything to encourage his grandmother, to make her feel welcomed. What was wrong?

Hepsie watched helplessly as her great-grandmother clutched her long skirt. Great-Granny Zennor turned back towards the apple trees. Hepsie followed her great-grandmother's pale blue eyes as they gazed around the garden, taking in the garage and Eb's former office overlooking the Common, the old garden shed by the elderflower bushes and, lastly, the remains of a rusty pump poking out of one of Eb's flowerbeds. She kept quiet as her great-grandmother's gaze lingered over the rusty pump. She wanted to ask one more question. But could she dare? Somehow there had to be some reason why Great-Granny Zennor believed her husband George had murdered her. And Hepsie thought she was beginning to guess why. If she didn't ask Great-Granny Zennor now, she may not have another chance.

"Did you fancy Neville Dangerfield?"

Great-Granny Zennor quickly turned to look at her. Hepsie sat awkwardly as her great-grandmother's eyes widened with terror.

"I'm sorry..." she begun to say, but Great-Granny Zennor's hand gripped the shiny grey folds of her skirt even more tightly.

Hepsie closed her eyes and breathed in deeply. When she reopened them, Great-Granny Zennor had gone.

Damn it!

Eb would not be pleased. Hepsie dropped back into

her deckchair, her head thumping against the cushion. She was still holding her mobile phone in her hand. The phone's metal case was hot and clammy. When she glanced at the screen, she saw that Mike still hadn't replied to her. What was he doing? She would have liked to have confided in him but Eb had told her not to tell Mike anything about Great-Granny Zennor's chats with them. Surprisingly, Mike hadn't asked. But Eb believed Mike would be less likely to make Great-Granny Zennor public if he knew less about her. She hadn't told him that Mike had been in regular contact with her ever since Sunday's séance. But as she had been careful to avoid genealogical shoptalk with Mike and he hadn't asked – even about obtaining copies of Great-Granny Zennor's poltergeist letters – she had seen no reason to do so. Couldn't she enjoy Mike by herself, now that he wasn't genealogically needed?

It was five weeks to the day since she'd first met Mike. Hepsie gazed up at the branches of budding fruit above her. Eb had told her the apples were Ashmead's Kernels. Her great-grandmother would have bitten into the soft flesh of the fruit over a century ago. Great-Granny Zennor was like her. Both their full lives had been cut off, although Hepsie was thankfully still alive. She had lost her independence and freedom and Great-Granny Zennor had lost her family and home. But what part did Neville Dangerfield have to play in all this? The thought that her Victorian great-grandmother might have had an interesting love life whilst she, the modern woman, languished at home, made Hepsie more determined to stoke up her relationship with Mike. Why should she miss out on a chance of excitement just because she'd made an error of judgement and exchanged her former independent life for a dutiful daughter's one?

Wednesday. The Cross Hands was quiet. Outside, the rain splattered on the empty garden tables and chairs. Hepsie was sitting at a small round table in a secluded corner of the pub. Mike was ordering their drinks at the bar. She checked her mobile phone but there were no more text messages from Sally. She had told Sally about Mike's recent contact but not about their séance and Great-Granny Zennor's return. Explaining to Sally everything that had happened to her and Eb during the last fortnight would have been too complicated. Anyway, Sally might not believe her. There was also the need to keep Great-Granny Zennor's return as secret as possible in case Sally – like Joan and Mike – felt the urge to gossip and inadvertently made the poor woman public before they had sorted out her problems. That was why she had told Sally about Mike. Sally had guessed something was happening because Hepsie had been ignoring her text messages. Instead of lying and saying: "Oh, nothing much, it's the same old boring life", Hepsie had thought it better to explain her silence by using Mike as an excuse.

Sally had joked about Mike.

"You've got to love the whole man, Hepsie. You can't change him."

"I know, Sally."

"If you don't accept his genealogy, it won't work for you both."

"He's cut back on it."

"It's still somewhere within him, Hepsie. You'd better take a course in genealogy. He'll revert to type as soon as he's got you."

What Sally didn't know, was that she was being used as an excuse, too. Hepsie had told Eb that she was meeting Sally at one of their regular pubs in Stroud. Eb had looked disbelieving, as though he had guessed. But he didn't challenge her. She wanted to keep her meeting with Mike secret, not only because she knew Eb didn't want Mike asking her about Great-Granny Zennor, but because she also didn't want anyone they knew seeing her in the pub with Mike. That's why she had persuaded Mike to meet her at the Cross Hands, on the Painswick Road between Stroud and Cheltenham. He had readily agreed. There was no point in her driving all the way to Cheltenham, as she had first suggested; he said it was fairer if he met her half-way. Hepsie had got the impression that Mike wasn't willing to meet up in a pub that he knew, too. The Cross Hands was ideal. And the weather was on their side. The rain was keeping people at home. Apart from a few regulars at the bar and a couple at another table, she and Mike were the only other drinkers. She hoped it would stay that way. The first of July might be wet and dismal, but she saw the new month as a new start for her.

Mike turned round from the bar and smiled at her. He paid the bartender and brought their drinks over to her. Gratefully, she took her glass of medium-dry white wine from him. Mike sat down and sipped from his pint of lager. They would have to limit themselves to one drink each. Hepsie hoped they would manage to last the whole evening until the pub closed. If there was plenty to say, then she suspected they wouldn't even need to order a soft drink. She smiled back at him. There was low music playing from overhead speakers. Mike was dressed casually in jeans and T-shirt. She opened a packet of crisps he'd also brought over and put it on the table between them. As she reached out to take a crisp, Mike did likewise. Their fingers touched for a moment but, unlike at the séance, she felt free to keep her hand close to his.

If she had been worried that Mike would shoptalk genealogy all evening, or reveal his true intentions weren't concerned with their mutual attraction but with finding out about Great-Granny Zennor, then she was extremely relieved. What did they talk about? Their drinks remained almost untouched as they discussed films, TV, the political state of the country and travel. Mike was very interested to know that she'd been to Africa, India and South America. He said he'd missed out on seeing the world. Hepsie wished she could show him these new places. She imagined exploring the world with Mike would be fun. He didn't say much about his private life. Or work. She didn't say much about hers. Both their thoughts wanted to stray away from home and family concerns.

Occasionally, Hepsie remembered to look over Mike's shoulders and glance around the pub. She couldn't see anyone she knew. She also felt that, unlike Amberley, there was no one here gossiping behind her back or giving her sidelong looks. Recently, every time she had gone to Amberley Post Office or walked in the village, she had kept her eyes and ears opened in case Joan had broken her promise and gossiped about Great-Granny Zennor's return. Her neighbour had been unusually quiet ever since speaking to Eb over a week ago. What was Joan up to? Hepsie inwardly shuddered at the thought of the chaos Joan was sure to create once the news of Great-Granny Zennor's return became public. Eb's genealogy would be blown out of all proportion and she would never be free of it, or of Joan, or of Amberley. Unusually for him, Hepsie could see Eb never speaking to Joan again. If only Great-Granny Zennor would reappear. Her great-grandmother hadn't been seen since last Saturday. She and Eb were wondering what they were going to say to Joan in order to scare her away without her reneging on her promise – if she hadn't done so already.

Mike smiled broadly at her as he picked up his glass to take a sip. The lighting was dim in the pub but his pale green eyes radiated enough glowing intensity as to be noticeable. Hepsie wondered how their evening was going to end. She would have liked to have gone somewhere else with Mike, but she knew Eb was expecting her back home as soon as the pubs closed. Sally didn't go nightclubbing during the week, especially on a quiet Wednesday. Eb would be worried, even if she made up some other excuse, such as her car breaking down. No, let her enjoy the moment whilst she could. There might well be others. Hepsie was about to take a sip from her own glass, when she noticed the startled look on Mike's face.

His pint glass was raised half-way to his mouth, as though he'd forgotten it was in his hand. She looked over to where he was looking. A woman was standing at another table not far from them. Hepsie smiled at her, hoping this woman would stop staring at them and get on with her own business. The young woman – she looked about the same age as themselves – smiled back. Surprisingly, there was a triumphant flicker in the woman's large brown eyes. Hepsie turned her gaze back to Mike. He had resumed his normal cheerful expression. She was about to say how strange it was for the woman to stare at them like that, when a female voice interjected: "Hello, Mike. I didn't expect to see you here."

Mike forced his wide lips into a welcoming smile. Hepsie turned her gaze towards the voice. The young woman from the other table was now standing next to theirs. She was taller than Hepsie and her slim frame was encased in skinny jeans and a low-cut red top. Her 'bling' jewellery was almost as shiny as her dyed blonde hair. Surely Mike didn't know anyone like that? The woman's make-up was perfectly applied, attractively enlarging her already large brown eyes. She fluttered her long mascara-clad lashes at Mike, as though she knew what power she had over him.

"I didn't think I would see you here," Mike amiably retorted.

The woman smiled knowingly at him.

"Well, aren't you going to introduce me?" She glanced sideways at Hepsie.

"Er, Hepsie...this is Selina. She's an old friend of mine."

Hepsie couldn't help raising her eyebrows in surprise. She smiled tightly at the other woman. Neither of them said a word.

Mike shifted uncomfortably in his seat. Hepsie could tell that he didn't seem too happy that she had met...his ex?

Selina was looking her up and down. Hepsie felt her clothes and body being appraised – critically. She was in no doubt that Selina saw her as shorter, plumper, and less beautiful in her bootleg jeans and Indian-print smock top. Hepsie hated her retroussé nose and – even though she had powdered it – her mole. She could see Selina thought she wasn't good enough for Mike.

"So, how did you two meet?" Selina's girlish voice enunciated her words insinuatingly.

"In a pub," Hepsie replied as Mike simultaneously said: "In a nightclub."

Selina smiled slyly from one of them to the other.

Why did Mike say that? Hepsie knew why she had lied. No way was Mike's ex-girlfriend going to find out about her genealogical connection to Mike and Eb's part in it. She imagined Selina would make her feel so embarrassed. But she had no idea why Mike had covered up his genealogical association with her and Eb. Was he embarrassed by his connection to them? Did he think his 'old friend' Selina would laugh at him for befriending an old blind man and his strange daughter?

"I think it was a pub," Hepsie began to say. "You were—"

"Of course!" Mike exclaimed.

"You were—"

"Well, it's a small world, meeting you here, too, Selina." Mike smiled at his ex. "Are you on your way to somewhere else?"

"No."

Hepsie thought she saw an uneasy flicker in Mike's pale green eyes.

"Are you with someone?" she asked.

"A friend." Selina paused. And then looking directly at Mike, added: "He's at the bar."

Hepsie scowled. Was there something still going on between these two? She didn't think Selina was the type to have a relationship with a fanatical genealogist. She couldn't imagine them curling up together in the evenings and having cosy chats about genealogy. Unfortunately, now was not the time to ask Selina about this. *Are you interested in genealogy, too? Is that how you met Mike?* If Mike really was a genealogist. Hepsie was having doubts. And not for the first time. Surely Mike would want to open out about his genealogical interest in front of Selina, who obviously knew him well?

Maybe there was another problem. Herself. She wasn't Mike's type. She had been deluding herself these past five weeks. Mike was trying to cut her off when she'd spoken about meeting him in a pub because he was afraid that Selina might be scared away if she thought something was going on between him and Hepsie. And why would Mike not want this? Because he was still attracted to Selina.

Hepsie felt her mole twitching on the bridge on her nose. Selina turned her gaze towards her.

"Mike and I shared a flat in Cheltenham," she said. "I would have liked him to move into my new one, but there was a slight problem." She waited for Hepsie's reaction.

The music played above them from the sound speakers. Hepsie clenched her mouth firmly shut. She gazed back at Selina as though nothing Selina had said could mean anything to her.

Selina wasn't pleased by this. She flicked her shoulder-length blonde hair with her manicured hand. She turned to Mike, who was gazing steadfastly at his lager glass. "Why don't you come over sometime and have a look at it?"

Mike looked up, a slow blush suffusing his cheeks. "Yeah, why not?" he replied.

Hepsie's self-confidence plummeted to her feet. She could almost feel her flip-flops – her best gold sequinned pair with two-inch wedges – curl up in disgust. She had to get out of here. How could *this*...Selina insinuate that she and Mike were still an item? That Mike could fancy her and that no-one else – least of all, a boring brunette, stay-at-home dutiful daughter like Hepsie – could fancy him?

"I've got to go," she suddenly said.

Mike looked at her in surprise. She picked up her handbag. Selina stood aside to allow her to get up from their table. Was it her imagination, but was there a flicker of disappointment in Mike's pale green eyes?

Ignoring this, as though it didn't matter what Mike felt, Hepsie gave Selina a tight smile as she passed by. Mike's blonde ex smiled back, her triumph lingering over her full lips.

"Goodbye," Mike called out as she walked away from their table. "Hope we'll meet again."

What did he mean by that? *Hope we'll meet again* sounded so casual – like he had only just met her in a pub for the first time. Didn't their text messages and phone conversations mean anything to him?

"Yeah," Hepsie replied, not bothering to look back. "See you!" As coolly as she could, she walked towards the pub door and slammed it shut behind her.

Outside, the air was fresh and cooling. Hepsie stood on the doorstep for a moment, letting the rain fall on her upturned face whilst she breathed in the damp wetness. The raindrops dribbled down her face like tears. She shook her head, trying to shake them off, but they dribbled down even faster. Glancing at her watch, she saw with sickening disappointment that it wasn't even 9.30 yet. What was she going to do? Eb wasn't expecting her back until late. Despite the rain mist over the hills, it was still light enough to drive without full car headlights. But how could she sit alone in her car when she had intended to spend the rest of her evening with...Mike? She couldn't help smiling cynically as she thought of how Selina's 'friend' might not like the presence of Mike in their cosy twosome. She had better get away from the Cross Hands before further trouble broke out.

Walking back to her car, she thought of Great-Granny Zennor and their conversation last Saturday. Her great-grandmother was as upset about Neville Dangerfield as she was about Mike. Didn't the course of true love ever run smoothly? Although, she was assuming that Neville Dangerfield had been Great-Granny Zennor's lover. Her great-grandmother hadn't actually given her an answer. Or, at least, a spoken answer. Hepsie wished she could find out more, particularly after her own embarrassing troubles this evening. First it was *Kate*; now it was *Selina*. Why was Mike being so thoughtless with her feelings? Sometimes, she didn't understand men. And she wondered whether Great-Granny Zennor thought the same.

Seventeen

Amberley 1892

He was walking along the track towards her. That was when she first saw him. Zennor was holding Elsie and Clara's hands as they walked between the swathes of wild garlic and bluebells in the beech copse. She was taking them to the village shops. The May sun shone through the gaps in the tall beech trees above them. But there was still a cool nip in the fresh breeze that shook the pale yellow catkins and made them flutter down to the ground. She had looked up because she had heard whistling. Melodic, sonorous whistling, that came from a strong, robust man. He was casually strolling towards them, with his big basket swinging manfully in his grasp. She knew who he was. George had told her. Neville Dangerfield had returned home to the Dangerfield Bakery after serving as a soldier. 'There'd been no wars', George had said and so, when old Mr Dangerfield had died, his youngest son Neville had returned home to help his two older brothers run the family bakery. George knew this because he'd been Neville's childhood friend, when they used to play 'soldiers' on the grassy slopes of the Bulwarks and prehistoric hill fort on the Common. And now Neville was on his way back from his early morning bakery round.

Birdsong joined in with his whistling as he approached her and the girls. Zennor slowed down, wondering how they were going to pass one another on the narrow track. Elsie and Clara had stopped chattering and were looking up at the Dangerfield baker with curiosity. Zennor blushed. She didn't know why. Maidenhood had long since left her and she *was* the mother of two young children. She should be safe, meeting a male stranger in the copse. Indeed, for George's sake, she should show the Dangerfield baker respect. She glanced up at him. He was taller than George, and broader. His dark brown corduroy suit was crumpled, like her father-in-law Ebenezer's, but he wore a bright red 'kerchief knotted around his muscular neck and a flat cap over his auburn curls. Flour lightly dusted parts of his corduroy suit and heavy hobnailed boots. He smiled at her in greeting. A broad, congenial smile. Standing aside to let her and the girls pass, he touched his forelock in respect.

He was making her feel like a lady. Zennor nodded back. She allowed her eyes to meet his. They interlocked for a second. She felt herself lifted off her feet. No, don't be stupid! The sunlight piercing through the beech trees spun around her. She smiled back at him. His auburn curls, peeking out from his cap, glowed ruby rich as they caught the strands of sunlight. She could have spoken to him. *I'm George's wife. How do you do?* There was a proper, social connection between them. But she walked passed him, her young daughters' hands tight in hers. As they walked along the track where he had only just trodden, she was conscious of his eyes following her along the

311

sinewy path between the swathes of bluebells and heavily scented wild garlic.

For weeks afterwards she couldn't stop thinking about Neville Dangerfield. They seemed to meet more often during their daily business around Amberley. At first they would merely smile at one another, or nod their heads in greeting, as they passed by the Post Office, or walked across the Common, or ambled through the sloping beech copses. Zennor half-expected to see the Dangerfield baker on these trips around the village. She became more conscious of her appearances: biting her lips to make them redder, tying an extra ribbon in her hair, and smoothing down the folds of her worn workday skirt. She didn't see anything wrong in what she was doing. Neville Dangerfield was, after all, George's friend and she was doing her husband good by putting on her best appearances and respecting his old school friend.

When Neville did speak to her, it was a shock.

"Good day, Ma'm," he said, courtesy filling every syllable of his rich, baritone voice.

She was too shocked to reply. His words echoed in her head like the pealing of a booming bell. She walked on by, conscious of his gaze upon her.

Afterwards, she thought how rude she was and how she must say something to him the next time they met, so that he wouldn't think George's wife was scaring him away. That opportunity, of course, was not too far in the future.

The next day, Zennor encountered the Dangerfield baker traversing the track by the Parochial School. The weather was warm and he was not wearing his thick corduroy jacket. He smiled in greeting. Zennor blushed. But she managed to say "Good day to you" as she passed by. His eyes flashed fire. Or, was it only the June sun dazzling his sight? The moment passed. She couldn't turn back to look. She hoped they would be able to speak next time they met.

By July they had progressed to exchanging pleasantries. The Dangerfield baker would doff his cap. Zennor could smell the hot, fresh bread in his basket as they spoke. She made sure she wore a flower in her buttonhole. This was for George's sake. She was putting on a good show for him. Despite the clamouring thoughts at the back of her mind, she couldn't see any harm in what she and the Dangerfield baker were doing. She was happily married to George and, having reached that stationary world at the centre of her heart – the one she'd always been looking for, particularly ever since her favourite brother and confidant Charlie died – she was not looking to change her life. By the end of July, Neville Dangerfield was delivering bread to Peace Cottage. Zennor made sure she was there to answer the door. His bodily strength forced itself out through the constraints of his rough linen shirt as he stood in the doorway holding his heavy basket of steaming bread.

She was amazed at how easy it was for them to speak to one another. Was this because he was George's friend? Yes, Neville Dangerfield was George's childhood friend and he had no more intention of stepping over his social demarcation than she had. Zennor considered he understood this. The Dangerfield baker was George's friend and she was George's wife and that was the bond between them. That was why they got on so well. And enjoyed one another's company. Even George said how pleased he was that she never scared away his village friends and associates. Yes, she reflected well on her husband. George could convene at the Blackwell Reading Room for his Working Men's Club evenings without losing face. In the meanwhile, she

313

could enjoy their Sunday Holy Trinity church services, in the knowledge that if she happened to glance up, she would catch Neville looking at her, seeing whether she was all right. She would smile back, pleased that she could acknowledge his presence.

However, the village thought otherwise.

Zennor first noticed the gossiping behind her back and the villagers' telling stares sometime in August, when the sun was high in the sky above the broad, sweeping Common. At first, she wondered what was wrong. Was her dress not quite right? Perhaps she should ask George for a new length of fabric to make into another day dress. Had she given Mr Clutterbuck the right change last Saturday when she'd bought their joint for the Sunday roast? Was the Anderson family behind in paying their credit to the shoemaker? She didn't think they were. Zennor was going to ask her mother-in-law Hephzibah, but she procrastinated. There had been no change in Hephzibah's demeanour towards her daughter-in-law, and Zennor wondered whether she had imagined the villagers' change in attitude towards her.

She continued to smile at her neighbours and the associates she met whilst doing her daily business in Amberley. But they began to reciprocate even less cordially. A pert nod of the head or, worse, hurrying on by, as though they hadn't seen her. Any spoken exchanges were cursory, smiles tight. The villagers kept their distance and briefly spoke to her as though she was the new girl in the village, again. A stranger, once more. She would enter a shop and the premises would immediately fall silent. Clutching her girls' hands, or her basket handle, Zennor would smile back graciously, wondering when she would be included in Amberley's latest secret.

314

Not once did she think she was being treated like this because of her association with the Dangerfield baker. At least, no one told her so. Why couldn't Neville Dangerfield, beside her husband, be her good friend? She'd been, after all, Charlie's confidant. And Neville Dangerfield was behaving as though nothing had changed. He betrayed no signs of uneasiness, that the villagers might be gossiping about him and his acquaintance, Mrs George Anderson. There must be nothing in the villagers' gossip. She must take her cue from him.

Village gossip soon reached George. She knew about it one evening in early September when she was in the scullery. Ebenezer must have spoken to George – maybe a client dropped a hint when he or she came to collect their mended umbrella from Ebenezer's workshop. Or, maybe one of Hephzibah's friends had told her. Anyway, Zennor knew it was bad, because George had not removed his jacket or cravat, as he might have done if they'd been alone after supper. Elsie and Clara were in bed and Ebenezer and Hephzibah were resting in the front parlour. Zennor was washing up the crockery and utensils from supper. Her lower arms were immersed in suds as she scoured a pan with a brush made by her father-in-law. The steam from the heated water had flushed her cheeks fiery red, but she reddened even more when she saw the look on George's face. Usually, after supper, they could enjoy some time together, when George was more relaxed from his long day's work at Davis & Co. and the family were out of the way. But this evening, Zennor could see from the mistrustful look in George's brown eyes, that he was in no mood for kisses and cuddles. She left off scouring and wiped her hands on her long apron.

"This has got to stop, Zennor."

"What has?"

George was standing by the scullery door. His thumb was tucked into his lower waistcoat pocket, as his father's generation liked to pose, making him look more authoritarian and, in no doubt, that he intended serious business.

"You're giving the family a bad name."

Zennor fidgeted with the strings of her long apron. Her fingertips were puckered from their soaking in hot water. She decided to be truthful with George. As best as she could. Maybe he could tell her what was wrong.

"It's the gossips, isn't it?" she ventured.

George swallowed hard before telling her. He didn't look hurt. But his voice dipped and rose as he explained.

"How can they think that?" she protested. "There's nothing going on between me and Neville. He's your childhood friend and I'm your wife and that's the relationship between us. Nothing more. I promise you."

She gazed directly at George's brown eyes. She so wanted him to believe her. He didn't flinch but there was no love in his eyes.

"I thought our friendship would be a good reflection on yourself," she added, hoping to appease him.

George was silent.

His silence unloosened her tongue like unravelling apron strings freed from their tight bow around a waist.

"I didn't know the villagers were gossiping about me because of my association with…I thought they understood." Zennor wrung her hands on her long apron. "Can't we stop the gossip? There must be something that can be done. Perhaps you could speak to them. Make them stop. Can you do that? I'm sure they'll listen. Tell them what I've just told you. Surely, they'll understand that. And stop their horrid..." She could barely get the word out. She looked at George pleadingly. "You know...*insinuations*," she whispered. Clasping her hands in front of her, she continued: "I love no one more than you George – and we've been happy here, haven't we? – here, in Paradise? – where you've given me a home and a family I can call my own...?"

George was shaking his head. "It's no good, Zennor. They're never going to listen to us. These village people are stuck in their ways. They can't be told. When we move to Stroud, after Mr Davis's death, life will be better for us. We'll get away from this narrow community and embrace a new world. You'll find yourself happier there."

No, I won't, Zennor thought. She didn't want to move away from Amberley, from her parents-in-law's house, Peace Cottage, where she had found what she thought was paradise. George didn't understand this. When they had first met, in their early courtship days, he had thought she would have been happier living in Stroud, where she worked, than in a backward place like Amberley. But since moving to Peace Cottage, he had discovered she was not like that. He knew she was reluctant to move to Stroud, particularly more so the longer she lived at Peace Cottage.

However, now was not the time to be arguing about moving to Stroud. George's proprietor, Mr Davis, was in good health, anyway, and their move to Stroud, to live over the draper's shop, wouldn't happen for a long time. Zennor didn't want to think about leaving Hephzibah and Ebenezer, and Peace Cottage, with its apple trees and loudly ticking grandfather clock, and the swallows swooping high above the broad, open

317

Common. Through the open back door she could see up the sloping grassy bank to the heavily laden apple trees, full of the promise of another year's reaping. Not knowing what to say to George, she kept mute.

"You'll have to break it off."

George's voice was as resolute as the look in his eyes.

Break it off? There and then, she knew she would find this difficult to do. She didn't want to relinquish her...or limit her daily acquaintanceship with Neville Dangerfield. Why should she be put in the wrong?

Defiantly, she said: "There's nothing to worry about. I won't break it off with him. If I do, the villagers will only think there was something going on between us, when there isn't. They'll be putting us in the wrong, when they've no right to." She paused, expecting George to contradict her. He remained tight-lipped. Looping up her desperation like a dropped stitch, she added: "Why don't you ask Neville yourself? He'll tell you nothing's going on."

George blanched. He shook his head. "I couldn't possibly do that. We may both be of humble birth, but in our manners we are gentlemen. I would be dishonouring our friendship by breaching this matter with him. He'll know, anyway. And, if he does, he'll be gentleman enough to curtail the villagers' maliciously wagging tongues." He stared back at Zennor. "I don't know why Neville Dangerfield returned to Amberley. He had a chance to be free. He was out in the world, away from this narrow village community. I was surprised he'd returned. But I suppose he's as much bound by the ties of family tradition as many of us are, here, in Amberley."

Zennor was left in no doubt by what her husband meant. *We must leave Peace Cottage. I am waiting to do so.* What could she say in response? For a flittering moment, she wished that the auburn-haired baker was her husband, and not the dapper man with a smart suit and neat moustache standing before her. She lowered her eyes, hoping George couldn't read her thoughts.

Seeing her reluctance to speak, George continued: "You will do this for me, won't you, Zennor? And for Papa and Mama? And," – here, his voice dipped – "for the girls? The village won't reconsider. I know – I understand them. You'll be best to act accordingly."

Zennor nodded in return. She dared to raise her eyes from the worn flagstones and meet her husband's gaze. The mistrustfulness in his honest brown eyes had been replaced not by love – as she would have hoped – but by a restless anxiety. He cared too much. She smiled back weakly. Did he take this as a sign of her acceptance?

She didn't know. He walked out of the scullery, without even looking back over his shoulder at her.

The following morning she accepted her daily loaf from Neville Dangerfield. He delivered early. She was up, ready for him, lighting the fire before George came down to shave and trim his moustache in the scullery mirror. Neville gave her a bunch of flowers. Fresh flowers he'd picked from the Common. Yellow and red Lady's Slipper, deep blue Milkwort, yellow Rock Rose, sweet scented purple Wild Thyme, nodding pale blue Harebells, and pink Field Scabious. She brought the flowers to her nose and sniffed them, gratefully. George had once picked flowers for her. He used to bring a bunch back home from his walk up Culver Hill from Woodchester Station. Did she remember his words from yesterday? Neville betrayed nothing more than his like of her. And she was glad of this. She didn't cancel their bread delivery. Was she thinking of doing so? As he walked back down the front garden path, Neville whistled the same tune she'd heard him melodiously whistling that first time they'd met in the beech copse.

One late afternoon in October, before the beech leaves had turned from pale yellow to rust, Zennor was sitting in front of her dressing-table mirror. She was looking at some pressed flowers she had concealed in a handkerchief. These had been pressed between the pages of her childhood prayer book, which she was keeping at the back of her lower dressing-table drawer for when Elsie would need it. Zennor fingered the strands of Wild Thyme, still sweetly scented and unfaded in their purple colouring. She stroked the soft pink heads of the Field Scabious. The nodding Harebells and wiry stemmed Milkwort had perished soon after Neville gave her the bunch of Common flowers. He hadn't given her another bunch. She was looking at these treasured stems whilst Hephzibah was downstairs and before George came home from Stroud.

Elsie and Clara's shouts rose up from the garden below her bedroom window. Zennor looked up. It had been a warm, sunny October afternoon and she had left her bedroom window ajar. The girls were shouting gleefully and giggling as they ran about the front garden. Soon she would have to put them to bed. She was looking forward to reading to them before her supper. Elsie had started at the newly built Parochial School last month, and Zennor was keen for her daughter to learn as much as she could. She wanted her children to enjoy reading, so that one day they could be the school assistant – or, even better, the head teacher – that her Pa had never allowed her to be. Zennor glanced at herself in the mirror.

She was proud to be a mother. Nothing had given

her more hope in her life than her children. They needed her. Elsie, with her floppy bow constantly falling out of her fine hair, and two-year-old Clara, with her stumbling toddler's legs, were depending upon their mother's help and love. And, Zennor suddenly realised, not only for now. In the years to come, little Elsie and Clara would still be depending upon her guidance, even when they were grown-up women, with lives and families of their own. She wouldn't desert them. Ever.

She closed her eyes and planted an imaginary kiss on, first, Elsie's soft forehead, and, then, on little Clara's. The girls had their eyes closed and were breathing deeply in their sleep. She stroked their fine hair and left them there, sleeping peacefully, and, hopefully, dreaming of the tales she had just read to them. Zennor opened her eyes and stared back at herself in her dressing-table mirror. She wondered whether there would be any more children to call her own...and George's.

Her gaze fell on the handkerchief on her lap. The sprigs of Wild Thyme and pink Field Scabious caught her eye. She smiled. She was about to lift a sprig of Wild Thyme to her nose when she heard George's warning in her head: *The village won't reconsider. I know – I understand them.* She dropped the Wild Thyme. Looking up at the mirror, she saw her reflection as others saw her. Mrs Mortimer, that God botherer from the newly formed Band of Hope group, was staring at her in disgust. Mr Clutterbuck, the butcher, was shaking his head. His meat cleaver came down heavily upon the carcass – thwack! – neatly hacking her problem in two. Even Sally Beard, her freckled-faced friend from lower down in the village, at Pinfarthing, and with whom she used to talk about motherhood, even Sally was ignoring her. Whenever Zennor rapped on Sally's front door, or looked for her in her garden, Sally was out.

The only person who hadn't ignored her when she'd passed by was little Mrs John Shipway. The deaf and dumb woman, her stomach swelling with her firstborn, had nodded respectfully at Zennor. Did Mrs Shipway know about the gossip? Had it not reached her silent world? Maybe she was showing Zennor a different kind of Christian kindness to that preached by her fellow Chapel followers.

Like a ton sack of potatoes falling from the warehouse doors on the upper storey to the waiting cart below, Zennor suddenly understood. She would lose her children. If she didn't act now, if she didn't acknowledge George's warning, then she was in danger of losing all this. All that she always ever wanted: her home, her family, her place in this community, her social standing, her children. All of this stationary world at the centre of her heart that she'd been searching for, ever since Pa took her childhood on a peripatetic journey.

And she would have to make a choice. Between 'all this' and the handsome Dangerfield baker, who was her friend. She wondered whether he would understand. Surely, he must know what the villagers were saying about them both. How could he not? Yet, he had continued to warm and nurture his friendship with her. Zennor bit her lower lip. She couldn't cry now. Elsie and Clara's shouts swooped up from the garden. Hephzibah would be coming to take them indoors soon. Twilight was already twitching at the curtains.

She knew she couldn't explain to him. Could she face him? She didn't think so. No, she mustn't. She might…weaken? They both might.

Hephzibah must answer the door tomorrow. She would ask her dear Mama-in-law to do so. Hephzibah would understand. Zennor could almost imagine the relief on her mother-in-law's face, as she applauded Zennor's return to common sense. The common sense that had been missing since...

Zennor almost laughed out loud. What would the God botherers call her? *The proverbial lamb?* The proverbial lamb who came home. She who heeds not, returned to the fold. She fingered the sprigs of Wild Thyme and Field Scabious lying on the handkerchief on her lap. She closed her eyes. Hephzibah called out to Elsie and Clara in the garden. They would be coming indoors. She must help Hephzibah undress and wash them and put them to bed. Before reading them a bedtime story. Her girls. Her hope in life.

Zennor opened her eyes. Methodically, she wrapped the pressed flowers in her handkerchief and pushed them to the back of her lower dressing-table drawer. She banged the drawer shut.

There was a dull ache in her heart. Something had left her soul between the setting of the late afternoon sun and the onset of chilly twilight. She wrapped her arms around her chest and rocked herself like a baby in a cradle. The girls' childish chatter could be heard in the house. Avoiding her reflection in the mirror, she stood up and walked over towards her bedroom window. In the waning light, she could see the shadowy fledgling copse on May Hill. The copse the villagers had planted in celebration of Queen Victoria's Golden Jubilee. In 1887, the year her eldest child, Elsie, was born. Zennor breathed in deeply, willing the mysterious hill to work its mystical powers on her. She would need a friend, now that Neville was not with her.

Eighteen

Hepsie switched off her mobile phone. Ever since Thursday, Mike had been sending her text messages. The more she ignored them, the more frantically he sent them. *I NEED 2 SPEAK 2 U. ABOUT SELINA. ITS NOT WHAT U THINK.* Well, if it was so important, then why didn't he call her? Hepsie knew she was right. He didn't call her because he was still attracted to *that* Selina. She should never have got involved with a fanatical genealogist. It hadn't worked out – although, not for the reasons she would have imagined. Now, it was not his genealogical obsession that was scaring her away, but his ex-bimbo-of-a-girlfriend reclaiming him. Why didn't she call him? Wasn't he worth fighting for? Hepsie clenched her mobile phone in her fist before throwing it onto her bed. No. She wasn't going to be the one to give way. Let her and Mike shake their stubborn minds at one another until their heads fell off.

She had told Sally. Sally, of course, could tell by Hepsie's silences that her evening with Mike at the Cross Hands hadn't gone well. When Hepsie explained why, Sally jokingly said wasn't that a relief, because now Hepsie wouldn't have to swot up on her genealogical background. However, there was another problem she couldn't tell Sally. Great-Granny Zennor hadn't been seen since Hepsie had spoken to her last Saturday – over a week ago.

Hepsie moved towards her faded turquoise desk. She gazed out of her bedroom window. Wednesday's rain had eased off into sullen sunshine. She could see the sunrays peeping out crossly behind the moving clouds. Eb hadn't been pleased. When she told him what had happened between her and Great-Granny Zennor last Saturday, he was worried. Worried that they had lost their ancestor just when they were getting to know her and before they could get to the bottom of her problems. Joan hadn't been in touch for nearly a fortnight, which only increased his anxiety. What was their neighbour up to? Secretly, Hepsie realised she would have to make contact with Joan soon, in case there was something behind their neighbour's uncharacteristic silence. Whenever she and Eb walked around Amberley or on the Common or entered the Post Office, they were on their guard. Where people treating them differently? Was Joan's gossiping voice lying behind the polite smiles and friendly greetings they encountered? If she spied someone in their garden, Hepsie would hurry on by, as quietly as possible, in case the gardener looked up and invited her to chat.

The copse on May Hill mirrored her glumly. If it had mystical powers, they certainly weren't working for her. She was cross with herself for scaring away Great-Granny Zennor. She should never have mentioned Neville Dangerfield. But she always seemed to be hurting her great-grandmother in some way: calling her names, such as poltergeist, threatening to exorcise her, prying into her private relationships. She would have liked to have had a heart-to-heart talk with her sisterly great-grandmother. Especially, after Wednesday evening's disaster. Hepsie wanted her and Great-Granny Zennor to talk like sisters. To talk about their love lives and to share their sorrows. They were the same age. Like twins, but not quite identical. Honey and chestnut.

Pulling out her desk chair, Hepsie sat down. She was still wondering about Great-Granny Zennor's interest in Mike. He was a stranger her great-grandmother had only met once and, then, only briefly. Great-Granny Zennor hadn't even spoken to him. So, what was it? Did Great-Granny Zennor think Mike knew more about her and Neville Dangerfield than he was letting on? But Hepsie couldn't ask him. They weren't speaking.

She looked at the paraphernalia on her desktop. She'd come upstairs to read Great-Granny Zennor's letters again, the ones her great-grandmother had written in her notebook. There were so many unanswered questions, which now couldn't be answered because she had foolishly scared away Great-Granny Zennor. If she re-read her great-grandmother's letters, she might find clues. Clues as to why Great-Granny Zennor believed her husband George had murdered her. Clues to the nature of her relationship with the Dangerfield baker. Hepsie was relieved she hadn't ripped out these letters, like she did with the last one Great-Granny Zennor wrote. She had been intending to do so. And thank God she hadn't given Joan any copies!

But what was it? She looked more closely at the paraphernalia on her desktop. That's strange, she thought, I'm sure my desk wasn't as tidy as that when I last sat here. And…

Her notebook was lying open on the centre of her desk.

But she had locked it away in her desk drawer last time. Hepsie's heart pounded within her. She grabbed her notebook and saw how many pages had been written on. The same neat copybook script of her great-grandmother's previous letters. Hepsie sighed. Why hadn't she thought of looking here before? Her notebook shook in her hands. She dared to read the first few lines.

Saturday p.m.

That was only yesterday. She'd been out shopping in Stroud. Eb had been busy in the garden.

Dear Hepsie,

This isn't going to be easy for me to write. I had hoped to tell you and your kind blind father, Eb, in person. But this was never to be. I suppose I am taking the cowardly path, but I must undo the wrong that has been done to me. My husband George thought he had guessed what had happened but he didn't know the whole truth. I didn't want it to happen. I need to tell my version of the truth. And that's why I'm writing in this journal to you, Hepsie. Though I have been told that you are my great-granddaughter, you are more like a sister to me, both in age and understanding, than any one I have met since I last lived at Peace Cottage. We could be twins. We're almost identical. Honey and chestnut, Ebenezer would say.

Hepsie bit her lower lip. It was a fortnight ago her great-grandmother had last written in this notebook. She hadn't thought Great-Granny Zennor would write in it again after being wrongly called a poltergeist. She read on.

It was in my seventh year of marriage that my life began to unravel. Like a loose stitch pulling apart the whole seam of my dress, I was left exposed. I didn't mean it that way. When I first came to Amberley I thought I had found that stationary world at the centre of my heart, the one I've always been looking for, but this world went wrong. There are some things I can't talk about, Hepsie, events that took place in my life before I came to Amberley. They came back to haunt me in the last eighteen months of my life. They were rustled from out of their hiding place by a howling gust of wind.

Joe. There. I've told you. He is – was – my elder brother. Rose came next. And then me. Followed by my long-lost confidant, Charlie. You would have liked him. Roelinda, Johnny and Alfie came next. And, then, last of all: Ivy. I can't believe she married the Dangerfield baker. Not after what happened.

But then she never knew what Joe did. It all came back to me. After that Christmas Day, on St Stephen's festival.

Great-Granny Zennor's letter had broken off here. Her handwriting had become slightly shaky. Hepsie saw blotches that might have come from tears. She read the next section.

Let me be frank with you, Hepsie. Joe did things he shouldn't have done. Ungentlemanly things. Please don't think ill of me, or of your ancestors. I would have kept that door locked for the rest of my life. When I threw away the key after leaving home

328

to work in domestic service, I thought I had escaped. The Evil had been left behind.

How wrong I was!

A gust of wind can start off in a small way but it's canny enough to penetrate the tiniest cracks and the furthest corners. This wind might blow gently at first, like soft whispers, but then it becomes more of a holla, until an almighty roar is whipped up and the dust and debris comes scuttling out of the cracks and corners. This is what happened to me. Who knows, Joe might have been locked away in that invisible room in my mind, if Neville Dangerfield hadn't come into my life.

There. You were right to ask. I didn't really mind. I would have liked to have talked to you about it face to face. But you do understand, don't you? You do understand how some things can never be said in spoken words? I didn't mean to make you look impolite. I did so want to tell you. And kind Eb. It's hard to think of both of you being my descendants but I can see there are likenesses. And after all this time, I really wanted to tell someone. To tell the truth. My side of the story. You will read on, won't you?

Hepsie nodded, as though Great-Granny Zennor was sitting there in her bedroom.

Flesh and blood. No matter what has happened, you and Eb are my flesh and blood. And don't let anything else change that. It gives me great comfort to know that I can entrust my telling of the truth to you both. Please tell Eb. He'll want to know.

Now, I must get onto the business of telling you.

Hepsie looked up from her notebook. The clouds were parting over May Hill and sunlight was falling onto the solitary copse. Below her, she could hear Eb's Audio Description narration on their television. The narrator's voice wasn't loud enough to cover the steady ticking of the grandfather clock, which seemed louder than ever. She glanced back at her notebook. There were many more pages to read. How had Great-Granny Zennor managed to write all this during one sitting? Hepsie read on.

In May 1892 a man entered my life. Although I was already married, we got on well. Too well, some others would have it. Neville Dangerfield. The younger brother of the Dangerfield Bakers. Returned to Amberley from serving as a soldier. He was handsome and a good conversationalist. We got on well. But the villagers gossiped. My husband George warned me. I was a good wife, I listened. Peace Cottage was my home and I never intended to leave this Paradise within the Five Valleys. We were happy, Hepsie, living here. But once a community has got the twist threaded through the needle's eye, there is no stopping it from stitching a whole fabric of lies.

I didn't want to say goodbye to my handsome Neville. But, if I remained his friend, then I lost the respect of everyone else, including those I loved most. It was with a reluctant heart that I let him go in the autumn of that year. And so my life might have ticked on, as regularly as Hephzibah and Ebenezer's grandfather clock, which still stands in this hall to this day.

Who knows why the clock hands whirl away the hours so quickly one minute and, then, so slowly the next? The autumn leaves burnished in the

*weakening sun, fell off the beech trees and shrivelled
in their dryness, as I waited for the first frosts to
appear. With the coming of the merry season, I tried
to hide my joylessness in festive preparations.
Helping my mother-in-law Hephzibah make the
Christmas pudding, finding holly and ivy to
garland the mantelpieces and doorways,
encouraging Elsie and Clara to believe in the
Christmas story. I did everything a good wife and
mother should do. Like a loving wife, I returned
my husband's kiss under the mistletoe on Christmas
Day. There's a saying that warring spouses should
kiss and make up under the mistletoe, and I think
George was hoping this would mend all our ills. I
remember he plucked a milky-white berry to show
he had taken a kiss from his wife. The mistletoe
sprig hanging above the kitchen door was still full
of berries. In our early married days, we were always
stealing a kiss under the mistletoe and the berries
would be quickly gone.*

*The next day – St Stephen's festival – I feigned
a headache. It was naughty of me. Particularly,
as George and I had made up under the mistletoe
the day before. But I was sick and tired – oh, I don't
know what – of everything – and I didn't want to
meet the cousins Ebenezer and Hephzibah were
taking the family to see that day. Hephzibah ordered
me to take lots of beef tea and put my feet up but I
didn't feel like sitting still. I went out into the cold
air and worked the pump until the ice broke and
water spluttered from the spout. I filled up my bucket,
my hands shivering raw and red in the harsh frost.
As I walked back to the house, I saw smoke from
my neighbours' chimneys rising up into the sullen
grey sky.*

It was no warmer in the scullery. I tightened my shawl, wrapped criss-cross around my bodice, and blew on my fingers. The scullery window was glazed with Jack-o'frost, an impenetrable pattern of feathers and whorls. I was going to heat the water up on the range, when I heard whistling. Deep, melodious whistling, which pierced the cold air more sharply than the cruel frost. I put down the bucket. I had left the scullery door open. My heart beat faster.

The whistling came down the back garden path and meandered its way to the scullery door. I gasped. My hands and body were shivering no more with cold than with feeling. He stood in the doorway.

I hadn't seen him – or, at least, not how I used to – since the beech leaves changed colour. Whenever our paths were in danger of converging – if I saw him in the distance on the Common or walking along the lane towards me – I would seek out a different route. Our bread was bought directly from the bakers, when I knew Neville would be on his round. And I stopped taking walks through the beech copse. In church, I didn't dare to glance up.

I tried to be strong. But it wasn't easy. Regaining the trust of the villagers was like waiting for a thick, crusty frost to thaw. My good friend Sally Beard could see that I was still not myself. "Where's my old girl?" she said. But we talked to one another in less friendly terms. A light had gone out and I couldn't find the taper to relight it.

Neville Dangerfield stood before me. He hadn't changed. His eyes looked at me in the same way they always had done. I opened my mouth to speak but only my warm breath materialised in the cold air.

"I did knock," he said. His voice was deep and melodious. "At your front door, but when there was no reply I came round the back."

He smiled at me.

I clutched at my skirt. I still couldn't speak. What was he doing here? Relief fluttered through me like a softly spiralling feather. He hadn't changed. And I was glad of it. But what was he doing here? No, I couldn't. Tempt not unto Evil.

"What are you doing here?" I asked, falteringly.

His smile grew wider at the sound of my voice.

"I saw your kin on their way to Minchinhampton. When I saw your smoking chimney I thought I would look in."

I gulped. We looked at one another. The fire in the kitchen range hissed and crackled and filled our noses with the warm smell of wood smoke.

"You are alone, aren't you?" he asked.

Tempt not unto Evil. I found my voice. "Just myself."

Neville looked at the ground. When he looked at me again, it was with an intenseness that made his eyes glisten and his ruby curls shake. I took an intake of breath. He stepped inside the scullery. And closed the scullery door behind him.

I was conscious of myself. Conscious of what I was wearing, my rough black laced boots, the long apron over my grey wool shawl, and the loose tendrils falling across my cold-slapped cheeks. My fingers felt dry and calloused as they shivered in the folds of my dark grey skirt. I bit my lower lip, not entrusting myself to speak.

"I had to see you," Neville said, "when I knew they were out. We can't go on – like this."

He waited for my reaction. I was as frozen to

333

*my spot as the solid ice in the water trough outside
Ebenezer's workshop.*

*"We can't go on avoiding one another like we
were strangers." Neville removed his cloth cap and
clenched it tightly in his strong fingers. "Come away
with me."*

*I should have remained silent. A voice within
me told me to do so. Told me to avoid his gaze and
to scare him away. But I couldn't. I couldn't let
the matter go without an explanation. From my point
of view.*

*"I can't. They'll think I'm no better than I should
be. And I can't – I'll lose everything: my family,
my home, my children." I uttered the last word with
a sob.*

*Neville looked surprised. But he moved a step
nearer to me.*

*"We can go away from here," he reiterated. "We
can go where the talking won't reach us – where
we can be alone. Come with me, Zennor, and we
can be as one." And, then, seeing the look on my
face, he added: "If it's the girls, Elsie and Clara
can come and live with us."*

I stepped back.

"You don't understand," I simply said.

*Neville smiled. "But I do, my dear Zennor. Isn't
this what we want? For us to be together? Who cares
what the God botherers and the other villagers say.
We were meant to be." His eyes glowed intensely like
the spitting hot embers in the kitchen fire.*

*"I can't leave Peace Cottage. This is my home.
This is the world I've always been looking for – I
can't, Neville. I can't leave it behind. Not now.
Please understand me."*

Neville's breathing was heavier and his muscular

334

chest was heaving beneath his crumpled corduroy suit.

"There's no need to be uncertain," he said. "Together we can be strong."

He had misread my signs. He had taken my denial for a woman's coyness. For a woman's fear of taking the unknown and of doing wrong in the eyes of others. But it wasn't like that. Why couldn't he see that I had wanted this stationary world at the centre of my heart for so long? I couldn't let it go. I couldn't let it be wrenched from my grasp like a silken handkerchief tugged out of my hand by the hollering wind.

My mistake was in talking to him. He had mistaken my conversation as a wish to pursue our illicit relationship. Passion blinded him. Stamped him like the branded cattle grazing on the Common. He was deaf and blind and I could be dumb for all my beseeching.

Neville stuffed his cap into his jacket pocket. He moved towards me. I opened my mouth to speak. But he took my face in his sturdy hands and kissed me.

How did I feel?

What could have been so sweet was bitter. Our first kiss. I tried to push him away but he was strong. His hands dropped from my face and his arms enveloped me like forceps. I pulled away. He held me tighter. I ducked his kisses. He tugged at my long apron and tightly wrapped shawl. I felt the passion rise between his legs.

He thought I was being coy. His passion would convince me. And we would find love in our mutual release. And, in that hope, I would change my mind.

*The flagstones were hard against my back. He
unbuckled his belt. His breath smelt of freshly baked
bread. And so did his auburn curls and coarse linen
shirt. His grip was firm. Was he hoping I would
melt like the hard frost on the window panes and
give in to him? I laid still. A cold sweat broke out
on my back.*

*In the coldness of the scullery, he took me, lying
on me as hot as his baking bread. What could have
given me so much happiness, only gave me pain.*

*When he had finished, I lay shaking on the
flagstones. I could see the mistletoe sprig hanging
from the kitchen doorway, its sticky white berries
held between splayed leaves like Eve's sin.*

*Neville left quietly. There were no more words
between us.*

Hepsie looked up from her notebook. Tears
streamed down her cheeks. For some unknown reason,
she thought of Mike. Of his pale green eyes and his
broad, congenial smile. She wiped the tears from her
cheeks and carried on reading.

*I was in bed when the family returned home.
Hephzibah asked whether I had a fever. I had
washed away all traces of him.*

Great-Granny Zennor's letter had broken off here.
Hepsie could almost read the deep breath her great-
grandmother had taken to begin the next section.

*As soon as I discovered I was with child, I knew
the baby was Neville's. Eve's sin had worked her
ancient rites and justice was as blind as passion.
Although George and I had been man and wife that*

*Christmastide, the timing was wrong. I hoped George
wouldn't realise this. The villagers were gossiping,
I was sure of that. Had Neville been seen arriving
or leaving Peace Cottage on St Stephen's Day? No
one spoke, but was it in their glances or manner
towards me? I lived in fear throughout my
indisposition. You may ask what stayed my hand
from killing the life within my womb? Before it was
there for all to see? Maybe I was hanging onto Neville
or, unable to hide my swelling stomach, fulfilling
George's hopes of a son and heir. And George was
so proud when his first son was born to carry on
the Anderson name.*

*But I lived in fear. I could see it in Georgie's
dear sweet face. To me it was writ large as Solomon's
words – for George and the whole of Amberley to
see. I would be accused of an immoral relationship
with the Dangerfield baker. And that stationary
world at the centre of my heart, the one I'd always
been searching for, would be lost.*

*So, you see, my dear great-granddaughter, my dear
Hepsie, how heavy a weight I have been carrying
with me all these many years. It's to you – and you
only – that I have been able to ease this iron weight
from the scales of my life and set the balance right.
You do believe me, don't you? I am telling the truth.
And you do understand there was no one who could
help me? My friends and family were my enemies.
One wrong word, one wrong suggestion, and I would
have lost far more than I already had. And then I
lost my life.*

Hepsie broke off from reading. Poor Great-Granny
Zennor! How could this have happened to her? Why
had no one helped her? And, what about Georgie...?

Hepsie's thoughts trailed off as she realised just what her great-grandmother's implications meant. Swallowing hard, she read on.

That's when I knew George had guessed. He didn't say so, but I thought there were hints. And I was going to tell him. The truth. That, yes, he was right, but, no, he was so wrong. And, then, I died. That wasn't meant to be. A mother leaving her children behind. And, I knew, I knew that he had played a part in it. My death. I couldn't – I didn't tell him in time.

Would it have made any difference? Would he have believed me?

None of us will ever know.

I hope you'll believe me, Hepsie. You and Eb are my only hope. It's funny to think that you are my flesh and blood. And Neville's. I can see his reddish highlights in your chestnut hair. Please tell Eb. I don't think he'll be hard on me. His sense of justice won't be as blind as his sight.

And you will forgive me? As I said, my life unravelled like a reel of thread falling from my hands and rolling away out of my reach. I watched it unwind, unable to bend down and pick up the reel before it completely unravelled.

Maybe we'll meet again, soon. I hope so. In the meantime, please do not think too badly of me. I depend upon your trust and understanding in this matter.

Yours ever,
Your loving great-grandmother,
Zennor Anderson

P.S. Will I see your friend Mike again? His pale green eyes remind me of Neville.

Hepsie put down her notebook on her desktop. Eb's Audio Description TV had faded away and all she could hear was the loud ticking of the grandfather clock. She glanced out of her bedroom window, where the warm July sun was now shining unsullenly over the solitary copse on May Hill. Her cheeks were still wet from when she had tried to wipe away her tears. She sniffed. What she had thought of as a love affair between her great-grandmother and the Dangerfield baker had, in fact, turned out to be something completely different – and far more tragic. And with wider-reaching consequences for herself and Eb than she could have ever imagined.

She bit her lip. What was she going to do? Eb would be so upset. He had so set his heart on finding out about his genealogical roots and in looking for a new self-identity. He thought he was an Anderson through and through. He cared more deeply than she did about her genealogical roots because he was in more need of redefining his self-identity. He hadn't said so, but she knew that since losing his sight and, therefore, his former status, he was aware of having lost part of himself. *Who was he? How could he make sense of his life? How could he reclaim something for himself? Could finding out about his genealogical background help him? Could it help him to define himself? Of who he was?* That was why he had hooked onto their family's coincidence in returning to their ancestors' former home. This is what lay behind his obsession. He had to know. Being an Anderson had become part of his search for his new self-identity.

Hepsie glanced back down at her notebook. She

couldn't tell him. Or, at least, not yet. Not until she had calmed down herself. She was in shock. Her great-grandmother had been raped. How could Neville Dangerfield do this to the woman he professed to love? But now the Dangerfield baker was her flesh and blood. Over eighteen months ago she had taken the decision to change the course of her life and which she now regretted. Eighteen months before the end of *her* life, Great-Granny Zennor had also taken a fatal step she'd regretted. Hepsie didn't understand how her...how Neville Dangerfield could have gone on to marry Great-Granny Zennor's younger sister Ivy. Was he hoping to possess the elder sister through the younger one? She didn't know what Ivy looked like or if the younger sister was similar in character to the older one.

Hepsie picked up her pen – the floral-scented one Sally had recently given her – and gazed at the blank page after Great-Granny Zennor's letter. She was going to pen a reply but she couldn't find the right words to express exactly...

It was no good. She had to get out of here. Go for a walk. On the Common. Get some fresh air. Her bedroom had changed. Peace Cottage had changed.

Throwing her pen onto her desk and leaving her notebook open, she left her bedroom. Blindly, she rushed along the landing and descended the boxed-staircase.

Deaf, she didn't hear him. She stumbled into him and he nearly fell backwards down the stairs.

"What is it?" Eb cried out.

She was buffeted against the weight of his body. She was crying. Loudly.

"Oh, Eb..." she managed to say.

He took her in his arms and comforted her.

Nineteen

Mike was back at Peace Cottage. He'd been here nearly half an hour and he still hadn't told them. The evening sun was warm outside but the living room's thick Cotswold stone walls insulated the room like a freezer bag. Mike sipped his coffee. Eb and Hepsie were sitting in the armchairs opposite him. Hepsie's face was suffused with an emotional intensity he hadn't seen before. When she had unexpectedly called him on Sunday evening, he was aware that a change had come over her. Firstly, she wasn't ignoring his text messages any more. Anxiously, he had explained that Selina wasn't his girlfriend and that he had no intention of resuming a relationship with her. He was sorry it had all gone wrong at the Cross Hands but could they meet somewhere else? To his surprise, Hepsie had suddenly come out with it. And told him everything.

Mike smiled at Hepsie, who warmly smiled back at him. She had told him everything. Everything about Great-Granny Zennor's confessional letter and the implications of its contents for herself and Eb. Hepsie had sounded very emotional on the phone. Ever since she and Eb became aware that something was bothering Great-Granny Zennor after their séance, they had kept quiet about her in the hope that she wouldn't be scared away before they could find out from her what was wrong. That's why they hadn't discussed Great-Granny Zennor with himself and Joan since their séance.

When he heard Hepsie's news, Mike had suddenly realised he had to tell her. The truth. He had started at her mention of Neville Dangerfield and how closely the baker was connected to them all. Only, Hepsie didn't know this. Mike suddenly knew the game was up. He decided he must tell her about his genealogical charade. He wanted to come out clean with his deception. Hepsie's outburst about Great-Granny Zennor, and her desire to make up with him, had swayed him. He also didn't want to risk losing Hepsie, as he nearly had done these last few days when she had ignored his text messages.

Through the open windows, Mike could hear evening birdsong. Their cheerful tunes mirrored the melody in his own heart. Of course, he could take the sensible option and lose Hepsie. He could take her news, pass it onto his aunt Kate and never contact the Andersons again. This would be the simplest and sanest action to take. But he couldn't. By her telephoning of him, Mike realised that Hepsie had missed him as much as he had missed her. Surely Hepsie would be relieved when she heard his news that he wasn't a fanatical genealogist?

He had told her he had something important to tell her and Eb. And that he needed to tell them in person. Hepsie was intrigued. They arranged that he would visit Peace Cottage this Tuesday evening. This would allow him time to talk to Kate. Although Hepsie, of course, didn't know this. Or, that his aunt Kate was presently sitting in his car on the Common.

Telling Kate hadn't been entirely easy. Firstly, he

342

had to tell her about Great-Granny Zennor's confession and the implications of it for them all. He didn't know how Kate might take this. She was the one who had instigated their genealogical charade and she had a right to know the outcome. But she might not like the result. Secondly, he wanted to come clean and tell her about his feelings for Hepsie Anderson. He was nervous about this because – and here, he faltered when he told her – because he knew he had betrayed her. He had become more involved with Hepsie than he wisely should have done. When he came to actually telling Kate, he told her everything. About his emotional emptiness, how he'd thought he'd been going somewhere only to be washed back up on the familiar shores of his home town; how bored he was with the repetitive cycle of his life; and how he couldn't afford to buy his own home. Hepsie offered him the chance of emotional happiness. He didn't want to lose this chance. To let it slip away from him like an outgoing tide and leave him stranded on his local shores.

Thirdly, he explained to Kate that this was the reason for his latest visit to Peace Cottage. He was going to tell Hepsie and Eb the truth. And expose his lie. He felt, since Great-Granny Zennor's confession had connected the Dangerfield and Anderson families together, that the time had come to tell Eb and Hepsie about Neville Dangerfield's confession and the reasons for his and Kate's genealogical charade. But Kate needn't worry. He wasn't going to tell the Andersons what lay behind her real reasons for wanting to find out the exact truth of Neville Dangerfield's confession. He would tell Hepsie and Eb he was helping his aunt to clear up a family myth, which Kate couldn't do by ordinary means.

Kate was in turmoil. She was shocked by his news.

She had hoped there wouldn't be any truth in the Neville Dangerfield and Zennor Anderson connection. But when she heard about Mike's plan to visit the Andersons, she became more like the Kate he used to know. The fighting Kate, who was more like his big sister than his aunt. She scolded him. Why hadn't he told her sooner? she asked. Mike argued that he couldn't call Hepsie and tell her he was cancelling his visit to Peace Cottage. He had already let her down once. And he couldn't risk losing her again.

His aunt saw how determined he was. She blamed herself. If it wasn't for her, he wouldn't be in this mess in the first place. Mike saw her protective instincts coming out of her long-closed shell. She was worried that, if he revealed his genealogical charade to the Andersons, he might be charged with a criminal offence. She would come with him to Amberley. But not – and here, Kate had looked at him pleadingly – not to meet the Andersons in person. She would wait in his car. Just in case. Just in case he needed back up or – or for her to explain. She didn't want him locked up for impersonating a genealogist.

So, there she was. Sitting in his car on the Common. He had parked by the War Memorial, so she could admire the views across the valley. Luckily, it was a beautiful evening. In some ways, Mike was relieved that Kate had decided to come with him. Perhaps her genealogical quest had worked out for the best. Although her genealogical research hadn't quite taken her mind off her incident, she was becoming more like her former self with every new discovery they made.

Mike took another sip of his coffee. He shouldn't keep Kate waiting. Or, the Andersons. But, as he swallowed his hot coffee, allowing the additive caffeine to pump up his strength, he realised his task wasn't an easy one. Hepsie's face was expectant. She was smiling encouragingly at him. Eb, however, was not his usual congenial self. Sitting morosely in his armchair, Eb had been unreceptive and lacking in his characteristic warmth and openness during their brief discussion about Great-Granny Zennor's confession. Mike wasn't surprised. He couldn't blame Eb for feeling like that. Great-Granny Zennor's news must have been shocking for him. Particularly, as he had been so enthusiastic about his Anderson roots. Mike felt bad that he had tricked this kind, blind man, who thought Mike was a fellow fanatical genealogist. Mike gulped as he swigged his remaining coffee. Perhaps Eb and Hepsie would be interested to hear the other side of the Zennor Anderson and Neville Dangerfield story. Maybe, Neville Dangerfield's deathbed confession might make up for all that had taken place.

Putting down his coffee mug on the low glass table between them all, Mike steeled himself to speak. He smiled nervously at Hepsie, before finding his voice.

"As you know, I have something important to tell you both." Mike moistened his lips. "It won't be easy, but I hope you'll understand why I did something. It's—"

He broke off as the grandfather clock began to chime from the hall. He counted the eight regular strokes under his breath. Eight o'clock. As soon as the eight stroke faded away, he resumed his confession.

"It's not something I'm particularly proud about, but there is a good reason for my actions. For me behaving as I did—"

Mike broke off for the second time. Eb and Hepsie weren't listening to him. Hepsie was looking towards the living-room door. There were tears in her round blue eyes. Eb was equally moved. He was also gazing

345

towards the living-room door, as though guessing something was over there. Mike looked to his left.

Standing by the open living-room door, her hand on the doorknob, was Great-Granny Zennor.

She stood hesitantly by the door, a questioning look on her face, as though she was unsure of how they would receive her. But her expression soon dissolved into emotion as she reflected the emotion in Hepsie and Eb's own faces. With her lower lip trembling and her pale blue eyes glistening with tears, she accepted the hug Hepsie gave her. The two women sobbed like long-lost sisters in each other's arms. Although one was dark-haired and the other fair, they were like a mirror image. Almost like twins, Mike thought.

There was a stillness in the living room for what seemed like a long time but was probably only a few minutes. Long shadows were lengthening across the room as the warm evening sun drew out the scent of lavender and other flowers in the garden.

Great-Granny Zennor and Hepsie released one another. There was relief in Great-Granny Zennor's face. Hepsie glanced at Mike. Her cheeks were wet with tears. She smiled at him. Mike's heart melted like an ice cream in the blazing sun. There was no need for an explanation from any of them. He got up from the sofa and allowed Hepsie, leading Great-Granny Zennor by the hand, to sit there in his place.

Mike was about to sit down in Hepsie's vacated armchair when he noticed that Eb was shaking. He placed his hand comfortingly on the old man's shoulder. Eb responded with a slight smile. But he was still uncharacteristically cool.

They sat in silence whilst the grandfather clock ticked away the minutes in time with the birdsong in the front garden. Mike knew he should get a move on and tell them. But Great-Granny Zennor kept on looking at him. As though there was something most compelling about his eyes. He smiled at her. She looked down and gripped Hepsie's hand even more tightly.

Mike thought of Kate waiting in his car and decided he must speak. Before the evening ended.

"What was it you were going to tell us?" Hepsie asked.

Mike swallowed the words he was about to emit.

"Can Zennor hear, too?"

He meekly nodded.

But then, seeing the warmth in Hepsie's face, the way she looked at him, and how uncharacteristically receptive she was after having embraced Great-Granny Zennor, he took heart. He must tell her.

Taking a deep breath, Mike began his confession. He told them about his genealogical charade, why he was doing it, about his aunt Kate's role in it, and how he had always intended telling them the truth. He glanced at each one of them as he spoke, occasionally stumbling over his words and pausing to see whether he'd got them on his side. Somewhere within him, a voice was telling him that he should have kept quiet.

Hepsie's warmth was dissolving into anger. Mike could almost see the mole on the bridge of her nose twitching with rage. He gulped. Great-Granny Zennor was clutching at her skirt. Her pale blue eyes widened in amazement. Eb was sitting silently in his armchair, his sightless eyes uncannily focussed in Mike's direction.

Mike mentioned Neville Dangerfield. And how the baker was his and Kate's ancestor.

"We're related!" Hepsie exclaimed. She released her hold of Great-Granny Zennor's hand.

"Your eyes – they're Neville's," Great-Granny Zennor whispered. She wrung her hands together.

Eb kept quiet.

Mike nodded. And bit his lower lip.

The emotion in Hepsie's round blue eyes was like a tornado. Mike thought she was about to take off and rocket through the beamed ceiling and upstairs rooms of Peace Cottage and out through the rafters and into the blue sky.

"What do you mean by this?" she asked.

And when he couldn't reply, she yelled: "How dare you!"

Mike leant forwards in his armchair. "Look," he began to plead, "I didn't like deceiving you and Eb, but, if I hadn't done this – and I *was* only doing this on my aunt Kate's behalf – I would never have met you – we would never have met one another—"

He didn't finish his sentence. Hepsie slapped him hard across his cheek.

For a moment, his tingling cheek took over his senses. Mike felt his face redden. But when he awoke from his stunned world, Hepsie was already laying into him with more angry words.

"What do you mean by this? How dare you! How could you deceive me and Eb? We—"

"But don't you understand?" Mike tried to explain.

"We put our trust in you. We thought you were our friend. You're nothing but—"

Mike turned towards Eb. The old man was stroking his thigh, up and down. He looked disturbed. Great-Granny Zennor was crying. In desperation, Mike turned back to face Hepsie. He tried to explain, just to her. He even tried to make a joke about how relieved she must be to discover that he wasn't an obsessive genealogist after all.

In all this confusion, none of them heard the doorbell ring. It was only when the caller continually pressed the bell, that they stopped talking. The chimes of the doorbell rang out mockingly, like the chimes of the grandfather clock stuck in a groove. They all looked towards the living-room door. Hepsie's chest was heaving and Mike could hear his own loud breaths. Great-Granny Zennor was sniffing as she tried to stifle her tears. There was an anxious frown on Eb's face.

The old man was the first to move. He groped for his long cane beside his armchair and eased himself up. Resignedly, he slowly walked towards the hall. The ringing of the doorbell had ceased. The caller must have heard their sudden cessation through the open windows. Eb's long cane tapped on the flagstones. Mike heard the front door opening and Eb asking: "Who's there?"

Someone replied. The front door was shut and Eb's long cane tapped back towards the living room. He walked in, followed by Kate.

She stood in the living room, in her pretty summer dress and strappy sandals. It had been a long time since Mike had seen her dressed up like this. She smiled nervously as she glanced around the living room and at their questioning faces. Mike could tell that she was struggling within herself, as her former self fought to get out of the constraints of the new skin that had grown around her since her incident. He smiled encouragingly at her, conscious that his cheek was still smarting.

"I couldn't wait in Mike's car any longer," she began to explain, her voice soft and hesitant. "I – I wanted to see this place and to meet…my distant cousins."

There was a sharp intake of breath from Hepsie. Mike bit his lower lip.

"I'm Mike's aunt – Kate. You're not charging him, are you? You know, for what he's done? It's my fault—"

"Kate!" Mike protested.

"No – no, it's my fault." Kate glanced at each of them. Mike was aware that she could see by their faces that their evening hadn't gone well. She remained standing, unsure of whether she could get them onto her side or not.

The grandfather clock struck the half-hour.

"Are we all sitting down?" Eb asked.

Taking this as a sign of encouragement, Mike stood up and offered Kate his armchair. She sat down. He remained standing close by her.

Hepsie was eyeing Kate with sulky interest. But whenever Mike tried to distract her gaze, she avoided all eye contact with him. Great-Granny Zennor sat mutely on the sofa, fidgeting with her fingers in her lap. Only Eb seemed to be settled comfortably enough in his seat to listen to Kate's explanation.

Kate took a deep breath before starting. "I don't suppose Mike's told you everything."

"There's more?" Hepsie interjected, anxiously.

Kate ignored both Hepsie's question and Hepsie's accusing eyes. "I didn't want Mike to tell you the real reasons," she continued, "that lay behind my decision to set up this stupid genealogical charade. To be honest…" – Kate's voice faltered – "to be honest, I wasn't really interested in the genealogical side of this connection – this connection between my ancestor, Neville Dangerfield, and the Mills and Anderson families."

She took another deep breath.

"It was hearing about my great-grandfather's confession that started me off."

Kate glanced at Great-Granny Zennor but there was no response. Great-Granny Zennor's eyes were focussed on the chimney-breast beam as she continued to fidget with her fingers.

"My mother – Neville and Ivy Dangerfield's granddaughter – told me one day. She had overheard her mother and aunt talking in the kitchen. The door was slightly open and my mother – Maria – happened to be passing by on the other side. She was in her late teens. She stopped to listen when she heard her mother and aunt talking about her dying grandfather, Neville. He was lying in bed upstairs. He had said something strange that morning, like a confession. Although he was dying, Maria heard her mother say that he had been quite lucid and not in a stupor or incoherently rambling. And his words had struck her as sounding true. But what a strange thing to say: *'I didn't mean to do that. But I thought it was for the best. You see"* – Kate hesitated before forcing the words out – *" 'I raped her. Zennor Anderson. "*

Hepsie gasped and clutched Great-Granny Zennor's hand. Her grip was returned but Great-Granny Zennor continued to stare at the chimney-breast beam. Eb had closed his eyes.

Kate was looking down at her lap, nervously fidgeting with her fingers. Mike placed his hand reassuringly on her shoulder. She glanced up at him, before continuing with her explanation, her voice slightly shaky.

"Maria heard her aunt reply: *'Wasn't that mother's sister?'* Neither her mother nor her aunt understood why Neville had said such a thing. And, if it was true. They couldn't imagine their father as a..." – Kate's voice faltered before she whispered – "...rapist. There had been no contact with the Andersons for many years. And certainly no hint of a scandal involving Ivy's sister and Neville. They couldn't understand it. Why had he said such a thing? But Maria's mother insisted that his words were lucid and had a ring of truth about them. And he seemed to be lifting some long-hidden guilt as he said them. She had taken his hand and squeezed it and this had given him some peace. He died the next day."

Kate paused, her lower lip trembling. Mike squeezed her shoulder.

"You don't have to tell them, Kate," he said.

She glanced up at him and squeezed his hand in return.

"I'll have to, Mike," she said. "They've got a right to know, particularly after we – I – have tricked them. I don't want them arresting you. What we've – I've – done won't make sense, if...I don't."

She glanced at the others. Mike could see that Eb had reopened his eyes and was looking very thoughtful. Hepsie, however, was still cross. He could almost feel her anger transmitting through her clasp of Great-Granny Zennor's hand. Great-Granny Zennor was shaking, the watermark patterns on her pale grey silk dress rippling like an incoming tide on the shore.

Maybe Kate found hope in Eb's demeanour, for she clenched her hands into tight fist balls on her lap and said: "I had to find out whether my great-grandfather Neville's words were true. I had to find out for my own peace of mind."

She gulped. Mike squeezed her shoulder, reassuringly. Although the late evening air coming through the open windows was still warm, he could feel her body shivering. The unlit living room became gloomier as the shadows lengthened with the waning of the evening sun.

"I couldn't live with the thought that my ancestor could have been" – Kate lowered her eyes – "a rapist. And that he admitted to being one. I couldn't!" She looked up to meet their gazes, her blue eyes tearful and pleading. "I had to clear his name. I had to find out everything about this...woman he mentioned." Briefly, her eyes met with Great-Granny Zennor's. "I hoped his confession was that of an old man incoherently rambling on his deathbed. Or, if not that, he'd been put in the wrong. But" – she looked directly at Great-Granny Zennor – "it was not to be. I'm so sorry..."

She leant forwards and reaching across, put her hand over Great-Granny Zennor and Hepsie's.

"You see, I was raped, too."

The ticking grandfather clock cut through the living room like a knife cutting through time.

Great-Granny Zennor took Kate's free hand in her own and squeezed it. Hepsie was staring at the chimney breast, her eyes wide with bewilderment. Eb had resumed stroking his thigh, but his expression, Mike was relieved to see, was full of sympathy.

"I hope you'll forgive me," Kate continued. "And" – her voice became quieter – "my great-grandfather. I wish life could have been different for you." She attempted a conciliatory smile at Great-Granny Zennor.

Great-Granny Zennor's pale blue eyes were full of emotion as she squeezed Kate's hand in reply.

Taking strength from this, Kate said: "I was attacked one night whilst I was alone in my home. He was a drug addict. I'd left my bedroom window open and he climbed up onto my wheelie bin, reached up to my window and—

"I couldn't stop him. He wanted money. But he took more than that.

"I haven't come out with this before...to strangers – but" – she paused – "I felt the same as you, Zennor – I didn't really want to carry it around with me for ever more."

She glanced up at Mike and said, more brightly: "Mike's been helping me, haven't you?"

Mike smiled kindly at her. He was relieved that Kate had got her explanation over and done with. He looked at her pixie face, with its wrinkles and shadows, and at her shiny short dark hair, and he was relieved to see something of the old Kate – her former streetwise urchin – returning to her expression. Even the atmosphere in the Andersons' living room felt better for her confession. The only problem was Hepsie.

Mike hoped he could now redeem himself in Hepsie's eyes. Surely she would forgive him after hearing Kate's explanation. He could see how upset she was by Kate's traumatic incident. And, surely, she must be relieved that he wasn't the fanatical genealogist she'd thought he'd been. But, then, Mike guessed these weren't the real reasons why she was angry with him. It was his deception. His deception of herself and of her trusting, blind father. He had made them look like fools. Even though he had no intention of doing so. He had tricked them.

Mike's cheek was still smarting. He wondered whether Kate had noticed it, whether his slapped cheek was red and blushing for all to see. Hepsie had her pride. Of course, she did. She wasn't going to melt in his arms without a fight, like the first ice cream licked by the heat of the summer sun. First, he must try and get her to look at him again. Maybe he should suggest they get some fresh coffee from the kitchen. This would give him a chance to talk to her alone. Give him the chance to explain...

As though reading his thoughts, the grandfather clock began striking the chimes of the ninth hour. Mike looked at Hepsie.

"It's been a confessional evening. I think we could all do with some fresh coffee," he began. "Hepsie—"

The doorbell rang.

The others glanced towards the living-room door.

"Hepsie—"

The doorbell rang, repeatedly.

Hepsie glanced at Eb.

Eb grimaced. He groped for his long cane and got up from his armchair. For the second time that evening, he tapped his way to Peace Cottage's front door.

The front door was opened.

"Eb! How good to see you. I bet you were worried you hadn't heard from me for so long."

Joan's gushing voice echoed throughout downstairs.

Hepsie groaned and, momentarily, shut her eyes.

Kate and Zennor released their hands.

Eb replied curtly to Joan before leading her into the living room.

"Oh, there's a party going on!" Joan exclaimed. She was all smiles, her pearly blonde bob gleaming like an ice cube in the gloom. There were no large glasses magnifying her large brown eyes this time. And she was dressed down in what looked like her gardening gear: a pair of long khaki shorts, a baggy navy-blue T-shirt and scuffed plimsolls.

She surveyed them all before introducing herself to Kate and saying to Great-Granny Zennor how good it was to meet her again. Mike blushed as he introduced his aunt to Joan. He was conscious that Joan seemed to be completely insensitive to the cross-current of emotions passing across their faces. Or, maybe, the unlit living room was too gloomy for Joan to see properly. No one offered her a seat. Eb had resumed his place by the fireside and was anxiously waiting on Joan's every word. Hepsie was biting her lower lip. She had told

355

Mike that she and Eb were worried that Joan hadn't been in contact with them for a fortnight.

Joan smiled conspiratorially at them, as though she had a present for their lucky selves.

"I was gardening when I happened to see your guests arrive," she said, "and I thought this would be a good time to tell you what I've done."

The grandfather clock ticked through the gloom.

"I've heard back from Radio Gloucestershire. They're willing to give us a five-minute slot. Isn't that exciting?" She clapped her hands.

"For what?" Eb asked.

"For an interview." Joan looked at them all, waiting for their applause.

When it wasn't forthcoming, she continued: "Yes, an interview. There will be myself, representing Amberley Family History Group; you, Eb, as the local genealogist; and Great-Granny Zennor, as the ancestor who's returned to her former home. Won't it be a wonderful set-up? Radio Gloucestershire think so. They're dead keen to get us on air.

"When's the best day for you both to be interviewed?" She glanced from Eb to Great-Granny Zennor.

Clutching at her skirt, Great-Granny Zennor stared at Joan in horror. Hepsie had closed her eyes and was mumbling under her breath. But it was for Eb that Mike felt most sorry. Poor Eb was stunned. This was too much for the old chap, particularly – and, here, Mike blushed guiltily – coming after Kate's and his own bad news. Joan knew she wasn't supposed to make Great-Granny Zennor's return public. She had reneged on her promise. But, Mike guessed, a fortnight was too long not to have heard from Joan and expect her to have kept quiet about the matter.

With his heart sinking heavily to his toes, Mike realised that the rest of the evening wasn't going to be any easier than the first part. And that his chances of making coffee with Hepsie and having a talk with her looked very unpromising. His only hope was that Joan's clumsy putting-of-her-foot in the matter might redirect some of Hepsie's anger away from him. They had a lot of reasoning to do.

Somehow, their families seemed to be the undoing of Hepsie and himself. As the sun set across Peace Cottage's garden and darkened the living room, Mike saw himself still stranded on his local shores.

In his telling of the truth, he had lost her.

Twenty

Standing in the utility room, Eb felt he was there. As though it had happened only yesterday, even though over a hundred years had passed. Leaning on his long cane, his hands tightly clasped over its ball handle, he tried to recall what the utility room looked like during his pre-blind days. Had any of the original scullery fittings been kept? He could feel the worn flagstones beneath his feet. And the back door was still there. But the enamel sink and draining board, and all the laundry paraphernalia such as mangle and washtub, had long since gone when he, Sofia and Hepsie had moved into Peace Cottage.

Eb closed his eyes. The washing machine rumbled behind him, sloshing his clothes without any hard human labour. He couldn't get Grandmother Zennor's words out of his head. He stood here in her former scullery, re-living what she had gone through. This room would never be the same for him. This was where his grandmother's world had fallen apart and where his father Georgie had been conceived. And where the Anderson family line had died out. Eb's throat felt dry. Through his grandmother's eyes, he experienced the events that had drastically altered his own perception of himself.

Who was he? He had been so close to finding a solution. Only for it to be turned upside down. Georgie's birth certificate – Grandpa George – even his very own surname: they were all lies. He had lost a part of himself all over again. In searching for certainty he had, like the blind man stumbling in the dark, only found more uncertainty. What was he supposed to do?

Eb opened his eyes. Grandmother Zennor had said some good things about his...er...biological grandfather. She had called Neville Dangerfield handsome, a good conversationalist; he was physically strong – and passionate, too. Eb sniffed. There was a smell of toast lingering over from breakfast. He supposed, with a wry grin, that he had inherited his love of baking bread from Neville. In all the times he had kneaded the dough and waited for his loaves to rise, the blood of the Dangerfield bakers had been coursing through him. Regretfully, he hadn't baked any bread since that fateful day in July, nearly two and a half months ago.

Of course, he could start researching the Dangerfield family. There were Dangerfields who lived locally – like the couple who gave him a lift back from his June church reading. However, the problem with this, was could he really tell them the truth? Eb imagined he wouldn't enjoy doing so. He wondered what would have happened if circumstances had worked out differently. If Grandmother Zennor had met Neville first and not George. Would their lives have been better? And more fulfilled?

When Grandmother Zennor visited him, which she did quite frequently, they didn't discuss what had happened. Or, at least, not directly. Eb smiled at the thought that although they were grandmother and grandson, their ages were reversed. Grandmother Zennor was forever thirty-two, locked in the midsummer of her life. He was – well, he was sixty-seven going on sixty-eight and he probably looked it, too, if Hepsie's attitude was anything to be judged by.

Eb enjoyed his developing relationship with Grandmother Zennor. They were getting to know one another. Occasionally, she dared to ask him questions about her family. *"Did my girls marry? Did they become school assistants or teachers?"* Eb felt bad about answering these questions, because he knew his replies were unhappy ones. *Yes, your eldest child Elsie did marry but her husband died in the First World War. She and Clara were childless. Both of them worked as shop assistants in their father's drapers.* Eb didn't like mentioning George. Did he still care that his presumed grandfather had been a murderer? Now that there was no biological connection between them. At least, the psychopathic genes hadn't been passed on. If Eb did care, it was only because Grandmother Zennor did. But he had found no proof, no written evidence or old wives' tale, to support his grandmother's belief. Eb liked to half-believe, and he thought Grandmother Zennor did, too, that she would meet her children on the other side. But what would she do if she met George and Neville? Eb shook his head. His grandmother's choice hadn't been an easy one. To choose between loving her family and loving Neville Dangerfield. And in playing by the rules, she had lost everything.

The washing machine rocketed into a whirling crescendo as it spun his clothes. He'd best move into the kitchen, not just because of the noise but because, if Grandmother Zennor suddenly arrived, he didn't want her to find him in the former scullery, re-living her past.

360

In the kitchen, Eb found two mugs and began to prepare fresh coffee for himself and tea for Grandmother Zennor. With the kettle set to boil, he eased himself into a chair by the kitchen table. He decided not to listen to the radio in case he missed Grandmother Zennor's arrival. There were times when listening to Radio Gloucestershire that he realised just how narrowly he and Grandmother Zennor had escaped from being broadcast across the county. Even now, in mid-September, the thought brought him out in a sweat.

After Joan's announcement, they had spent the remainder of the evening explaining almost everything to her: Mike's deception, Kate's tragedy, Grandmother Zennor's confessional letter and the far-reaching implications this had for all of them. Joan had to be told the truth in order to convince her not to go ahead with her plans for media exposure. Eb was certain he could trust her to cancel their Radio Gloucestershire interview. Not just because she was sympathetic towards them, but because she was also aware that, perhaps after all, this wasn't the sort of news that reflected well on Amberley's public reputation.

Eb chuckled. It can't have been easy for Joan to turn down their radio interview and he wondered what sort of excuse she'd used. If Radio Gloucestershire had thought she was a nutcase who had made up the whole story. He chuckled even though he knew that making Grandmother Zennor and her return public would have caused a media sensation and put Amberley – and themselves – on the international map for ever more.

When Hepsie had asked Joan why she had reneged on her promise to keep quiet, Joan explained that she thought they had wanted more time to get to know their ancestor and to find out as much as they could about life in Victorian Amberley. Meanwhile, having misread their intentions, she proceeded to do them the favour of making their exciting genealogical news public by contacting Radio Gloucestershire. Eb knew Joan was disappointed. And, in particular, by Mike's deception. Mike had seemed such a promising candidate for Joan's promotion of Amberley Family History Group. She could see this attractive, young man bringing the genealogical masses to Amberley.

However, no amount of disappointment could keep Joan from routinely checking on Peace Cottage. Eb was aware of a more understanding attitude behind her bossy helpfulness, softening the neighbourly boundaries of their friendship. Uncharacteristically, she didn't press him into attending any of her forthcoming Amberley Family History Group monthly meetings or day trips. Was she slowly waiting for him to recover from his genealogical drama, in the hope that he might, in time, be able to tell his story? Eb shook his head. He knew the matter was far too personal for him to ever make public. Maybe he might astound Amberley Family History Group with an occasional snippet of information about Victorian Amberley. They would marvel at him, wondering where the information came from, and he would be coy about it. No, he must carry the knowledge to his grave, like his own ancestors had done.

The kettle reached boiling point. Eb stood up and, mentally counting his steps, moved towards the sideboard. Carefully, he prepared himself a two-mug cafetière and placed it on his tray. He was using a Dycem tray-liner, so that his mug, the cafetière and a plastic milk bottle wouldn't slide around and knock each other off the tray when he was walking back to the kitchen table. The coffee smelt good. Rich and exotic. Eb retraced his steps towards the table and lowered his tray until he could feel it resting on the hard surface. When he was seated, he pushed down the cafetière's plunger and poured himself a mug, listening for the bleep of his liquid level indicator. He hadn't prepared Grandmother Zennor's tea because he didn't know when she might arrive and, anyway, she often offered to make her tea herself. Eb guessed this was because she wanted to help him and not because he made a bad pot of tea.

Eb brought his mug towards his lips. Handel's *Zadok The Priest* jingled into life inside his trouser pocket. Eb cursed as coffee sloshed over the side of his mug as he banged it back down on the table. He was never fast enough answering his mobile phone. Reaching inside his trouser pocket, Eb pulled out his phone and flicked it open.

"Hello, Kate."

He knew the caller was her because he used different ringtones to help him recognise who was calling. *Zadok The Priest* wasn't his obvious choice for Kate, but he had run out of ringtones. He supposed he could get Hepsie to add some more suitable ones to his phone.

"Hello, Eb." Kate's voice was clear and calm.

"Are you all right?" Eb asked.

"Yes, I'm coping."

"That's good." Eb nodded sympathetically, although he was alone.

"I've got some information on the Dangerfields." Kate paused, as though she was uncertain of his response. Eb held back from saying anything. "It's their family tree. If you want it, I can e-mail it to you."

Eb considered for a second. Did he really care any more? However, he replied: "Yes."

Kate's voice betrayed her relief. "I meant to tell you before but...um...I thought you might need to get over what happened. Do you have a family tree maker programme?"

"Yes."

"I can send it over as a GEDCOM file."

"That's great. I'm looking forward to receiving it." Eb hoped he sounded enthusiastic enough. He didn't want to disappoint Kate. It wasn't her fault, anyway.

"Give me a call when you've listened to it. I'm sure there will be things you'll want to discuss."

"Of course."

"Well...speak to you again soon."

"I hope so, Kate. I always enjoy my chats with you."

"Bye for now."

"Bye, Kate."

Eb flicked his mobile phone shut. And sighed, deeply.

No, he didn't want to disappoint Kate. She had guessed how he felt and she was trying to revive his interest in his genealogical background. Maybe, to make up for what had happened and all that he had lost. After that terrible evening in July, Kate had rung him to re-apologise about her and Mike's behaviour and for giving him more grief than he deserved. But how could he be anything but kind towards her? Particularly, after all that she had gone through. They had been in contact with one another ever since. Although, never in person. Eb wished Kate could visit him at Peace Cottage but she couldn't get there without Mike's help.

Slowly, through their chats over the summer, Eb got to know Kate better. He heard about some of the details of her rape ordeal, how she was still coping with it, her counselling sessions, and the progress of her approaching court case. Kate was worried about the latter. Initially, she didn't feel she was strong enough to go through with the public court case and to re-live the trauma she had wanted to forget, if only she could. Eb had done his best to offer sympathy. Kate needed his support. However, since the debacle of their genealogical charade and the revealing of Grandmother Zennor's own unfortunate past, Kate had found a new strength growing in her. Perhaps she could face her fear of speaking in court. Of being cross-examined. Mike, her Victim Support Officer, her prosecution lawyer, all said there was a strong enough case to convict...Kate couldn't call him by name. She told Eb she was unsure whether she would testify behind a screen or meet her attacker face to face. After her medical examination, the police had video-interviewed her and this could be used in court instead of her being there. But Kate realised that by setting an example she would be encouraging other victims to come forward and prosecute their attackers. There was also the question of waiving her right to anonymity. All these were big steps for her to take.

Kate told Eb she would carry the image of Grandmother Zennor in her mind to help her through. She realised she had the chance, unlike his grandmother, to vindicate herself. To gain a sort of justice during her lifetime. Maybe, afterwards, in the future, she could re-build her life. Sell her home at Cherry Tree Close and move away from Cheltenham. She would like to work again. All these were incentives for her to approach her forthcoming court case with greater courage than she thought she had left within her.

Eb hoped she would win. At court and in the future. It was too bad that her attacker had pleaded not guilty.

Modern society was becoming a monster. Eb was relieved that he lived somewhere like Amberley. No, his problems weren't as big as Kate's. He was lucky for that. Eb took a sip of his coffee. The strong, hot liquid flowed refreshingly down his throat. He and Kate had also talked about Hepsie and Mike. Neither of them liked to interfere in the younger generation's relationship problems, but Kate was worried that she couldn't save Mike's relationship with Hepsie.

When Eb tried to talk to Hepsie about Mike, suggesting they should ring him and invite him over, Hepsie was having none of it.

"What do you mean, Eb?" she retaliated; "He tricked us. We don't want anything more to do with him."

"Anyway," she continued, "what have we got to talk about now that he's not the budding genealogist you thought he was? I think he might find life in Amberley very boring."

In truth, Eb wished Hepsie could be independent again. He had never intended his only daughter to stay here, at Peace Cottage, for the rest of her life. Or, at least, until he had passed away. It wasn't fair on her. She had so much to give to the world, so much to live for. Although he knew he depended on her, not only physically but emotionally, too, he didn't want her wasting the prime years of her life on an old man like him. There were times when he'd bitten his lower lip to stop himself from blurting this out to her. *"You don't have to stay with me,"* he'd wanted to say, *"Take your chance and re-find life before it's too late."* He knew she was miserable as she resigned herself to a lifetime of looking after him.

The grandfather clock struck the eleventh hour. Hepsie was returning a manuscript to her freelance employers, Salmon Mill Publishing Company, in the

Golden Valley. Eb hoped she would linger there a while. As he sipped his coffee, he thought that although he would miss Hepsie if she did leave Peace Cottage, he wouldn't be lonely. How could he be, when he had three women keeping an eye on him? There was Grandmother Zennor, Joan and Kate. Three women looking after him couldn't be bad. No, he was a lucky man. And he was lucky that he'd had a family, however small, around him. Particularly, in times of need, such as when his sight deteriorated. Sofia and Hepsie had kept him sane, buffered his suicidal thoughts and despair in the cradling strength of their love. And he'd been lucky to come home. Sofia hadn't. Eb touched her face in his memory. Despite the shock of finding out the truth about his genealogical roots, he was lucky to have family and, even if Anderson blood was not coursing through his veins, he could still call himself an Anderson. They had been the ones, after all, to give him a name and a sense of belonging. Did genes matter? There was the question of his love of baking bread, presumably inherited from Neville Dangerfield, but would Hepsie, Mike or Kate be baking bread in his place after his own death? Eb could imagine himself teaching Kate how to bake bread, but Mike and Hepsie...?

Grandmother Zennor's constant visits had been a surprise for him. Eb wondered whether she was staying around until Hepsie and Mike made up. Waiting for them to find the happiness she had lost. She had been at Peace Cottage from the blossoming to the ripening of the fruit on the apple trees. Where else could she go? She had told him about the lovers, Morveren and Matthew Trewella, living beneath the waves in the Atlantic Ocean. He couldn't imagine Grandmother Zennor living the life of a mermaid. Singing her love laments to the wind and to Matthew Trewella's fellow villagers on the coast. Maybe she would try and find her lost children. Whatever she did, Eb hoped she would always come back to visit him.

The ticking of the grandfather clock was growing louder. Eb swigged the remaining dregs of his coffee. As he put his mug back down on the table, the grandfather clock chimed the quarter-hour. Time was permanent and so was his grandfather clock. Over the years, the clock's owners had come and gone but the clock continued to mark time, its pendulum swinging to the beat of the changing generations. Grandmother Zennor, his ancestors, his father Georgie, and Sofia had all come and gone. And even he would, one day. They were transitional, whereas Old Father Time kept on ticking. The Keeper of Time, logging life. Eb wondered whether he would see Sofia again after he died. And whether they would haunt – or, rather, visit – Peace Cottage like Grandmother Zennor did.

Eb poured himself another mugful of coffee. He shouldn't really be drinking this strong stuff. No doubt, he would find in today's newspapers several articles telling him not to drink this amount of caffeine, in case he developed blocked arteries, or suffered from increased insomnia, or his toes fell off. If he had lived in Amberley years ago, he would have drunk the pure, clean water from the springs situated along the narrow lanes and steep paths. He would scoop up the crystal water with his hands or use the metal cups thoughtfully chained to the walls, and hear the Band of Hope singing in the Wesleyan Chapel: *"Water bright, water bright, from the crystal spring!"*

Lavender and marjoram filled his nose. Silk brushed against his shoulder and petticoats softly swished beside him. She came into view. He could see the sheen of her dress. She took his hand in hers and squeezed it. Eb looked into her pale blue eyes, and was reminded of his own. As he had once seen them when looking at his reflection in the mirror. Or, when he saw himself in his dreams. For him, memories and dreams were interchangeable. He enjoyed taking in the pale grey sheen of Grandmother Zennor's dress, her honey-toned hair and the roses blooming in her cheeks. He squeezed her hand in return. She smiled. And Eb smiled, too, glad that his dreams and Grandmother Zennor had brought colour to his life.

Twenty-one

The ladder wobbled as Hepsie reached across to pick another apple. Cupping her hand, she lifted up the apple and twisted it gently, so that the ripe fruit came away with its stalk intact. She placed it in the wicker basket hanging over her arm. The basket was lined with newspaper so that the wicker wouldn't bruise the apples. Gripping her bare feet on the wooden rung, she steadied herself with her free hands against the ladder sides. She had wedged the ladder between the bent branches of the apple tree, making sure the ladder was evenly balanced on the long grass. Peace Cottage's sloping back garden was not ideal for ladders. The ladder wobbled again as she climbed up another rung to reach the uppermost branches. Looking towards Peace Cottage, she could see the crown of May Hill's copse peeking over the roof.

The first weekend in October was like an Indian summer. Hepsie breathed in the fresh air and looked up at the blue sky and fishbone clouds. She closed her eyes as the warm afternoon sun bathed her in apple-scented goldenness. It was no use. These Ashmead's Kernels needed picking before they were blown off by the late autumn winds or killed off by the first frosts. Carefully, Hepsie cupped another russety apple. Eb had done some research on the background to Great-Granny Zennor's apple trees. They were first bred by a Gloucester lawyer, Dr William Ashmead, at the beginning of the nineteenth century. Almost extinct by the 1950s, Ashmead's Kernel was making a comeback, as buyers opted to return to traditional apples. Hepsie could feel the rough skin in her hands. She wondered whether Great-Granny Zennor would help her and Eb to eat the fruit this year.

She had seen Great-Granny Zennor quite a few times since that fateful evening in early July. Her great-grandmother's confessional letter had upset her more than any boring facts, such as census returns, parish records, death certificates and, even, Great-Granny Zennor's grave, could have done. She and Great-Granny Zennor never spoke about what had happened that July evening or about Great-Granny Zennor's past. Neither of them mentioned Mike. Although, Hepsie knew that her great-grandmother – like everyone else – was waiting for her to make up with him. No one said anything. Eb had suggested she call Mike and invite him to Peace Cottage. There was that unspoken silence between them, where no one said what they really thought. Well, she wasn't going to do that! Mike had tricked them. And that was the truth of the matter. Hepsie angrily tugged at the apple in her hand, pulling it away from the stem less gently than she should do.

Her pride was hurt. Ok, she wasn't telling Eb this, or anyone else. But Mike had made her look a fool, several times over. Kate, Selina, the whole charade. Hepsie dropped her picked apple into her basket, not caring whether it bruised. She realised she had confused love with escape. She was using her attraction towards Mike as an excuse to escape from

371

her present life at Peace Cottage. He was the means, and not the end. At least, that was what she convinced herself.

Hepsie moved up another rung. She was almost at the top of the apple tree. The sky felt nearer to her. She wanted to climb into the sky. To step out into the blueness and escape from Peace Cottage for ever more. She wanted to get away from the ticking grandfather clock, which regularly counted the minutes of her passing youth, reminding her that time, and her life, were passing by. If she wasn't careful, she could end up like a fallen Ashmead's Kernel, left to rot in the long grass beneath this bountiful fruit tree.

Her hand found an apple whose position nearer the sky and sun had made it larger. As she twisted it off its stalk, its rough, greenish-brown skin dissolved into Mike's face. She almost thought it was going to grow fingers, too, and ruffle Mike's hair so that his top hair stood up like brush bristles. Hepsie shook her head. This wouldn't do. She wanted to tell off the apple. *"Please, look like a dessert apple!"* she wanted to yell from the top of the apple tree. Why did her memory do this to her? And then she heard his voice, low and mellifluous, dosing the Ashmead's Kernel in honey and cream. Often, she would be in the middle of doing some mundane chore, when Mike's voice would pop up in her mind like a tune she'd heard on television. The melody, the words, the rhythm, would replay themselves in her mind until she had grown to like the song and couldn't stop singing or humming along to it. Hepsie threw her picked apple into her basket.

Above her, in the distance, a small aeroplane rumbled across the sky, leaving a white tail. Hepsie wished she could reach up and grab this white tail.

"Wait for me!" she wanted to say, as the aeroplane sped off to follow the broadening estuary of the River Severn on its way down to meet the Atlantic Ocean. Mike hadn't been in contact since July. Not even with Eb. Hepsie continued to stare after the aeroplane long after it had disappeared from her sight. She knew Kate was in contact with Eb. And sometimes he would talk to her about Kate's problems. Probably, in the hope that she might soften her attitude towards Mike. But Hepsie wasn't having any of this. She was sorry for Kate but, if the genealogical charade had never been set up, then Mike would never had...However, Hepsie was disappointed that there had been no message passed to her from Mike by Kate. He wasn't even trying to get in touch with her. Was he waiting for her to forgive him? To make the first move? Hepsie grabbed the sides of the ladder in anger. As much as she tried not to, she couldn't help wondering what he'd been up to these last three months.

Her basket felt heavy on her arm. She ought to empty it but she didn't want to descend the ladder. Not just yet. There was something soothing in being near to the sky. She wondered whether Eb was waiting for her to ask him about what Mike was doing. Or, didn't Kate and Eb mention Mike during their chats? Everyone was waiting for her to melt like an apple-favoured blancmange left out in the summer's heat. Didn't anyone have any principles?

Despite her aching arm, Hepsie reached out for another apple. She couldn't help thinking that, if Sofia had been here, all this would never have happened. Sofia would have stopped Eb's genealogical obsession from taking over their lives. She would have buffeted his fears from enveloping him. And, Hepsie ruefully thought, I wouldn't even be living here. She added another apple to her full basket. She remembered her mother used to enjoy baking with apples. Making apple chutney to be sold on Joan's WI stall during the Harvest Festival. Or, sticky toffee apples for fund-raising events at the Parochial School. Hepsie wondered what she was going to do with all these Ashmead's Kernels. Would she have to give them away? Or, maybe, she and Eb should start a toffee-apple-making business. There was a time when Eb was responsible for picking these apples. Hepsie remembered helping him as a child. In the years when Eb became blind and Sofia fatally ill, the apples had been left to fall off the trees.

Sally. She could offer a basketful to Sally. Her freckled-faced best friend might even be persuaded to join her and Eb in their toffee-apple-making enterprise. Hepsie smiled at the thought of how Sally had taken her news about Mike. She had told Sally – quite honestly – that she and Mike hadn't made up. But she hadn't told Sally about Mike's last visit to Peace Cottage. Sally believed Hepsie had fallen out with Mike over Selina and their Cross Hands evening. Hepsie decided she wouldn't tell Sally the whole story. It was too complicated. And, anyway, Sally might not believe her. There was also the need to keep Great-Granny Zennor's return and the truth about her and Eb's genealogical roots secret.

"What a shame, you've lost your crusading genealogist," Sally had said. "However, I suppose you could never have seen eye to eye with the genealogy business."

Hepsie had to bite her tongue to stop her from telling Sally the truth. "Actually, I was right; he was a con man."

But she knew Sally would want the full explanation.

And she knew what Sally's response would be: "Look, old girl, all that genealogy has gone to your head and given you hallucinations."

Hepsie leant against the ladder and closed her eyes. She allowed the warm sun to bathe her tiredness. Her basket was too heavy and her arms too aching. In the bushes in the garden she could hear the birds calling to one another. She didn't want to leave her exulted perch. Opening her eyes, she glanced over her shoulder at the view behind her. Beyond the roof of Eb's former office and their garage, she saw the Common stretching away towards Whitfield's Tump. Cattle grazed and lowed in place of the Methodist preacher, George Whitfield, who had attracted large crowds during the early eighteenth century. Squinting, she was able to make out the heavily laden blackberry bushes and elderberry trees. No doubt, if she were to look on the Common early one morning, she would find fresh mushrooms to pick. The villagers were lucky that they had the Common. At one of Joan's Family History meetings, Hepsie had learnt how the local millwright, Jehu Shipway, had saved the Common for his fellow villagers. Arguing for Commoners' Rights to be recognised, Mr Shipway had fought convincingly against the purchase of the Common by the local Lord of the Manor. There had been Commoners' Rights in Amberley for centuries: villagers grazing their cattle and horses on the Common, or foraging for dead firewood in the beech copses, or taking their pigs there to feed off the fallen beech mast, or quarrying for limestone in the hillsides. The villagers were lucky that their Common had been bought by the National Trust and kept as an unspoilt—

"Hi! Hepsie!"

The ladder wobbled as she stopped herself from

nearly falling off it. Grasping the ladder sides, she took a deep breath.

"Hi! Hepsie! Can you hear me?"

Mike's voice was loud and clear. It drifted up to her, along with his earthy scent, and beyond into the blue, Indian-summer sky.

Of course, she could hear him! Hepsie scowled, annoyed that she hadn't put on any make-up or brushed her hair, which was untidily pulled back into a ponytail. She clung to the ladder sides, conscious that Mike was probably looking up at her from below, eyeing her faded, torn jeans and her old cerise T-shirt that had shrunk in the wash. She had better reply to him.

"Hi, Mike." Her voice was unexcited.

"I rang your front doorbell but there was no reply. I was walking back along the lane when I saw your head poking above the apple branches."

"And that's when you jumped over our garden wall?" Hepsie asked, sarcastically.

She peered down at Mike between the apple boughs. He was looking up at her. He was wearing a white T-shirt and black jeans. He smiled at her. One of his broad, congenial smiles. Hepsie scowled. Avoiding his pale green eyes, she focussed her gaze on some apple leaves. Secretly, she was pleased that he hadn't changed.

"I've got something to tell you," Mike said.

"Again?" Hepsie couldn't help sounding anxious. He had said that last time they'd met.

"I'm taking a sabbatical from my job."

What did that have to do with her? Slyly, Hepsie glanced down at Mike. He was running his hand through his hair. She knew he was waiting for her to climb down the ladder. Well, she wasn't going to do that! Instead, she said: "Is that a good idea? There's

376

a recession on at the moment. You might lose your job."

Mike stopped running his hand through his hair and smiled up at her. "I've been thinking of taking one for some time. There's also Kate. She's going to court soon and I want to be there to support her. After that's over..." Mike paused. "I want to get away from Cheltenham."

His words stabbed her heart like an apple corer digging out the centre of an Ashmead's Kernel. Hepsie was silent.

"I've got a small deposit I was...er...saving for a flat," Mike continued, "but I've decided instead to go travelling. See that world I've always wanted to see."

He looked up at her, expectantly. But Hepsie could only think: *"Why not me?"* Why wasn't she going travelling? Like she once had done as a carefree student. She scowled at him. How dare he! Particularly, when he knew she was stuck here at Peace Cottage, looking after Eb and forsaking her own independence.

"Do you want to come with me?" Mike asked.

Hepsie nearly fell off her ladder. She managed to steady herself, although her left arm was aching from the weight of her heavy basket.

"What do you mean? You know I can't!"

She couldn't. Because of Eb. Because it would mean having to make up with Mike. And forgiving him. How did she know he wasn't conning her, again?

Angrily, Hepsie began to descend the ladder. Her fruit-laden basket swung awkwardly from her arm as her bare feet gripped each wooden rung. Flushed, she reached the lower half of the ladder, only to find Mike holding the ladder sides. Her back was encircled by his arms and chest. Their bodies were almost touching.

She waited for him to move away. He didn't. She glanced over her shoulder. Mike kissed her.

His lips tasted of apple and honey...and life.

She kissed him in return.

The grandfather clock was silenced as time stood still.

Mike relieved her of her heavy basket of apples. She descended the remaining rungs. All around her she could smell the fragrant scent of Eb's hybrid Tea Roses and his bright orange-vermilion Autumn Sunlight roses climbing over the garden wall. As she stood next to Mike, the long grass tickling her bare feet, she picked up an Ashmead's Kernel from her basket and took a bite of its soft flesh. The apple was juicy and slightly tart. She offered her apple to Mike. He smiled at her and took a bite.

Taking a bite of the apple was like taking a bite of Paradise. Hepsie looked around her and saw the garden how Great-Granny Zennor had once seen it. The fresh air, the birdsong, the scented flowers, the abundant fruit trees, the Common stretching away beyond the house, the soft green hills shimmering in the sunlit distance, the blue, Indian-summer sky reaching up to touch the sun. Paradise had returned to Peace Cottage.

Above her and Mike, the apple leaves gently stirred. Hepsie thought she felt Great-Granny Zennor's presence. But she heard only an aeroplane flying overhead. Mike took hold of her hand. Together, they looked up between the apple branches and watched as the aeroplane arched across the sky, painting a white plume behind it.

And they looked at one another, excitedly.

Epilogue

Zennor followed George along the track. She hadn't managed to catch up with him since leaving Zennor Quoit. Her chestnut mare was slower than his grey steed and less easy to control. Zennor pulled on her reins to check the animal. The wind buffeted her body, making it harder to stay on her horse. She gritted her teeth and gripped the reins more tightly.

The wind hollered fiercely across the open, treeless moorland. As she steered her mare along the narrow, winding track, the hem of her dress was snagged by prickly yellow gorse. Ahead of her, she could see the massive granite boulders, balanced on top of one another like unrisen bread, that she and George had stopped to look at on their way to the Quoit. Beyond this, Zennor saw the blue-green Atlantic Ocean glimmering in the late morning sunlight. She and George were completely alone in this windswept universe.

George's grey steed broke into a canter. He was heading towards the derelict engine-house they'd passed on the way up. Zennor urged her mare into a canter. She didn't want to be left alone in this eerie, desolate place.

Mindful that she still hadn't told George the truth.

About what had happened. She knew he had noticed and guessed. He had seen it in Georgie's face. Why else had he brought her here? He was getting rid of her. He was taking her away from her girls and from Georgie. When Georgie needed her most. She had hoped to talk to him over their packed lunch of fresh pasties and saffron cakes at the Quoit. But George had been keen to move on too quickly. Why was that? Why didn't he want to linger? Why didn't he want to talk to her? Zennor was worried. She recalled the sacrificial tomb, with its pit-black entrance hole, and her hands trembled around her mare's reins.

A bird, hidden in the yellow gorse and purple heather, startled her mare. The animal reared, whinnying. Zennor was thrown backwards. The reins slipped out of her hands. She landed amongst the bracken and gorse. And broke her neck against one of the innumerable small granite boulders strewning the moor. On this deathly pillow she lost consciousness, letting Georgie, the moor and the world slip away.

Back at Zennor Churchtown, some weeks later, the local poet, Henny Quick, was stood outside the porch of St Senara's Church. He was holding a batch of broadsheets. Looking around at the local people gathered amongst the tombstones, he pitched his voice against the strong wind and started his oration.

"Verses on the fatal accident and death of Zennor Anderson, aged thirty-two years, stranger – or, *emmet* – to this Churchtown. It's whispered abroad her husband played a hand in her accident – and many a local looked the other way. He got her a nervous mare and on the top of Zennor Hill the work of evil hands was done. In the waves of the Atlantic Ocean, off the coast of Zennor Head, you can hear her singing alongside the wanton mermaid, Morveren, and her lover, Matthew Trewella. Together, they sing their lost love's lament. And their voices are carried inland by the wind."

Acknowledgements

A big thank you to my first readers:

Rose Hill, Gwen Lamie, Ann Fernley-Jones, Helga Sten, Lesley and Forest Campbell, George Mandel, Nomi Paynton and Zena Flax.

I am also very grateful for the support of my late father, Richard Quick.